Linda Finlay lives on the Devonshire coast and is the author of eleven novels. From lacemaking to willow weaving, each one is based on a local craft which, in order to write authentically and place herself firmly in the shoes of her heroines, she has learned to do herself. However, it is people and their problems that make for a good story and, with so much interesting material to work with, it is easy for Linda to let her imagination run as wild as the West Country landscape which has inspired her writing. *Farringdon's Fortune* is her twelfth novel and the second in the Farringdon series. Linda says it has been fun delving further into life at Nettlecombe Manor in East Devon and exciting taking middle daughter Victoria to London for the Season where she makes her debut into Society with some surprising outcomes.

T0006162

Farringdon's Fortune

Linda Finlay

ONE PLACE. MANY STORIES

HQ
An imprint of HarperCollins*Publishers* Ltd
1 London Bridge Street
London SE1 9GF

www.harpercollins.co.uk

HarperCollins*Publishers*
Macken House, 39/40 Mayor Street Upper,
Dublin1, D01 C9W8, Ireland

This paperback edition 2022

1
First published in Great Britain by
HQ, an imprint of HarperCollins*Publishers* Ltd 2022

For Mum

Chapter 1

How could one woman spend so much money in such a short time? Edwin stared aghast at the invoices spread out on the desk before him, his earlier good mood evaporating like morning mist in the warmth of the sun. Clearly his wife Charlotte was seeking revenge for him having sent her away. Neglecting the two young daughters she had given him was not something he could forget nor yet forgive. At six and four years respectively, Sarah and Maria needed – indeed deserved – love and parental guidance. He also couldn't overlook the fact that Sam, his estate manager's son, would still be here today if Charlotte hadn't allowed them to wander off.

He pressed his hand to his eyes as the memory of that horrific day returned yet again to haunt him. His girls playing alone by the well, Sarah tumbling down into it then Sam's broken body being winched out of the shaft. Charlotte's denial that she'd done anything wrong had been the final straw. He knew he would have to see her at some time to discuss the future, but the truth was, he was not relishing it.

How different life had been with his first wife, Beatrice,

a warm, loving woman who had adored spending time with him and their three daughters, Louisa, Victoria, and Beatrice before the riding accident that had tragically cut her life short. They'd been so happy, despite her not siring him a son. Whether or not that was down to the curse placed on them by gypsies when his father had turned them off his land, he'd never know. The fact remained he still had no heir.

Shaking his head, he forced his attention back to the present and the papers before him. He'd expected bills for new clothes, fripperies even, but commissioning a self-portrait? Even by Charlotte's standards, that was taking things too far. Despairingly, he ran his hands through his hair, which, at fifty, was still luxuriant, the silvering at the temples making him look more distinguished than in his youth. There was no question he would have to settle the outstanding charges; as her husband it was his duty. A fact of which Charlotte would be only too aware. Well, she would also be made aware her allowance would cease altogether if she didn't rein in her spending.

'Papa.' He looked up in surprise as eighteen-year-old Victoria burst through the door like a windstorm, eliciting a whimper from Ellery, his aged black Labrador, who was ensconced beneath his desk. Although elegantly dressed in a green morning gown, chestnut curls swept back neatly in a chignon, his daughter's cheeks were flushed, a frown creasing her brow.

'Whatever is the matter, my dear? Are you not well?'

'Step Mama has written,' she cried, her dark eyes troubled as she held out a sheet of cream embossed paper. 'Apparently, I am to be in London by the end of next week and need to take all these items she's listed. There are so many things required for the Season and . . . ' she broke off, shaking her head in dismay.

'Let me look,' Edwin said, taking it from her trembling hands. He gestured for her to sit beside the log fire gently burning in the cream-grey stone grate that had been carved by masons at his quarry on the outskirts of the Nettlecombe estate. It might be the damp chill from the sea fret encasing the Jacobean manor in a damp shroud that was causing Victoria to shiver, though it was more likely the shock of finding out her departure was to be so sudden. Quickly he scanned Charlotte's copperplate handwriting, his eyes widening at the lengthy list.

'Are four ball gowns, six day dresses, six skirts with co-ordinating blouses really necessary?' he asked, frowning as he reeled off the first items.

'It is not those I am worried about, Papa. I am also to take a white silk robe suitable for my debut along with appropriate accoutrements. Why, I don't possess a white robe, let alone a silk one, and, even if I did, I wouldn't know what accessories to put with it. I mean, it is not every day you are presented at court, is it? I simply cannot go,' she stated, folding her arms tightly across her chest.

'Now then, Victoria, I will not hear defeatist talk from a Farringdon,' Edwin chided, placing his hand on her shoulder. 'We will commission a suitable gown to be made straight away.'

'But Papa, you don't understand. I don't have any white silk and, even if I did, it's much too late to arrange for a dressmaker to call. The best ones will already have been engaged.

Oh, it's impossible. Step Mama never liked me, and has probably done this on purpose,' she cried, anger darkening her brown eyes to black. 'My application for presentation was accepted ages ago, which means she must have received the invitation before she left.'

Edwin's frown deepened. Victoria was right, of course. Such important events were organised well in advance. Charlotte would not only have known the date, but her meticulous mind would also have filed it away. Despite initially having made a great of show of being a dutiful stepmother, it had become increasingly evident that Charlotte's first duty was to herself. Well, he certainly wasn't giving her the satisfaction of spoiling his daughter's debut.

'Leave this with me,' he told her. 'I will make arrangements then reply to Charlotte with details of our arrival. In the meantime, tell Vanny to prepare those garments you deem suitable.'

'Thank you, Papa,' Victoria said, getting up and kissing his cheek. 'You always make things sound possible.'

'They usually are.' He watched fondly as she left the room. He thought for a moment, then rang the bell.

'Ah Ferris, please ask Louisa to join me and arrange for a tray of coffee to be brought.' At twenty, his eldest daughter had a sensible head on her shoulders and might be able to offer a solution.

Settling into his button-back chair beside the fire, he closed his eyes, letting the peace and tranquillity of his office, with its comforting smell of wood and leather, wrap around him. However, it wasn't long before his thoughts returned to Charlotte. Even before he'd sent her away, she'd been seething

4

with resentment that there was to be no grand ball to celebrate the betrothal of Louisa to Captain Henry Beauchamp, who had expressed their preference for a small party for close family and friends. Now he realized the ball was more about increasing her social standing than celebrating the couple's future happiness. Not for the first time had he cause to question his second marriage. There was no denying he had fallen for her charms when he was still in the depths of despair after losing Beatrice. He had been flattered that a young beauty should be attracted to a man, who, although not old, was certainly past his prime. Only later did he realize becoming lady of the manor had been the real attraction.

Once again, he couldn't help reflecting how different things had been with his first wife. They'd met at a ball during her first Season, fallen in love and been blissfully happy before her untimely death. Now, Edwin understood the wisdom of making a suitable match and that was what he wanted for his daughters – although he knew that, at seventeen, exuberant Bea had very strong views on what she wanted to do with her life.

A sharp rap roused him from his musing, and he looked up in surprise as Nanny bustled through the door in a manner that defied her advancing years. She was dressed in her customary attire of dove-grey tailored skirt and white blouse; hair neatly coiled into a bun.

'How many times do I have to tell you, Nanny, this is what we have maids for,' he chided, jumping to his feet, and taking the tray from her.

'And how many times do I have to tell you that I like to make myself useful. With Sarah and Maria under the tutelage of Miss Birkett and Louisa overseeing the running of Nettlecombe in Her Ladyship's absence, I have little enough to do.' Edwin smiled knowing that, despite her protestations, the woman kept a watchful eye over them all. 'Now tell me what is ailing you, young Edwin?' she asked, pouring his drink.

His smile widened. In Nanny's eyes he was still a young boy, and she always knew when he was troubled. Before he could answer there was another knock at the door and Louisa appeared, immaculately attired in a navy day dress with crisp lace collar, dark hair braided at the nape of her neck.

'You wish to see me, Papa?' she asked.

'Yes, Louisa, I do,' he replied, gesturing for her to take the seat her sister had recently vacated. Smoothing down her skirts, she accepted a cup of coffee then looked askance. 'Don't go, Nanny,' he added as the woman made to leave. 'You may be able to help.'

He briefly outlined the contents of Charlotte's missive and, by the time he'd finished, both women's lips were set in a tight line.

'Step Mama is preposterous, trying to prevent Victoria from being presented,' Louisa exclaimed.

'If you'll excuse me, Lady Louisa, I don't think it's Her Ladyship's intention to prevent Victoria from being presented. After all, that would restrict her own social opportunities, would it not? May she not simply wish to outshine her?'

'You are right as usual, Nanny,' Edwin agreed, sipping his drink thoughtfully. There was no way Charlotte would risk missing out on the glamorous balls and parties that would be held throughout the Season. 'You think it's her way of getting back at me?' he asked.

'It will certainly be a rush to get everything ready in time,' the woman replied diplomatically.

'But not impossible if we all pull together,' Louisa said. 'Victoria and I are due to visit the Quarry Crafters in Combe this morning to see the progress they are making with the orders for the workers' shirts.'

'Setting up that charitable institution has certainly made a difference to those widows,' Nanny told her. 'Earning their own money without having to resort to walking the streets or begging has given them a sense of purpose, not to mention a hot meal for their children every day.'

'Everyone deserves a chance in life,' Louisa said quietly. 'However, I was thinking that Ida Somers, their supervisor, is a competent seamstress and might well be able to help with Victoria's predicament.'

'And if she can't, she's bound to know someone who can,' Nanny added, nodding knowingly.

'Just remember to keep Quick close by at all times,' Edwin cautioned. Always conscious of his daughters' safekeeping he knew the conscientious footman would keep them safe.

Chapter 2

By the time the two eldest sisters descended the granite steps, the haze had finally given way to golden sunshine that gilded the grey stones of the old manor house. With its elegant symmetry, soaring chimneys and mullioned windows, Nettlecombe nestled in the shelter of lush green hills at the head of a long combe that led down to the sea.

Mindful of the less fortunate circumstance of the villagers, the sisters climbed into the old cart they used when visiting the hamlet of Combe. Hardy footman Quick flicked the reins and they set off at a brisk trot. Despite his strong physique, he was an amiable man who happily moved between his duties, yet he wouldn't hesitate to risk his own life defending the Ladies Farringdon if circumstances warranted it.

'Do you think Mrs Somers will have time to help?' Victoria asked as they travelled down the long driveway that was bordered on each side by magnificent lime trees bursting with life. 'The women have just received that new order and—'

'Stop fretting,' Louisa soothed, patting her sister's hand. 'She will be in her element. You know there's nothing Mrs Somers likes better than being involved in something she considers important, and it doesn't come more important than a debut gown.'

They turned into the lane leading to the hamlet of Combe with violets and bluebells snuggling in the shade of the hedge banks. Fields dotted with sheep and cattle spread out far and wide, stone cottages for the estate workers set neatly on one side. The sound of banging and ringing rose from the valley below where the Farringdon quarry mined the finest stone that was shipped far and wide. It gave employment to many local men as well as travelling masons keen to work the material favoured for its colour and ease of carving. Leaving the cacophony behind, they veered sharply into the village, passing the thatched forge where grey smoke rose high into the sky and tethered horses awaited the attention of Tom, the blacksmith. Opposite, his wife Lily, the school mistress, was calmly ushering her pupils back inside their cottage, which also served as the classroom, after their morning break. Victoria shook her head.

'I don't know how she keeps them in line like that. And that's another thing: if Ida Somers is busy working on my gown, who will supervise the workers?'

'Stop worrying. The women love you and will want to help,' Louisa assured her as they travelled along the meandering lane. Moments later they pulled to a halt outside the smart hall, which Sam, the young estate worker, had helped convert from a tumbledown barn and which had been named in his honour when he had died bravely saving their young stepsister.

'I'm not sure how long we will be,' Louisa told Quick as he handed her down.

'That's all right, Lady Louisa. I'll take a walk around and stretch me legs, but I'll not be far away. His Lordship's most insistent about that.'

As Louisa's eyes adjusted to the dim light after the sunshine outside, she counted ten women sitting at the two long tables set down the middle of the room. Their heads were bent over their sewing, and she couldn't help thinking how much progress had been made since she'd first set up the Quarry Crafters mere months previously. Then, they'd been suspicious, feral even, each looking out for themselves. Now, under Ida Somers' watchful eye, they worked as a team and the atmosphere was quite convivial. Of course, earning money and receiving a daily meal both for themselves and their offspring every noon helped. The regular sustenance gave the women energy to concentrate on their sewing, the children their lessons, and the delicious aroma emanating from the pot over the fire made Louisa's mouth water. Lizzie, one of the young widows who'd been given the responsibility of catering for the women, had proven to be a good cook and her stews with barley and beans were always popular.

'Morning, Lady Louisa, Lady Victoria.' The supervisor, a tiny woman in a black dress, came scurrying over to greet them, her bird-like eyes bright with curiosity.

'Good morning, Mrs Somers. Everyone looks happy,' Louisa replied.

'They are. Which is more than yer does, if yer don't mind my saying,' the woman replied, scrutinizing Victoria closely.

'Actually, Mrs Somers, I do have a problem and wondered if you might be able to help.'

'Sit yerselves down and spill the beans, but not them in the stew, mind,' the woman cackled, pulling out a chair at the furthest end of the table and ignoring the curious glances being cast their way. 'So, how can Ida help?' Sensing the gravity of the situation she leaned closer, nodding thoughtfully as Victoria outlined her problem.

'So, you see, Mrs Somers, I really am in a pickle,' she finished. 'I told Papa I needn't go, but he insists.'

'Cors yer must. Yer whole future depends on it. If we gets hold of some silk, I'll make yer a suitable gown. Time's short so it wouldn't be anything fancy but there's nothing wrong with me stitching. I wonder . . . ' she hesitated and bit her lip.

'What do you wonder, Mrs Somers?' Louisa prompted.

'If we should pay young Jane Haydon and her new shop in Salthaven a visit. I hear she has kept working despite losing . . . ' she paused. 'Well, since Sam's accident,' she finished quickly, aware of the sensitivity of the subject.

'Poor Jane,' Louisa murmured. 'It would be lovely to see her again.'

'It would, and she might have some suitable fabric. If she doesn't, she'll probably know where we can get some.'

'Of course,' Victoria cried, brightening. 'It is only right we should give her our custom, and even if she doesn't have any material, I shall need appropriate underpinning for silk is notoriously unforgiving.'

'I could always make you some stays,' Jeannie offered eagerly, not the least bit embarrassed to own she'd been listening in on their conversation. 'They be renowned in these parts.'

'That is truly kind of you, Jeannie, and we'll bear that in mind, won't we, Victoria?'

'Oh, er, yes,' her sister replied, trying not to shudder at the thought of the coarse straplike contraptions the woman was reputed to produce.

'However, Salthaven is a few miles further along the coast, so we really do need to be leaving,' Louisa continued, rising to her feet.

'But what about the work here?' Ida Somers frowned, gazing anxiously around the hall.

'Ladies, please may I have your attention?' Louisa requested. As the room fell silent and heads turned in her direction, she smiled. 'I am pleased to see you all working so diligently and may I congratulate you on your neat stitching,' she added, gesturing to the growing pile of vests and shirts on the table before them. The women grinned, delighted at the praise. 'The quarrymen are so delighted with their new garments they've spread the word and we have received our first order from local fishermen.' The women's smiles widened, for although it had taken them some time to master the sewing, they had persevered and now took great pride in what they were doing. 'However, I require the services of Mrs Somers for the rest of today and trust that in her absence you will continue working to meet the next deadline?'

'You know you can rely on us,' replied a young woman called Rosa, and her colleagues nodded in agreement. They were on to a good thing, and they knew it. Opportunities for women were scarce in small communities such as this. Although a few skilled women were struggling to eke a living from making pillow lace, demand for that was waning since machines had been introduced in the factory further up the county in Tiverton. Fear of ending up in the workhouse was never far away.

'Thank you, ladies. Should you encounter any problem, please consult Rosa.'

'Me?' Rosa squeaked, her eyes widening in surprise.

'Yes, Rosa, you have a good grasp of everything. Should anything require the particular attention of Mrs Somers, note it down in this book for when she returns,' Louisa said, opening her reticule.

'You'd trust me with this?' the girl gasped, staring at the delicate silver case on the table in astonishment.

'Of course. Now, we really do need to be on our way,' she said, heading for the door.

'Well, I'da be. Who'd have thought yer'd need me?' Ida Somers muttered, fastening her shawl around her shoulders. 'Ooh, it's that nice Mr Quick,' she cooed, patting her hair into place beneath her bonnet when she saw the driver waiting. 'Ta, I'm sure,' she said, smiling flirtatiously up at him, as, defying propriety, she clambered in before the ladies.

Raising a brow at her sister, Louisa climbed up beside her. The woman was outrageous, and from the flush creeping up his neck, Quick was embarrassed by such overt attention.

They set off through the lush countryside, but the trees, with their froth of blossom, golden gorse and glimpses of the aquamarine sea far below passed unnoticed, as Victoria showed Ida Somers the list of things she was required to take.

'I've ticked off those garments I already have, but, as you can see, there is much left to purchase.'

''Tis more items than I'da can imagine one person needing for the whole of their life, let alone one Season,' she murmured, shaking her head in disbelief. 'And 'tis all goin' to cost a small fortune.'

'Papa insists we are not to worry about that,' Louisa assured her. 'The important thing is to ensure Victoria has everything she needs for her debut.'

'What that I'da had such a father,' the woman muttered. 'Still, don't yer worry, Lady Victoria, I'da make sure yer be the belle of all them balls,' she said, brightening.

'As long as we can find suitable fabric for my coming-out gown,' Victoria sighed, returning to her list.

'Didn't yer never want to be presented at court?' Ida asked, turning to Louisa. 'I mean, what with yer being the oldest an' all.' As the woman's beady eyes bore into her, Louisa bit her lip. Really, her impertinence knew no bounds. However, in fairness, she had been willing to help.

'As soon as I met Henry – Captain Beauchamp – I knew he was the man for me, so there seemed little point.' She sat back reflecting. With his chiselled cheekbones, piercing blue eyes and fair hair that stubbornly curled at the ends, he was the most attractive man she had ever met. Of course, the last time she'd seen him, he'd been about to join his regiment, the Grenadier Guards, in Southampton. How handsome he had looked in his uniform of red jacket with stiff gold collar and tasselled epaulettes over tight black trousers. Remembering he was now in Gallipoli and the danger he was facing, her dark eyes clouded, and she let out a sigh.

'And now yer fretting about him out there fighting with them Ottomans. Oh yes, I'da might be a poor old dressmaker but she knows what's happening in the world.'

'I'm sure you do, Mrs Somers, and, yes, I pray each night that Henry will be spared,' she replied, her hand reaching for his dress button that she always kept with her.

'Which was more than my hubby were at the quarry,' Ida sighed. ''Tis always the good ones taken first. Like poor Sam. I'da been wondering how Jane's coping,' the woman sighed, oblivious to Louisa battling her emotions. 'And I'da always wanted to see that fancy shop of hers. Cors, she makes corsets while I'da be the experienced dressmaker,' she said, puffing up with importance. 'Ooh, we's nearly there.'

Thank heavens, thought Louisa, averting her gaze for the woman's incessant chattering was making her head throb.

Crossing the two-arched bridge over the river, they slowly descended into the town of Salthaven with its magnificent mix of Georgian and Regency buildings. Beyond, the blue waters of the bay shimmered in the sunshine while gulls squawked as they wheeled on the thermals. The cart slowly made its way along the promenade, crowded with shoppers and people taking the air. It was a fashionable resort with ladies attired in the latest mode.

'Jane should do well here,' Louisa commented, holding onto the side of the cart as they veered off to the right.

'She deserves to after all she has been through. Ah, here we are,' Victoria declared as they clattered to a stop outside a three-storey Regency building with a fan-shaped window above the ornate front door. The sign in neat gilt script proclaimed Madame Rosetta, *Corsetiere*, then underneath, Jane

Haydon, Proprietor. It was situated between an apothecary and gentleman's outfitters, but Victoria was too busy staring at the enchanting items displayed in the bay window to notice. 'Goodness, look at that fringed parasol and those reticules with twinkly beads,' she exclaimed. 'And just think, Step Mama isn't here to oversee my purchases.'

Chapter 3

Chester Square, London

Feeling like a canary in a cage, Charlotte prowled around the little sitting room adjoining the guest bedroom her sister had assigned her for the Season. Whilst Emmeline had done everything to make her welcome, the dated decor and furnishings upset her sensibilities. Situated on the third floor of the tall town house in Chester Square, there was no denying the rooms were well situated with views over the green and a glimpse of the limestone church of St Michael. However, compared with those at Nettlecombe, they were tiresomely small and sparsely furnished. Thankfully, fittings for her new wardrobe with Madame Helene and sittings for her portraiture with the handsome Mr Maclise had meant she'd had to spend little time here since her arrival. Now, with Victoria's appearance imminent, space would be even more limited. It was her intention to ensure Victoria secured a good marriage during the Season therefore admirers would need to see her in the best possible light when they called.

Whilst the drawing room downstairs was presentable, even if it was dreadfully outmoded with its faded gold decor and insipid water colours of daffodils and dahlias, they would need more seating for suitors. Still, Nicholas and Emmeline could hardly object when their daughter Hester would be receiving them too. Her musing was interrupted by a knock on the door.

'Enter,' she invited grandly. 'Oh, it's you,' she added as her sister stepped into the room.

'Who were you expecting, Her Majesty the Queen?' Emmeline teased. Ten years older, blonde tresses threaded with silver in places, her blue eyes sparkled with amusement giving her a softer appearance. 'Although the way you are dressed you could well be,' she added.

'A lady should be the epitome of femininity at all times,' Charlotte replied, smoothing down the wide silk skirts that accentuated her tiny waist.

'Well, you always did place great emphasis on appearance. Goodness, not another delivery?' Emmeline cried, noticing the beribboned boxes from a couture atelier.

'Talking of appearances, you do realize there is insufficient seating in your drawing room for entertaining guests?' Charlotte sighed, countering the question with one of her own. 'I really don't know how you put up with the privations.'

'We are hardly living in poverty, sister dear. In fact, I'm rather proud of our house here in the square, and of Nicholas too. Other lawyers and scholars live nearer the busy city in places like Bloomsbury, you know. Besides, we have always found the drawing room adequate for entertaining. Gracious, wherever did that come from?' she asked, gesturing to the gold and pink porcelain timepiece with its scroll and floral decoration that now stood on the mantel.

'I needed something to brighten the place,' Charlotte

replied. 'I had the one in the great hall at Nettlecombe specially commissioned.'

'Hmm,' her sister murmured then frowned. 'I did request vases of fresh flowers be placed in here whilst you were out.'

'I had the maid remove them. You should know by now their sickly smell gets up my nose. It is bad enough having all this flowery wallpaper everywhere,' she grumbled, grimacing at the silver-grey walls overlaid with blossoms and birds.

'It used to be the nursery, but we turned it into this comfortable sitting room to give you extra space and privacy whilst you are here.'

'I do appreciate that, for the rooms are somewhat smaller than I'm used to,' Charlotte acknowledged. 'Anyway, my portraiture will be arriving shortly and will look perfect above the fireplace.'

'Chambers mentioned she'd been asked to escort you again. Whilst I don't mind sharing a maid, she does have enough duties of her own to carry out.'

'Servants need to be fully occupied or they get up to no good,' Charlotte told her. 'Besides, Mr Maclise said I had such delicate features he required a few sittings to ensure he did justice to my likeness.'

'And no doubt charged a fortune for each one.'

'Edwin can afford it,' Charlotte said airily, trying not to smile at the thought of his horrified expression when he received the bill. Serve him right for putting his daughters before her, she thought, still aggrieved at the way he'd sent her away.

'Well, I wouldn't wish to sit still that long,' Emmeline replied. 'Nor waste Nicholas' money.'

Charlotte shot her a disparaging look. Emmeline's husband might be hardworking, but he spent his spare time helping those less fortunate, receiving only a pittance for his efforts. While her sister endorsed his ethics, it didn't leave them much to spend on the finer things. Funding Hester's Season would have been impossible if the girl's godmother, the Countess of Kilcoyle, hadn't proposed sponsoring her as well as furnishing the requisite wardrobe.

'When exactly are Edwin and Victoria arriving?' Emmeline asked, perching on the chaise. 'It still seems strange you didn't travel together.'

'I told you, I came ahead to prepare. It takes time to select the style and fabric for new gowns.' Having visited London's most elite modiste, she would be admirably attired for all the balls and parties the Season would afford. After her dreary existence in the depths of the countryside, she intended to have some fun.

'As we will merely be chaperones on the sidelines, surely it is Victoria on whom you should be concentrating. I mean, what about her debutante gown? Dressmakers are extremely busy at this time of year. We had to book one for Hester months back.' Charlotte shrugged but Emmeline persisted. 'She must need guidance, and, as her stepmother—'

'Gracious, Emmeline, do stop fussing,' Charlotte interjected. 'Edwin's girls never listen to me. I have sent Victoria a list detailing everything she needs to bring, so have hardly neglected my duties.'

Emmeline frowned. 'Is everything all right between you and Edwin? You used to send such glowing reports of your life in Devonshire, yet in the weeks you have been here you've hardly mentioned him.'

'I have to confess, family life is hardly exciting. Nobody appreciates the efforts I go to.'

'One can hardly expect gratitude for being a mother. It goes with the territory.' Emmeline smiled. 'As long as mine get fed on a regular basis, they are happy. Of course, William, Thomas and Robert live their own lives now.'

Charlotte sighed. 'At least you have heirs.'

'Ah, so that's the problem. I wondered why you hadn't asked after your nephews,' Emmeline said gently.

'It would have been so satisfying to present Edwin with a boy, especially as his first wife didn't,' Charlotte murmured.

'You are still young enough to have another child,' Emmeline pointed out.

The gentleness of her voice hardened Charlotte's heart for she couldn't bring herself to admit that, far from showing loving attention, Edwin had sent her away for neglecting their daughters.

'I'm sure he hardly notices I'm not there.'

'Well, in that case, a little time apart will make him realize just how much he misses you.'

Giving a sad little smile, Charlotte rose to her feet and crossed to the window. She peered down at the street below where hansom cabs and carriages rolled by, and smartly dressed people with places to be strode purposefully along.

'Being buried in the depths of the Devonshire countryside is dreary; at least you have the excitement of life pulsating around you here,' she sighed, choosing to ignore the crossing sweepers dodging the traffic to clear the street of dung and debris.

'Forgive me if I don't feel much sympathy, sister dear; after all, you have married into a life of privilege. Now tell me, did Edwin say how my lovely little nieces, Sarah and Maria, are? And the delightful Nanny?'

'I am given to understand a governess has been engaged, so, with no further role to play at Nettlecombe, I presume the old witch has been sent packing. Don't look at me like that,' she snapped, as Emmeline stared aghast. 'She was too ancient to be of any use. Why, she even went out and left them by themselves one afternoon,' she added, the story she had concocted becoming a reality as she spoke.

'Goodness, that doesn't sound like the Nanny I met. She absolutely adores those girls.'

'Anyway, in answer to your earlier question, I have requested Edwin and Victoria be here by next Sunday.'

'It will be lovely to see them again and I know Hester is excited about sharing such an important time with her cousin.'

'Indeed, now can we please change the subject?' Charlotte said, settling herself back in her seat. 'Do you have any social events arranged for us this week?' She stared hopefully at her sister.

'I thought we would be finalising our plans for the girls. There is much to consider, after all. Besides, I've hardly seen you since you arrived, and it would be nice to spend time together. As you know, I have my afternoon shifts at Haven House, the local women's refuge. You are welcome to come with me; an extra pair of hands is always useful.'

'You seem to forget I'm a lady of the manor now.'

'Not much chance of that, sister dear,' Emmeline chuckled. 'However, there is nothing like helping those in need for putting one's own problems into perspective.' Just then the angel on the clock trumpeted the quarter hour and Emmeline jumped to her feet.

'Heavens, what a frightful sound. Well, I'd better go and change. Nicholas has invited a new work colleague for dinner. Apparently, the man has removed to the area and has yet to make any friends. Some company might cheer you up,' she added.

'It will be an opportunity to wear one of my new ensembles,' Charlotte conceded, sitting up straighter and patting her hair. 'This idea of skirts with matching bodices gives one a much better choice.'

'Lucky you.' Emmeline grimaced down at her green skirt, which had seen better days but was still serviceable enough to wear to the house she'd turned into a sanctuary for fallen women. 'Shall I send Chambers to assist when she has done her best with me?'

'Yes, do, although we won't have to share a maid much longer, I have requested Shears accompany Victoria.'

'That will make all our lives easier. We will see you downstairs for preprandial drinks in an hour.'

As the door closed, Charlotte smiled. Some new male attention might be interesting.

Dressed in her new lilac evening bodice, which tapered to a point over the matching domed skirt, Charlotte checked her reflection in the mirror. The low neckline and bare shoulders showed off her porcelain skin while a jewelled comb sparkled in her fair tresses. A string of lustrous pearls would have set the whole outfit off to perfection but, annoyingly, Edwin seemed to have forgotten the akoya ones he'd promised to buy her. However, the Farringdon pearls she'd seen in the Nettlecombe vault were even finer, and, as lady of the manor, her entitlement. If, as Emmeline suggested, Edwin had missed her, he would surely be in a conciliatory mood when he arrived. Spirits lifted at the thought, she picked up her wrap and tripped lightly down the stairs.

Following the sound of light-hearted chatter, Charlotte paused in the doorway, her gaze meeting with that of their guest. With his wavy hair and dark, fathomless eyes, he was undeniably a most attractive man. As Nicholas spotted her, both men rose to their feet.

'Lady Farringdon, may I present my colleague Alexander Clarke. Alexander, this is Emmeline's sister, Lady Charlotte Farringdon.'

'I am pleased to make your acquaintance, Lady Farringdon,' he said, his look of appreciation sending a quiver down her spine.

'Please call me Charlotte; I am not one to stand on ceremony,' she replied, smiling demurely and ignoring Emmeline's snort of amusement. As the dinner gong sounded, Alexander proffered his arm.

'What a shame you missed the preprandial,' he murmured.

As napkins were placed and the soup served, Charlotte covertly studied the man sitting opposite. His dark jacket was impeccably cut, shirt snowy as the crisp tablecloth, the gold of his cufflinks glinting in the candlelight. Below her status, of course, but his admiring look was balm to her wounded pride. Seeing Emmeline frown, she gave her brightest smile.

'I understand you have recently removed to the area, Mr Clarke. Have you travelled far?'

'From the south coast; Brighton, in fact. And my friends call me Alexander.' She nodded and turned her attention to the duck consommé.

'Charlotte is staying with us for the Season,' Emmeline told their guest as their dishes were cleared and the roast lamb served. 'Both our daughters are to be presented.'

Charlotte shot her a look, for the man must be in his mid-thirties and heaven forbid he should think her an older woman, but she needn't have worried.

'That is both exciting and surprising,' he murmured, quirking his brow. 'I can't believe you have daughters reaching maturity.'

'Victoria is my stepdaughter. There is little difference in our years,' she said, smiling sweetly. As Emmeline spluttered, she glowered and gave her a kick under the table. However, Alexander nodded gallantly then turned his attention to the sherry trifle decorated with glistening cherries and angelica that was placed before him.

Having declined dessert, Charlotte sipped her wine and focused on the wallpaper. Really Emmeline's taste was as lacking as her tact, she thought, studying the green diamond shapes on a burgundy ground.

'I must compliment you on a wonderful meal, Emmeline,' Alexander said, pushing his empty dish to one side. 'I couldn't help noticing your interest in furnishings,' he added, turning his attention to Charlotte. 'In Brighton we have a building called the Royal Pavilion. It was built for The Prince of Wales and is the most exquisite edifice with ornate banqueting hall and a music room festooned with glorious chandeliers. There is simply nowhere like it.'

'What about that magnificent structure built for the Exhibition of Fifty-One? Now there's splendid architecture, referred to as The Palace of Crystal by the playwright Jerrold, and quite rightly in my opinion,' Nicholas countered.

'Although it's been relocated to Penge Common,' Emmeline told them. 'The whole thing is being rebuilt on the Peak there; it could well be worth a visit.'

'Perhaps we could go together,' Alexander suggested, and, although he looked at each of them in turn, Charlotte was sure his gaze lingered on her a moment longer.

'I would be happy to offer use of my carriage,' she told them. 'It is stabled in the mews behind.'

'Well, that is something for future consideration. However, you must forgive us, ladies, Alexander and I have business to discuss in my study,' Nicholas said, rising to his feet.

'Will you join us later?' Emmeline asked.

'Regrettably not tonight, my dear.' He lowered his voice. 'We have received instructions regarding a case of fraud in the city. It's a messy business, which is why Alexander has been called in. As you can imagine, there is much to deliberate.'

'Thank you again for a splendid meal, Emmeline,' Alexander said. 'And it has been lovely to meet you,' he added, his eyes full of promise as he stared at Charlotte.

'Shall we go through to the drawing room?' Emmeline asked once the men had left.

'Actually, I'm rather tired and think I shall retire for the night,' Charlotte replied, impatient to relive the details of the evening in the privacy of her chamber. As she rose to her feet, her sister laid a hand on her arm.

'Be careful, Charlotte,' she cautioned.

'I'm sure I don't know what you mean.'

'I know that look of old, sister dear. Remember you are a married woman with a stepdaughter about to be presented at court.'

'Honestly, Emmeline, you always did have a vivid imagination,' Charlotte retorted, making for the staircase. She hadn't had so much fun in ages. Edwin hardly noticed her these days and Alexander's admiring looks had reminded her she was still an attractive woman.

Chapter 4

Salthaven, Devonshire

Hearing voices rising from the shop below her workroom, which they still called the *magasin* in memory of her former benefactor Madame Pittier, Jane Haydon looked up from the corded taffeta corset she was endeavouring to finish. She knew Miss Brown – the apprentice who had been with her since she'd opened her business in this seaside town earlier in the year – was quite capable of dealing with those ladies who visited the establishment. Even those, expecting to be fitted for their underpinnings immediately. With dark eyes that missed nothing, despite being known as Mouse, her polite manner was a foil for her steely determination. Before they knew it, clients had been shown the range of fabric available and were clutching a card detailing their appointment. Today, however, one voice sounded particularly insistent, and it was then she realized who that person was.

Quickly covering the delicate material with a sheet, she checked her crisp white blouse for any stray thread from her sewing, straightened her navy skirts and hurried down the stairs.

'Goodness, Louisa, Victoria and Mrs Somers, how kind of you to visit my establishment,' Jane greeted them.

'It is an enchanting place. A veritable treasure trove,' Victoria cried excitedly.

'I'm sorry, Miss Haydon, I did explain you only see clients by appointment . . . ' Mouse began, looking anxiously at her employer.

'I wouldn't trouble you, Jane, but we find ourselves in a predicament,' Louisa told her, turning from the fringed parasol she'd been admiring.

'And they need yer and me to help,' Ida said, puffing out her chest importantly before inhaling deeply. 'It do smell lovely in here, just like a rose garden and I see yer still wears a pink bud at yer throat. And look at all these colourful things yer got,' she added, gazing at the mannequins draped in their pink chemises, the bolts of fabric neatly stacked on the shelves, drawers of ribbons, lace and velvet open to entice the customer. She turned back to Jane and frowned. 'Yer lookin' peaky though, how are yer managing?'

Jane shrugged, knowing her pallid skin and the dark smudges beneath her eyes told their own story of sleepless nights and that cold empty feeling that came with knowing she would never see her beloved Sam again. She squared her shoulders and forced a smile. Business was her focus now.

'Hello, Jane, I do apologize for imposing,' Victoria ventured.

'But you're not,' Jane hastened to reassure her. 'Why don't we go through to the Receiving Room, and you can tell me what the problem is. Please ask Millie to bring us some refreshment, Miss Brown,' she said, smiling reassuringly at the young girl. Then, knowing there wouldn't be enough seating in the cosy room, she picked up the cushioned chair from beside the counter and led the way.

'Make yourselves comfortable,' Jane invited, gesturing to the chaise decorated with a cherry shawl. The warmth from the fire, necessary for when her clients disrobed for their fitting, intensified the fragrance of the dried rose petals in the crystal bowl, lending the place a welcoming ambience.

'What a pleasant room,' Louisa said, taking in the bright furnishings and embroidered divider in the corner. 'How have you been keeping?' she asked.

'Busy. I find it's the best way, thank you,' Jane replied quickly, blinking back thoughts of the accident. Her emotions were still too raw to speak of Sam. Their sympathy, however well intentioned, would be her undoing. 'Now, you spoke of a predicament, how can I help?'

Once again, Victoria found herself outlining the contents of her stepmother's letter.

'So, you see, without a white silk gown and appropriate accoutrements, I cannot make my debut,' she finished, giving a slender shrug of her shoulders.

'They came to me for help and I'da suggested yer might have something suitable,' Ida Somers said quickly. 'I mean yer has to start with the dress before you can even think of anything else, don't yer?'

'Ideally, yes,' Jane agreed.

'Yer've got some lovely fabrics in yer shop, but I'da didn't see no white silk.'

'I'm afraid I don't have any of the quality you require. I'm still building up my stock, you see.'

'Do you know where we might purchase some?' Louisa asked. 'Papa said to tell you that he will pay whatever is necessary.'

'Here we is,' the maid announced, bouncing into the room in her frilly white apron, cap perched on wayward curls. Setting down the tray with a flourish that set the cups and saucers rattling, she turned to the visitors. 'Yous can tell yous Pa we don't charge for refreshments. We met at poor Sam's funeral, didn't we?' she added.

'We did indeed,' Louisa smiled politely.

'Thank you, Millie. You can leave me to pour,' Jane said quickly.

'Righty-o. Nice seeing yous again,' the maid chirped.

'Fancy yer having staff,' Ida exclaimed, taking the cup Jane proffered.

'Yes, I'm lucky, I couldn't manage both my business and the house without them. Now, about your predicament,' she said, turning back to Victoria.

'Is there any way you can help?' the young woman asked.

Jane quickly shook her head, feeling terrible when she saw Victoria's look of disappointment.

'Well, I'm sorry to have disturbed you,' she said, but Jane, busy battling with her conscience, didn't hear.

She couldn't, could she? Surely, she couldn't be expected to. It wouldn't be right. And yet, it would be of no use to her now, would it? And she was meant to be a businesswoman. Before she could change her mind, she shot to her feet, causing her guests to stare at her in surprise.

'I've just remembered something. If you'd like to follow me to the workroom,' she invited, leading the way out into the

31

hall and up the stairs. Moving her sewing aside, she hurried over to the shelf in the furthest corner of the room, but, as her hands reached out, she started, sure she'd heard clacking of looms and voices singing in a foreign tongue. 'Oh,' she gasped, turning back to the others. However, unaware of anything amiss, they were waiting patiently. Shaking her head, she snatched up the parcel and placed it on the long table. Steeling herself, she peeled back the layers of soft paper and cotton sheeting, a shower of dried rose petals scattering around them. There was a stunned silence as they gazed in wonder at the lustrous white silk.

'Oh my, that certainly be some quality material,' Ida exclaimed, reaching out as if to stroke it, then withdrawing her hand at the last moment. However, the temptation proved too great, and she tentatively ran a finger over the soft fibres. 'This has been woven by the finest of craftsmen. Where did yer get such fabric?' she asked, her sharp eyes scrutinizing Jane. Luckily, before she had a chance to reply, Victoria spoke.

'Gracious, look at that delicate gold thread running through it.'

'It gives the fabric a luminosity that would sit well against your skin, Victoria. Is it for sale?' Louisa asked. Not trusting her voice, Jane nodded.

'It will make the perfect debut gown,' Victoria exclaimed, her dark eyes glowing amber with excitement. 'You can turn this into one, can't you?'

'With careful cutting, there should just be sufficient for that,' Jane murmured, fighting down the temptation to say she had changed her mind. This was business after all. 'And, of course, you will need underpinning in the correct colour,' she added, remembering Victoria's previous choice.

'Trust me to choose charcoal last time,' Victoria groaned. 'Although the look of horror on Step Mama's face when she saw the corset was worth it.'

'Why don't we go back downstairs and finish our tea whilst we discuss what needs to be done and by whom,' Jane said, unable to bear looking at the fabric any longer. It wouldn't be fair to let her own emotions dampen Victoria's excitement.

'We'll require a pattern for the dress,' Jane said, once they had reclaimed their seats in the Receiving Room.

'I did bring a copy of *The Ladies' Companion* with me, just in case,' Victoria said, quickly opening the reticule on her lap. 'My understanding is that a debut robe should be a relatively simple one. With a train, of course,' she added, passing the copy that was opened at the relevant page. A train as well? Jane's heart sank.

'Simple in style perhaps, but quality silk such as that requires skilful working, but then you're an experienced dressmaker, Mrs Somers,' she said, turning to the woman who, to her surprise, stared back in horror.

'I've worked on quality fabric, of course, but never one such as this. Although I'll help with pinning the hem, of course. And as yer know I'm good at the toiles,' she added quickly.

'But there won't be time for toiles,' Jane cried. 'It will take ages to make a gown with a train and suitable corset by myself.'

'Unless yous had one of them sewing machines yous always

talking about,' Millie said, waltzing into the room to collect the tray.

'Is this true?' Louisa asked, turning to Jane.

'It would make the task more achievable. However, I don't have one, so the issue isn't relevant,' she said, glaring at Millie, who grinned back unrepentantly before scuttling away. She really would have to speak to that girl, she thought, before turning her attention back to her visitors.

Having agreed the silk would make a wonderful debut gown in the design Victoria desired, Louisa suggested to Ida they have a look at the accessories in the shop whilst Jane noted her sister's measurements.

'Do you wish to choose the fabric for your corset?' Jane asked, when she'd meticulously written down the details.

'I'll leave that to you if I may. You know what will work best with that wonderful silk. To think you had it hidden in your workroom. It's almost as if it was meant to be,' Victoria exclaimed, clapping her hands in delight. 'Perhaps you could help me select the right accoutrements, as Step Mama calls them. I can't wait to see her face when I appear in all my finery. Do you think you can make my gown, in, well . . . it will have to be finished in a week, for we have to be in London next weekend?'

One week! Jane swallowed hard, then, seeing Victoria's quizzical gaze, thought quickly. 'You will need to come in for a fitting on Thursday then.'

Was it her or were the walls closing in? 'Shall we join the others?' she suggested, rising quickly to her feet.

In the shop, the ladies were delving into the drawers, gasping in delight at the array of finery. Finally, their selection made, the glass-fronted counter was hidden beneath an array of brightly coloured chemises, silk gloves, ornamental hair pins, fringe-trimmed parasols and reticules of various shapes.

'Oh, I nearly forgot,' Victoria exclaimed. 'Apparently, I need a headdress with feathers, would you believe? There isn't time to go to the milliners so could you possibly manage to make one like this?' she asked, again tapping her finger against the picture in the magazine.

'It looks simple enough,' Jane replied, praying she would be able to deliver all she was promising. At this rate she would be burning the midnight candle for many nights to come.

'Blimey, this little lot's goin' to cost a king's ransom,' Ida Somers whistled, shaking her head, and sending the cherries on her bonnet bobbing furiously.

Jane stared down at her notebook where she'd been surreptitiously jotting down the cost of each item. Never had she taken so much in one transaction, and that was without pricing the fabric and making up the gown and corset.

'Which Papa will be happy to pay,' Louisa said, misinterpreting Jane's expression. She smiled, yet her delight at being able to purchase more supplies was overshadowed by the thought of sewing the special silk. Victoria's dress was going to take nearly all that was in the parcel, which meant she was going to have to be inventive with the train. And it all had to be done in a few days.

'I can't thank you enough for your help, Jane. If you can have these items wrapped, I will send Quick back later to collect them. And your invoice too, of course,' she added, lowering her voice and staring knowingly.

'I can't wait until Thursday,' Victoria told her excitedly.

By the time the happy group left, with Ida Somers promising to return to help the next day, Jane was exhausted.

'Do I have any fittings other than Mrs Tattersall-Smythe booked in for this afternoon?' she asked Mouse.

'Yes, Lady Cotterill at three thirty,' the girl replied, consulting the appointments diary. 'Miss Frobisher is booked in on Friday, but I can send her a note if that would help,' the girl replied, sensing Jane's agitation.

'That wouldn't be professional and if word got round, it could ruin my reputation, for my business is still as a corsetiere. This gown is a special commission, and I will just have to work into the nights and over the weekend to get it finished,' she added, ignoring the girl's incredulous look. 'Now, this shop is looking decidedly untidy; I'll get Millie to pack the purchases ready for collection while you tidy up before Mrs Tattersall-Smythe arrives. You'd better restock the window as well. Customers can't buy what they can't see,' she added, gesturing towards the depleted display. 'I'll be upstairs in the workroom finishing her corset should you need me.'

'Here, that was a good morning's work,' Millie cried, almost colliding with Jane in the hallway.

'It was,' she agreed. 'However, you really must learn to curb your tongue in front of clients, Millie. Fancy suggesting a sewing machine would make all the difference.'

'Well, it would,' replied the maid, unrepentant as ever.

'I know, but it simply isn't done to mention these things. We're tradespeople, remember?'

'Nothing wrong with that,' Millie sniffed. 'They'd have no fancy things to wear if it weren't for the likes of us. Want me to check them numbers?' she asked, nodding at the list Jane was clutching.

The girl might be irrepressible but there was no denying she had a good head for figures, Jane thought, as she hurried up to the workroom. Unable to bear the sight of the silk shimmering in the sunshine, she rewrapped it and placed it back on the shelf. Forcing herself to concentrate, she settled back to her work, and, if her thoughts strayed as her needle completed the finishing touches, she pushed them firmly away again.

It was early evening and, having checked downstairs was tidy, Jane was about to lock the door when it flew open, sending the little bell ringing furiously.

'My sincere apologies for arriving at this late hour, Miss Haydon.'

'Lord Farringdon?' she exclaimed, staring at the smartly dressed man in surprise. 'I was expecting your coachman.'

'And Quick is here now,' Lord Farringdon stated, as the man, now in smart blue livery, staggered in behind him, his face hidden behind the bulky object he was carrying. 'Perhaps you could direct him to your workroom?'

'My workroom?' Jane stuttered. 'I don't understand.'

'I thinks I might,' Millie chirped, appearing in the doorway. 'Here, let me help,' she offered, hurrying to help Quick manoeuvre the cumbersome article. 'Yous working late an' all then?'

'Seems we all have extra duties to perform this week,' the man replied somewhat breathlessly.

'Forgive the intrusion, Miss Haydon,' Lord Farringdon smiled apologetically. 'Louisa and Victoria came to see me the moment they arrived home. Although delighted you'd agreed to make Victoria's debut gown, they are concerned being without a sewing machine would hinder your progress. Knowing time is of the essence . . . ' he gestured to Quick's departing back.

'I'm pleased to be of service to your daughter, my Lord, but I cannot accept charity.'

'I would prefer you thought it a gesture of goodwill, Miss Haydon,' he replied, respect flashing in his eyes. 'As a person who deals in business myself, I know only too well the pressures deadlines can bring and, if something or someone can assist, then surely that is the way forward.'

'Well, if you put it like that . . . ' Jane wavered.

'I do. My daughter's happiness means everything.' There was an awkward pause as he stood staring at her. He cleared his throat.

'How are you keeping, Miss Haydon? Things can't have been easy for you since . . . well, that terrible accident,' he murmured, his voice sympathetic as he studied her face.

'No, Lord Farringdon, they haven't,' she admitted. 'But life has to go on, doesn't it?'

'It does,' he agreed solemnly, his expression telling Jane that he really did understand.

There was the sound of heavy footsteps as Quick reappeared, this time his arms filled with all the wrapped purchases.

'I'll bid you good evening, Miss Haydon, and my apologies once again for taking up so much of your valuable time.'

'Good evening, Lord Farringdon. Thank you for the loan of the sewing machine. I will see it is returned when Victoria's dress is finished.'

Surprise flashed in his eyes, then he shrugged.

'As you wish, Miss Haydon.'

'Well, that was a stupid thing to say,' Millie squeaked, as the bell tinkled behind him. 'He's only gone and bought the latest machine. The one that does that fancy stitching yous been on about.'

'I have my pride, Millie,' Jane said.

'And that helps pay the bills, I suppose?' the maid scoffed.

'I'll be up in the workroom,' Jane replied. 'Which will help pay the bills,' she retorted. It wasn't fair to take it out on Millie, she knew, but mention of Sam had unsettled her again, and she needed to be by herself.

Ignoring the gleaming machine set on its own little table, she hurried over to the shelf and took down the parcel of precious silk. Unwrapping it for the second time that day, she could contain her grief no longer and hot tears ran like rivers down her cheeks.

Chapter 5

Edwin stared out of the carriage window but all he could see were those sad, sapphire eyes. Before he knew it, they were sweeping up the driveway flanked by the burgeoning lime trees towards the gates of Nettlecombe, its archway and pillars topped with stone griffins that were purported to protect the Farringdon family. Then he caught sight of the fence now surrounding the well in the far field and shifted restlessly in his seat. Unbidden, memories of the tragic accident that had befallen Miss Haydon's betrothed, Sam Gill, came flooding back. Such a waste and he knew only too well the acute pain that loss of a life cut short inflicted. He sighed, thinking it a blessing she had her business to focus on.

Remembering her indignant look as she declared she didn't accept charity, he shook his head. Judging from her depleted stock, it was evident the young woman needed assistance and returning the sewing machine when she'd finished making Victoria's dress, a service she'd agreed to fit in alongside her existing work, was not good business practice. He couldn't help feeling a sense of responsibility for the circumstances she found herself in and would insist she keep the machine he'd called in favours to acquire so quickly.

Bathed in the rosy glow of the setting sun, the Jacobean manor house looked inviting and welcoming. As Quick pulled to a halt and the imposing entrance door opened to receive him, the thought of a relaxing evening with a glass of cognac had never felt more appealing. However, as he stepped down from the carriage, his estate manager hurried towards him.

'May I have a word, my Lord?' he asked, looking uneasy as he took the clay pipe from his mouth.

'Of course, Wilfred. Come inside.'

'No, I won't, if you don't mind. Don't like to leave Edith too long by herself. She still gets agitated and that's why . . . why I need to give you notice to find someone new to run your estate.'

'Are you sure?' Edwin frowned. 'I mean if it's a question of money—' he began, realizing that they were now having to manage without his son's wage.

'No, it's not that,' Wilf replied quickly. 'You've been more than generous. It's the wife, she can't bear to look out on . . . well, where Sam died. And I goes around thinking he'll appear at any moment.' He stopped and sighed. 'We thought we'd see if we can find somewhere near our daughter, Mary. She's with child and it'll give Edith something positive to focus on.'

'Yes, I understand. Although, I shall be sad to lose such a competent manager.'

'Well, I'm getting on now and, of course, Sam were going to take over. Besides, me joints is seizing up after that fall.

41

Been a bad year all round.' He gave another sigh, his lips quivering. Abruptly he jammed his pipe back into his mouth.

'Perhaps a new start would be a good idea. Mary is living on the outskirts of Combe, is she not?' Edwin asked. Wilf nodded and he continued. 'I'll see that a dwelling near to her is made available—'

'I'll not have a salary for . . . ' Wilf interrupted, waving away the whisps of smoke that rose on the evening air between them.

'Rent free for the sterling service you've both given the Farringdons over the years,' Edwin finished. 'As I said, I will be deeply sorry to lose you, but leave it with me and I'll speak with you tomorrow about arrangements. Shall we say five o'clock in my office?'

'Thank you, my Lord.' He gave a weak smile and made his way back towards the stone cottage that had been his home since he and Edith married.

It was late by the time Edwin, glass in hand, finally settled himself into his easy chair beside the fire in his office. The younger girls would have been put to bed hours since and, as the house was quiet, clearly the older ones were otherwise engaged. He'd have a supper tray sent in later.

What a day, he thought. First the discovery of Charlotte's preposterous spending and then her bombshell that Victoria was expected in London for her debut earlier than anticipated. Despite the woman trying to cause trouble, arrangements for Victoria's new gown and accoutrements were now in hand and he had sent word to his housekeeper in Grosvenor Square, informing her of their imminent arrival. As the date for the presentation coincided with Bea's interview, they could all travel together. Despite his misgivings, she was adamant she wished to become a nurse and had countered every objection he'd raised until, finally, he had promised to write to his old friend, Professor Todd. Her determination and stubborn streak were certainly inherited from her late mother, who'd instilled the idea in her daughters that, despite being female, they could do anything they set their mind to.

His monthly inspection of the quarry to discuss any problems with its manager Wakeley was arranged, but now he also needed to find a new estate manager. Loyal and hardworking, Wilf would be difficult to replace. Edwin couldn't imagine him doing nothing though. Perhaps he could find him some other role on the estate. Clearly life at Nettlecombe was about to change.

*

The first rays of early morning sun were filtering through the workroom window when Jane woke with a start. Heavens, she'd fallen asleep at her worktable, she realized, staring anxiously down in case she'd ruined the delicate silk. Luckily, she'd been resting on the cotton it was encased in and it hadn't been marked. However, snippets of her strange dream haunted her. The clacking of looms, foreign voices singing, Madame smiling and reaching out her hands. Clearly her nerves had made her overwrought, she thought, shaking her head to clear it. Only then did she realize she was still clutching the precious bobbin Sam had carved for her. A cherished gift she would keep for ever.

Stretching to ease her aching back, she gasped when she

saw the monstrous shape looming before her. It took a few seconds before she realized it wasn't a gigantic eye staring at her but the wheel of the sewing machine. Rising stiffly to her feet, she went over to inspect it properly.

The arm, needle and plate were mounted on top of a polished wooden table, and it was obviously worked by operating the foot pedal. Seeing the thickness of the needle, she sighed. Despite Lord Farringdon's kindness and the urgency of the situation, there was no way she could risk using that on the delicate silk. How she wished Millie had kept her mouth shut.

Whilst Madame had taught her basic dressmaking skills when she was her apprentice, and she made her own clothes, Jane had never attempted anything as momentous as a debut gown before. Although simple in design she would need to sketch the pattern to the measurements she'd taken. There would barely be enough of the special silk, which wouldn't be easy to work anyway, so there was absolutely no margin for error. It was imperative she got it right first time. At least Ida Somers was coming to help later. Being an experienced dressmaker, the woman would know exactly what to do.

Despite her misgivings, she couldn't resist reaching out and running her finger over the soft fabric, tracing the delicate golden thread that ran through it. As the vision of a young man with loving hazel eyes and mischievous smile swam before her, she blinked back the seemingly ever-present tears. Sighing for what would never now be, she hurried through to the bedroom to wash and change into her dark skirt and pink satin blouse.

'Ooh, that Quick be a fine fellow,' Ida Somers exclaimed, sending the little bell tinkling as she burst through the door a couple of hours later. Her cheeks were as rosy as the cherries that bobbed on her bonnet.

'Did you travel in Lord Farringdon's carriage?' Jane asked, staring at the woman in surprise as the sound of hooves receded.

'No, his cart. The ladies ride in it when they're working with the Quarry Crafters. Don't want to offend them by using the plush carriage. Anyhow, after Quick dropped them off he were told to bring me here. I'm to help yer each day until Victoria's dress is made. Suits me fine 'cos, like I said, that Quick's quite a man. Shy though; when I said how nice it was, us riding together, he didn't reply.' She shook her head, setting the cherries bobbing wildly again. 'Still, males can be a bit slow on the uptake and yer has to put the notion of romance in their heads, don't yer?' she winked slyly.

'It's good of Louisa and Victoria to let you come here to help,' Jane replied, as soon as she could get a word in.

'They suggested yer might like to work up at the manor, but I didn't think yer'd like that,' Ida added quickly when she saw Jane's horrified expression.

'No, I wouldn't be able to concentrate,' Jane shuddered. Her little shop with bales of coloured fabric lining the shelves, glass-fronted counter topped with a vase of fragrant rose potpourri and the little pink chair for her clients had become her sanctuary. 'Let's go up to the workroom and make a start,' she said, forcing her thoughts back to the present. 'You'll be all right, won't you?' she asked Mouse, who was tidying the rolls of ribbons in the drawer.

'Yes, Miss Haydon.' The girl's eyes lit up and she nodded enthusiastically.

Jane smiled, for there was no denying that Mouse reminded her of her younger self when she'd loved nothing better than being in charge of Madame's *magasin* when she'd had a fitting. As she made her way up the stairs, it occurred to her that this title, whilst appropriate when the business had been in Exeter, wasn't right for Salthaven. She would have to give it some thought.

However, there was no time for reflection, for on entering the workroom Ida gaped in astonishment.

'Oh my . . . would yer look at that fearsome beast,' she exclaimed, crossing the room for a closer look. 'And it's threaded up ready. Well, it might be the latest thing but yer still won't get me using it.' She glared down at the treadle and sniffed. 'Whoever heard of stitching with yer feet.'

'We've a lot to do before we even get to the sewing,' Jane pointed out, wondering what the woman did intend doing to help.

'I'da says, tidy mind, tidy work', Ida Somers stated, nodding to the table where Jane had already laid out her tools.

At least they agreed on something, Jane thought. As was her way, the work box sat to her right and her sharpest shears, chalks, marking silks, paper, pins and measuring tape were all set in a line. Alongside the picture of the gown in *The Ladies' Companion* lay the pattern she'd sketched out earlier. She'd also found some suitable ostrich feathers which, when trimmed and attached to a toning length of fabric, would make up the headdress. Finally, her gaze came to rest on the silk spread out ready for measuring and cutting. Its gossamer sheen looked quite ethereal today and a shiver shuddered down her spine. Come on, Jane, you can do this, she steeled herself.

'That must have cost a pretty penny. Where did yer get it then?' Ida Somers asked, her bird-like eyes staring candidly at Jane.

'I found it hidden in the back of a cupboard when we were moving from Exeter. Madame was dead by then, so I had no way of knowing why it was there.'

'Well, it's the finest silk I'da ever seen. In fact, it would make a—' she broke off her eyes widening in realization. 'Oh, yer was going to use it for yer wedding dress, weren't yer?' she said. Unable to trust her voice, Jane nodded. 'That's a worthy thing you done offering it to Lady Victoria,' the woman said, patting her hand. 'And in Ida's experience, good breeds good. Now, yer'll want to make a start on the measuring and marking, so I'll get on with that headdress.'

'I thought we would be working on the dress together,' Jane began but Ida had tucked one of the plumes behind the cherries on her bonnet and was dancing down the room. 'I'da be goin' to the ball,' she chortled.

'Perhaps you could begin by trimming them,' Jane suggested, suppressing a sigh as she turned back to the silk. Ida Somers was right, of course, it was better being put to good use than languishing on the shelf. And it wasn't as if she was going to need it herself. Her heart had died along with Sam and her business was now her future. Still, this was a prestigious commission that could only enhance her reputation. As long as she got it right. And finished in time.

She turned her attention to laying the pattern on the silk in the most efficient way. However, the fabric was slippery and kept sliding along the table so that she had to start over again.

'Yer should smooth out the paper it came wrapped in and put it on that,' Ida called from the other end of the table.

'Good idea,' Jane agreed, wondering why she hadn't thought of it herself. By the time she'd finally got the pattern laid out and held down with weights, for even silk pins might leave holes in such a delicate weave, she was feeling hot and bothered. She never had this much trouble working on her corsets. Determinedly, she picked up the chalk ready to mark out the seam allowance.

'Yous tea is getting cold,' Millie chirped, peering round the door.

'I asked to have refreshments set out in the kitchen at noon,' Jane replied, fighting down her exasperation at the interruption.

'The bell on the church clock tolled that ages ago,' the maid pointed out.

'Well, I can't stop now; I've got far too much to do.'

'Come on, Jane, you need a break and there's nothing better than a curative cuppa to get things into perspective,' Ida chided.

Jane stared at the fabric still waiting to be cut out and sighed.

'Just ten minutes then,' she conceded, putting her hand to her head. All that concentrating had left her feeling as though someone had stabbed her with every single pin in the jar.

Chapter 6

Fortified from luncheon, yet nervous of cutting into the delicate fabric, Jane set about remeasuring everything.

'That's it dear, measure twice, cut once,' Ida Somers chirped as she scuttled to the other end of the table and took up the headdress again. Admittedly, it was looking good, but Jane would have welcomed some help. Yet the woman was humming happily as she worked which at least left her free to concentrate.

Satisfied her measurements were correct, Jane picked up the shears and took a deep breath. The rasp of metal on silk as she made the first cut sounded loud, making her jump. Fearful of making a mistake, progress was slow and laborious but, by the end of the afternoon, the pieces had been cut. Picking up the strips that were left, Jane was disappointed to find there was less remaining than she'd hoped. She was either going to have to make the train smaller than the one in the picture, or somehow incorporate another fabric into the design.

'Yer'll need to tack them sides together before yer sew the seams,' Ida commented, leaning over her shoulder. 'Best use the hand-basting technique; silk will pucker else. Ooh,

I can hear me lift.' She grinned, straightening her bonnet and pinching colour into her cheeks.

'But I don't know what that technique is,' Jane cried, staring at her in dismay.

''Tis only loose stitches to hold the pieces together,' Ida explained. 'Oh, give it here,' she sighed, settling on the seat beside Jane and threading a fine needle. 'Like this, see,' she said, her needle moving surely in and out. 'It's the best way to make sure yer final seams will be smooth. 'Now, I mustn't keep Mr Handsome waiting.'

As the clatter of boots on the stairs receded, Jane suppressed a sigh and turned back to her work. The stitches looked like a dotted line, and yet as she tried to replicate them, she realized it was not as easy as Ida Somers made out. It was going to take an age to do so before she made a start, she needed to check that all was well in the shop.

'Is everything all right in here?' she asked Mouse.

'Yes, Miss Haydon, although it's been hectic. Two ladies were most insistent they be fitted for new corsets this week but knowing how busy you are with the gown, I made appointments for next week. One really wasn't happy, but I told her your good reputation meant you were in great demand.'

'And just let slip the commission was for Lady Farringdon,' Millie trilled. 'The Receiving Room's neat as a pin and I've doused the fire 'cos supper's nearly ready. That Mrs Somers said yous must eat regular like, so I've made a pot of pease pudding,' she added, giving Jane a stern look when she opened her mouth to protest that she didn't have time.

*

The next day, Jane was already at her worktable when Ida Somers arrived.

'Goodness, girl, hasn't you moved since yesterday?' the woman asked.

Jane smiled but didn't respond, for the truth was the sky had been lightening to grey by the time she'd completed the hand basting. She hadn't realized Victoria was so tall until she came to tacking the sides and the slippery fabric meant her progress had been slow and laborious. However, now everything was ready for sewing, the seams and the sleeves were ready for inserting. Millie urged her to try using the sewing machine, but she couldn't, could she? Her glance involuntarily went to the gleaming machine.

'You ain't thinking of using that fearsome beast?' Ida shrieked.

'It would surely be quicker than hand sewing.'

'But suppose it goes wrong and messes up that lovely silk?'

Jane hesitated. Speed against safety? It was tempting and yet she really couldn't take the risk.

'You're right, Mrs Somers,' Jane agreed. It might be slower but at least she was certain of the result. And it needed to be completed to the hem stage before Victoria came for her fitting.

As Ida Somers put the finishing touches to the headdress, Jane painstakingly sewed, her confidence growing with every stitch so that, by that afternoon, it was ready for fitting. Triumphantly, she threw the gown over the mannequin and smoothed it down, revelling at the smoothness of the silk. But as she stepped back to admire her work, she let out a cry.

'It looks all wrong,' she wailed, 'yet I'm sure I followed the pattern.' She glanced from the model to the magazine.

'Them shoulders is too wide,' Ida declared, beady eyes assessing. 'Victoria's much narrower across here,' she added, her hand sweeping across the straps. 'It needs to be more like this.' Jane watched as with a few deft strokes, the woman gathered and pinned until the gown draped as it was meant to.

'Oh, Mrs Somers, you're amazing,' Jane gasped.

'Na, experienced,' Ida chuckled. 'Can't have the girl baring her all in front of the Queen of England now, can we?'

'Goodness, I never thought about her dress being seen by Her Majesty,' Jane gasped.

'Doubt she'll even notice. Has hundreds of girls presented to her each day. Probably spends the time wondering what delights she's getting for her dinner,' Ida snorted.

'You are funny,' Jane chuckled, giddy with relief that she hadn't ruined the silk after all. 'I really do appreciate your help though. It would have taken me ages to work out what was wrong.'

'Like I said when you was staying at my cot when Madame Pittier was ill and you had that interview with Lady Charlotte Farringdon, I'da been sewing since before yer was born so there's not much I'da don't know. Look how I helped you make them toiles.'

Jane suppressed a grin, remembering how she'd asked the woman to thread needles and count pins to stop her constant chattering while she concentrated on making the toiles. Still, having gained the commission from Lady Farringdon, she had ended up staying longer with Ida than intended and the two had formed an unlikely friendship.

'Not that I'm changing me mind about using the beast,'

she sniffed, jerking her head towards the sewing machine and bringing Jane back to the present. 'Yer can have that pleasure.'

'I might try using it on the veil,' Jane said quickly in case the woman should report back to the Farringdons and they think her ungrateful. However, Ida wasn't listening. Having heard a cart clattering to a halt in the street below, she was now peering out of the window.

'Just finished in time, that's me lift,' she grinned, turning and placing the headdress in Jane's hands before straightening her bonnet. 'Gotta make the most of me chances.' Then with a broad wink, the woman was gone.

Jane stared down at the feathers neatly attached to the white band, marvelling at the woman's invisible stitching. For all her ways, Ida really was a talented seamstress and Jane was grateful for her help. At least that was one thing ready, she thought, placing it on the table then turning back to the mannequin. It was amazing the difference those few tweaks had made. Reaching out, she couldn't resist running her fingers over the silky folds of the gown. Although it wasn't finished, she could see it would be perfect for Victoria. And yet, she couldn't help wishing that circumstances were different and that she would be the one wearing it.

Still, it was no good dwelling on the past, Jane thought, moving towards the sewing machine. Picking up a piece of calico, she set it in place then gingerly put her foot on the treadle. Although she had no intention of keeping the fearsome beast, as Ida Somers called it, Lord Farringdon had taken the trouble to bring it all the way from Nettlecombe and it would be churlish not to see how it worked. Besides, if it saved time and enabled her to produce more corsets, she would make extra profit. And that was the key to becoming the successful businesswoman she intended.

Reaching the end of the seam, she stared down at the treadle, thinking how much easier and quicker it had been guiding the material with both hands whilst using her feet to power the machine. When funds permitted, it would indeed be prudent to purchase one herself, for she still had to repay Lady Connaught, who had advanced her the money for the rent on the premises.

She yawned, the stresses of the day and working long into the early hours catching up with her. Her eyes grew heavy. Strains of that haunting song echoed in her head. Madame had hummed a similar tune as she'd sewn, she thought, jerking herself awake. She shook her head to clear it then saw something glinting under the table. Reaching down, she retrieved a little package tied with the same gold thread that ran through the silk. Gently easing it from the paper, there was a tinkling sound as tiny, shiny buttons spilled onto the table. Made of mother of pearl, they were exquisite and a perfect match for the silk fabric. Ideal for the bodice of Victoria's gown, in fact. It was then she spotted the sheet of paper that had been secreted beneath them. Although it was fragile and yellowed with age, she could just make out the faint outline of writing and realized it was a letter. Squinting, she tried to decipher the faded words that were written in a foreign language.

Ma très chère Rosa

J'ai terminé mon apprentissage et j'écris pour vous faire savoir que quand je reviendrai vous voir, ce sera en tant que tisserand à part entière.

Donc, ma très chère Rosetta, je peux enfin vous demander d'être ma femme. Dans l'espoir et l'anticipation que votre réponse sera favorable, j'envoie ceci avant mon arrivée. J'espère que vous trouverez la soie à votre goût. Maître m'a aidée à la tisser, le fil d'or qui la traverse est connu sous le nom de sceau rouge et quand il reflète la lumière de la chandelle, il me rappelle vos tresses d'or.

Votre Jean Pittier

Ma très chère Rosa? Donc, ma très chère Rosetta? Madame had been called Rosetta. Had this been written to her? Frustratingly, she could only make out a few French words which she remembered hearing Madame use. It was signed by Jean Pittier. Madame's sister, perhaps? She didn't recall her former employer ever mentioning one and yet the note must have been enclosed with the parcel of silk.

The chiming of the church clock in the market square jolted her back to the present. She must get on. Victoria was coming for her fitting the next day and, although the shadows were already gathering in the corner of the room, there was much to do before she could retire for the night. Placing the letter in her work box for safe keeping, she lit yet another candle then carefully removed the silk gown from the mannequin.

Pushing aside the glass buttons she'd intended using, she began sewing on the beautiful pearl ones. How much finer they were.

Just the train to go now. She'd found some satin fabric with a weave that would complement the silk and cut it into long panels; now all she had to do was join them together. She stifled a yawn, her previous late night's working catching up with her once again. However, would she manage to get everything done?

'*Use the machine, girl. That's what it's here for.*'

Madame's strident tones cut through the workroom, making Jane jump.

'*Or are you too scared?*'

'I most certainly am not,' Jane cried, gathering up the fabric panels and marching over to the fearsome beast. However, stitching the fragile fabric proved to be very different to the calico she'd tried previously. Cursing as she caught her finger under the needle and frowning at the resulting bubble of blood, she jumped up and wrapped a rag around it. Perhaps she should resort to hand sewing after all.

'*If at first . . .*'

'All right, Madame,' she replied then laughed to think she was still jumping to her former boss's orders. However, she wasn't going to be beaten by a stupid machine. Amazingly, as if the woman was guiding her, she finished the seams in seemingly no time at all. Holding the train up to inspect by the light of the candle, she smiled at the perfect rows of stitching.

'*Well done, girl.*'

Smiling at Madame's praise, Jane covered her work then snuffed out the candle. Sparing with her praise, her employer had always known when she needed encouragement. It was almost as if working on the silk and reading her letter had conjured up the woman's presence.

*

'Gracious me,' Beatrice cried, bursting into Victoria's usually immaculate dressing room, and staring at the gowns, gloves, and hats strewn on every surface. 'This is so unlike you,' she added, picking her way through the maze of footwear and hat boxes that littered the floor.

'I know,' her sister wailed. 'Despite Step Mama's list, I don't see how it's possible to ensure I have everything required for the entire Season. I shall be away for three months at least.'

'Calm down. It won't be the end of the world if you forget something. Cousin Hester's bound to help. Besides, you will have access to London's finest modistes. Not like me who will merely require a dress, apron and cap, always assuming Professor Todd thinks I have what it takes to become a nurse when he interviews me.' She flopped down on the chest that stood ready and waiting.

'Of course you do, Bea. You'll make a fine one,' Victoria loyally declared. 'Sarah and Maria always come to you when they're feeling off colour.'

'But I want to do more than that. I want to heal people when they're hurt.' Bea frowned. 'I felt so helpless when Mother fell from her horse.'

'I know,' Victoria said, patting her shoulder. 'You really will make a wonderful nurse, though how you got round Papa is beyond me, and I really can't see Step Mama approving.'

'She's too wrapped up in her own affairs to worry about me. Anyway, aren't you excited about being launched into society?'

'I will be if I can decide what to take. Vanny is anxious to pack ready for our things to be sent on ahead of our arrival.'

'Yes, she is, m'lady,' the maid confirmed, appearing in the doorway. 'It will be more than my job's worth not to have everything ready by noon. Now, tell me which of these white shoes you wish to take,' she asked, holding up three pairs of satin slippers.

Bea laughed. 'Oh Vanny, white is white surely.'

'You might mock Lady Beatrice but there are many shades of white and it is important to get the right one. Which pair do you think will match your debut gown, Victoria?'

'Goodness, I hadn't even realized there was a difference, Vanny. Whatever would I do without you?' she replied, then let out a squeal. 'You are coming with me to London, aren't you?'

'Lady Farringdon has sent word that Shears is to accompany you.'

'But she can't do my hair or . . . ' Realizing it was improper to voice her thoughts in front of her lady's maid, her voice trailed off.

'Would you like to come to London for the Season, Vanny?' Bea asked.

'I most certainly would, m'lady,' she replied, her eyes shining at the prospect. 'However, Shears is senior lady's maid so . . . ' she shrugged. 'Now please could you tell me which of these you wish to take?' Victoria studied the slippers, noticing for the first time their varying hues.

'Those will best match the golden thread in the silk,' she said, pointing to the creamier coloured of the pairs.

'I shall wrap them in their cloth bag to protect them and then return to help in here,' Vanny told them, staring pointedly at the piles of clothing before she left.

'Why don't you suggest to Papa that Vanny accompany you? It is your debut, after all and Shears is . . . well, more suited to the needs of an older woman,' Bea said, giving a wicked grin.

'Step Mama would swoon if she heard you say that.' Victoria chuckled. 'I would certainly feel more confident if Vanny were there to dress me. Do you think I dare ask Papa?'

'I do. Look, I know you hate confrontation, but you need to be more assertive if you are to survive a Season in London. Why not start by tackling him at dinner tonight?' she challenged, blue eyes alight with mischief.

'All right, and in return you can help me decide what I should take.'

'My things have already been taken downstairs, so why not. Oh, really Victoria, you're surely not taking Miss Darcey?' she laughed, picking up the porcelain doll with its froth of pink lacy skirts and matching feathered hat.

'I most certainly am. Dearest Mama gave her to me before she died and she's my most treasured possession.' Victoria stared around the room and sighed. 'Everything's going to change, isn't it?'

'Yes, and isn't it exciting? Imagine living in London.' Bea's eyes glittered navy with enthusiasm. 'Now come on, where's that list?'

'My debut outfit will have to travel with me. Oh Bea,

you should see the silk Jane is using. In fact, I have a fitting tomorrow morning; why don't you come with me?'

'I'd love to, and it would be good to see Jane again.'

'It will mean being interrogated by Mrs Somers en route,' Victoria pointed out, laughing as Bea grimaced. 'Although she appears to have set her bonnet at Quick and spends her time trying to catch his attention.'

'That will make the journey interesting then,' Bea grinned.

Chapter 7

'You look like an angel, except obviously I know you're not,' Bea chuckled, as Victoria emerged from behind the pink embroidered screen in the Receiving Room.

'Oh Jane, it's beautiful,' the girl gasped, turning this way and that in front of the long mirror.

'Yes, we've done an excellent job,' Ida agreed, puffing out her chest. 'It needs a slight adjustment on yer waist what with yer being so slender like, and we still need to pin the hem. Not that we used pins on the body, of course.'

Jane bit down a retort. Trust the woman to take the credit when she had been the one sewing by the light of the candle until daybreak. Now her eyes felt gritty, her nerves taut as a tightly wound bobbin. Had Madame really been in her workroom with her? Whether she had or not, the train looked splendid, she thought, attaching it to the back of the gown.

'You've worked wonders,' Victoria said, giving Jane a knowing look. 'These buttons set off the bodice perfectly. Wherever did you get them?' she asked, running her fingers admiringly over their pearlescent sheen.

'I think they must have been sent with the silk. There was

a note too, but it's written in French, and I can't make out all the words.'

'How exciting. Perhaps we can have a look.'

'Bea, really,' Victoria reproached.

'When you've finished here, of course,' Bea added quickly.

'Of course,' Jane agreed, watching as Ida placed the headdress on Victoria's chestnut curls. The trimmed ostrich feathers set off the girl's colouring and complemented the gown perfectly.

'I can't believe this is really me,' Victoria said, shaking her head.

'Yer looks a real picture, even if I do say so myself,' Ida Somers nodded. 'Cors, I knew yer would when I was making it.'

'I am most grateful to you both,' Victoria said quickly. 'Except, I must confess my chest feels somewhat bare.' She frowned, running her hand over the exposed flesh. Although the neckline was now high enough to conceal her womanly charms, Jane supposed the girl was used to wearing gowns that covered her completely.

'Perhaps a necklace might help,' she ventured. 'Now, if you wouldn't mind stepping onto the stool, I'll start on your hem.'

'I'll help, I've a good eye for a hem,' Ida offered. 'None better in the business, in fact.'

Through a mouthful of pins, Ida regaled them with tales of past customers until Jane was tempted to suggest she might swallow one if she didn't shut up.

'Oh my, now you does look a picture,' Ida said, when Jane sat back on her heels to check the hem looked even. 'It's a shame about yer wedding dress, Jane, but yer must admit this is the next best thing for that beautiful silk.' Silence descended like a shroud as Victoria stared at Jane in dismay.

'You mean this was intended for your betrothal gown?' she gasped, running her fingers awkwardly over the fabric.

'Sorry, girl, I'da didn't know it was a secret,' the woman muttered.

As Jane blinked back the tears that threatened, Beatrice took the older woman by the arm and led her towards the door, saying she was thinking of ordering a new chemise and would appreciate her opinion on which fabric to choose.

'I am so sorry,' Victoria murmured as the door closed behind them. 'I didn't know . . .' Reaching out, she drew Jane close.

'How could you?' Jane whispered. 'However, I can't think of a nicer person to be wearing it.'

'But you might need it in the future. I mean we are the same age and . . .'

'My work is my life now. I have been given this opportunity and intend making the most of it.' She forced a smile. 'Now turn round and mind the pins, while I help you out of your gown.'

As Victoria disappeared behind the screen, Jane carefully laid the dress over the back of the chaise. She allowed herself a last wistful sigh for what might have been then tidied away her things.

'You mentioned a letter earlier,' Victoria said, reappearing in the elegant primrose ensemble she'd arrived in. 'I speak fluent French; would it help if I had a look?'

'Please,' Jane cried, hurrying over to her work box, and retrieving it.

Victoria studied the note for a moment then smiled.

'It is a love letter to someone called Rosa. How thrilling,' she cried, as she began reading aloud. 'My Dearest Rosa, I have finished my apprenticeship and write to let you know that when I next see you, it will be as a fully fledged weaver. So, my dearest Rosetta, at last I can ask you to be my wife. In hope and anticipation your answer will be favourable, I am sending this ahead of my arrival. I hope you find the silk to your liking. Master helped me weave this, the gold thread running through it is known as pail red and when it catches the light of the candle it reminds me of your golden tresses. Your Loving Jean Pittier.'

'Oh, how romantic,' Victoria exclaimed, handing the letter back to Jane. 'Do you know who Rosa was?'

'I think it must have been Madame Pittier, my former employer.'

'You say Madame, so she married this Jean then?'

'No, she wasn't married. Madame was a courtesy title for business purposes.'

'I seem to remember you saying that she'd brought you up.' Victoria frowned, recalling the conversation they'd had at the manor earlier that year.

'Yes, my mother was her maid but ran off leaving me behind. Madame took me on as her apprentice. But wait a minute, Jean is a girl's name so how could they be going to marry?'

'Jean is French for John,' Victoria explained. 'I wonder what happened?'

'I don't suppose we'll ever know,' Jane said sadly, wondering if that was why Madame had affected her French mannerisms. It didn't explain why she had heard the clacking of looms and foreign voices though. Unless it was Madame sending her signals from the afterlife she'd so believed in. The question though, was why?

'Well, whoever Jean was, he was obviously a fantastic weaver as well as being romantic. I can't say I've ever heard of the expression pail red before, but perhaps you have?'

'It is not one I'm familiar with.'

'Well, I might not have golden tresses, but I shall certainly enjoy being dressed in such beautiful fabric. I am really grateful for all you've done, Jane.' She paused and bit her lip. 'And really sorry you didn't get to wear it.' Jane nodded and tried to swallow the lump at the back of her throat. 'Do you need me for another fitting, only I have a hundred and one things to do before I leave Devonshire?'

'No, there's just the hem to stitch and your corset to make. Everything should be ready by Monday.' She smiled, omitting to mention she would need to work over the weekend to fulfil her promise.

'Wonderful. If you can have them packed ready for travelling, Quick will collect them. Along with your invoice for all you have done.'

'Enjoy all those balls, and who knows, you might even find yourself a prince.'

'I was thinking perhaps an earl or duke. That would be one in the eye for Her Ladyship, what with Papa only being a baron. And you would, of course, be invited to the wedding. Oh, I am sorry, that was tactless,' she stammered, her hand going to her mouth.

'Don't be. What's done is done. I shall concentrate on being the finest corsetiere in Devonshire.'

'And I shall recommend your services to all the ladies of London,' Victoria declared. They may have been poles apart in social standing but the smile they shared was one of complete understanding.

Jane watched in astonishment as Ida Somers followed Victoria and Beatrice towards the door. Surely the woman was staying to assist?

'That nice Quick is here and I'da got to make the most of me chances,' she chortled, giving Jane a sly wink. 'Miss Brown can help finish the sewing; that's what she's here for, isn't it?'

'I never said anything,' Mouse replied, looking worriedly at Jane as the door shut behind them.

'I'm sure you didn't. Nevertheless, you are here to learn to make corsets as well as selling merchandise,' she replied, remembering Lady Connaught had sent the young girl here to improve her sewing skills. Neglecting her duties and offending her patron could cause her to withdraw her sponsorship, without which she would have no choice but to close her business. 'Once I have completed Lady Victoria's commission, you can assist me in the workroom when we are closed to clients.' Routinely, she glanced around, ensuring everything was tidy and in its place.

'Didn't Lady Beatrice purchase any fabric?' she asked, frowning at the bales behind the counter.

'No. Although Mrs Somers asked Lady Beatrice what colour chemise would suit her as she might be needing something silky and sophisticated soon.'

'And was Lady Beatrice able to help?' Jane asked, quirking a brow in astonishment.

'To be honest, I got the impression she was trying not to laugh.'

'I see,' Jane replied, trying to keep a straight face herself. Really, the woman was incorrigible. She must be well into her forties if she was a day. The ringing of the bell brought her back to the present as Millie burst through the door, hazel eyes burning with the excitement Jane knew from experience meant she had some gossip to impart.

'Guess what?' the maid exclaimed, resting her basket on the counter. 'I only gone and got meself a follower.' However, any further revelation had to wait as the bell tinkled again and two ladies dressed in the latest mode stepped elegantly into the shop. As Mouse stepped forward to assist, Jane ushered Millie into the hallway.

'I know you're excited, Millie, but you really should use the door from the yard,' she chided, remembering Lady Connaught's advice.

'But I'm housekeeper now,' the girl reminded her, removing her bonnet, and tossing her wayward curls. 'Anyhows, it was me speaking nicely to Bert, the butcher's boy, that got us a nice bacon joint for our meal. Well, he chopped a bit off the knuckle, but it will stew up nicely with some split peas. Bert says—'

'That all sounds lovely,' Jane said quickly. Seeing the girl's crestfallen expression at having her news interrupted, she added, 'I really am busy, Millie. There's still Lady Victoria's commission to finish so perhaps we can have a good chat over supper later.'

'But yous hardly stops to eat these days. And yous know what they say about all work and no play,' Millie muttered, hefting her basket and strutting off towards the scullery.

Jane shook her head. However, there was no time to dwell

Chapter 8

Following his manager into the quarry, Edwin shivered as the chilly air hit him. Squinting as his eyes adjusted to the dim light after the bright sunshine outside, he was shocked to hear shouting come from the area the stonemasons used. Even above the racket of the quarrymen's hammering and sawing, the sound of angry voices echoed and bounced off the walls of the vast cavern, causing Wakeley to quicken his step. Knowing escalating arguments could lead to the men downing tools, Edwin frowned. The masons currently on site were the best in the area. Reputation of their work had spread wide and far, and he prided himself on the quality of both the stone and carvings that were exported from his quarry. A reputation, he knew, could be lost in less time than it took to light one of the foul-smelling tallow candles that were stuck to the walls with wet marl.

'Shut it or sling it.' Wakeley's sudden bellow stopped the two men squaring up to each other in their tracks. As they stood glowering, neither prepared to move away from the arched stone tracery, Edwin stepped forward.

'What seems to be the trouble?' he asked.

'I were here first,' the stocky, younger man blustered. Defiantly, reaching out a calloused hand to lift down one of the arch-shaped stones used to trace the elegant windows of the finest churches and cathedrals.

'Yer weren't,' the older man spat, wiping sweat from his brow. 'Yer sneaked behind when I was laying down me block. Go and work on a different piece.'

'But me block's drying. Can't carve stone that's dried out.'

'Grow up, the pair of you, or I'll knock your blinking heads together,' Wakeley barked. 'You're not paid to quarrel.'

'Can always find another quarry. Crying out for good masons, they are.'

'I'm sure, being intelligent gentlemen, you can sort this out between you,' Edwin said placatingly. Although the men were highly strung, he knew they were also highly skilled and he was anxious to keep them.

Knowing the men needed to use sections from both sides of the archway, he signalled Wakeley to assign each a piece to work on. With a grunt the masons returned to their own workstation, placed their tracery on top of the stone blocks and began cutting to shape.

'Pig-headed, the pair of them,' Wakeley muttered as they retraced their steps to the entrance of the quarry. The crescendo of hammering and cutting coming from the quarry men working below made further conversation impossible.

Edwin bided his time until the inspection was complete, and they were back in the manager's office before raising the matter.

'You need to take better control, Wakeley. It is no good having the best quality limestone in Devonshire if the carving isn't finished on time. The barge is already on its way to collect the order and God knows we need the money to pay the wages, yours included. You know as well as I that it is imperative we keep the cash flow going or it will be curtains for everyone.'

He was the largest employer for miles around and responsibility for his workers and the continuation of the quarry hung heavy on his shoulders.

'I'm leaving for London next week, so we need to go through the ledgers, and you can tell me what new orders we've received.'

Two hours later, Edwin snapped his fingers at Ellery who was sprawled out in front of the fire and began retracing his steps up the steep lane. His joints felt stiff and there was no doubt the cold and damp underground penetrated his bones more these days.

'Nearly there, old boy,' he told his loyal companion who was panting at his side. 'Both feeling our age, aren't we?

Despite his worries, his spirits lifted when he reached the driveway of Nettlecombe. The borders were a riot of colour, the fragrance of flowers mingling with that of freshly cut grass. He admired the topiary bushes, which had recently been clipped, then, remembering his meeting with Wilf, lengthened his stride.

The happy sound of birdsong filled the air, some calling for a new mate, others busy seeking brandlings for their offspring. Even the new lambs bleating in the nearby field sounded full of joy. The season of renewal and rebirth. Suddenly Edwin was seized by an overwhelming sense of loneliness, making him yearn for the warmth of a woman's affection.

Not the cold, calculating kind that Charlotte offered with its expectation of expensive jewels in return. After he'd seen his two daughters settled in London, he would pay his mistress a visit. Anticipation flowing through his veins, he skipped up the steps like a man half his years.

First, his meeting with Wilf and then a celebratory dinner with his older daughters. He had also arranged a family tea party with Sarah and Maria the following afternoon for it was important the younger girls were included in the farewell festivities. If that were the right word, for life at the manor without Victoria and Beatrice was going to be very different and he was going to miss them.

'There is a letter from Her Ladyship,' Ferris announced, breaking into Edwin's thoughts as he stepped into the hallway flanked by elaborate oak panelling, the sound of Ellery's paws cushioned by the recently laid plush Axminster carpet. His ancestors seemed to frown down at him from their ornate frames and, as ever, he felt responsibility for the future of Nettlecombe settle heavier on his shoulders.

'Thank you,' he replied, taking it from the salver the butler held and placing it in his pocket to read later. A vase of golden narcissi had been arranged in front of the monstrous cherub clock and the heady mix of beeswax and flowers made Edwin smile as he strode towards his office. The manor felt like home again.

No sooner had he settled himself behind his desk than there was a knock on the door and Wilfred Gill, his old estate manager, was announced.

'Come in and sit yourself down, Wilf,' Edwin invited as the man stood uneasily before him.

'The missus says she hopes we haven't put you to too much trouble,' the man said, snatching his cap from his head.

'I can't deny the estate will miss your expertise. However, I have a proposition for you to consider,' Edwin said, sitting back in his chair and studying his manager thoughtfully. 'Louisa tells me the hall in Combe is becoming ever busier now that various groups hold their meetings there, which mean the women have to re-arrange the tables and chairs before they can commence work. Not a problem itself, but they are paid for every piece they produce and understandably resent any delay. There is also the issue of cleaning up along with occasional minor maintenance. What the place needs is a caretaker, and I was wondering if you would consider the position.'

Wilf sat in silence, twisting his cap round and round on his lap until Edwin wondered if he'd offended the man.

'I realize the hall being named after Sam might pose a problem, and I have no wish to be insensitive.'

'Not at all, my Lord. Sam worked hard to refit the barn and it would be like I was keeping his memory alive.'

'As it would entail working evenings and weekends, you would move into the vacant cottage opposite the church.'

'I don't know what to say,' Wilf murmured, shaking his head. 'It'll be a new start and Edith and me will be able to nip across to Sam's grave and speak with him each day.'

'That's settled then. I'll be interviewing for a new estate manager when I return from London; if you could hold the fort until then I'd be grateful,' he said, getting to his feet and proffering his hand.

*

Edwin entered the elegant dining hall to find his three daughters already seated. The long table was set with a crisp white cloth, crystal glasses gleaming in the light from the silver candelabra.

'Apologies for keeping you waiting, my dears. I went upstairs to say goodnight to Sarah and Maria and the little ones had so much they simply had to tell me.' He grinned ruefully.

'I shall miss the little monkeys,' Bea said, sitting back to allow the asparagus soup to be ladled into her bowl.

Haunch of venison with turnips in butter was followed by the lightest of lemon creams. Cook had excelled herself, and if Victoria seemed jumpy, Edwin put it down to nerves at what lay ahead. Whilst he appreciated that being presented must seem a daunting prospect, given her shyness, mixing in society would only increase her confidence.

However, as soon as they'd finished their meal, she turned to him, her chin lifting in a way he knew meant she had something on her mind.

'Papa, I know Step Mama has asked for Shears, but I wish for Vanny to accompany me to London,' she said, her words coming out in a rush.

'I'm not sure we should go against Charlotte's wishes,' Edwin frowned. 'Besides, Louisa will still be here,' he reminded her.

'With few social engagements until Henry returns, I can manage with Shears well enough,' Louisa replied, swallowing hard at thoughts of her beloved so far away. 'I think, in this case, Victoria's wish should take precedence. Vanny knows how Victoria likes to dress, how her hair should be done, and it is her Season after all,' Louisa said.

'Besides, Shears is ancient and Victoria needs to look of the minute if she is to catch the eye of a handsome earl or duke,' Bea told him.

'Earl or duke?' Edwin murmured, quirking his brow. 'Goodness, Victoria, I hadn't realized you were so ambitious.'

'Well, I—' she began, only for Beatrice to interject again.

'Of course she is. And Step Mama will only be attending the balls and parties as her chaperone. She will have to watch from the sidelines.' She grinned, clapping her hands gleefully.

'Beatrice,' Edwin admonished.

'It's true, Papa,' Louisa told him. 'This is Victoria's time to shine.'

Although he agreed, Edwin wasn't sure about the protocol of Vanny taking Shears' place. The woman was senior, after all. And of course, Charlotte was bound to have a tantrum. But then she wasn't here to make the decision.

'Very well, Victoria, tell Vanny she may accompany you. Now, I believe you were going to tell me about your gown.'

'Jane has worked her magic,' Victoria began and proceeded to describe her dress in detail. 'The gold thread running through the silk gives it a luminosity.'

'I almost didn't recognize her, she looked so ladylike,' Bea chuckled.

'The only thing is the neckline seems a little low,' Victoria frowned.

'You usually wear high collars that cover your throat, so I expect it would seem strange,' Louisa pointed out. 'However, you are a young lady now and such presentation is expected, within the bounds of modesty, of course,' she added. Edwin suppressed a smile as his eldest daughter assumed a motherly role.

75

'Oh, but of course. We can't have you making eligible gentlemen's eyes pop out,' Bea giggled.

'Luckily, you don't have any such worries for, of course, as a nurse you will wear a uniform,' Louisa replied.

'Always supposing you pass your interview with Professor Todd. He has a reputation for only engaging the most competent, suitable applicants, and a young lady like yourself . . .' Edwin's voice trailed off as Bea gave him a withering stare.

'Clearly you are expecting Professor Todd to find me lacking. Well, Papa, I never asked to be born a lady. It has been my ambition to become a nurse since Mother's accident and that is what I intend to do. I'll show you, see if I don't.'

Edwin cleared his throat. He admired her determination but did indeed have grave reservations that such a situation would be appropriate. Whilst he had acquiesced and written to his old friend, the professor, was he hoping she wouldn't pass his scrutiny and the decision would be made for him? And what Charlotte would say when she found out, he dreaded to think.

'I'm sure you will, Bea,' he finally acceded when he saw she was waiting for an answer. Tonight was a celebration and he was not going to spoil it. He rose to his feet, and they looked askance. 'Firstly, I would like to propose a toast to my beautiful daughters,' he said, raising his glass to each of them in turn. 'I would also like to wish both Victoria and Beatrice every success in their new ventures. Nettlecombe is certainly going to miss you, as will I. However, Louisa is doing a superb job overseeing the household in Charlotte's absence and I am sure you will return with wild stories of your adventures. Although, not too wild,' he added, assuming his sternest paternal expression.

'Spoilsport,' Bea giggled.

'Now, I have a gift for each of you,' he said, smiling at the squeals of delight as he passed a velvet box to each of them. 'A memento from your dear Mama, which I know she would wish me to give you this evening.'

'Mama knew I loved her emeralds,' Louisa cried, tears of joy welling as she ran her fingers lovingly across the necklace.

'Oh Papa,' Victoria exclaimed as she opened the velvet box containing a string of South Sea pearls. 'Mama always looked beautiful when she wore these. They will be perfect in the neckline of my debut gown.'

'And I always loved her sapphire brooch.' Bea smiled. 'Mama said the colour matched my eyes. Attached to a velvet ribbon, it will make the perfect choker.'

'These were your mother's dearest treasures. Wear them in her memory, for I know that, wherever you are, she will be with you, spurring you on to achieve your goals in life.' His voice wavered as he struggled to control his emotions, for in truth, she was always in his heart.

Chapter 9

London

Edwin sat back in his carriage as it rattled over the cobbles, smiling indulgently as his daughters gazed wide-eyed at the hustle and bustle of city life going on around them. The thoroughfare was busy with horse-drawn buses jostling alongside carts and cabs. The screech of grime-streaked costermongers, barrows piled with vegetables and fruit mingled with the laughter of pedestrians attired in their Sunday best clothes thronging the pavements. It was a far cry from the comparatively quiet lanes of Devonshire they had left a few short days ago.

'Imagine being part of all this,' Bea cried, her eyes alight with excitement as she looked from left to right.

'It's noisy and a bit daunting though, don't you think?' Victoria shuddered as a hansom sped past, dust rising like a cloud behind them.

'Don't worry, you'll soon get used to it, and it will be good for you to experience a different way of life,' Edwin reassured her.

'Think of all the magnificent beaux you'll meet,' Bea

giggled, nudging her sister as they passed two smartly dressed young men in top hats, one of whom winked cheekily at them. 'And all those glamorous parties you'll be going to. It'll be a ball.'

'You are right, and I do want to explore every part of the city,' Victoria replied, brightening at the thought.

'Perhaps not all, for I trust Aunt Emmeline will keep you away from the seedier areas,' Edwin told her firmly.

'Spoilsport, I thought Victoria was here to have some fun,' Bea teased. 'Don't worry, I am only joking,' she added, holding up her hands in mock surrender as he gave her one of his sternest looks.

'I'm pleased to hear it,' Edwin replied, making a mental note to speak with Nicholas, his brother-in-law, about being scrupulous in his vetting of possible suitors. He knew the seamy side of a gentleman's life in the city could involve riotous drinking and rowdy behaviour and, although he was sure the company his daughter would be keeping would not involve any such thing, it was his parental duty to ensure she was kept safe. He wished he had asked Quick to drive them, but Louisa's need was greater, and he felt better knowing his eldest daughter had protection whilst he was away.

'Goodness, Vanny, you look as if you've seen a ghost,' Victoria exclaimed as her lady's maid suddenly sat bolt upright, a frown creasing her usually placid features.

'I'm fine, thank you, m'lady,' Vanny stammered, but Victoria wasn't convinced.

'You're not worried about seeing Step Mama, are you?'

'Seeing Lady Farringdon?' she squeaked, almost jumping off her seat. Noting their surprised expressions, she composed herself. 'I mean, I don't think Lady Farringdon is going to be pleased to see me when she asked for Shears.'

'Papa will explain, won't you?' Victoria said, turning to him.

'Indeed,' Edwin confirmed. 'With so many important functions to attend, it is perfectly reasonable to have your own maid with you. Ah, your aunt and uncle's house is just along here,' he added as they turned into the quieter, more salubrious environs of Chester Square, its terrace of tall buildings facing onto a pleasant green. Although there was no front garden, with its basement, four storeys, large, arched sash windows, and dormers in the attic to accommodate the servants, the building was nevertheless impressive. The driver pulled to a halt alongside steps leading up to a square front door, its brass knocker and letterbox gleaming in the afternoon sun.

'Please see that my gown is hung up straight away,' Victoria instructed Vanny, indicating the box tied with pink ribbons containing her precious debut outfit.

'Come along, we mustn't keep Charlotte waiting,' Edwin insisted, ushering them from the carriage, leaving the coachmen to unload their things.

'I'm sure Step Mama can't wait to see us,' muttered Bea, raising her brow theatrically.

Edwin shot her another one of his looks. Although he didn't relish speaking with Charlotte about her spending, for Victoria's sake he was determined their meeting should be pleasant.

The butler opened the door, then, with a deferential smile, took their outdoor things. They followed him across a tiled chequered floor, sweet perfume from the vase of brightly coloured flowers on the mahogany table permeating the hallway, then up a wide flight of carpeted stairs. As they reached the top, a young lady rushed towards them, red curls bouncing round her shoulders.

'You're here at last,' she cried.

'Hester,' Victoria greeted her cousin before she was engulfed in a warm embrace.

'I'm so pleased to see you. We are going to have such fun. It's lovely to see you too, Bea, and you, Uncle Edwin. Father and Mother are waiting in the drawing room. It's all right, Jarvis, I'll show them in.' As the butler nodded and retraced his steps, Edwin smothered a smile. At nineteen, Hester might be a year older than Victoria, but her exuberance reminded him of a red setter puppy. Her warmth would no doubt help his daughter cope with Charlotte's overbearing and often cold manner.

Not knowing what mood his wife would be in, Edwin braced himself. However, when they entered the room, to his surprise, Charlotte was nowhere to be seen.

'Edwin, welcome.' Nicholas proffered his hand in greeting. 'Victoria and Beatrice, my favourite nieces,' he greeted, smiling warmly.

'Good afternoon, Uncle Nicholas,' they replied.

'It's lovely to see you,' Emmeline beamed. 'Do make yourselves comfortable.' She gestured for the girls to be seated on the red and gold striped sofa.

'Thank you, Emmeline,' Edwin replied. As he seated himself in the matching wing chair that was placed alongside, he couldn't help thinking how warm and welcoming his sister-in-law was compared to Charlotte. Despite the fact the furnishings had obviously seen better days, with sunlight flooding through the tall sash windows, the room felt cosy and homely.

'You must be weary after your journey,' Emmeline smiled.

'We spent the night at my house in Grosvenor Square to give the girls time to recover. The past couple of weeks have been hectic since we received notification that the presentation was to be sooner than we had anticipated. However, everyone rallied round, and we've managed to get Victoria's debut dress made in time.'

'Oh, but I thought Charlotte had . . . ' Emmeline began then stopped and shook her head. 'Well, it's lovely to see you, and wonderful that you are here too, Beatrice.'

'It is fortunate Beatrice's interview with Professor Todd in Harley Street is this week and we have been able to travel together.'

'An interview? Goodness, how exciting. Charlotte never mentioned that.' Emmeline frowned, looking flustered.

'Surprise, surprise. I intend becoming a nurse, Aunt Emmeline,' Bea told her. 'Although nobody seems to think me capable.' Edwin shot her a reproving look before returning his attention to Emmeline.

'Charlotte is not here then?'

There was an awkward pause as Emmeline exchanged a look with Nicholas.

'Er, no, she said she had an engagement this afternoon.'

'I see,' he replied.

'I told you she wouldn't be awaiting our arrival with bated breath,' Bea muttered.

'Why don't you show Victoria her room and then we shall have some refreshment?' Emmeline said quickly to her daughter.

'Good idea, and I can tell you who's on the marriage mart this Season,' Hester giggled.

'We've prepared the room next to Charlotte, but I know Hester's hoping Victoria might prefer the chamber adjoining hers,' Emmeline told Edwin as the girls excitedly made their escape. 'After living with a house full of brothers it will be fun for her to have another young female to discuss fashion and fellows with. I'm much too old for my opinions to be of any import, you understand.'

Although she smiled, the way her words tripped over each other indicated the woman was ill at ease, which surprised Edwin for he'd always got on well with her.

'It is most kind of you to accommodate them. I hope Victoria staying won't pose any problem. She has been swinging from delight to despair over being presented and knowing you will be there along with Charlotte to guide her, is a great relief. As I mentioned in my letter, I will, of course, cover all expenses.'

'Both Victoria and Charlotte are welcome. Now, if you'll excuse me, I really need to discuss menus with the housekeeper.'

'Is everything all right, Edwin?' Nicholas ventured as the door closed behind his wife.

'Why do you ask?' he replied.

'Call it intuition.' His brother-in-law shrugged. 'You wanted to discuss business so let's get down to the detail whilst we are by ourselves.'

Edwin explained that Victoria had led a somewhat sheltered existence in Devonshire and was unused to the faster paced life of London.

'She's keen to see everywhere but . . . '

'You want me to ensure she stays away from the unseemly sights,' Nicholas said, shooting him a wry grin. 'Don't worry, old chap, I've had a similar orders from Emmeline about Hester. It's always been easier with the boys. I mean you want them to experience a bit of life before they wed, don't you? Not that I told Emmeline that, of course,' he chuckled.

Edwin nodded, then re-iterated that he didn't want Nicholas to be out of pocket and expected to be apprised of all expenditure incurred during the Season.

'This should cover initial outgoings,' he said, taking a banker's draft from his pocket and passing it over. 'I would also like to set up a separate fund for Victoria. As she has yet to gain her majority, it would need to be administered by an adult and . . . '

'You mean me?' Nicholas offered, and Edwin nodded.

'It might seem strange, but I'd feel better knowing Victoria has the funds she needs, money that Charlotte . . . ' he stopped realizing he was in danger of being indiscreet.

'I fully understand,' Nicholas nodded, and Edwin could see the man appreciated more than he had explained. 'I'll get the papers drawn up and sent over to Grosvenor Square before you leave.' Any further discussion was curtailed as Emmeline returned.

'Tea and sandwiches are on their way, or perhaps you'd prefer coffee?' she asked.

'A cup of tea will be most welcome,' Edwin smiled, pleased

to see that his sister-in-law was looking more relaxed. 'I would just like to say again how much I appreciate you welcoming Victoria into your home.'

'We will love having her here and the cousins sharing their debut . . . ' she broke off as the door burst open and Charlotte hurried into the room.

'Step-cousins, they are step-cousins,' she reminded her sister.

'Oh, Charlotte, you are back,' Emmeline said quietly. 'We were wondering what had kept you. You are just in time for afternoon tea.'

'Charlotte, how nice to see you again,' Edwin said, rising to his feet. His voice was cordial, his lips assuming a smile so that most people would think he was indeed pleased to see her. Only the tic in the side of his cheek revealed his true feelings.

*

Charlotte had been having such a lovely time listening to the band playing in Hyde Park that she'd stayed longer than she should have. Her escort had been so charming and attentive, it had been hard to tear herself away. Then that stupid little maid had seen them. Still, she would deal with that.

Knowing she was unforgivably late and recognizing in Edwin the signs of a man pushed to the limit, she decided that attack would be the best form of defence.

'I trust Victoria has brought everything I listed for the Season. It took a great deal of thought to work out all she would need for we really can't have her letting down the Farringdon name.'

'Charlotte . . . ' Emmeline spluttered, looking at her aghast. Edwin rose quickly to his feet.

'If you'll excuse us, Charlotte and I require some time alone,' Edwin said, taking her arm. Shaking herself free, she marched from the room, leaving him to follow.

'Well?' she snapped, settling herself on the sofa of the upstairs sitting room. How old he looks, she thought, as he stood before her, leaning on his cane. She had never liked the stupid silver-topped thing. Although impeccably dressed, despite her counsel to visit his tailor, his clothes were last season's. 'For heaven's sake, be seated do.'

To her annoyance he continued standing, taking in her portrait over the fireplace and the ornate clock.

'I can see why I have received so many invoices,' he said curtly.

'So, you begrudge me a few new fripperies now? I would remind you that it is your daughter's presentation I am here for. As you can see, the decor and furnishings are sparse, and I needed to purchase a few comforts.'

'That's not very charitable, Charlotte. This house is charming – a home, in fact – and it's kind of Nicholas and Emmeline to allow you to stay for the Season. If you remember, I did suggest you stay in Grosvenor Square, only you delighted in telling me that Hester's godmother has a new palatial property in Belgrave Square that not only puts mine to shame but boasts private gardens for its residents. And, as Hester's sponsor, much of the entertaining will take place there.'

'Which is true. It is my responsibility to ensure Victoria is presented in the best possible light, and, as Hester's godmother is Countess of Kilcoyle . . . well, need I say any more? However, one thing concerns me. There could be occasion for Victoria to receive suitors here and, as I am sure you noticed, the drawing room downstairs does not have enough chairs to accommodate them so more will need to be purchased.'

'There looked to be sufficient,' Edwin replied.

'For heaven's sake, it would be improper if not downright disgusting for her to have to take a seat recently vacated by a gentleman. The cushion would still be warm from his behind,' she declared, shuddering at the thought.

'Really, Charlotte, now I've heard everything. There is to be no more spending and that is it.'

'You mean you'd deprive your own daughter?'

'Should Emmeline feel more seating is required, then she may request some be sent from Grosvenor Square,' he replied. 'However, you will not purchase any new. I will not have your profligacy leading me to the brink of bankruptcy.'

'It was you who sent me away in the first place,' Charlotte reminded him.

'And we all know why that was. Which reminds me, being the good mother that you clearly are not, don't you wish to know how Sarah and Maria are?'

'Surely there is no need when being the good father you clearly think yourself, you have engaged the services of a suitable governess. I take it you've got rid of that hideous old Nanny,' she retaliated, not wishing to be wrong-footed again.

'Nanny is enjoying a more restful way of life,' he confirmed.

'Well, I trust Victoria has had a white silk debut gown

made?' She paused then, and, knowing there was a dearth of talented dressmakers near the manor, gave a sneer.

'Considering the short notice you deigned to give us, I think we have done very well,' he countered.

'You mean you managed to commission the making of one with matching train and headdress?' Charlotte frowned, not liking his triumphant expression.

'Indeed. Victoria will definitely be the belle of the ball.'

'Who made them then?' she demanded.

'Miss Haydon and—' he broke off as she gave an incredulous snort.

'Miss Haydon makes corsets. I hardly think she would have the skills to sew a gown fine enough for Victoria to be presented to Her Majesty.'

'You will see for yourself soon enough,' he replied. 'Now, to return to your spending. If you don't desist, Charlotte, I shall stop your allowance completely.'

'But it is the Season. We will be invited to balls, recitals, soirees. Suppose Victoria needs new shoes or a cape or something?' she threw at him, knowing he was unlikely to refuse one of his beloved daughters anything.

'Nicholas has my authority to deal with such things. It is your extravagance we are discussing here. I warn you again, Charlotte, keep within your allowance or it will be cut completely. Now, Beatrice has some news of her own so if you wish to see her before we leave, I suggest you accompany me back downstairs.'

'But you haven't asked me whether I'm prepared to come back to Nettlecombe yet,' she said, thinking of the Farringdon pearls she'd been hoping to elicit.

'That's because you haven't asked me if I'm prepared to take you back,' he countered.

'Why you . . . ' she began, but she was talking to his back. How dare he treat her like that, she fumed, throwing her reticule after him. And after all she was doing for his daughter too. You will regret this, Edwin Farringdon, she vowed.

Her thoughts turned to Alexander who clearly adored her, and she smiled. It was just a shame that stupid little maid had seen them together.

Chapter 10

Waking from a deep sleep, Victoria stared lazily around the room. It was grander than the one next to her stepmother, the primrose-coloured walls and golden drapes matching the coverlet on her bed, making it cheery and bright. It was also next to Hester's, and her cousin's sunny nature and sense of fun was a welcome change from her stepmother's bad moods. She didn't know exactly what had happened between Charlotte and her Papa, only that the woman had declined to join them for afternoon tea or dinner, remaining upstairs all evening.

Hester's brothers had arrived in time for preprandial drinks, and they'd spent an enjoyable evening together before Papa and Beatrice had taken their leave. Realizing it would be some time before she saw them again, Victoria's spirits had fallen, but Aunt Emmeline had told her how much they'd been looking forward to her visit, explaining what coming out for the Season entailed. Heavens, she shot bolt upright, her mouth dry, her heart thumping a tattoo. Today she was being presented to the Queen. A knock on the door sent her nerves racing but it was only Vanny.

'Good morning, m'lady, I thought you'd like some tea and toast,' she said, smiling as she placed a silver tray on the table beside her.

'I couldn't eat a thing,' Victoria protested, blinking as the drapes were pulled back.

'You must have something. It is going to be a long day and you'll need to keep up your strength. I've hung your dress out ready and asked that water be heated for your bath.'

'Thank you, Vanny. Has Step Mama said anything about you being here instead of Shears?' The maid shook her head and gave a funny little smile.

'Somehow I don't think she will object,' she murmured, turning to leave.

Well, that will be a first, Victoria thought as the door closed. She picked up the cup, but the sight of the milky liquid made her stomach churn and she put it down again. How glad she would be when the ceremony was over, and she was officially launched into society. Thank heavens she had her cousin to accompany her, she thought, nibbling valiantly at the toast. There was another knock and, as if her thoughts had summoned her, Hester popped her head around the door.

'Isn't it exciting?' she cried, copper curls wreathing her head like a halo as she flopped herself down on the bed in a way that would have made Charlotte frown. 'I've already bathed but I'm forbidden to touch my gown until Chambers comes to assist. Mother seems to think I'll tear the hem or spill something on it.'

'And is that likely?' Victoria asked.

'Yes,' Hester grinned. 'It's a glorious day out there. Perfect for a carriage ride although Aunt Dorothea warned it's likely to be a slow one. Oh, you haven't eaten all your breakfast.'

'I couldn't manage any more. My insides feel like butterflies are having a ball of their own. Aren't you nervous about today?'

'I'll be glad when the presentation's over,' Hester replied, snatching up the remaining triangle of toast and popping it into her mouth. 'I'm more excited about the ball my aunt is giving in our honour afterwards. She throws the most splendid parties and think of all those handsome gentlemen we are going to meet. I do hope Roscoe will be there. He's . . . Oh, I'd better go, Mother's calling. See you downstairs after we've been primped and preened.' As the door closed again, Victoria couldn't help wishing she'd been blessed with her cousin's confidence.

The next couple of hours passed in a flurry. After bathing, Victoria was corseted to within an inch of her life. Luckily, Jane Haydon had done a perfect job and her underpinning fitted like a glove. Then, wrapped in a sateen robe she endeavoured to sit still whilst her hair was dressed. Finally, she stepped into her debut gown, so nervous by now that she couldn't stop trembling as Vanny attached the train then fastened her mama's pearls around her neck.

'You look absolutely stunning,' Aunt Emmeline cried, as Victoria, train over her arm, picked her way carefully down the stairs in her satin slippers, the feathered headdress making her look taller and more elegant than usual.

'Just like a princess,' Hester added, clapping her hands in delight.

'Thank you. And you look wonderful too,' Victoria told her cousin.

'At least white suits you especially with that gold thread running through the fabric,' Hester groaned, staring ruefully at her own gown, which although beautifully made, stood stark against the warmth of her colouring.

'You both look charming,' Emmeline insisted, frowning as another figure in white silk regally descended the stairs. 'Haven't our girls done us proud?'

'Yes, yes,' Charlotte nodded impatiently, inspecting her reflection in the mirror on the chiffonier. Her eyes narrowed and she spun around to face Victoria.

'Why are you wearing my Farringdon pearls?' she asked, her voice dangerously quiet.

'Papa gave them to me. They set off my—'

'Take them off this instant,' she insisted.

'But they were Mama's and—'

'As the current Lady Farringdon, they are mine,' Charlotte told her in a voice that brooked no argument.

'Is there some problem?' They span round to see a majestic lady peering at them through her lorgnette. Dressed in a gown of magenta silk trimmed with black lace; her silver hair was pinned with a matching clip.

'Dorothea,' Emmeline greeted the woman warmly. 'You look magnificent.'

'And you are as elegant as ever, Emmeline.' She turned to Hester and nodded. 'You look delightful, dear. I do hope you have been practising your glide and curtsy?'

'I have, Aunt,' Hester grinned ruefully. 'And I think I have improved.'

'Thank heavens for that. I was minded to forewarn the palace stewards to remove their occasional furniture in the interest of safety.' The woman chuckled then turned to Victoria. 'You look charming, my dear. The fabric of your gown is quite exceptional,' she marvelled, holding her lorgnette closer. 'Such workmanship. You must let me have the name of your modiste.'

'Madame Helene made my outfit,' Charlotte told her, smoothing down the folds of her skirts. The older woman frowned; her disapproval evident.

'Dorothea, you remember my sister, Lady Charlotte Farringdon,' Emmeline intervened quickly.

'Indeed, I do,' she replied, her voice cool.

'It is lovely to see you again, Dorothea.' Charlotte smiled.

'Countess of Kilcoyle,' the woman corrected. 'However, you may address me as Lady Newton Berwick,' she said, looking Charlotte up and down with disdain. 'As a mother and chaperone, shouldn't you be more suitably gowned?'

'Well, really, I—' Charlotte began but the woman held up her hand.

'Perhaps you would be good enough to tell me what all the fuss was about when I arrived. I could hear the clamour from the steps outside,' Dorothea interjected, cutting her off with a glare.

'Really, it is nothing for you to concern yourself about, Lady Newton Berwick. I was merely ensuring Victoria understands the importance of returning her necklace. They are the Farringdon pearls, you know.'

'Very fine ones too, by the look of them,' the woman said, studying the string with her candid gaze. 'Dashed stupid time to bring up a trivial matter like that though, especially with one's own daughter,' the woman tutted. Before Charlotte could correct her, she turned back to the girls. 'Now, my dears, your presentation cards have been handed into the palace. Remember, you must walk gracefully and with decorum towards the Queen, execute a full court curtsy – without wobbling or tripping over your train, please, Hester. Kiss her hand if it is offered, rise, then back out of the room without turning away. That is most important, but then I am sure you have prepared your daughter, Lady Farringdon?'

'I have written everything out for my *step*daughter,' Charlotte replied, placing emphasis on the word step. 'She will have ample time to prepare herself in the carriage. I understand, there are between one and two hundred girls presented each day and the procession will take time.' Giving the woman a haughty look, she handed Victoria a slim, green leather-bound book.

'A bit late for that,' Dorothea tutted, clearly unimpressed. 'Enjoy your presentation, girls, then we shall toast your launch into society at your ball tonight. Now, it is time we were leaving. Your carriage will follow my barouche, Lady Farringdon. And as you will be with the other chaperones later, you might wish to change into something more suitable.' With another frown at Charlotte's ensemble, she turned to leave.

'Thank you, Dorothea,' Emmeline said quickly, before an indignant Charlotte could respond. As the countess descended the stairs, she turned to her sister. 'It doesn't do to make an enemy of Dorothea,' she warned.

The roads leading to the palace were even more crowded with carriages than they'd feared. Charlotte, furious at having been relegated to riding behind her sister in the much statelier barouche, glared at the crowds and cursed Edwin for sending her away with the Farringdons' second coach, which was less grand. Never had she felt so humiliated and playing second fiddle to her sister did not sit well with her at all. She was lady of the manor, when all said and done.

Seeing her stepmother's mutinous expression, Victoria immersed herself in the green book, which set out the rules of etiquette for young ladies rather than instructions for the presentation itself. Luckily Hester had advised her what to expect from today. How lovely it must be to have a mother and godmother full of encouragement rather than a step-mother who saw her as some sort of competition.

'Did you have to select such strong-smelling flowers?' Charlotte asked, wrinkling her nose at the bouquet of white blooms beside Victoria.

'Aunt Emmeline kindly arranged for them to be delivered and I think they are quite beautiful,' she replied, stroking the silky petals of lily of the valley.

'Well, you can throw them to the crowds after the ceremony,' Charlotte declared haughtily.

Really, the woman was impossible, Victoria thought and, not trusting herself to comment, she turned to look out of the window.

The tumult was growing, the press of carriages containing ladies dressed in white becoming so great they slowed to a crawl. When, finally, they reached the palace and were handed down, Victoria carefully folded her train over her left arm, then tightly clutching her bouquet, followed Dorothea, Emmeline, and Hester. With the ease of someone born to it, the Countess of Kilcoyle took Hester's arm and sailed through the crowds, leaving Charlotte and Victoria to follow.

Inside the Long Gallery where they were to wait, everywhere was a wave of white, and Victoria's stomach began to churn again. She glanced at Hester who gave a nervous smile. After what seemed an eternity, they were led into the Presence Chamber where they carefully let down their trains. In turn, each was spread out by the Lords-in-waiting with their wands, then their names were read out and Victoria was convinced she was going to be sick. Legs trembling, she moved forward, hardly noticing the regal personage surrounded by a sea of faces, as she silently recited: curtsy low, hold for a moment, back away, do not stumble. Her stepmother stood staring at the Queen expectantly until she was moved away.

'Well, really, Her Majesty didn't even look at me,' Charlotte hissed, as they followed Dorothea and Hester back outside.

'When will you learn this day is not about you, Lady Farringdon?' the countess retorted. Relieved that their ordeal was over, Victoria and Hester couldn't help chuckling at Charlotte's indignation.

'There, that was easy, wasn't it? And I didn't stumble once,' Hester exclaimed as she was handed back into the barouche. Weak with relief, Victoria climbed into the coach beside her stepmother and slumped back against the padded squabs.

'She's gloating, you know,' Charlotte lamented.

'Who is?' Victoria asked, thankful her stomach had settled at last.

'Her Majesty, of course.'

'Why would Queen Victoria be gloating?'

'Not her . . . that conceited countess. Not only didn't the Queen speak to me, she failed to offer you her hand for a kiss, unlike Hester,' she retorted, glaring at the barouche ahead.

'Poor Hester, she was shaking so much I thought she'd keel over. It's a shame Aunt Emmeline could only watch from the sidelines, though.'

'Yes, isn't it?' Charlotte smirked, visibly brightening.

'At least we can relax now and look forward to the ball,' Victoria said quickly, not liking the expression on her stepmother's face.

'Goodness only knows how long it will take to get through this crush,' Charlotte groaned, gesturing to the carriages, lined in every direction as far as the eye could see. 'You'd better read more of that book I prepared for you. Now you have been launched into society, it is your duty to find an illustrious husband.' She looked around as if expecting there to be suitors already flocking towards them.

Not wishing to engage in any further conversation, Victoria closed her eyes. What a fuss. All that preparation and effort for a few seconds of ceremony she could hardly remember. As if that weren't bad enough, judging from the gleam in her stepmother's eye, she would have Victoria marching down the aisle at the earliest opportunity. It was another half an hour before they began to move and, even then, progress was stop and start. Exhaustion from the events of the day crept up on her and she fell asleep.

Victoria was jolted awake by the carriage pulling to a stop. She just had time to peer up at the imposing building of white stucco with its fine porch projection, before being ushered from the coach by an impatient Charlotte.

'Smooth your headdress, girl, and hurry do. We lost sight of the barouche hours ago.'

Still dazed from her sleep, she followed her stepmother

up the steps and into a grand vestibule. Despite the shadows only just beginning to gather, the wall lanterns were lit, casting pools of golden light along the hallway, gleaming off the marbled floor. A footman in blue and gold livery hurried towards them

'The countess is waiting for you,' he announced, leading the way up the curved staircase above which the largest, most magnificent chandelier Victoria had ever seen, blazed with seemingly hundreds of candles. Clearly the barouche had arrived before them, Victoria thought, relieved to have Hester's company again. As Victoria patted her pearls into place, she felt her stepmother move closer, so close that she could feel her breath on her neck.

'Those pearls are mine and you will hand them over the moment we return to Chester Square,' she hissed.

Hearing the venom in her voice, Victoria swallowed, but before she could reply they were being shown into a comfortable drawing room decorated in the palest of mauves and pinks.

'Ah, there you are,' Dorothea greeted them. 'Come and join us, Hester, Victoria, my belles of my ball. Heavens,' she said, frowning at Charlotte through her lorgnette, 'you are still wearing that white dress. You took so long getting here, I naturally assumed you had detoured to change into something more suited to your position as chaperone.'

'Of all the . . . ' Charlotte began, but Dorothea had turned back to Victoria and Hester.

'You have done your families proud today,' she told them, looking up as a head popped around the door.

'You remember Tristan, Emmeline? He has shortly

returned from Italy. Lady Farringdon, Victoria, may I present my younger son.'

Victoria turned from Dorothea and found herself staring up into the bluest eyes she had ever seen. A tingle of excitement ran down her spine and, for the first time that day, she felt truly alive.

Chapter 11

Realizing she was staring at him, Victoria smiled demurely and dropped her gaze.

'It is lovely to meet you,' she murmured.

'The pleasure is all mine,' Tristan Newton Berwick replied, his voice warm.

'This is your younger son, you say,' Charlotte stated, clearly unhappy at being ignored.

'Indeed, and Tristan made an earnest effort to ensure he arrived home in time for our debutante ball tonight. Alas, the same cannot be said for his brother Giles.' Dorothea tutted. Yet, Victoria hardly heard, she was covertly absorbing every detail of the handsome man she judged to be somewhere in his early twenties, the way the fairness of his hair contrasted against the collar of his black jacket, his well-defined features, strong jaw, aquiline nose, and generous mouth.

'It is so lovely to see you again, Tristan. I hope you will call one day soon and tell us about your travels,' Emmeline invited.

'I'd be delighted,' he replied, giving a bow.

'It has been a long, if eventful, day and you haven't had

time to eat so I have had a small repast prepared for you,' Dorothea told them. 'Can't have you fainting during the dancing now, can we?'

'Oh, thank you, Aunt, you're a lifesaver. I could eat a whale, I'm that hungry,' Hester replied.

'I'm afraid we're clean out of whales so you'll have to make do with smoked salmon and caviar,' the woman quipped, her lips quivering. 'Although, I would remind you that it is not polite for young ladies to discuss their hunger in company,' she added, resuming her countenance. 'Now, Hester, Victoria, as the guests of honour, when you have refreshed, you will join me in receiving our guests in the ballroom. You and Charlotte will sit with the other chaperones, Emmeline.'

'Of course, Dorothea,' Emmeline replied brightly while Charlotte pouted.

'Tristan, show everyone to the small dining hall, but no partaking of any food yourself; I shall expect you back directly, to assist me.'

'Yes, Mother,' he replied. 'She's both matriarch and slave driver,' he told Victoria, as he escorted them along the thickly carpeted hallway, but his grin betrayed the fact that he was fond of his mother. Then he stopped and turned to Victoria.

'A charming young lady such as yourself will undoubtedly be inundated with requests to dance, so I wonder if I might have the pleasure of claiming one now?' he asked, staring pointedly at the card Charlotte had tied to her wrist with a golden ribbon.

'Why, yes, of course,' she nodded, passing it over and watching as he quickly wrote his name.

'Goodness, and that's before the ball's even begun,' Hester exclaimed, staring at Tristan in astonishment.

'I would be honoured if you would permit me one too,' he told her.

'Why, thank you, Tristan. Is Ross coming?' she asked as Tristan duly added his signature to her card.

'Oh, how to wound a man,' he replied, clutching his hand to his chest theatrically. 'Here I am trying to be the most chivalrous of gentleman, and you dare to ask me about my cousin,' he declared, throwing open the door to a comfortable room where a table was set with bone china and cutlery that gleamed beneath yet another magnificent chandelier. A sideboard was laden with salvers of the promised smoked salmon and caviar along with cold meats, freshly baked bread, and curls of glistening golden butter.

'Jenkins will take care of you,' he added, indicating the liveried man standing to attention. 'Oh, and should you need it, you'll find a ladies' powder room opposite,' he added, grinning at Hester who, having been unable to resist sampling the caviar, had a tell-tale speck of black on her upper lip.

'Thank you, my good man,' Charlotte said graciously, as if addressing a butler. With a quirk of his brow and deadpan expression, Tristan bowed theatrically and left. Victoria had to bite her lip to stop herself from laughing out loud. Not only was Dorothea's son good-looking, he obviously had a sense of humour, and she couldn't wait to dance with him. Oblivious, Charlotte moved towards the table and waited until Jenkins pulled out a chair for her to be seated.

'Good old Aunt Dorothea,' Hester cried as they selected some choice delicacies. 'She always says you can't function on an empty stomach and I for one will drop down dead if I don't eat something soon.'

Later, as Charlotte and Emmeline sat discussing the presentation, Hester turned to Victoria and whispered.

'What was in that green book?'

'Rules of Etiquette for a Young Lady,' Victoria said, raising her brows. 'Rule No. 1: We should be elegant hostesses, pay avid attention to what our caller has to say and never disagree with him for the male mind is superior.'

'Is that so?' Hester said, rolling her eyes. 'There's nothing Roscoe and I love more than a good disagreement, makes things more exciting and—'

'Don't you know it is rude to whisper?' Charlotte asked, narrowing her eyes.

'Is that in your little green book too, Aunt?' Hester asked, smiling sweetly.

'You would be advised to read and learn from it, Hester,' Charlotte told her. 'Ah, at last,' she exclaimed, as the footman arrived to escort them.

'You must tell me more later,' Hester whispered as they made their way towards the ballroom, where Dorothea instructed Victoria and Hester to join her in the receiving line just inside the entrance.

'The table for chaperones is over there,' she told Emmeline and Charlotte, gesturing to a waiter who was circulating with a tray of drinks to take them to their seats.

To her delight, Victoria found herself standing next to Tristan who gave her a wide grin before turning to greet the first arrivals. The orchestra was playing softly, and Victoria just had time for a quick glance around at the highly polished wooden dance floor surrounded by tables set with snowy white damask cloth and cut crystal glasses that winked in the light of the chandeliers, before a queue began to form.

As the guests proceeded along the line, their jewels twinkling in the light of myriad candles, she found herself smiling and shaking hand after hand. Through the sea of debutantes still in their white gowns who were presented by their chaperones dressed in darker outfits, she was acutely conscious of Tristan's presence. He was so close she could smell the tang of his fresh, citrusy cologne, feel the warmth emanating from him. Gentlemen sporting black dress coats with low-cut waistcoats displaying their pristine white shirt fronts, bowing low and congratulating her, all passed by in a blur, so impatient was she for Tristan to claim his dance. Just when Victoria thought her arm was going to drop off, the arrivals tailed off and Dorothea turned towards them.

'That's it, everyone is here now. Naturally, as hostess I must mingle, so Tristan will escort you over to where Emmeline and Charlotte are waiting.'

'My pleasure,' he replied, looking pointedly at Victoria.

'And please make sure our guests have all they need.'

'Yes, Mother. Come along, ladies.'

As they followed him across the crowded ballroom, it seemed to Victoria as if everyone turned and stared.

'We're being watched,' she murmured to Hester.

'Of course we are, silly. Being new on the marriage mart, the ton will be eyeing us up: the men to see who takes their fancy; and the ladies sizing up the opposition. For that's what this is all about really, isn't it? A competition to secure a spouse.'

Victoria frowned. 'I hadn't thought of it like that.'

'When Aunt Dorothea was "grooming" me for society, as she called it, she warned me to be on my guard and not trust anyone. Personally, I think it looks far more interesting through there,' Hester declared, nodding towards an ante room where long tables groaned with an array of dishes along with huge jugs of iced lemonade.

'Not hungry again already, I trust?' Tristan teased.

'Not quite yet,' Hester replied, her eyes lighting up at the young man approaching. 'Ross,' she greeted him warmly. He was as dark as Tristan was fair and Victoria was just thinking it surprising that they should be related when he turned and smiled at her.

'And who is this delightful young lady, may I enquire?' he asked.

'This is my cousin, Lady Victoria Farringdon,' Hester told him, then lowered her voice. 'Her mother, or rather stepmother, is the blonde woman in the white dress shooting daggers at you. Victoria, this is Roscoe Beliver James.'

'Delighted to make your acquaintance, Lady Victoria. I wonder if I might reserve a dance for later; that is if your card is not already fully marked, of course.'

'Er, no, I mean yes, of course,' Victoria stuttered, aware that Hester was looking crestfallen. Before he could take her card though, Charlotte appeared at her side.

'Good evening?' she said, making it sound like a question.

'Lady Farringdon, Roscoe Beliver James,' he said, bowing low. 'Delighted to make your acquaintance. Please forgive me, I was so surprised when your charming daughter informed me that she had room to accommodate me for a dance later,

I quite forgot to introduce myself.' He paused. 'I haven't made some frightful mistake. You are Victoria's mother?' he asked, flashing a disarming smile whilst managing to look amazed at the same time.

'Stepmother actually, although, as you can obviously tell, we are more like sisters,' Charlotte replied, patting her fair tresses.

Victoria tried not to laugh at the way her stepmother had succumbed to the man's blatant flattery.

'Indeed,' Roscoe nodded gallantly. 'Well, you must be most proud of Victoria. She has certainly caused quite a stir here this evening, which is why I would be honoured if she would grant me a dance.'

'Well, hand this charming young man your card, Victoria,' Charlotte said, clearly annoyed the attention had moved away from her. He signed it with a flourish then turned to Hester.

'I suppose I'd better claim one from you as well, minx, although my poor toes have barely recovered from last time,' he said, grimacing at Hester.

'That was months ago, Ross. I'm much more accomplished now,' she protested. 'Oh goody, the dancing is about to start,' she added as attendants armed with brass snuffers moved to extinguish some of the candles, leaving the dance floor bathed in muted light. Then a trumpet sounded, and a buzz of excitement ran round the room.

'I believe I have the pleasure of the first dance,' a deep voice said.

Victoria looked up to find Tristan bowing before her and once again felt that shiver of anticipation. However, that was nothing compared to when he led her to the dance floor and she lightly placed her arm upon his.

Never had she found a quadrille so thrilling. There might have been other couples in their square, but afterwards she couldn't remember who they were or what they looked like. The tang of his cologne was enticing, his blue eyes mesmerizing as they gazed into hers, even the flash of gold from the buttons on his waistcoat was distracting, but, luckily, she was an accomplished dancer, and the steps came naturally. When the music stopped, he bowed gallantly then proffered his arm. She felt as if she was walking on air as he led her back to where her stepmother and Aunt Emmeline were waiting.

'Thank you, Lady Victoria. Regrettably, as host, it is my duty to see that no lady guest is left unattended,' he told her. Then as he bowed to take his leave, he murmured, 'However, be sure I shall see you again before the night is out.'

'Oh,' she exclaimed, but didn't have time to dwell on his words as she was claimed by Roscoe for the next dance. And so it continued, with one gentleman after another claiming her, until, just when she thought she would faint from the heat, supper was announced.

'Thank heavens, I was becoming quite bored,' Charlotte announced as Victoria's partner led her back to her seat.

'May I accompany you to the dining room or fetch you a glass of iced lemonade?' he enquired.

'Sorry, old chap, I think you'll find that's my prerogative,' Tristan said, appearing as if by magic.

The man looked about to argue but shrugged and disappeared into the crowd. Tristan grinned disarmingly. 'Might I get you some refreshment, or better still, why don't you come and see what is on offer?'

'That would be delightful,' Charlotte replied, starting to rise.

'Please don't get up, Lady Farringdon. Allow me to select something to tempt you. In fact, Victoria, why don't you come and show me what your stepmother and Aunt Emmeline like.' Before Charlotte could protest, he'd taken her arm and was guiding her towards the room where people were queuing for the banquet. As Hester and Roscoe joined them, Tristan murmured, 'Such is the path of true love that even in a crowd we cannot be alone.' He said it so solemnly, she couldn't help but smile. He really was quite droll as well as extremely good-looking.

'Aunt Charlotte is glaring daggers,' Hester giggled. 'I don't think she likes having been relegated to the role of chaperone.'

'Let us fill her plate then. Hopefully, that will cheer her up, and keep her occupied,' Tristan added, dropping his voice again. 'Now, there's a varied spread here so what can we tempt her with, do you think?'

Back at the table, Charlotte ignored the delicious morsels they had so carefully selected and turned to Tristan.

'So, you are the second son of the countess, I believe?' Victoria having just taken a sip of her iced lemonade nearly choked.

'Really, Step Mama,' she admonished.

'That is quite all right, Victoria. By the fate of a mere eighteen months, I was born the spare,' Tristan replied good-naturedly.

'And being the fourth out of five sons, I don't even have that honour,' Roscoe chipped in.

'Why, I do believe the band is about to resume,' Emmeline said quickly, relief showing on her face.

'Then you must excuse me, ladies, duty calls,' Tristan said, rising to his feet and perfecting a bow. 'I will see you later,' he murmured to Victoria.

'Hester, I do believe this is our dance,' Roscoe said, proffering his arm. Victoria couldn't help noting the alacrity with which her cousin accepted.

'Really, Charlotte, this is neither the time nor place to discuss such family matters,' Emmeline chided. However, Victoria didn't hear her response for she was claimed for the next dance. Refreshed from her drink but furious with Charlotte for questioning Tristan in such an inappropriate manner, she threw herself into the dancing for the rest of the evening. Finally, having just reclaimed her seat, she was surprised to hear the last dance being announced.

'I believe this is ours.' As that deep voice sounded beside her, she looked up to find Tristan grinning down at her.

'But we've already danced,' she frowned.

'You mean you cannot bear to risk another with me?' he asked, quirking his brow.

'Well, yes but my card—'

'—promises to save the last dance for me,' he finished. Quickly she checked and saw that he had indeed put his name against this one. Excitement flooded through her as she took his arm and let him lead her onto the dance floor. This time the music was slower, softer and as his arm came to rest lightly at the back of her waist, she felt sensations she had never experienced before.

'You do realize you are the talk of the ball?' he murmured.

'The way your dress catches the glow of the candlelight makes you stand out from all the other debutantes. You look divine, like a cherub. My dear Victoria, I shall have to act quickly for it is clear you will have many suitors beating a path to your door.'

Thinking he was joking, she smiled, then gave herself up to the music, the dance and the feel of his touch that seared through the delicate silk of her gown.

Chapter 12

Too excited to sleep after her dance with Tristan, Victoria had lain awake, reliving every moment, finally falling asleep as the first steaks of dawn lightened the sky. Consequently, she woke late and, knowing she'd only just be in time for breakfast, hurriedly dressed. As she made her way down the stairs, she was met with the heady fragrance of flowers. To her astonishment, the hallway looked like a hot house with tussie-mussies and beribboned bouquets covering the table, chiffonier and seemingly every other surface.

'Good morning, everyone. I do apologize for being late,' she greeted as she entered the dining room.

Aunt Emmeline smiled. 'Good morning, Victoria. If you can't have a lie-in after your debut, then I don't know when you can. And have you seen all those beautiful flowers? The doorbell has been ringing non-stop.'

'You mean they are all for us?' Victoria asked her cousin as she took her place at the table.

'No,' Hester sighed, looking up from her coddled eggs. 'Every single card is addressed to you. Not that I'm jealous. Well, actually, yes, I am.'

'Don't be silly, the next one is bound to be for you,' Victoria replied, gratefully accepting a cup of coffee.

'Good morning, my dear,' Nicholas said, looking up from his paper. 'It says here that the ball thrown by the Countess of Kilcoyle was a sensation with everyone who is anyone in attendance. Good heavens,' he continued reading. 'A dark-eyed debutante from Devonshire, known as the Girl with the Golden Gown, is being tipped as the one to watch this Season. With chestnut hair and heart-shaped face, this femme fatale had every eligible bachelor clamouring to sign her dance card.'

'Let me see that,' Emmeline said excitedly, all but snatching the paper from him. 'Heavens, Victoria, it is you, for it also says Lord Farringdon has promised a very generous dowry.'

'He has?' Victoria frowned. 'He never mentioned it.'

'Perhaps he thought it inappropriate for your delicate ears,' Nicholas suggested. 'Although, I am surprised he didn't mention it to me.'

'Oh, and they have described your wonderful dress, saying the golden thread, which reflected the candlelight when you danced, is pail red, the like of which has not been seen for many years,' Emmeline exclaimed.

'Goodness, yes, that was mentioned in the letter from the weaver. You see—' Victoria began.

'What on earth are all those flowers doing littering the hallway? That sickly scent has quite put me off my breakfast,' Charlotte cried, crinkling her nose as she swanned into the room.

'It would appear Victoria attracted many admirers at the ball last night. Shall I have the floral tributes sent upstairs to your sitting room?'

'Certainly not. I have already told you their cloying odour turns my stomach. It's worse than the cheapest cologne,' Charlotte grimaced, then turned and, seemingly having forgotten her lack of appetite, helped herself to kidneys and bacon from the chafing dish on the sideboard.

'You must be so proud of Victoria. Both she and her beautiful gown have caused quite a stir,' Emmeline said quickly, holding out the paper for her sister to see.

'I was surprised Edwin didn't mention the generous dowry he is bestowing upon Victoria,' Nicholas said, giving Charlotte a penetrating stare.

'Did he not?' she asked, a secretive smile curling her lips as she scanned the print. 'However, it would appear they are making more fuss about that gown. Since when is golden thread called pail red? Gold is gold when all is said and done. It just amazes me that a dress cobbled together by some local dressmaker and a corsetiere should cause such a stir.'

'It is exquisitely made. Even Dorothea commented on it, and she has such an eye for detail,' Emmeline protested. 'How they managed it in such a short time, is beyond me. I mean, where did they get that exquisite silk fabric?'

'Jane Haydon, the corsetiere, intended using it for her wedding dress, but then Sam, her betrothed, was killed and—'

'Yes, yes, I'm sure we've all heard the story many times,' Charlotte snapped. 'Where is my coffee?' she asked, glaring at the maid, who nearly tripped over the rug in her haste to please.

There was a discreet tap on the door and the butler

appeared brandishing an elaborate display of lily of the valley.

'Excuse me, madam, we are running out of space in the hallway, and I wondered where you would like these put?'

'Oh, those darling creamy pearls are just like the ones in our bouquet. Are they for me by any chance?' Hester asked, her sea-green eyes wide with hope.

'The card is addressed to Lady Victoria,' he replied.

'Oh, well, never mind,' she sighed, resuming her breakfast.

'Thank you, Jarvis. Unfortunately, Lady Charlotte has an aversion to the fragrance of flowers so perhaps you would be so kind as to take it through to the drawing room,' Emmeline instructed.

As the door closed behind him, Charlotte placed her cup in the saucer and turned to Victoria, her expression grave.

'Talking of pearls reminds me you have yet to return the Farringdon ones.'

'But I told you, Papa gave them to me. They were Mama's and—'

'As Edwin's wife, they now belong to me. Anyone can tell that they are of immense value—'

'If that is the case, then they should be deposited in a security box at the bank for safety,' Nicholas interjected, taking back his newspaper, and staring at Charlotte.

'Why thank you, Nicholas, but that won't be necessary.'

'I beg to disagree. Edwin has entrusted me with Victoria's financial affairs during her stay here, and that includes ensuring anything of value is kept safe.'

'I don't think you heard me, Nicholas. As Edwin's wife, those pearls are mine,' she reiterated, her expression glacial.

'Yet, as I understand it, he gave them to Victoria. Now, until I can clarify the matter, I insist those jewels are placed in the safe keeping of the bank,' he insisted. 'I am on my way there now as it happens, so perhaps you would be good enough to get them for me, Victoria.' Although he spoke quietly, his expression brooked no argument.

'Yes, Uncle, of course,' she replied, jumping to her feet. Whilst she'd enjoyed wearing her mama's pearls, there was something about the way Charlotte coveted them that made her feel uneasy. Papa had wanted her to have them, and she too would feel happier knowing they were out of her stepmother's reach.

'I suppose you think you have been clever,' Charlotte hissed as she followed Victoria, and they made their way up the stairs to their little sitting room. 'Well, you are going to regret this, young lady. Just see if you don't,' she added, snatching the card from each floral gift as they passed.

'But how will I know who has sent which?' Victoria asked, knowing good manners dictated she acknowledge each one.

'You won't, but that doesn't matter. Each gentleman has his title engraved or printed on his card and you, my dear, will receive the most elite of suitors and accept the best proposal of marriage offered.'

Victoria stared at her stepmother aghast. 'I think that's a bit presumptuous,' she remarked, perching nervously on the edge of a chair.

'As it happens, your opinion is of no concern. You are now out in society, a sign to eligible bachelors you are in the market for marriage. As your stepmother, it is my duty to make sure you make the most desirable one. There is no reason whatsoever to delay the matter.'

'I will only marry a man I admire and am fond of,' Victoria protested, as images of the man with golden hair and deep-blue eyes swam before her.

'Is that so? You should remember you are only eighteen years old and under my jurisdiction. Now, let us look through these cards and decide who we will receive when they call.'

Realizing Tristan's might be amongst them, Victoria conceded. Eagerly, she picked up a pile and flicked through them, her spirits plummeting when it became clear his wasn't there. However, with a gleam in her eye that made Victoria uneasy, Charlotte began sorting them into some sort of order. Unable to watch her stepmother any longer, she jumped to her feet and went over to the window.

'Really, Victoria, fidgeting like that is most unladylike. Go and change into your most attractive afternoon dress and be ready to receive suitors when they call,' she instructed.

In her room, Victoria opened the wardrobe and flicked desultorily through her afternoon gowns. She didn't like the way her stepmother had been grinning like a cat who'd got the canary as she'd picked out the plushest of visiting cards. And she didn't want to be paraded in front of a lot of suitors. After selecting her demurest – a pale green with buttons from waist to neck and full sleeves that narrowed at the wrists – which would surely deter the keenest of admirers, she sank down in the chair.

'Can I come in?' Hester asked, peering round the door. 'I had hoped we could spend the afternoon together, but I hear you will busy entertaining. Mother has roped me in to help at the refuge. Not that I mind particularly, it's just that I'd much rather be fending off an army of callers like you.' She sighed, flopping onto the bed. 'The poor maid has been instructed to place floral arrangements all around the hall and then on each stair up to the drawing room so that suitors can see the full extent of the competition.'

'Don't,' Victoria groaned. 'Step Mama's just told me I am to marry the most eligible one that proposes but . . . '

'You've fallen for Tristan, haven't you?' she cried, clapping her hands in delight.

'He is rather gorgeous.' Victoria smiled wistfully. 'But there was no card from him. Besides, Step Mama says . . . '

'That under the rules of primogeniture, it's his older brother Giles who will inherit the title, estates and lands when he marries, and titles and riches are what matters to Aunt Charlotte,' Hester finished for her.

'Precisely. I suppose I should have realized that would be her objective but it's my life and I have no intention of marrying someone just to please her.'

'What you need is a strategy. Have a coughing fit, pretend to be hard of hearing, laugh hysterically like a hyena. Men hate that.'

'Step Mama would kill me. I thought I'd wear my plainest gown,' Victoria said, indicating the one she'd chosen.

'You call that plain?' Hester gulped. 'It's finer than my best ballgown. That's it. You can wear one of my day dresses. We are nearly the same build but have completely different colouring. Come on, let's go and pick the one that does its dastardliest.' She grinned, jumping up and pulling Victoria towards the door.

'But what about Vanny? She will be coming to dress me shortly.'

'We'll save her a job then, won't we?'

At two minutes to three, Victoria tripped downstairs to the drawing room where her stepmother was peering excitedly through the window.

'And not before time, a rather splendid carriage has just pulled up. Thank heavens Edwin agreed to lend Emmeline extra chairs.' She turned and nearly did a double take. 'Oh, good heavens, whatever are you wearing?' Charlotte gasped.

'It's my new look, don't you like it?' Victoria asked, trying not to laugh at her stepmother's horrified expression.

'You look . . . you look . . . ' Charlotte shook her head and sank into a chair, words failing her as she took in the oatmeal-coloured high-necked dress that drained the colour from Victoria's face and the fawn ribbon tying up her hair in an unbecoming knot. However, just as she and Hester had planned, there was no time for her to change before the first visitor was announced.

'The Marquis of Ardingly,' Jarvis announced solemnly. He stood holding the door open and yet it was some moments before an elderly gentleman, leaning heavily on his cane, hobbled into the room. As he stood panting for breath, Victoria didn't know whether to laugh at the ridiculousness of the situation or her stepmother's shocked expression.

However, Charlotte recovered her composure, smiled graciously then offered him a chair.

'Thank you,' he wheezed. 'Find stairs a killer these days.' He paused to catch his breath then turned to Victoria. 'Now my dear, you must be the belle of the ball everyone is talking about,' he said, leaning closer and staring at her through rheumy eyes. The poor man was half blind, Victoria realized. She needn't have bothered borrowing Hester's gown after all.

'Isn't that right, my dear?' Charlotte said.

'Er, yes,' Victoria replied, snapping back to the present and hoping she was saying the right thing.

'Victoria also sings like a lark and plays the pianoforte. Her stitching is neat and—'

'Don't need all that,' the Marquis rasped, waving his hand dismissively. 'Castle is already comfortably furnished.'

'Castle?' Charlotte repeated, her eyes widening.

'You'll have to speak up, I've left my ear trumpet behind,' he said, hitting the floor with his stick, then turning to peer at Victoria again. 'Son's gone and got himself shot so need a young filly to provide another heir. What do you say then?'

As Victoria tried desperately to think of a polite way of declining, there was another knock at the door.

'Lord Ellis Barcley,' Jarvis announced. As a distinguished-looking man of middle years, with hair greying at the temples, proffered an enormous bouquet, the marquis struggled to his feet.

'Sensible girl taking time to consider,' he wheezed. 'Save me a dance at the next ball and you can give me your answer then. Cheerio.'

'I fear he will be dead before then,' Lord Barcley chuckled. 'Now, my dear, let me tell you about myself.'

Over the next couple of hours, as suitors of varying ages and rank arrived then left after the customary ten or fifteen minutes, Victoria endeavoured not to yawn. Oh glory, not another one, she groaned when Jarvis knocked yet again. Then she saw Tristan standing in the doorway and her heart flipped. He was carrying a single bloom which he presented with a flourish.

'Why, Lord Newton Berwick, your generosity knows no bounds,' Charlotte commented, her voice dripping with sarcasm. 'You must surely have seen all the other magnificent floral arrangements on your way up the stairs.'

'Indeed, I did espy the amazing array of tussie-mussies and nosegays, Lady Farringdon,' Tristan replied, unperturbed. 'However, no hot house full of flowers can compare to Victoria's flawless beauty. With this single, perfect bloom, I wish to demonstrate the integrity of my intention to court her.' He turned to Victoria. 'I'd be honoured if you would accept this pink rose, the symbol of grace and sweetness,' he said solemnly, bowing low as he presented it to her. However, as she reached out to take it, he grinned wickedly. 'Have I come on sackcloth and ashes day, per chance?' he whispered, gesturing to her gown.

'You might as well have,' she murmured, mortified that he should see her dressed this way. Surely, he wouldn't wish to court her now.

'Well, that's certainly a fine speech, young man,' Charlotte stated.

'Thank you, Lady Farringdon. It would be the greatest of honours if you would permit me to call upon your daughter again on Thursday afternoon and take her for a carriage ride around Hyde Park, with yourself acting as chaperone, of course.'

'Oh, that would be lovely,' Victoria cried, her heart flipping.

'Indeed, it would,' Charlotte replied. 'However, regrettably we have a prior engagement that afternoon.'

'We do? But . . . ' Victoria began then stuttered to a halt as Charlotte shook her head.

'I'm sure Lord Newton Berwick is quite aware he is not the first suitor to have called upon you this afternoon.'

'Quite so, Lady Farringdon. Might I enquire when Lady Victoria would be free to receive me again? I myself am available on Saturday afternoon, for example.' Making a great show of reaching for her diary and flicking through the pages, Charlotte shook her head.

'Saturday is out of the question, I'm afraid. Shall we say Tuesday week?'

'But that's . . . ' Victoria began.

'The first date we have free,' Charlotte finished.

'Tuesday week it shall be then,' Tristan nodded. 'Thank you for receiving me.' Under the guise of perfecting a bow, he shot Victoria a salacious wink which set her pulses racing and then he was gone, leaving behind the tang of his cologne.

'I didn't know we had any engagements on Thursday,' Victoria said, as the door shut behind him.

'And I didn't know my stepdaughter would appear in front of eminent suitors looking like a drab. I have never been so humiliated in my life.'

There was no answer to that, and realizing her stepmother was exacting her revenge, Victoria clutched the precious pink rose to her chest and hurried from the room.

Chapter 13

The musicians on the dais fell silent as the young woman began playing a solo on the violin. However, her fingers trembled, and Victoria winced as the ensuing notes sounded like she was strangling a clowder of cats.

'No young lady should be seen in public holding an instrument like that,' Lady Dorothea derided, frowning through her lorgnette. 'Just look at the angle of her neck that is most definitely not an elegant pose. Girls, please note there is a good reason females play the pianoforte; the keyboard allows one to adopt a graceful posture which gentlemen enjoy observing.' Hester nodded at her godmother then turned to Victoria and raised her brows.

'I'm sure they would prefer to dance or play cards,' she murmured, only to receive a nudge in her side.

'Now you see why I insisted you practise until you were note perfect, Victoria,' Charlotte said, looking smug. 'Still, at least this is an opportunity to be seen,' she added, sitting up straighter in her chair.

They were attending a private recital at the family home of Lady Alice who had been presented on the same day as

Victoria and Charlotte. However, the girl, pretty but slightly on the plump side, was clearly self-conscious, blushing unbecomingly as she continued picking her way clumsily through the Menuetto.

'Schubert will be shuddering in his grave,' Dorothea exclaimed, shuddering as another screech rent the air. 'Whatever is her mother thinking allowing the girl to show herself up like that?' As the audience began fidgeting in their seats, Hester leaned closer to Victoria.

'Do you think we dare cause a distraction by dancing?' she whispered, gesturing to the space on the highly polished floor in front of the trio.

'No, Hester, you may not,' her godmother remonstrated. 'It is already hot enough in here as it is,' she added, flapping her lace fan so that the silver handle twinkled in the candlelight.

'Let's hope supper is announced soon,' Hester murmured, 'I'm ravenous. Although Lady Bampton-Highcliffe is not renowned for laying on a generous spread. Oh, thank heavens,' she added as Lady Alice ceased playing and the audience politely applauded.

'Come along, Victoria, we must mingle,' Charlotte said, rising to her feet. 'Please remember to behave with decorum for you don't know who you might meet. Although, I am pleased to see you have heeded my advice and dressed more becomingly,' she added, nodding at Victoria's emerald skirts as she nudged her towards the next room where supper had been laid out. Clearly, she still hadn't been forgiven for appearing in Hester's gown when suitors had called. Still, it was strange she hadn't taken Vanny to task as she would normally have done.

'What a boring evening with one meagre mouthful of food each by the look of it,' Hester lamented, as they waited their turn at the buffet table. 'If only Tristan and Roscoe were here to lighten the mood.'

'Yes,' Victoria agreed, feigning a sudden interest in the paltry selection of canapés to avoid the gaze of a thin man who was trying to catch her attention. It might have been the height of fashion to sport moustache and mutton chops in the style of Prince Albert, but ginger facial hair held no appeal. Helping herself to a Patum Peperium croute, she was about to make her escape, when her stepmother laid a hand on her arm. As the man smiled and introduced himself, Charlotte looked him up and down speculatively, before nodding and edging Victoria away from the others.

'Might I present my stepdaughter, Lady Victoria Farringdon. This is Captain Crockett, my dear. Now, please excuse me, I've just seen someone I must catch up with.'

'Delightful recital, what?' the man said.

'Well, actually,' she began then realized he might be a friend of their hostess and nodded. As the man stood grinning and twiddling his moustache, Victoria nibbled at her croute, but the relish was so highly spiced it caught in the back of her throat, making her gasp.

'I say,' the captain frowned. 'Dashed nuisance, what?'

'Don't stand gawping, man, fetch the lady a glass of fruit cup,' Dorothea ordered, appearing at their side.

'What? Oh, er, yes,' he mumbled, hastily disappearing.

'Allow me.' A glass was thrust in Victoria's hand, and she gratefully took a sip. Then another and another until it was drained.

'Thank you,' she said, smiling at the dark-haired man who was staring solicitously at her with hazel eyes.

'My pleasure, although I fear the cup too warm to slake one's thirst.'

'Victoria, to whom are you speaking?' As the strident tones of her stepmother pierced the gathering, causing heads to turn their way, the gentleman perfected a bow.

'Forgive me for not introducing myself, Lady Farringdon, but I thought it best to save your daughter from choking first.'

'Quite right, Tim Tom,' Hester said, appearing beside them. 'This is my cousin, Victoria Farringdon. Victoria, this is Timothy Thomas Rydon, known to his friends as Tim Tom.'

'Not very flattering, I'm afraid,' the man said, grinning ruefully.

'Captain Crockett was getting my stepdaughter a drink,' Charlotte said peevishly.

'Well, he's taking his time, Aunt Charlotte,' Hester said, peering around. 'Poor Victoria could have choked by now if it hadn't been for Tim Tom here.'

'Indeed. Well, please don't let us detain you,' Charlotte replied, her eyes glacial as she stared at him.

'It has been a pleasure meeting you,' he replied, perfecting another bow, then departing.

Whispers of appreciation rippled through the cluster of debutantes as he passed by but, when he took no notice, they turned their attention to Victoria.

'Isn't she the one they are calling the girl in the golden gown?' asked a pretty woman, green eyes glittering as she smiled superciliously at Victoria.

'How many men does she intend snaring?' her fair-haired companion replied as she nodded in recognition.

'Cheap trick pretending to choke, wish I'd thought of it.' The woman's high-pitched snicker reminded Victoria of a braying horse.

'Hortence, Phoebe, Ophelia, it is time we took our leave.' As an older woman with a fox fur stole draped around her shoulders shepherded them away, Victoria breathed a sigh of relief.

'Apparently, it is acceptable to be derogative about a fellow debutante providing one does it with a smile on one's face,' Dorothea sighed. 'Standards have slipped since my day. Time to thank our hostess and take our leave, I think.'

'What an evening,' Charlotte grumbled. 'I cannot believe you let that charming captain leave like that.'

'I'm sorry, Step Mama, but I do have the right to choose whom I spend time with.'

'Well, he would have been a better catch than that other man. Tim Tom indeed; what kind of name is that?'

'I disagree,' Dorothea replied. 'Not only is Viscount Timothy Thomas Rydon a handsome young man; it is rumoured he is actively searching for a wife this Season.'

'Viscount? You should have said. How was I to know?' Charlotte spluttered, peering around as if he might reappear.

'It's all in the breeding, Lady Farringdon,' Dorothea replied acerbically. 'Although, I must agree with Victoria, it is her choice whom she wishes to spend time with, and she obviously has the better taste.'

'Aunt really is the mistress of put-downs,' Hester murmured as Charlotte flounced away. Victoria smiled, thinking how wonderful it was to see her stepmother wrong-footed for once.

*

'Dorothea has invited us to join her for a ride around Hyde Park this afternoon,' Emmeline said, perusing the letter that had just been delivered.

'It is right and proper the girls be seen out in the park, and the countess's barouche does create a favourable impression,' Charlotte said, smiling graciously. She took a sip of her coffee then frowned. 'Did you say this afternoon? Regrettably, I have a prior engagement.'

'Where are you going?' Victoria asked, staring at her stepmother in surprise.

'That is no concern of yours,' Charlotte snapped, putting her cup down with a clatter. Victoria and Hester raised their brows. The woman had been in a terrible temper since finding out she'd favoured a captain over a viscount. Not that Victoria cared. Although Tim Tom had been pleasant and had saved her from nearly choking, he hadn't set her pulses racing like Tristan. And, thanks to her stepmother, she still had to wait for days to see him again.

'But it is a beautiful day and, as you yourself have said, the girls should be seen in the park; surely you could re-arrange your, er, appointment?' Emmeline suggested, shooting her sister a knowing look.

'Impossible, I'm afraid,' Charlotte replied, dabbing her lips with her linen napkin.

'In that case I shall convey your apologies to Dorothea.'

'You mean you will go without me?' Charlotte spluttered, looking incredulous.

'Emmeline is quite capable of chaperoning,' Nicholas said, looking up from his paper. 'Not only will it be right and proper, but it will also create a favourable impression, which is more than can be said for your engagement,' he retorted, throwing down his newspaper and striding from the room.

'Well, really,' Charlotte snapped.

'You know how he feels, and quite frankly . . . ' Seeing Hester and Victoria watching curiously, Emmeline stopped mid-sentence. 'Go and make yourselves useful, then make sure you are suitably dressed and ready to leave at two o'clock sharp,' she told them.

*

Being a sunny afternoon, the Rotten Row was busy with gentlemen riders displaying their prowess, ladies sporting bonnets trimmed with peacock feathers intent on being seen as they paraded in their carriages, while others were promenading in their afternoon best. Shafts of sunlight glinted through the velvety green leaves, setting off Victoria's moss-green outfit to perfection. With her hair dressed in side-coils under a bonnet edged with burgundy that matched her calf-skin gloves, she felt every inch the debutante.

'It is good of you to arrange this wonderful outing, Aunt,' Hester smiled. She was wearing a tiered cape jacket in rust and deep bonnet tied with a matching ribbon that complemented her copper colouring perfectly. 'I wonder if we will see anyone we know?' she added, staring around curiously.

'Hmm, I wonder,' Dorothea replied. 'Although the objective is to be seen yourself, Hester, so it would be better if you were a little more discreet. Of course, when one gets to my age one simply cannot do without a parasol, which provides the perfect cover,' she added, winking as she twirled it around, staring blatantly from under it.

'Please don't encourage her, Dorothea, she's quite incorrigible as she is,' Emmeline laughed good-naturedly.

Victoria smiled at their easy banter, not for the first time wishing Charlotte was more relaxed and carefree. It was not like her stepmother to miss the opportunity of being seen and she wondered what prior engagement she had. Whatever it was, she'd certainly dressed up for it, disappearing without saying goodbye. If Victoria hadn't spotted her from the drawing room window, she wouldn't have known she'd left the house at noon. Determined to enjoy this beautiful afternoon, she sat back and gazed around. There were families out walking, children playing, dogs barking at the ducks swimming on the waters of the Serpentine.

'Look at them,' Hester hissed, inclining her head towards the gentlemen on mighty steeds, their polished riding boots gleaming in the afternoon sun as they proudly exhibited their equestrian prowess.

'I believe that is exactly what they are wanting you to do,' Dorothea remarked acerbically. 'One trusts they do not venture too close to the water and get a dowsing.'

'That would be splendid fun to watch,' Hester chuckled.

'Goodness me,' Dorothea cried, holding up her lorgnette. 'I do believe that's Tristan and Roscoe heading our way. What a surprise.'

Victoria's heart skipped as she watched the two men approaching.

'Good afternoon, ladies. What a lovely surprise,' Tristan said, his gaze lingering on Victoria as he pulled on the reins.

'I say, this is a surprise,' Roscoe echoed.

'And such a lovely one,' Hester cried, clapping her hands in delight.

Victoria might have pondered at the emphasis being placed on surprise, had they not heard a startled shout. Turning, they saw a young child chasing excitedly after a dog; both were headed right in the path of an oncoming carriage.

'Oh no,' Victoria cried, her hands going to her mouth in dismay. But Tristan had already turned his horse and was galloping towards them, Roscoe following. Heart pounding, mouth dry, she could only watch and pray they would be in time. Suddenly, the dog barked, causing the horses to rear up in fright. The coachmen frantically pulled on the reins but the little boy, intent on catching his pet, didn't stop. Tristan was the first to reach them and, for a moment, all they could see were hooves flaying, hear the frantic cry of the father and frenzied neighing of the horses. Then, Tristan leaned down and, in one deft movement, scooped up the little boy, setting him on the saddle before him.

Heart hammering, Victoria watched as the man ran up and snatched his son, cuddling him tight to his chest as if he'd never let him go again. As the coachmen brought the horses under control, Tristan and Rosco trotted back towards the barouche.

'Are you having an enjoyable perambulation, Mother?' Tristan asked nonchalantly, only the flush on his face betraying anything had been amiss.

'Yes, thank you,' Dorothea replied. 'However, observing that drama has made me thirsty, and I find myself sorely in need of refreshment. Shall we all return home and partake of afternoon tea?' she suggested.

'Good idea, Mother. I'd better ride on ahead though; a wash and change of clothes are sorely needed. I'll see you later,' Tristan said, looking directly at Victoria. 'Come on, Roscoe, you're looking the worse for wear too.' As the two men rode off, Emmeline turned to Dorothea.

'What a brave young man,' she sighed.

'Yes, he is rather. Not that you must pass comment; his head is big enough as it is,' Dorothea told her sternly. Yet Victoria noted the proud look on her face as she stared after her son.

'Roscoe was brave too, going after them like that,' Hester declared loyally.

'He was indeed,' Emmeline agreed.

It was only when refreshments had been served and they were all sitting in Dorothea's comfortable drawing room, that Victoria began to relax. She couldn't resist glancing at Tristan and her heart flipped when she saw he was gazing back at her. Looking quickly down at her plate, she was wondering how she could possibly eat the cake she'd selected, when a hand reached out and took it.

'Allow me,' Tristan grinned, popping the fancy into his mouth in one fell swoop.

'Tristan, really,' his mother admonished. 'If you are going to behave like that, I shall insist you go outside.'

'Certainly, Mother,' he replied, jumping to his feet.

'I thought you'd never ask. As our taking of the afternoon air was curtailed, would you permit me to show Victoria the gardens, Aunt Emmeline?' he asked politely.

'And knowing Hester's fondness for food, perhaps I could show her the chestnut trees for later in the year,' Roscoe added.

'Which she has already seen,' Dorothea pointed out. 'Oh, very well, but we shall be watching from the window.'

Outside, the two couples crossed the path then grinned gleefully before taking separate gravelled walks.

'This is delightful,' Victoria cried, inhaling the fragrance of the summer flowers.

'I must say I do find the scenery here today particularly delightful,' Tristan said, darting her a look that sent her pulses racing.

Trying not to blush, she followed him further along the path. Her skirts brushed against the lavender bushes releasing more perfume into the air so that she began to feel quite heady. Stopping by a wooden pergola, he turned to face her.

'I must confess that when we arranged a surprise encounter, we didn't expect it to be quite so dramatic.'

'You mean our meeting in the park was planned?' Victoria asked, staring at him in astonishment. Then she remembered how much had been made of their 'surprise' meeting earlier.

'Faint heart never won fair maiden, or in this case, the delightful lady whose hair gleams like burnished chestnuts in the sunlight.'

'Oh,' Victoria murmured, thinking she had never heard anything so romantic.

'Despite your stepmother's obvious objection, I wish to

spend time with you, Victoria. Luckily Mother likes you and is happy to assist.' He shot her a disarming smile then produced a perfect orange rosebud from behind his back and presented it to her with a flourish. 'To show my admiration and desire. Do you have any objections to our getting to know each other better?'

'None at all,' she murmured. They were standing so close she could smell the freshness of his clean shirt, the tang of his cologne. She stared into his eyes that reflected the cerulean of the sky above them, her heart beating faster. Not only was he the most handsome man she had ever met, but he had displayed courage and fortitude, traits she found admirable in a man. 'I can't think of anything I would like better,' she told him.

They were so engrossed in each other they didn't notice the figure watching closely from an upstairs window of the house, a calculating expression on his face.

Chapter 14

As the carriage bowled along the streets towards Marylebone, Edwin was still berating himself for losing his temper with Charlotte. Reasoning would have been better, but her high-handed manner and spendthrift ways had got under his skin. He could think of no other woman who would insist on purchasing unnecessary clocks and commissioning a portraiture for a place they were only staying in for three or four months. Not for the first time he wished he'd seen through Charlotte's veneer earlier, for beneath her pretty and fragile skin she was brittle and vain. That iridescent blonde beauty and sweet smile that had captured his affection was merely a veil for selfishness and a heart as cold as marble. Was it really any excuse that she'd caught him at his lowest ebb? Shouldn't he have questioned her so-called devotion after they'd only known each other a short time? Well, it was no good him encouraging Victoria to be more assertive if he couldn't practise what he preached himself.

Shaking his head to clear his dark thoughts, he glanced out of the window and saw the soot-stained buildings packed close together, clouds of smoke belching from their chimneys and swirling around the carriage. The persistent noise from the build-up of traffic and shouts of the pedestrians dodging between the mass of horse-drawn vehicles made him shudder. How he preferred the quiet of the lush green rolling hills of Devonshire where farmers tilled their land and only vagrant sheep ventured onto the lanes. Bea, who had been lost in thought, looked up and gave him a nervous smile. Naturally, she was apprehensive about her forthcoming interview with Professor Todd and, reaching out, he gave her hand a reassuring squeeze.

'Suppose I'm not good enough to become a nurse?' she burst out.

'A Farringdon is always good enough, Beatrice,' he told her, treating her to one of his serious looks. 'However, you must admit nursing is not the usual choice for a well-bred young lady.'

'It is all I've thought of for so long,' she sighed. 'Although I was young when Mama died, I remember that feeling of hopelessness at not being able to do anything for her. It was then I knew what I wanted to do with my life. When I visit her grave, I talk to her about my ambition and, it probably sounds silly, but it feels as if she is listening, and spurring me on.'

'That is not silly at all, Bea. I talk to her too and, when I leave, my thoughts are usually gathered.' He let out a long sigh and they fell silent again.

'You still miss her, don't you, Papa?'

'Yes, I do,' he admitted. 'Although I am lucky to have you, for you remind me so much of her. Spirited and determined, yet gentle and sympathetic.' In fact, all the attributes required for nursing, he thought.

'Thank you, Papa,' Bea smiled. 'I shall miss you if I'm accepted.'

'Nettlecombe would be noticeably quieter without my rumbustious daughter,' he told her, still not willing to admit there might be a possibility of her being accepted.

'And you will look after Firecracker?'

'For at least the hundredth time, yes. It would be more than my life's worth not to look after your precious steed. Look, I do believe we have arrived,' he said, as the carriage turned into Harley Street and pulled up outside a tall brick building flanked with iron railings. Edwin led the way up the steps towards the imposing front door with fanlight above and rang the bell.

'Good luck, my dear. Although I know you won't need it,' he assured her, as the door opened, and they were admitted into the high-ceilinged hall with its gleaming tiled floor. Everywhere was quiet as the grave, save for the man's highly polished shoes, which squeaked as he walked. The huge chandelier hanging over the stairs seemed incongruous in such an environment.

'Lord Farringdon and his daughter Lady Beatrice,' the attendant announced in answer to his knock. As they were shown into an airy office dominated by a huge wooden desk, Beatrice found herself staring at a silver-haired man wearing a dark three-piece suit and round silver-framed spectacles.

'Edwin,' he greeted, rising, and proffering his hand. 'And you must be Beatrice.' He smiled. 'I trust Devonshire is looking as delightful as it was last time I was there, which alas is far too long ago. Life is so busy these days. Do take a seat.'

'Thank you for seeing us, Professor Todd,' Edwin smiled, knowing from experience that where business was concerned, it was best to keep matters formal. The man nodded then turned his penetrating gaze on Beatrice, who, aware that the next minutes would decide her future, sat up straighter and folded her hands neatly in her lap.

'Perhaps you would like tell me why you wish to become a nurse, what you think it entails and what attributes you have to offer such a worthwhile profession.'

Edwin listened with pride as Beatrice answered his questions, hesitantly at first then becoming more passionate as she got into her stride. Clearly, she'd done her homework.

'Hmm. That's all very laudable; however, you are obviously a genteel young lady, used to the finer things of life. Nursing is extremely hard, not to say dirty work. The hours are long, the pay poor and living conditions basic at best.

'But you can't reject me because of my upbringing, surely?' Beatrice cried. 'All I ask is a chance to show you what I'm capable of. I am ready and willing to start straight away, this very minute.' Silence descended as the professor steepled his fingers and stared intently at her for so long Edwin became worried his daughter had been too forthright. However, eventually the man nodded.

'Very well. I had been toying with a couple of options but the Hospital for Gentlewomen During Illness is desperately in need of help. However, I must warn you that the superintendent, Miss Nightingale, is a very efficient but formidable woman who brooks no argument. You will be expected to do as she bids. She has plans to set up a training school for nurses but, as we are not sure when that will happen, initially it will be a case of having to learn on the job.'

'That is fine by me,' Bea replied.

'In that case, I will get someone to show you where the hospital is. If, after that, you still wish to nurse, a starting date will be arranged.'

'Nothing will change my mind, Professor. As my bag is in the carriage, I shall go and collect it now,' she said, rising to her feet. 'Thank you very much for seeing me.'

'I'll direct the coachman to take you to the hospital,' Edwin said, shocked by how quickly things were moving.

'Thank you, Papa, but it's time I stood on my own two feet. I'll be sure to write and let you know how I'm getting on.'

'That is a fine daughter you have there,' Professor Todd told Edwin as Bea departed with her guide, and the door shut behind her. 'However, she has a lot to learn. Do you realize, she didn't ask what her wage would be or where she'd be lodging?'

'Oh heavens,' Edwin groaned. 'I don't think she's ever had to think about such things before.'

'She'll soon understand the importance,' the professor replied, a grin twitching his lips. 'Beatrice seems one determined young lady and I have no doubt she will go far.' And Edwin agreed, little realizing just how far she would be going.

It was with mixed feelings that Edwin headed back to Grosvenor Square. On the one hand, although apprehensive for his daughter, he was proud of the way she had conducted herself with Professor Todd. On the other, another chapter of his life had ended.

He shook himself. Hadn't he always scorned those parents

who tried to hold their offspring back? Tonight, he would enjoy one of Mrs Crawford's delectable meals then tomorrow he would call on Victoria to see how she was getting on. But there again, upon reflection, she was only just getting used to life in London and a visit might unsettle her. Sometimes the hardest yet best thing to do was to let go. Giving Charlotte time to cool down would probably be a good thing too. He would take some time for himself, call upon his mistress for some loving affection, which suddenly he felt a great need for. Not only did she give him the warmth that was so lacking in his marriage, but she listened with interest to what he had to say and, being an intelligent woman, would participate in meaningful conversations that did not revolve around material acquisitions.

*

It was the smell that Beatrice noticed first. From the moment she walked along the corridor, it tickled her nose, catching the back of her throat so that she thought she might retch. But she had no time to dwell on it, for the straight-backed superintendent, severe in her plain dark dress, appeared to show her around.

'This hospital has twenty beds and caters for mainly governesses, some wives or daughters of clergy and occasionally those of naval or the military,' Miss Nightingale began without preamble, her demeanour severe as she strode along the hallway at such speed Beatrice could hardly keep up. She must have been in her thirties yet had the energy of a young girl and it was clear her candid gaze missed nothing.

'The weekly charge is one guinea for a single like this,' she added, throwing open the door to a small but neat room containing one bed, then moving on before Beatrice had had time to draw breath. 'Or fourteen shillings for a bed in a three- or four-bed ward like this.' Again, the door was thrown open but this time there was a row of beds each partitioned by a curtain. 'We require two letters of introduction giving details of social position and income plus a guarantee that expenses will be paid every week. Now, what has this got to do with nursing, you're thinking.' She turned and treated Bea to another penetrating stare.

Beatrice blanched; could the woman read her mind?

'The answer is everything, Miss Farringdon. This is a large, three-storey building which takes a great deal of coal to heat the water and cook the food, which of course also needs to be purchased and prepared. I also insist on cleanliness in everything, from the washing of floors, bedding, equipment and, most importantly, your hands. You may have detected the faint smell of diluted chloride of lime that we use?'

Faint? Bea thought, but she only had time to nod before the woman resumed talking.

'Back to running costs. It is vital to ensure this expenditure is met along with our nursing fees and medical supplies, of course. Understand the finances and you're halfway to understanding how this place functions. Think of it in the context of your wages having to support your living costs and you won't go far wrong.'

Wages? Living Costs? Bea stared at the woman in surprise. Professor Todd hadn't mentioned those, had he?

'Where are you staying?' the woman asked, as if again reading her thoughts.

'Well, I hadn't thought that far. You see Professor Todd only offered me the position an hour or so ago and . . . '

'I trust he explained that you are on probation until I deem you suitable,' she cut in. Without waiting for an answer, she continued. 'I strongly believe that dirt breeds disease so remember, cleanliness is paramount, both in your work and your appearance. Now, I have matters to attend to. Nurse,' she called to a young woman who hurriedly straightened her cap then came scurrying over.

'How many times do I have to tell you not to run, Nurse Grey,' she scolded. 'Walk briskly at all times. Miss Farringdon is here to learn the ropes, so please take her under your wing. There is a spare bed in your room, is there not? Find her a suitable dress and cap then show her where everything is kept and how I like things done.' With that she strode off down the hallway.

'She's scary but her heart's in the right place – as long as you do things her way,' Nurse Grey chuckled. 'Come on, I'll show you where we sleep. I'm Ruby, by the way,' she added.

'Beatrice but everyone calls me Bea. I'll just get my things.' She hurried back to the lobby, her thoughts in a whirl. She hadn't even considered having to share a room. Still, she'd promised herself she would do anything necessary to fulfil her ambition and at least Ruby seemed a pleasant girl.

'My, that's grand,' Ruby cried, eyeing the shiny leather bag, then leading the way up a flight of stairs that led off the hallway. 'There are more wards through there,' she told Bea, indicating a doorway before climbing another, narrower staircase. 'Always pays to have a candle with you when you're on nights. Black as the hobs of hell it gets and right spooky, an' all.' Although it was only late afternoon, the shadows were already gathering in the hallway, and Bea shuddered at the thought of having to walk along here alone in the dark.

Chapter 15

'Right, this is us,' Ruby announced, elbowing open a door that led into a room under the eaves.

'Goodness, there are five beds in here,' Bea exclaimed. 'I've never slept in a room with someone else before,' she said, shaking her head in disbelief.

'Blimey, girl, there were ten of us at home, all topping and tailing in two beds. Now, there's usually three or four of us in here, but if the wards fill up, they sometimes send one of the Sisters of St Thomas to help. You can have the bed under the skylight, see the stars when they're out. If you're not too whacked after your shift to stay awake, that is. Anyways, you unpack, and I'll find a dress and cap that'll fit you.'

Bea was still staring around the room when Ruby reappeared a few moments later.

'Something wrong?'

'Where do I hang my clothes?' she asked, only for Ruby to chortle with mirth.

'Oh my, where do you think you are, The Burlington? Look, love, I can tell from your accent you aren't used to slumming it, but you're going to have to make do with one of those like the rest of us.' She gestured to the small wooden cabinet beside the bed. 'And when you've done that, you can try these on for size.'

Bea stared at the plain grey dress, white apron and mob cap and swallowed hard. To think she'd worried her navy fitted travelling dress wouldn't be smart enough.

'Er, you wouldn't help me, would you,' Bea asked, turning round so that Ruby could undo the buttons.

'Blimey, girl, you used to having a maid or something? Crikey, you are, aren't you?' she chuckled, duly obliging. But as Beatrice stepped out of her dress, she gasped. 'I never seen such fine underthings and me lather's got a stall at Spitalfields.'

'Your lather?' Bea frowned.

'Yea, father. Here, that corset moulds to your body like a glove. There's not a bone sticking out, not like in me stays; they cut me in half every time I bend over. And would you look at that pink chemise? Oh sorry, that was rude of me.'

'That's all right.' Bea smiled. 'I'm rather fond of it myself. Especially as my stepmother thinks it's too grown-up for me.'

'How old are you then?'

'Seventeen.'

'Well, I'm sixteen and me finger and thumb – that's me mum, by the way – has treated me like a grown-up for ever. Wouldn't mind borrowing these threads on me day off.' Ruby flopped down on the bed and stroked the fine fabric of Bea's gown. 'So how much do you know about governesses then?'

'Well, the one we had . . . oh, I see what you mean,' Bea said quickly, as Ruby raised her brows. She really was going to have to remember where she was. 'Perhaps you could tell me about the ones in here while I get changed,' she asked, trying not to wince as the coarse material of the dress pricked her skin.

Tying on the apron and placing the cap on her head, she listened as Ruby described their various illnesses and idiosyncrasies.

'One woman's charge hit her over the head with a cricket bat. Had a lump the size of the ball, she did.'

'Nurse Grey, you are not paid to regale probationers with tales about our patients.'

Jumping up quickly, they saw an older nurse, hands on hips, glaring at them from the doorway. 'If it is not too much to ask, perhaps I could trouble you to report to the ward where patients are dying for their supper.'

'That's an unfortunate choice of words,' Ruby chortled, only to receive another gimlet glare. 'I've just been explaining the ropes to Nurse Farringdon here,' she added.

'Well, Nurse Farringdon, all I can say is that if you wish to know how things are done properly around here then you'd be better off asking someone who knows. And tuck your hair up under your cap. This is not a fashion parade, you know.'

As the woman stamped back down the stairs, her footsteps echoing round the attic room, Bea turned to Ruby.

'Who on earth was that?'

'Miss Ratcliffe, the matron, but we call her Ratty. She's Miss Nightingale's second in command and the worst person to get on the wrong side of. She'll make you do all the dirtiest jobs and stand over you to make sure you do them properly.'

What a way to start, Bea thought, her spirits plummeting. She had so wanted to make a good impression on her first day too.

Quickly Bea folded some of her clothes into the cupboard then placed her bag containing the rest of her things beside the bed.

'Don't leave it there,' Ruby cried, looking horrified. 'Hide it under the cover for now. Come on, we daren't upset Ratty any more.'

Determined to prove herself, Bea followed the girl back down the stairs where Ruby was dispatched to the wards whilst she was directed to fetch the meals being winched up from the basement kitchen by a windlass.

'This thing's a lifesaver, believe you me,' a nurse with eyes shiny as sloes, chocolate-coloured skin and a cheery smile told Bea as she retrieved a large dish from the hatch. 'Running around like headless chickens we were, before Miss Nightingale had this installed. She might seem daunting at times, but that woman certainly gets things done. I am Salena, by the way. Just joined us, have you?'

'Yes, and my name's Bea.'

'Well, good luck. Now, I'd better get this lot delivered while the food is hot or Ratty will have me for tomorrow's breakfast. You can take that to Miss Bishop in room eight over there,' Salena told her, nodding towards the remaining dish that was covered with a cloth.

Miss Bishop was lying back against her pillow, her fair hair spilling from under her cap. She smiled weakly as Bea carefully set the tray down on the cabinet beside her bed.

'Shall I help you to sit up?' Bea asked.

'I've no strength to eat,' the woman sighed.

'It's eating that gives you energy, or so my governess used to say.' Seeing that she'd got the woman's attention, Bea leaned forward and helped to ease her into a sitting position. The woman coughed then shivered. Snatching up a fringed shawl from the end of the bed, Bea placed it around her shoulders to add a layer of warmth to the white high-necked nightgown, then gently she straightened her cap. 'There, that's better.' She placed the tray on the woman's lap, but she just stared forlornly at it.

'Come on, you must eat,' she coaxed, holding a spoonful of broth to her lips. Like a little bird, the woman opened her mouth. They repeated the process a few times until the bowl was half emptied then the woman slumped back against her pillow.

'Sorry, I can't manage any more.' Pleased to see there was now some colour in her cheeks, Bea smiled.

'You've done well,' she assured the woman, who nodded then closed her eyes. As Bea got up to go, Miss Bishop opened one eye.

'I've been governess to three young girls. Mischievous but a delight to teach. Now they're all grown up and my services will soon no longer be required, I shall need to find a new position. You don't know of a family seeking a governess, do you?' She looked so sad Bea's heart went out to her.

'I believe there is always demand for good ones, such as yourself. However, you will need to build up your strength.'

'You are right, of course,' Miss Bishop agreed. 'Thank you, my dear. It is kind of you to spend time with me. Everyone is always so busy.'

Bea pulled the cover up over her, then, tiptoed out with the tray. However, when she reached the door, she saw Miss Ratcliffe was standing there watching.

'Perhaps you would be good enough to remember you are here to assist the other nurses. If we all spent time talking, nothing would ever get done.' Bea's heart sank. Surely, it wasn't wrong to spend a few minutes with a patient.

However, there was no time to dwell on Matron's remarks, for no sooner had the supper things been cleared than she was helping with the patients' ablutions before settling them for the night. With the coarse dress chaffing her skin and her hands already red and sore, she was just wondering how much longer she could carry on when she bumped into Ruby carrying a pot covered by a cloth.

'Blimey, girl, my shoes are pinching something chronic and my belly's rumbling louder than last night's thunder,' she moaned. 'Thank heavens it's nearly time for our supper then we can go to roost. You hungry?'

Only just realizing she hadn't eaten since leaving Grosvenor Square that morning and that she was ravenous, Bea nodded.

'The dining room . . . ' However, the rest of her sentence was lost in a loud cry of indignation.

'Nurses Grey and Farringdon, if you have time to stand around then I trust all the patients are settled and ready for their nightly medicines.' They turned round to see Matron emerging from a side room carrying a wooden chest.

'Lory, I swear that woman's a witch,' Ruby muttered. 'Yes, Matron,' she called sweetly.

'Then you may assist me on my round, Nurse Grey.'

'Glory be,' Ruby groaned. 'Be a love and take this to the sluice. I'll see you down in the dining room, it's just along from the kitchen,' she said quickly, before going to join the woman.

Trying not to retch at the unsavoury smell emanating from the pot, Bea hurried to dispose of it. However, as she walked briskly along the corridor, she heard someone crying. Unable to ignore the anguished sounds, she put the pot on a nearby shelf then popped her head around the door. In the fading light, she could just make out a figure hunched over on the bed, sobbing her heart out.

'Whatever is the matter?' she asked, hurrying to the woman's side. Tears were streaming down her face, and she was clearly in distress. Taking the handkerchief from her apron pocket, Bea gently dabbed her cheeks then sat down on the bed.

'Are you in pain?' she asked, taking her hand, and gently stroking it. 'Shall I get Matron?' she asked, half rising, only for the woman to clutch her hand tighter. It was obvious she didn't want to be left by herself and, not knowing what to do, Bea began to sing softly as she had to Firecracker when he'd become agitated. Gradually, the sobs subsided until, with a final hiccup, the room fell quiet.

'I'm so scared, please stay with me until I fall asleep?' The plea came out of the shadows, urgent and insistent.

'Of course,' Bea said quickly, fearful the woman would become upset again. 'Can you tell me why you are so distressed?' There was a heavy silence followed by a long, drawn-out sigh.

'Because the physician is coming to see me tomorrow and I just know he's going to say I'm well enough to return to work.'

'But that is good news, surely,' Bea replied.

'No, it most certainly is not . . . '

'Nurse Farringdon, a word if you please.' She looked up to see Matron standing in the doorway, candle in one hand.

'I'm sure everything will be fine,' she said, giving the woman a reassuring smile before sliding off the bed.

'Nurse Farringdon, do you have any idea what is wrong with that patient?' Matron asked, closing the door. Although her features were hazy in the light of the candle, Bea could feel the heat of her anger.

'No, but she was crying and—'

'You went to assist,' Miss Ratcliffe finished for her. 'However, without knowing the full history of her case, you could have said the wrong thing, inflamed an already delicate situation. And sitting on patient's beds is strictly forbidden as is abandoning a pot filled with faeces.'

'But I was . . . ' Bea, said glancing towards the shelf.

'Nurse Grey is seeing to it. Miss Nightingale wishes to see you, so you'd better look sharp.'

'Yes, Matron,' she replied.

Hurrying along the corridor towards the superintendent's office, Bea's thoughts were spinning like a top. Her first day and she was in trouble already. Surely, she wasn't going to be asked to leave? Smoothing down her apron, she knocked on the door.

Chapter 16

'Enter.' The strident tones did nothing to ease her worries.

'You wished to see me, Miss Nightingale?'

'Ah, Nurse Farringdon, come in and take a seat,' the superintendent invited, looking up from the papers she'd been reading. To Bea's surprise, she smiled. 'I have been reading Professor Todd's letter of recommendation. He speaks highly of you, yet says you have a lot to learn. But then don't we all? Tell me, how have you found your first day here?' Even in the dim light, her gaze was candid, and Bea decided to be truthful.

'I seem to have made some mistakes, but in future I will ensure my hair is tucked under my cap and not sit on a patient's bed. I didn't realize I was doing anything wrong by helping Miss Bishop to eat. She did have more colour in her cheeks when I left.'

'I'm not sure where you got the idea it was wrong to encourage patients to eat. Nutrition is vital for recovery, and we have a very competent cook. Taking the time out of a busy schedule is the sign of a good nurse.'

'Oh, but . . . I thought . . . '

'You were in trouble?' Again, that smile.

'Well, yes. Being my first day I wanted to get everything right but . . . ' she sighed.

'You seem rather agitated, Nurse, is there something else?'

'Well, yes.' Knowing Matron was likely to be speaking with the superintendent, Bea decided she might as well tell her everything.

'And so, you see, I left the pot on a ledge and tried to help a patient who was upset but I didn't know the history of her case and was told to think before acting next time.'

'Ah, now I see where this stems from. Out of interest, which patient did you try and comfort?'

'The one in ward fifteen. She was crying her heart out, fretting that the physician will say she's well enough to go home when he sees her tomorrow.'

'And that strikes you as peculiar?'

'Well, yes, surely that means she's better.'

'Sometimes psychological damage goes far deeper than the physical.' Seeing her confused look, Miss Nightingale continued. 'Miss Blackett, like some of our previous patients, has suffered at the hands of her employer. And I mean that literally. There are men who think the governess, or more usually the maid, is there for their own pleasure. If the woman refuses and he gets angry . . . well, I'm sure you get the picture.'

'But that is terrible,' Bea gasped.

'Regrettably, that is the way of things. She is lucky not to be expecting an unwanted baby but obviously her employer won't have her back.'

'I'm sure she wouldn't want to return to her post either,' Bea retorted. 'Besides, she can always get another job.'

'Without a character? Highly unlikely. Which leaves her without a roof over her head.'

'Then where will she go?'

'The poor house probably. Although if she becomes hysterical in front of the physician tomorrow, he might recommend she be put away in an asylum, for her own safety, you understand.'

'But that's awful,' Bea cried, staring at the superintendent, aghast.

'Some would say she has been lucky having the fees for her stay here paid, but one can only twist the hand of a guilty man so far. I'm afraid both the money and duration for Miss Blackett's time here are at an end.'

'But surely there is something you can do,' Bea cried.

'Until the law of the land or men's attitude can be changed, then no, there is not. Professor Todd intimated you were naive, and I can see that you are. This is a hard world and if you want to survive as a nurse then you are going to have to toughen up or give up.'

'Give up? But I've always wanted to be a nurse,' Bea protested. The woman leaned forward and stared her straight in the eye.

'You have had a privileged and sheltered upbringing and know little of what life for the working classes is really like.'

'So, you think my background counts against me?' Bea cried, her chin rising in defiance. The superintendent surveyed her for such a long moment, Bea was convinced she was going to send her home for insubordination. Then the woman smiled and her whole demeanour softened.

'I am going to share with you something few people

know, but which, under the circumstances, might be of help. My background too is one of privilege. I was born into a well-connected family in Florence who removed to England when I was still young. We divided our time between our two homes in Derbyshire and Hampshire. I was educated by my father who had advanced ideas about women's education, slaking my thirst to learn as much as I could about mathematics, history, languages, you name it.' She shrugged. 'I also helped tend the sick, both in our family and those of the estate workers. However, when I later expressed a desire to take up nursing, my parents were horrified, stating it was not a desirable activity for a woman of my standing.'

'But you must have talked them round or you wouldn't be here now,' Bea replied.

'Eventually, I was able to enrol at an institute in Germany where I learned important nursing skills, about patient observation and the value of good hospital organization. I'll let you into a secret, Nurse Farringdon: this is my first nursing position.'

'Goodness, that's incredible. You look so efficient and . . . well, knowledgeable about everything.'

The woman smiled. 'The moral of my story is that our background makes us who we are today yet need not be a barrier to future aspirations. However, in order to best help our patients, we also need to know about their background. I suggest you get Nurse Grey to take you out onto the streets of Marylebone and beyond where you'll see some of the most poverty-stricken areas. Then will you appreciate how these people live and what they endure to survive. Only by understanding that can you truly help. Now, go and get some supper before it is all gone. Goodnight, Nurse Farringdon.'

'Good night, superintendent, and thank you. I really appreciate you sharing your story and will, of course, keep it to myself.'

No longer feeling hungry and wanting to be by herself to reflect on what she'd been told, Bea made her way up the stairs. Reaching the second floor where it became narrower and darker, she heard scratching and rustling, followed by a creak. Spinning round, she tried in vain to see if someone was following her, but all she could make out were swinging silver cobwebs festooned with huge, black spiders. She shuddered, wishing she'd brought a candle with her as Ruby had suggested. Then something scuttled over her foot and fighting down a scream, she dived into the bedroom and hid under the covers. Had she made a mistake coming here after all?

When Bea woke the next morning, her back was aching, she could hear gentle snoring. The mattress felt so much harder than her normal feathered one and she could see streaks of early morning light filtering through the window above her. A window on the ceiling? Where was she? From below came the clatter of hoofs and the rattle of cartwheels over cobbles, boys bellowing the morning news. Wincing as she propped herself up on her pillow, she peered around, saw Ruby sleeping alongside and the mound of another body in the bed by the door. Of course, she remembered now: she was at the Hospital for Gentlewomen.

Misgivings from the previous night forgotten, her heart skipped in delight. She had taken the first steps to becoming a nurse and clearly must have been overtired for hadn't she seen mice and other vermin in the stables back home? Although she knew she had a lot to learn, Miss Nightingale's disclosure the previous evening had given her the incentive. She would go out onto the streets and discover what the people in this part of London were like, see how they lived so that she too could become a good nurse.

'Where did you get to last night?' Ruby whispered, breaking into her thoughts. 'Seems right daft missing a meal you've paid for. It gets deducted from your pay whether you eat it or not, you know.'

'The superintendent wanted to see me and then I was so tired I came straight up to bed,' Bea told her, omitting the bit about the shadows.

'Blimey, girl, what have you been up to?' Ruby asked, hazel eyes wide. 'Don't tell me old Ratty did her usual tatty?'

'Pardon?' Bea frowned.

'Ratty tatty, like the letter box,' Ruby said, imitating an opening and closing mouth with her hand. 'She's always dropping us in it. Talking of which, you didn't have to leave that full pot on the ledge like that.'

'I'm sorry, but one of the patients was crying and I went to see what was wrong.'

'What's all the noise about?' a muffled voice enquired as a tousled head emerged from under the bedclothes.

'Sorry, Edith, didn't mean to wake you. This is Bea, she started yesterday.'

'Hello, Edith, how nice to meet you.'

'Likewise, I'm sure,' the older woman replied, eyeing Bea curiously. 'Well, no peace for the wicked,' she added, dragging on her dress, and tucking frizzy brown hair under her cap. 'And you two had better look sharp, Matron will be checking the wards before Dr Lennox swoops.'

The day couldn't have been more different from the previous one for it seemed Bea was expected to act as a messenger, fetching this and carrying that for whomever asked.

'Don't worry,' Ruby murmured, taking a bandage from her. 'It will calm down once the physician has finished his rounds. His nibs thinks we were all put on this earth to minister to his whims,' she said, giving one of her cheeky grins.

'Nurse Farringdon, a pot to ward six immediately,' Matron ordered, her querulous tones sending Bea scurrying. 'And walk, do not run.'

'No, Matron,' Bea replied, raising her brow. Was it her imagination or was the smell of chloride of lime even stronger today, she wondered, setting off down the corridor? After duly seeing to the patient in ward six and disposing of the contents, she was summoned to help tidy the beds in the upstairs ward before Dr Lennox reached there. The three occupants were all sitting up, hair neatly combed under their white caps, beribboned white bed jackets neatly tied over their white nightdresses.

'Can you help me straighten their covers?' Salena asked, breaking into a smile when she saw Bea.

'I do feel terrible today,' the first woman said.

'Don't you worry, Miss Price, Dr Lennox is bound to have something to cure that ill humour that's plaguing you.'

'Well, the last powder did me no good whatsoever,' the woman grumbled.

'Nor me,' the young patient in the next bed let out a long sigh.

'I've given up wondering what normal is. I'm sure I felt better before I came here,' the third one murmured. 'It's the miasma from the Thames, floats in through those windows they insist on keeping open.'

'Come now, ladies, you'll all feel better once you've seen Dr Lennox,' Salena told them cheerfully. 'And I've heard there's stew and dumplings for luncheon.'

'There always is something tasty when the physician's here. If one weren't suspicious, one would think it was made for his benefit.'

Bea had to admire the way Salena handled the patients as she helped plump up pillows and tidy things away into the cupboards. It seemed everywhere had to be even more pristine than usual for the eminent visitor. She wondered what he was like.

She didn't have to wait long to find out for as she left the ward, Matron summoned her into the room where the physician was examining Miss Bishop.

'Ah, Nurse Farringdon, Dr Lennox here is interested to hear your theories on nutrition,' she said, her look unfathomable.

'My theories?' Bea frowned.

'Miss Bishop has said she is feeling stronger today and that it is all down to you. Apparently, you not only insisted she eat her supper but assisted in spooning the broth into her mouth. Of course, we don't normally have the time to pander to our patients' needs like that,' she told Dr Lennox, giving Bea a disapproving look.

'Well, Nurse?' Dr Lennox queried. 'What do you think. Would you presume to know better than her physician?'

'No, of course not,' Bea protested. 'It's what Nanny always did with the little ones at home when they were too weak to eat. I thought if I assisted Miss Bishop, she would get some nutrition inside her, which would make her stronger.'

'Elementary thinking,' Dr Lennox snorted. 'If only treating patients was that simple. I'll have you know that we physicians are highly trained and need a licence from the Royal College of Physicians to practise,' he added, puffing out his chest so that his stethoscope bounced against it. 'May I ask how long you have been, er, practising to be a nurse?' As his bulging eyes stared knowingly at her, Bea swallowed.

'I started yesterday,' she admitted.

'Yes, well, clearly you have much to learn. Treating a patient entails taking a detailed case history, making a thorough examination and then, and only then,' he retorted, jabbing his finger at her, 'can I decide the best course of action and write out a prescription for the apothecary to dispense. Now whilst I do what I have been trained to, run along and make a bed or something.'

Bea opened her mouth to protest but Matron waved her away. She was here to learn, wanted to even, but that pompous, supercilious man in his black frock coat, buttons straining over his corpulent body, had no right to talk to her like that.

'Blimey, girl, what's up, you got steam coming out your ears?' Ruby exclaimed, as Bea stomped down the corridor.

'It's that physician,' she spluttered. 'I've never been spoken to like that in my life before.'

'You get used to it. Puffed up like one of those peacocks and full of his own importance he is. Why the tinctures me Nan makes work better than any powders he prescribes. I'm going to see her on Sunday to get some of her salve for my poor skin.' She held up her red, chapped hands for Bea to see. 'You'll need some before much longer so why not come with me?' she suggested, hazel eyes gleaming.

'I'd love to,' Bea replied, remembering Miss Nightingale had advised her to see what life was like in the outside world, as she'd put it. 'You called her Nan, though; don't you have one of those funny names for her?' she teased.

'Get a clout round the head good and proper if I called her anything but Nan,' Ruby snorted. 'Her pie and mash is to die for though,' she added, grinning.

Chapter 17

The weather was overcast and windy as they set off from the hospital that Sunday. Having declared Bea would attract unwanted attention in her blue travelling gown, Ruby had insisted Edith loan her a shawl to cover it. Now, with gusts blowing up from the Thames, bringing with them the unsavoury smell of salt and sewage, Bea was glad of the protection it afforded as she held it up to her nose. The noise and bustle of Marylebone hit them as soon as they turned the street. Omnibuses, hansoms, carts, and private carriages clattered over the cobbles and the air was thick with the stench of horse dung, rotting fruit and rubbish. Crossing sweepers tried valiantly to clear the debris, while barrow boys, flower sellers and girls with bunches of watercress shouted their wares. A beggar held out his skeletal hand, eyes pleading as they passed, but as Bea hesitated, Ruby urged her on.

'Don't stop or they'll all be after you.'

'But he's all skin and bones,' Bea protested, looking back at the body that seemed little more than a bundle of rags as it slumped pitifully against a wall.

'Because he'll spend anything he gets on liquor or worse.'

'Where will he sleep?'

'In a doorway if he isn't moved on, or under the arches. Don't look like that. Life is hard round here,' she said, taking Bea's arm as the crowd grew thicker and pressed against them. 'It's not all bad. Some will cadge enough for a pie or bed at the penny dosshouses, others will slump over a clothesline because it's cheaper. You'll be all right,' she added, mistaking Bea's shudder. 'Just keep looking straight ahead and don't make eye contact with anyone. Come on, this way, Nan lives at the Rookery.'

'That sounds nice. Is it that what her house is called?' Bea asked.

'If you weren't a stranger round here, I'd think you were taking the mickey,' Ruby muttered, shaking her head. 'The Rookery's another slum area.'

'This place is like a maze,' Bea muttered as they turned yet another corner and came upon market stalls, their canvas roofs flapping, heard shrieking and rattling as more sellers pedalled their wares. Here costermongers laboured over their barrows as they tried to sell passers-by their Sunday dinners, making her think longingly of Mrs Cookson's roast beef with her potatoes crisped to perfection in beef dripping. Then she saw the cheese and fish laid out on trays, sweating in the humidity, offal dripping blood onto the already filthy pavement. The whole place was covered in clouds of flies and the stench was unbearable. Bea felt nauseous, all thought of eating gone, and yet couldn't help staring around in horror.

'People have to eat,' Ruby said, seeing her expression. 'In fact, I'm just popping in here to get me Nan some sweetbreads,' she added, indicating a nearby shop.

Bea frowned. 'But this is the Sabbath, and everyone's trading.'

'Don't make no difference here. The Good Lord ain't going to appear and hand out bread and wine, or pay their rent, is he?'

A few minutes later, Ruby re-appeared carrying a parcel wrapped in old newspaper. They walked on in silence, the market and shops giving way to large houses in various states of disrepair, some with roofs that had fallen in, others had broken windows yet seemingly all had lines of clothes strung across the streets between them. Barefooted urchins in tattered rags dodged in and out, heedless of the shouts from unkempt women standing gossiping in the doorways.

'So many children,' Bea exclaimed. 'Where do they all live?'

'Here, of course. The tenements are divided into rooms probably with eight or ten to each. The ones above ground are lucky 'cos in winter the heavy rain gushes down and floods the basements. Then when the temperature drops, the water freezes. Many a poor soul's died frozen stiff to their pallet.'

'That is terrible.' Bea shuddered. 'Can't anything be done?'

'They stuff up the holes in the windows and walls with any spare rags, but it doesn't help much.'

'But can't they build more houses for these people? I mean, they are human beings for crying out loud,' Bea cried. Ruby gave a harsh laugh.

'Tell that to the greedy landlords or them businessmen who reckoned they were helping the housing situation when they stuck these up. All out to make as much money as they could, they bought up the market gardens for a song and built on that. Cheap buildings thrown up on marshy land, it's not surprising so many collapse. Anyhows, me Nan's not complaining 'cos her place is right on the edge, claims the soil is the best for growing her herbs and plants. Lord knows what gets thrown onto it, mind. Come on, it's just down the alleyway here.'

Bea followed her friend down a dark, narrow passageway with blackened walls on either side. It was strewn with debris and, judging from the unsavoury smell, goodness only knows what else. Then, as they emerged into daylight once more, Ruby knocked on a bleached wooden door that fronted another street.

'Nan,' she cried, throwing her arms around the diminutive woman who answered. Her white hair was fluffed up around her face and she was wearing a coarse black dress covered by a large snowy apron.

'No need to make such a fuss, Ruby Grey,' she scolded. 'And who is this you've brought to see me?' The woman scrutinised Bea with the same inquisitive, hazel-coloured eyes as her granddaughter, then nodded as if satisfied.

'This is Bea Farringdon,' Ruby introduced. 'She's just started working at the hospital.'

'Then very welcome you are, ducks.' Smiling, she stood aside, and Bea saw they had stepped straight into the living room, which was small but welcoming. Although faded brown curtains hung at the windows, the cushions on the chair were a riot of colour as were the rag rugs on the stone flags. A few sticks were crackling in the grate in front of which a kettle began singing.

'What a charming room,' she said politely. 'It's so vibrant.'

'Thank you,' the woman said, clearly pleased. 'I run up the remnants my Tommy gets me from his stall. Might be poor but don't have to be plain, I always says, but it don't do to draw attention to yourself round here,' she added, catching Bea glancing at the window. 'Now sit yourselves down while I make us a brew. Er, you do drink tea?' she asked Bea.

'Cors she does, Nan. She's not the Queen, you know.'

'And how do you know what the Queen drinks, young lady?' the woman chided.

'A cup of tea would be lovely, er . . . sorry, I didn't catch your name?'

'Call me Nan, ducks, everybody do.'

'Well, I might not know what the Queen drinks, but I know what my Nan likes,' Ruby said, holding out the parcel.

'Now, our Rubes, don't I tell you not to go spending your hard-earned money on me,' the woman chided. Yet she couldn't contain her delight when she peeked inside the wrapper. 'Ooh, me favourite. Ta ducks, I'll feast like a queen meself tomorrow.'

While Ruby helped her Nan with the tea, Bea couldn't help gazing around the room. It really was tiny, and she could now see that the cushions were placed to cover the springs that poked through the worn covers of the sofa. There seemed to be some bed at the other end of the room too. Surely the woman didn't live and sleep in the same room? Bunches of herbs were strung on a rack over the fire, plants lined the windowsill and from an old iron pot hanging near the grate, the most delicious smell of cooking emanated.

'So, tell me Bea, where are you from and why does an upper-class young lady like you wish to spend her time nursing? It can't be for the pay,' Nan asked as they sat enjoying their drinks.

'Nan!' Ruby cried.

'That's all right,' Bea chuckled. 'Our family home is in Devonshire. It's a lovely manor house set in rolling green hills, but has not been a very happy place since Mama died and Papa still hasn't a son to pass the estate on to. He thinks that is because of a curse put on the family by some gypsies when my Grandpapa turned them off his land.'

'What kind of curse was that?' Nan said, eyes alert as she sat up straighter.

'That from there on no male heir would be born to a Farringdon.'

'And have they? Had any sons, I mean.'

'No,' Bea sighed, shaking her head. 'Naturally, that is a sadness to Papa.'

'Well, you can tell him from me, that curses can be lifted by kindness.'

'Really? How would that work?'

'He could always invite gypsies to camp on his land again. It would be worth a try, wouldn't it? Anyway, dear, you were telling us how you became a nurse,' she urged.

Both Nan and Ruby listened intently as she explained about her mother's fatal riding accident and how helpless she'd felt. 'Since then, I've had this need to be able to help people burning away inside me. Does that sound silly?'

'Not at all,' Nan murmured. 'There's a real need for physicians and nurses, for those who can afford them, of course. Though if them new quacks didn't dismiss all our old ways of healing, everyone would benefit.'

'I did tell you Nan made her own herbal remedies, didn't I?'

'You did, and I'd love to see some. If that would be all right?' Bea asked, turning to Nan who was regarding her thoughtfully.

'I like you, Bea, and would be willing to show you my own little physic garden, as long as you promise not to tell anyone. Regrettably, women like me are still regarded with deep suspicion.'

'What, even in London?' she asked.

'Especially in London,' Nan replied. 'Physicians are hailed as miracle workers for prescribing their pills and powders, yet if a woman makes remedies from nature's bounty she's cast as a witch. And we all know what that means. Strung up by the rope,' she added, seeing Bea's bewilderment.

Bea followed Nan out of the same door they'd come in by, and round the side of the building with its bulging walls. Fleetingly she wondered why they hadn't used the back door but then the stench from the open gullies hit her full in the face and she quickly pulled the loaned shawl over her nose.

'Being on the end means I get me own garden, see,' Nan said, not seeming to notice Bea's discomfort as she gestured proudly towards what looked like clumps of weeds and twigs sprouting from sludgy soil. 'Grows all the herbs for my remedies here; that old lavender serves me good and proper,' she whispered, pointing to the straggly shrub on the edge. Bea nodded, amazed that something so withered could produce anything. She peered around, then crouched down and pulled back a huge dock leaf to reveal delicate green fronds beneath. 'Seen the like before?'

'Cook always makes parsley sauce to go with our gammon,

and rosemary for our roast lamb,' Bea said, delighted she recognized at least two of the tiny plants.

Nan snorted and gave her a wry look before gently pulling back more of the straggly foliage.

'These yellow beauties are the sticklewort; cure all sorts they can: sores, coughs, even treat wounds. I can see you don't believe me,' she said, regarding Bea shrewdly.

'It just seems incredible that one plant could possibly do so much.'

'Ah, but it's how you distil it, see, ducks,' the old woman grinned and tapped the side of her nose. She looked around again, then parted more foliage, this time revealing tiny mauve flowers. 'Bruisewort or Boneset, its uses are obvious; now this one here's good for the gripes . . . oh,' she cried, jumping to her feet as they heard voices. 'Best go in,' she muttered, scuttling back down the side of the path like a little mouse.

'I made us another brew,' Ruby said, picking up the brown tea pot and pouring the steaming liquid as they reappeared. 'Didn't you bring any herbs in with you?'

'Heard old Jackson and his missus coming down the alley so had to come in. You know how they loves to poke their noses in where they ain't wanted. Don't worry, ducks, I already made up the salve for your hands,' she said, taking a little blue jar from the shelf and placing it on the table beside her. 'And I dare say you'll be needing some too,' Nan said, looking at Bea's hands then passing her a similar one. 'They won't stay all white and smooth like that for long but if you rub in some unguent day and night that should help.' She sighed, flopping down on a chair beside the table and picking up her tea.

'What did you think of Nan's plants? Of course, it's not full moon so she hasn't done her charm dance yet.'

'Cheeky beggar,' Nan muttered, blowing on her tea to cool it.

'Something's smelling good, Nan.' She looked at the woman hopefully.

'I don't know, our Rubes, don't they feed you at that hospital?' the woman grumbled good-naturedly. 'Sit yourselves down. You can cut some of that bread, I'll dish up once I've finished my tea. Though I'm clean out of gammon and the butcher had no leg of lamb.'

'Don't be daft, Nan. We never have those. Knuckle of bacon or scrag end if we're lucky,' Ruby replied, giving the woman a funny look.

'That was me telling your Nan what we had with parsley and rosemary at home,' Bea confessed. 'I didn't think, I'm afraid.'

'No need to apologize for what you're used to,' Nan said, going over to the fire and taking the lid off the pot. As a wonderful aroma filled the tiny room, Bea's stomach rumbled. 'Bitty-piecey broth,' the woman announced, ladling the thick soup into unglazed earthenware bowls, and placing them on the table next to the chunks of coarse brown bread. 'Well, get stuck in, ducks,' the woman invited, dunking her bread into the broth and scooping it up. 'Might be a bit hard but the yeast in it's good for your insides.'

'Blimey, Nan, where did you learn that?' Ruby asked, staring at her in astonishment. The woman tapped the side of her nose again. 'You nurses aren't the only ones that know what's good for you.'

'Talking of good, this broth is delicious. What's in it? If you don't mind me asking.'

'Ask away, ducks,' she told Bea. 'Got some fall offs from the veg barrow and cut them up, hence the bitty-piecey; bits of this, pieces of that, get it?' she chortled.

Ruby grinned. 'Bet you added some of your herbs.'

'Talking of which, you were about to tell me what that other herb was when we were interrupted,' Bea said.

'That be the hedge nettle, known as heal all, thrives in that damp soil and is good for the chilly need,' Nan nodded.

'You said herbs could be used for treating more than one thing. How does that work exactly?' she asked, fascinated by the thought. The woman wiped her bowl with the last of her bread then regarded Bea for a long moment.

'Come and see me next weekend and I'll show you.'

'Really? Oh, that would be wonderful. Thank you and thank you so much for your kind hospitality. I've had a lovely time.'

'So have I, ducks, and thanks for them lambs do das, our Rubes. I'll enjoy them tomorrow. Now, grab your salves and get a shufty on or you'll have that matron on your backs. Take this,' Nan said, pressing a fabric pouch into Bea's hand. 'Scents of cedarwood and lavender to mask them unsavoury smells. It'll also ward off disease and ill humours so you might find it useful at the hospital. Just don't tell Matron.' She chuckled and gave a broad wink.

Chapter 18

As they hurried back down the alley, Bea held the little sachet to her nose, inhaling deeply. The woody, spicy perfume was potent and did indeed disguise the putrid odours.

'What did you think of me Nan then? Quite a character, isn't she?' Ruby grinned.

'I thought she was lovely,' Bea replied. 'But why didn't she go out of the back door to her little garden?' Although privately, Bea wondered how that tiny strip of mud could ever be considered a garden, she was too polite to mention it.

'What back door? There's only the one room so why would she need more than one door in a cottage so small. You are funny. Tell you what, next time you go to Devonshire, you can take me with you so I can count how many your home has. Don't worry, I'll try and speak all la de da, so I don't embarrass you.'

'Oh Ruby, you'd never do that. In fact, my sisters would love you. Victoria, who's eighteen and in London for the Season, is staying with Aunt Emmeline who lives not that far from the hospital. I promised to pay them a visit so you can come with me then, if you like.'

'And how many doors does Aunt Emmeline have?' Ruby asked, darting her a look of amusement. 'If you're serious, I'd like that.'

They'd reached the tenements, where the women were bringing in their washing, while the ragged children stared curiously and held out grubby hands for money.

'Don't even think about it,' Ruby hissed as Bea hesitated. 'The men will be home from the alehouses, their bellies full of beer and liquor, their thoughts on what's below them, if you get my meaning.'

Turning the corner, they walked on, the atmosphere seeming different to earlier. Gone were the market stalls and costermongers, now filthy children scouted the gutters for dropped coins or scraps or food. Unsavoury-looking louts with florid cheeks leaned against walls of taverns, leering at loitering females whose charms were actively spilling over their blouses.

'Do you think the women realize they are encouraging those men to look at them?' Bea asked.

'Cors they do,' Ruby snorted. 'They're flower sellers, silly.'

'Where are their flowers then?' Bea frowned, certain Ruby was teasing her again.

'That's the polite way of saying they're prostitutes. Honestly, you aren't safe to be let out. Come on, we don't want to be seen staring or they'll think we're for the taking too.'

'What are they doing?' Bea asked, catching the sight of men with nets, skulking in the shadows.

'Beak hunting,' Ruby replied, then sighed when she saw Bea's bemused expression. 'Stealing fowl from that patch of land over there by the ditch.'

'Goodness, I didn't know they raised poultry in London,' Bea murmured, slowing to take a closer look.

'Well, as far as I know, they don't grow on trees at the palace. Now, do come on, you're drawing attention to us,' the girl urged, taking Bea by the arm and all but dragging her along. 'Oh blimey, that's all we need; look straight ahead and don't stop.'

They hurried on, ignoring the men worse the wear for liquor who called out lewdly, the singing and bawdy remarks emanating from the open doors of the alehouses, drunkards urinating onto the piles of steaming dung outside. No wonder everywhere stank, Bea thought, inhaling the herbs again.

Eventually, and somewhat to Bea's surprise, they arrived back at the hospital unscathed. She'd never walked so far in all her life; her feet were aching, and she was sure she'd never be able to get her boots off. All she wanted to do was climb into bed and sleep, but, as they entered the entrance hall, Matron was waiting. She stared pointedly at the clock.

'Evening, Matron,' Ruby called cheerily. 'Made it by the skin of our teeth.'

'As usual, Nurse Grey. I would have thought you'd be setting a better example to our new probationer. Now go and change; you are needed on the wards to help settle the patients for the night.'

'But it's our day off,' Ruby protested.

'Call yourselves nurses?' The woman's strident tones rang out, causing a cleaner who was scrubbing the floor to dart them a pitying look.

'Blooming slave driver,' Ruby muttered as they hurried up the stairs and changed into their uniform.

The hospital smell didn't seem so bad after the malodorous air outside, Bea realized, but she had no time to dwell on the matter as she was directed to help collect the supper dishes. Duly going from ward to ward, she smiled at the patients who asked how her day off had been, so that by the time she reached room eight, she felt as if she was back with friends and had almost forgotten her aching feet.

'Good evening, Miss Bishop,' she greeted the woman. 'Oh, you must be feeling better, you've managed to eat most of your supper tonight.'

'I have indeed and it's down to you, my dear. Despite what that fancy physician said, I did feel my strength returning after you fed me that broth. It was only then I realized just how weak I had become.'

'Well, I'm glad I've done something right since I came here,' Bea told her.

'I told that physician you were the kindest nurse here,' the woman said, her eyes bright.

'That was nice of you, Miss Bishop,' she replied, wondering how Dr Lennox had responded to that. 'Now, is there anything else I can do for you?'

'A chat would be nice. It gets so lonely in here,' she sighed, gesturing round the empty room.

'I dare not stay tonight, Matron's on the warpath, but I'll make time for one tomorrow,' Bea promised when she saw the woman's disappointed look.

'I'd appreciate that,' Miss Bishop replied, smiling bravely.

Bea deposited the tray on the windlass, then went about collecting the rest from the other wards. The patients all seemed pleased to see her, desperate for news of the outside world. She recounted some of her day, making the markets sound exciting and how Ruby's Nan had made delicious bitty-piecey broth from vegetables that had fallen from the barrow.

'Perhaps you could tell the cook here exactly what was in it. It would be nice to have something different,' Miss Price told her.

'The food here is palatable but boring as we always have the same thing,' her colleague Miss Crawford added.

'You know what day of the week it is by what we get fed,' the third patient in the ward, Miss Sandford said. 'Never would I think I'd be happy returning to nursery food, but I'd give up my best lace handkerchief for a boiled egg and soldiers.'

Having learned from Salena that the best way to deal with the ladies was to humour them, Bea nodded as she collected their empty dishes. For all their peculiar ways, it was satisfying getting to know patients and seeing them become brighter in spirits. Finally, she reached ward fifteen.

'Good evening, Miss Blackett,' she called brightly as she entered the room. 'Oh, I'm sorry,' she stammered, as she found herself staring into the face of a stranger.

'Miss Blackett was discharged from here this afternoon,' Matron said from the doorway. 'As you can see, Miss Grimble here has been admitted. I will discuss her, er, requirements with you later. Can Nurse Farringdon get you anything while she is here, Miss Grimble?'

'I thought I was here to get some peace and quiet,' the woman snapped.

'I'll leave you to it, then,' Bea said, smiling through gritted teeth as she closed the door behind her. 'Where did Miss Blackett go?' she asked Matron.

'She was admitted to the local asylum where they have the appropriate regimes and equipment to treat her.'

'What do you mean?' Bea asked.

'Restraints to stop her escaping and, of course, she'll be bled to let out the bad. If and when she's calmer, her treatment will be reconsidered.'

'But there was nothing really wrong . . . ' Bea began.

'Nurse Farringdon, I hope you are not suggesting you know better than the physician yet again? If you wish to remain here, I strongly suggest you show respect for your elders and betters.'

'I will, I mean I do. But Miss Blackett was—'

'Come into my office,' the woman said, pushing open the door behind her.

'Nurse Farringdon, whatever you might think, all of us here at the hospital have the best interests of our patients at heart and do all we can to help them. However, we are bound by rules and governed by those deemed more qualified. We might not always agree, but it is not our prerogative to say so. Do you understand?'

'Yes, Matron,' Bea muttered. 'But . . . '

'There can be no buts.' She sighed, then continued, her voice softer.

'Understandably, one can and does get attached to patients, especially when one first starts nursing. However, it is neither professional nor desirable to do so. Patients move on or die and if you become emotionally attached you will end up needing care yourself. And that will help nobody. Miss Nightingale intends setting up a training school for nurses and hopefully it will be soon, for it might surprise you to know, that, if you obey the guidelines, I think you have the makings of a fine one. Now, there are pots waiting to be collected from the upstairs wards and please ensure they are thoroughly washed this time.' The woman gave a nod and Bea knew she'd been dismissed.

Out in the corridor, she stood still for a moment trying to take in what Matron had told her, but then she was called to assist in changing a patient's nightdress and there was no time to think.

It was only later as she lay in bed, listening to Ruby's gentle snores, that she had time to reflect on her day. She shuddered at the sights she'd seen, the appalling conditions some people endured. Then, smiled at the thought of Nan, whose tiny patch of herbs was her pride and joy. Could they really be used for healing? She couldn't wait to find out. And then there'd been that talk by Matron. Her heart flipped excitedly, for surprisingly the woman she'd come to think of as an ogre had told her she had the makings of a fine nurse.

Chapter 19

Charlotte prowled around her upstairs sitting room wondering how to spend the afternoon. Victoria had insisted on helping Emmeline and Hester at Haven House and, until recently, she would have welcomed their departure, enabling her to meet with Alexander without any questions being asked. However, he had become possessive, demanding more of her time than she wished to give, leaving her no option other than to terminate their dalliance. Still, that was his loss, she thought, gazing up at her portrait above the fireplace. The artist had captured her likeness beautifully, portraying her as a woman in her prime, smiling beguilingly as if she was keeping some wondrous secret. Which she had been, of course. There was nothing like the sweet murmurings of a lover to bring a flush to one's cheeks. She let out a long sigh. At least that meddlesome maid would have nothing to poke her nose into. A knock on the door roused her from her reverie.

'Lord Newton Berwick wonders if you might spare him a moment, Lady Farringdon,' Jarvis said. 'He is waiting in the downstairs drawing room.'

'Really? Surely propriety dictates he leaves his card prior to calling; after all, I am extremely busy.' The butler glanced around the empty room and, although his expression remained bland, he somehow managed to convey his scepticism, before bowing and leaving.

Really, that Tristan boy should know better, Charlotte fumed. Well, he could wait. However, having nothing better to do, she patted her hair and smoothed down her skirts then sailed regally down the stairs.

'Lady Farringdon, please forgive my intrusion. I called to see Aunt Emmeline, quite forgetting this was one of her afternoons of good works at Haven House.'

'Oh,' Charlotte murmured, taken aback by the handsome man standing before her. Although his appearance was similar to Tristan, this man's features were sharper, his cheekbones more chiselled, his skin tanned from time spent in the open air. He carried an air of authority and the admiration shining from his clear blue eyes as he gazed at her made her pulse race.

'Giles Newton Berwick at your service, Lady Farringdon,' he said, bowing low.

'Please do take a seat, my Lord, and tell me how I may be of assistance,' Charlotte purred.

'Thank you,' he replied, waiting for her to be seated before folding his long limbs into the chair opposite. 'Having just returned from my travels abroad, I find myself somewhat disorientated, for normally I would have remembered Aunt Emmeline wouldn't be home at this time. Are you staying with her by any chance?'

'I am her sister and here for the Season. My stepdaughter Victoria has just been launched into society,' she finished quickly, unwilling to admit to this handsome man her role was that of chaperone.

'Surely you cannot mean you are stepmother to the golden girl of the Season,' he exclaimed. 'I mean, if you will forgive my frankness, you look far too young and pretty.'

'How kind of you to say so.' Charlotte smile widened and she tossed her head coquettishly. 'Of course, I am much younger than her Papa so there are really very few years between us. Goodness, where are my manners? I haven't offered you any refreshment.'

'Thank you, but regrettably I am unable to stay much longer,' he said.

'That is such a shame,' she murmured, all thought of good manners and propriety disappearing as disappointment flooded through her.

'Perhaps I might have the pleasure of seeing you at Mother's ball later in the year,' he suggested. 'It is to be held at our country seat in Surrey.'

'You will not be attending the society balls and soirees before then?' she asked, her brain going into overdrive as she thought what a marvellous match he would make for Victoria. Not to mention elevate her own status in society.

'They really are not to my taste. All that dodging of doting mothers trying to foist their ingenue daughters on me.' He shook his head then leaned forward. 'I prefer the company of real women rather than vestal virgins,' he said, shooting her a meaningful look that sent the blood tingling in her veins. 'Although, of course, I understand the importance of marrying one when the time comes.'

'And when might that be?' she asked quickly, as he began

rising to his feet. As if sensing her impatience, he sat back in his seat and shrugged.

'It will need to be this year,' he admitted. 'However, I intend having fun before the noose is lowered.' He grinned ruefully. 'To be honest, that is the reason I am avoiding Mother, the dreaded Dowager Countess. She can be persistent and once she knew I was back in town, well, let us just say I made my visit as short as politely possible.' He shrugged again. 'I am currently hiding in my house on the edge of town. Goodness, forgive my candour but you are very easy to talk to, Lady Farringdon.'

'Charlotte, please,' she murmured. 'We can't be that far apart in age after all.'

'Indeed,' he agreed, giving her another admiring look. 'It is refreshing to be able to talk to a young lady so understanding.'

'You may feel free to speak to me any time you wish, Giles,' she replied coyly.

'Thank you. I would like that, but . . . ' he looked around then leaned towards her again. 'Walls have ears and servants have mouths.'

'Goodness, don't I know it,' Charlotte tutted, thinking of her maid. 'However, it seems you need a wife of purity and good breeding, and Victoria a husband who understands women . . . ' she let her voice trail away.

'Yes, I see what you mean.' He looked at her speculatively.

'And of course, Edwin – Lord Farringdon – will be settling a substantial dowry upon her marriage.' There was a moment's silence broken only by the ticking of the clock.

'If I might venture, you are a very attractive woman.

I wonder if perchance we could make plans for the future whilst having a little fun too?'

Charlotte hid a grin for that was just what she had been thinking. Even though her heart was skipping as fast as her racing mind, she inclined her head and pretended to consider. Despite his younger years, he was obviously a man of experience, and knowing the chase was an important part of the game, she smiled demurely, but did not answer.

'Thank you for seeing me. However, I must not outstay my welcome and would be pleased if you would convey my best wishes to Aunt Emmeline. This is where I can be found,' he said, handing her a card embossed in gold. 'Although I'd be grateful if you would keep this information to yourself. I am free Wednesday and Saturday afternoons. Convenient, as that is when I understand my brother and your stepdaughter take their carriage ride in Hyde Park before returning to Mother's for afternoon tea.'

'They do?' she cried, looking at him sharply. Suddenly so many things were making sense.

'Oh dear, I'm sorry if I've shocked you,' Giles murmured, looking anything but.

'Heavens, no, I am aware of all that goes on here,' Charlotte lied.

'My housekeeper, Mrs Perkins, is a dear so your reputation is assured. Conveniently, she is also deaf as a post.' He grinned at her knowingly.

Charlotte spent the rest of the afternoon plotting and planning. So, Victoria was seeing Tristan behind her back. Well, two could play at that game. If she played her cards right, she could have some fun whilst ensuring Victoria's future was mapped out for her. Even Edwin would surely congratulate her on securing a future earl for his beloved second daughter.

'You look like the cat who got the canary,' Emmeline commented, staring at Charlotte over the supper table that evening.

'Probably been spending money again,' Nicholas grunted from behind his evening paper.

'Actually, I had an interesting conversation with Lord Newton Berwick.'

'Tristan called?' Victoria asked, her brow creasing in disappointment.

'No, his brother Giles. He forgot it was your afternoon for charitable works,' Charlotte told Emmeline.

'That's not like Giles,' her sister responded. 'Oh well, no doubt we will see him soon.'

'Yes, anything Tristan has, Giles wants,' Hester said acerbically, giving her cousin a knowing look.

'We had an interesting time at Haven House,' Victoria ventured, sensing an argument brewing. 'Some of those poor women were covered in bruises, one even had a broken arm.'

'I know, it's terrible the lengths some men go to have their way. Then there are the women who've been abused on the streets.'

'Well, they should be more careful,' Charlotte snapped, wrinkling her nose at her sister in disgust. 'Why can't they stay at home like decent women?'

'Some don't have homes to go to, others with children to feed earn money in the only way they can,' Emmeline said, letting out a sad sigh.

'Well, I won't have Victoria visiting there again. It is not seemly mixing with gutter women like that.' Charlotte shuddered. 'Anyone could have seen her.'

'But Step Mama, these people need our help; they—'

'I simply forbid it, Victoria. A lady's reputation can be tarnished by association. You are out in society now, please remember that. I see you have finished eating, so you'd do well to study your Book of Etiquette. That is a more appropriate way to spend your time. I would suggest Rule 9: The Bed Chamber. Knowing how to keep your husband happy will be more beneficial than mixing with fallen women who have no morals and behave like alley cats.'

Nicholas threw down his newspaper in disgust and, as a heated interchange ensued, Victoria and Hester raised their brows then hurried from the room.

*

On Wednesday, Charlotte took out her most seductive outfit then tore it off and changed it for a demure high-necked day dress. Deciding that was equally wrong, she pulled on a new two-piece then shook her head.

'Can I help you, Lady Farringdon?' Vanny asked, slipping into the room as Charlotte threw another dress down in disgust.

'My closet is an absolute shambles, Vanstone. I have absolutely nothing decent to wear. See that every single outfit is freshly laundered and hanging neatly by the time I return.'

'But Lady Far—' she began, staring dubiously at the woman's bodice which was inappropriate for daytime.

'The only *but* that I can think of is that of your position, Vanstone,' Charlotte retorted, snatching up a silk wrap and disappearing down the stairs. Keeping the maid busy was the only way she could think of to prevent her prying into her affairs. The girl knew too much already and if she wasn't so clever at dressing her hair and accessorizing her costumes, she would have been dismissed long since.

Luckily, her carriage was waiting outside as she'd requested, and as she left Chester Square behind her spirits lifted. What could be better than ensuring her stepdaughter's future was secured? And if she had a little fun into the bargain, well, she deserved it, surely? She'd certainly had enough of acting as a chaperone. Furthermore, having learned that Victoria was going behind her back to meet Tristan gave her ammunition for the future. Ammunition she wouldn't hesitate to use to get her own way.

Chapter 20

Jane inhaled the soothing fragrance of eau de rose as she cast a critical eye around the *magasin*. Although Mouse had ensured the shelves were replenished and the window display updated with what limited accessories they had left in stock, there was no doubting more were needed.

Picking up the bills that had just arrived, she took herself through to the Receiving Room. Running a business was considerably more expensive than she'd envisaged. If she was to succeed, she either had to cut costs or increase custom, as well as being more effective in managing her finances. Millie and Mouse relied on her and giving up was not an option.

Clearly, there was a growing demand for special occasion accessories by the fashionable ladies who either lived or vacationed in the area, and she could extend her repertoire to cater for the carriage trade.

While she had no desire to become a dressmaker, Lady Victoria's commission had made her realize she could offer a more varied and inclusive service. Salthaven might only be fifteen miles from Exeter, but the more affluent clientele differed significantly in their requirements.

Sinking onto the chaise, she began jotting down ideas. Engageantes, removable sleeves that added service to gowns, and modesty pieces to replace the bulkier camisoles, were becoming *de rigueur* – plus accessories ladies simply must have so they leave her emporium wondering how they'd managed without them. That was it: in order to reflect the new scope of her business, from now on the *magasin* would be known as Miss Haydon's Emporium.

'Lady Connaught, Miss Haydon,' Mouse announced, standing back so that the woman could enter. She was wearing an eau de nil silk dress with pearl buttons from collar to the gently flaring waist, which, whilst a nod to the changing mode, was elegant and flattered her fair colouring. Perhaps she had called to discuss a new corset, Jane thought, her spirits lifting as she welcomed her visitor with a smile.

'My apologies for visiting unannounced, only I found myself with a free half hour and thought I'd see how my protégée, Mouse, is progressing.'

'She is doing very well, Lady Connaught. Mouse has already learned to stitch a basic corset and is eager to learn how to use the sewing machine. Won't you take a seat?' she asked, indicating the chaise she'd vacated. 'May I offer you some refreshment?'

The woman shook her head.

'To be frank, Miss Haydon—' Miss Haydon? Jane frowned; Lady Connaught might be her patron, but it was unlike her to be so formal. '—I was somewhat surprised and disappointed at the lack of merchandise displayed in the window and the sparse selection of fabric in your shop. Are you awaiting a delivery?' Trying to return her candid gaze, Jane cursed under her breath. The woman was undoubtedly shrewd when it came to matters of business.

'Actually, I am in the middle of refurbishing and expanding my emporium.' The woman appraised the room with its modest furnishings then quirked her immaculate brow in surprise.

'It is all very much in the initial stages,' Jane went on quickly. 'Planning and ordering.'

'Hmm. After hearing about the wonderful debut gown you made for Lady Victoria, I confess I was expecting to see you displaying exotic fabric like the pail-red silk you used. Although I understand it hasn't been seen for many years.'

'It belonged to Madame Pittier,' Jane explained.

'Ah yes, Lady Louisa explained about the letter. Interestingly, Lady Montgomery, who was a client of Madame's since she established her business, mentioned talk of a handsome French weaver but, being so long ago, she couldn't recall the details. Not that we spend our time tittle-tattling at these soirees, you understand. Although Lady Louisa did confide that Victoria has been hailed as the Girl with the Golden Gown, tipped to be the one to watch this Season. Her concern is that you hadn't charged enough for such exquisite silk.'

'Lord Farringdon settled the account immediately,' Jane assured her, hoping that would be the end of the matter. Lady Connaught might be her benefactor, but she didn't want her prying into her financial affairs, at least until she was back on her feet again.

'Well, that will help with your overheads,' Lady Connaught said brightly as she rose to her feet. 'However, I feel it my duty to remind you that under our terms of agreement, you must prove the business is profitable after your first six months of trading. Then, should you be in a position to take on another poor unfortunate girl from the orphanage, you will be doing a great service. Philanthropy is all about helping each other, is it not?'

Jane nodded, understanding the woman's meaning.

'It is, and I am truly grateful for the opportunity you have afforded me. And, when my emporium becomes successful, I intend opening an apprentice school for girls from local orphanages.'

'What a splendid notion,' Lady Connaught beamed. 'Although, I fear that will take some time. Now, I must take my leave, or I shall be late for my appointment.'

As the door closed behind her visitor, Jane smiled, visualizing the workroom upstairs filled with young girls eager to learn how to sew. How satisfying it would be to give them the means to earn their own living, she thought. It would lend new meaning to her own life. Give her a sense of purpose. For the first time since losing Sam, she felt warmth stealing through her body.

First things first, Jane chided herself, returning to her notebook. In order to expand her business, she had to increase production, which was where the sewing machine came in. Having used it successfully for Victoria's train, she could see how much quicker it would be to produce her corsets, camisoles, chemisettes and modesty pieces. Though every single garment would still be bespoke and finished by hand. She had no desire to compete with the factories that were now churning out mass-produced items at reduced cost. They were fine for the everyday woman, but she wanted to attract the elite. A frisson of excitement tingled her spine. It would take hard work to increase her repertoire, but she wasn't afraid of that.

Snatching up copies of *The Ladies' Companion* and *Godey's Lady's Book* Victoria had let her keep, she ran upstairs to the workroom. After studying the pictures carefully, she began sketching out her own patterns. She only needed the basic concept then she could apply her own vision. Finally, she began running them up in calico. She was so busy she hardly noticed the dimming room until it forced her to stop and light the candle.

'Yous been up here for ever,' Millie said, eyeing her warily from the doorway. 'Mouse locked up hours ago.' Her glance went to the machine and the sample garments alongside. 'Thank the Lord yous seen sense at last.'

'Come and tell me what you think of these?' Jane said, holding up the candle so the girl could see. 'Of course, they're only samples.' But Millie had spotted a camisole in emerald silk she'd made earlier.

'Coo, imagine Bert's face if he saw me in this,' Millie cried, swaying this way and that as she held the garment against her apron.

'I trust you wouldn't be so brazen, Millicent,' Jane chided. 'It would be improper, not to say downright immoral.'

'Sorry, Mother Superior,' Millie giggled. 'Oh Jane, yous face is a picture. Saucy, I may be, but sinful I ain't. He'll have to put a ring on my finger before he can sample me in satin, I can tell you that for naught,' she declared hotly.

'I'm relieved to hear it. Now, most of the chemisettes and modesty pieces will be in serviceable linen or cotton for wearing with day dresses. What do you think of this?' Jane asked, holding up a sample engageante.

'Be a bit lopsided wearing just one, wouldn't yous?' she chirped, pulling the detachable sleeve up over her wrist. 'And what's this? Looks like one of them kidneys in Bert's window, only them's brown, of course,' she asked, scrutinizing the curved piece of calico.

'It's a dress preserver, to be tacked on the inside.'

'Coo, it's good to know the toffs sweat just like us normal folk, though they's probably get hot dancing and drinking rather than scouring pots and scrubbing floors. This machine is going to make a difference, isn't it?'

'Except it is on loan,' Jane replied, trying to calculate how she could afford to purchase one. Suddenly the elation of the past hours dissipated, leaving her drained and exhausted so that she didn't hear the maid muttering about stupid pride as she left.

Deciding she might as well make the most of the machine before it was collected, Jane spent the next few days perfecting the new accoutrements. As she thought chemisettes were quicker to make than the bulkier chemises and she had ideas for individualizing the garments with embroidery or lace trim, letting the client choose her own embellishment. Dress preservers and modesty pieces were easy to run up on the machine, but it was the engageantes that caused her the most trouble. No matter what fabric she used, the finished results didn't meet her high standards.

It was half-day closing and, as the clock on the church finished chiming the noon hour, Mouse appeared by her side. Jane had promised to teach her how to make accessories and use the machine.

'I do love the smell in here, it's heaven,' the girl told Jane, her face alight with excitement.

'The only angels we have to do the sewing is us, so we'll start with the dress preservers,' Jane told her, smiling at her enthusiasm as she laid out the fabric on the long table. 'In order to maximize usage, it's imperative to lay down the pattern correctly.' With Mouse watching intently, Jane demonstrated how this was done. 'Once you have cut them all out, I will show you how to use the machine.'

Jane went back to the table and began adding the trimmings to a corset that needed completing, but it seemed no time at all before Mouse had finished and was hovering, impatient to use the machine. As ever, the apprentice only needed showing once and, no sooner had Jane risen from the seat, than the girl had taken her place.

'Ooh, I love this,' Mouse cried, carefully guiding the fabric with her hands. Her enthusiasm was infectious and there was no doubting her ability even if the whirr of the machine took some getting used to as Jane tried to concentrate.

'I can't believe how quick it is,' Mouse cried, placing her third pair of preservers on the table an hour later. Jane smiled, enjoying the companionship of the girl working alongside her.

'When you have made a dozen pairs you can cut out a chemisette in the cotton and we'll see how you get on sewing that together.'

'What, on this?' she asked, tapping the top of the gleaming machine.

'Of course, what else?' Jane asked, shooting her a wry smile. 'Meanwhile, I shall try making another pair of engageantes, in broderie anglaise this time.'

'That's a funny name; what does it mean?'

'Broderie anglaise is French for English embroidery. The oval patterned cut-outs give it a delicate lacy effect. Although it's not as fine as lace . . . oh, that's given me an idea,' she cried.

She glanced over at the dwindling fabric on the shelf and sighed. This was the last piece of broderie anglaise, and they were almost out of lace. Stocks of silk and cotton were dwindling at an alarming rate. Having bought accessories and paid bills with the money from Lord Farringdon, she would have to eke everything out until the end of the month when, hopefully, clients would settle their invoices. If only people would pay when they made their purchases instead of asking to be billed. Then she remembered Lady Farringdon's refusal to even contemplate the subject of money and sighed again. Life really was easier for the upper classes.

Under Jane's instruction, Mouse diligently laid out the pattern then cut carefully around it.

'Now you need to pin and tack the neckline, then along the edges of the fabric. When you become more experienced you will be able to dispense with this part of the operation,' Jane told her. 'Whilst you're learning it's easier, not to say more cost effective, to unpick tacking stitches should you make a mistake, rather than waste the fabric if it doesn't lie flat. Not that I'm sure you would intentionally,' she added quickly, seeing the girl frown.

'Will I have me wages deducted if I do waste any?' Mouse asked quietly.

'Of course not,' Jane replied. 'Why do you ask?'

'At the home we were supposed to be paid for our work, but they kept fining us for making mistakes, even when we knew we hadn't. I'm always careful you see,' she said, looking so solemn, Jane's heart went out to her. 'They'd tell us we were in debt and cut our food, giving us smaller and smaller meals until sometimes we didn't get anything to eat all day.'

'That's dreadful,' Jane exclaimed. No wonder the poor thing had been so thin when she'd arrived. 'I can assure you that will never happen here. We might have to scrimp and scrape come the end of the month, but we always have something in our bowls. Now, let's see how you get on sewing that chemisette.'

As Mouse hurried back to the machine, Jane began work on the broderie anglaise engageantes. The fullness of fabric needed gathering tightly at the wrist to fit under the bell-shaped 'pagoda' sleeves of day dresses. The shape for those worn with evening gowns varied according to the cut but she'd worry about those later. Just as Jane was satisfied she'd produced a pair she'd be happy to sell, Mouse brought over her completed chemisette.

'That looks professional, well done,' Jane told her. 'As we have both had a productive afternoon, let's we go and see what Millie's cooked for supper.'

They were greeted by the aroma of yet more bacon broth but were too tired and hungry to object.

'I heard the fearsome beast whirring away all afternoon, so I takes it yous pleased with it now,' Millie grinned knowingly at Jane.

'It does serve a purpose,' she admitted.

'And I love using it,' Mouse exclaimed, quickly looking at Jane in case she'd said the wrong thing. But Millie was already recounting the day's happenings in Salthaven, including the fact that Bert had asked her to tea on Sunday.

'Only wants me to meet his ma; I mean, what does that tell yous?'

'That she wants to see who's been nicking all the offcuts of bacon,' Mouse quipped. Jane stared at the girl in surprise for it seemed she was coming out of her shell at last.

'I'd take you along,' Millie retorted. 'Except yous too pretty and I don't want no competition.'

'But you are pretty, Millie. Besides, I can't cook like you and that's what men want isn't it?'

'In my experience, they want everything they can get their hands on. You ever had a follower?'

'No,' Mouse squeaked.

'Blimey, girl, keep your hair on,' Millie cried.

'Is Mouse your given name?' Jane asked.

'No, the housemaster called me that because he said I was afraid of my own shadow. The orphanage called me Hope.'

'How lovely; was that Hope for the future?'

'No—' the girl sighed '—hope they had room for me.'

'I think Hope's a lovely name,' Millie told her.

'And that is what you shall be known as from now on, Hope Brown.' Jane smiled at the girl.

'Now I really feel as if I've started a new life,' she beamed.

'Good. Now I must go and check on supplies. Hopefully, we should have enough samples of our new lines to exhibit alongside our current stock.'

'Aren't yous going to advertise them new accessories?' Millie asked.

'That would be expensive, and I am operating on a shoestring.'

'Or corset lace,' Millie trilled. 'But how will people knows what's here if yous don't publicize?'

'By creating mystery and intrigue, word will soon spread. Ladies love being the first to be seen wearing a new line. I shall tell them what they are purchasing is unique, and, as the item itself will be bespoke, I won't be lying.'

'You crafty old thing,' Millie exclaimed. 'They won't be able to resist bragging to their friends.'

'That's the plan. Always supposing we have enough fabric and trimmings,' she sighed.

However, a detailed inspection of the stock revealed she hardly had enough to fulfil her current commissions let alone make the additional accessories she had planned. Why hadn't she checked before? She'd have to pay a visit to the wholesaler first thing in the morning.

With no money, she would have to ask for credit. But then that's what the gentry did, didn't they?

Chapter 21

Jane thanked the haulier who'd given her a lift to Exeter and clambered down from the cart.

'Yer be careful, this ain't no place for a maid like yer,' he told her.

'I'll be fine,' she called up to him. He tipped his hand to his flat cap and urged the old bay cob to walk on, leaving Jane standing on the bustling wharf. It was much busier than she'd thought it would be this early in the morning, and she stared around in dismay. The sun was barely a blush on the horizon and yet the huge ships moored to the quay by thick ropes, were already having their cargoes unloaded. Burly men, their bear-like arms operating the derricks, were shouting orders as heavy crates were dropped onto wagons waiting on the dockside. The horses then hauled them into the huge warehouses, or out past the Customs House and over the bridge towards their various destinations. A sudden gust of wind tugged at Jane's bonnet and, as she reached to save it, another one lifted her skirts, drawing unwanted attention as she hastily smoothed them down. Blushing at the catcalls and whistles, she gritted her teeth. She'd come here on a mission and refused to be thwarted by a mob of leching louts.

'What's a pretty girl like you doing hanging around here?' a gruff voice asked. Spinning round, Jane saw a swarthy man eyeing her up and down with obvious interest.

'Looking for a bit of business, are yer?' he leered, leaning closer so that the smell of unwashed body wafted her way. Common sense told her to turn and run, only the thought of her livelihood and those depending on her kept her rooted to the ground.

'I'm seeking to buy some fabric,' she ventured, trying not to shudder at the gleam in his bloodshot eyes and quickly taking a step backwards.

'And what kind would yer be wanting?' he grinned, scratching his greasy grey hair.

'Silk and cotton mainly,' she replied. 'Perhaps you could point me in the right direction.'

'I could certainly do that, darlin'.' He gave a throaty chuckle and moved closer, his arms snaking out to grab her.

'Hawker.' At the sound of the stentorian voice, the man swore but dropped his arms.

'Just helping the young lady,' he told the tall, broad-shouldered man who was striding towards them.

'Get back to your sweeping or I'll sack you for wasting time,' the man ordered. He turned to Jane, grey eyes assessing. His tailored clothes and demeanour denoted someone in authority and Jane wondered if she was trespassing.

'This is no place for a young lady, miss.'

'Miss Haydon, proprietress of an emporium in Salthaven,' she told him, drawing herself up to her full height. He stared at her for a long moment, and she could tell he was trying to work out if she was telling the truth.

'Well, with due respect, Miss Haydon, isn't that where you should be, rather than hanging around the wharf?'

'I have come to purchase fabric,' she retorted, determined to show him she meant business.

'And do you usually purchase direct from the warehouse?' he asked, quirking a brow.

'Well, no,' she admitted. 'However, I find myself in a predicament.'

'Look, Miss Haydon, we seem to be attracting attention,' he said, waving his silver-topped cane towards a group of sailors staring unashamedly in their direction. 'I am Cedric Fairfax, proprietor of the warehouse over there.' This time he used his cane to indicate a row of red sandstone and brick buildings. 'Allow me to escort you there and we can discuss your, er, predicament.' Seeing her hesitate, he gave a wry grin. 'It will be safer than staying here. Some of these men have been at sea for months and are – how shall I put it – desperate for some fun and frolics, if you get my meaning.'

'Thank you,' she replied with as much dignity as she could muster, for his lips were twitching with amusement. Moments later she was following him into a cavernous storehouse stacked to the rafters with huge bales of cloth.

'You can take your pick of the finest fabrics the world has to offer.' Mr Fairfax gestured with his cane once more. 'I only buy the best but then, of course, my prices reflect that,' he told her, suddenly the savvy salesman. 'Now what are you requiring exactly?'

'Silk, cotton and perhaps some broderie anglaise,' she murmured. 'But, as I said earlier, I have a predicament.'

'Sorry, Miss Haydon, I thought that was your predicament.'

'But it's not the main one. You see, I don't actually have the money to purchase fabric outright,' she admitted. His brows quirked in astonishment.

'So, you *were* touting for business in order to pay for it that way,' he asked, placing emphasis on the 'were'. 'Well, pardon me for mistaking you for a lady—'

'But I am a lady,' she cried. Then seeing his cynical look, she decided to level with him. 'Of course, I intend paying for my purchases but can only do so when my clients settle their invoices. I didn't mean to run short of fabric. Recent circumstances made me somewhat preoccupied. Then I had this idea for expanding my range to attract the carriage trade and ran up samples without checking the stock . . . ' she stuttered to a halt as he shook his head. 'It was a stupid idea coming here, I'm sorry to have bothered you,' she muttered, turning to go.

'Wait,' he commanded. 'What have you brought as collateral?'

'Regrettably. I don't have anything of value to offer as a guarantee so I can only apologize again for wasting your time.'

'You intrigue me, Miss Haydon. Why don't we make ourselves comfortable and discuss this in more detail?' Pushing open the door to what was clearly an office, he gestured for her to take a chair then seated himself behind a desk. Her attention was caught by the huge book seemingly stuffed with material that was placed in the centre. Seeing her enquiring look, he opened it to reveal squares of brightly coloured fabrics, all neatly labelled and priced. 'My samples folder.

Time is money and it saves me having to show merchants the entire stock held out in the warehouse. It is easier and quicker for them to flick through the swatches and select what they wish to buy. My men then cut, package, and deliver. Now tell me, how does a lady as young as yourself come to have an emporium in a prestigious town like Salthaven? I know the rent on premises there isn't cheap.' Again, he studied her with those clear, grey eyes so that Jane felt he was seeing right inside her.

'It's a long story, Mr Fairfax, but Lady Connaught had enough faith in me to offer to become my sponsor. In return, I am training one of her other protégées.'

'Lady Connaught is well known for her philanthropic works,' he agreed, sitting back in his chair and steepling his fingers. 'You say you don't have anything of value to offer as surety, yet you must have some possession that is dear to you?'

'I do have a bobbin that is priceless to me. It was carved by someone special,' Jane murmured, her voice tailing off. He watched her for a few moments longer then leaned forward as if coming to a decision.

'Suppose I let you have the fabric you came here for in return for that bobbin?' he asked.

'No!' she cried then took a deep breath and continued in a calmer voice. 'I'm sorry, I could never part with it.'

'Suppose I let you have the fabric you need today in exchange for this bobbin as surety. When you make payment in full it will be returned?' Jane stared at him in astonishment. 'That's fairer terms than you'd get from a pawnbroker and there would be no risk of my selling it.'

'But why would you do that?' Jane frowned.

'I admire your grit, Miss Haydon. Not to say your downright audacity.' He smiled and shook his head. 'With determination like that, your business will surely succeed. Besides, if Lady Connaught sees fit to back you, then who am I to question her judgement. By the way, what exactly is your line?'

'I am a corsetiere,' Jane told him.

'Indeed.' His eyes lit up and he grinned. 'I will advance you the cloth with the bobbin as collateral on condition you make a silk corset for my lady, how about that?'

'Your wife?' she asked.

'My lady, and I have the very silk for it too.' He winked before becoming the businessman again and pulling a piece of paper towards him. 'Now give me your address then we can select which fabrics you want. I will tell you the full amount owing when you have made your choice. My driver will collect the bobbin when he delivers them and you have my word that, as soon as I receive the full payment, it will be returned.'

'But why would you do that for me when I've told you the bobbin is only of sentimental value?' Jane asked the question that had been nagging at her.

'That, in my experience, is the most certain way of ensuring repayment. Well, Miss Haydon, do you agree to my terms?' he asked, rising to his feet, and proffering his hand.

Jane hesitated. Could she really bear to part with her precious bobbin even for a matter of weeks? But then if she didn't, how could she accept any new commissions and keep her business going?

Chapter 22

Refreshed from his break at the coaching house whilst the horses were changed, Edwin climbed back into his carriage and watched as they traversed the wide streets of Honiton. With the rectangular church of St Michael's staring down from its imposing position on the hill, it was a pleasant market town renowned as a staging post for lace being sent to London.

How pleased he was to have left the hubbub of the city far behind and to be back in the relative peace and quiet of Devonshire. Whilst he'd enjoyed being cosseted by his mistress, and it had certainly made a pleasing change to have some stimulating conversation, his visit had highlighted the sad fact that his marriage was a sham. Charlotte hadn't even had the courtesy to be home when he'd called at Chester Square after the presentation to hear how the celebrations had gone. Whilst it had been good to hear Victoria's news, he'd been furious to hear Charlotte had demanded the Farringdon pearls for herself. Even she must realize their birth mother's jewellery would naturally pass to her daughters. Thankfully, Nicholas had given his assurance that he would take care of them whilst Victoria was in London.

He thought again how radiant she'd looked, making him promise to return to meet this Tristan she'd incessantly spoken of. He was pleased she was happy for he'd worried she might find society life overwhelming. Of course, Hester was a good companion and dear Emmeline a steadying influence, obviously doing the job Charlotte should have been.

His thoughts turned to Beatrice. Knowing his strongwilled daughter, she would be bossing everyone in the hospital around by now. Although, from what Professor Todd had said, the forthright Miss Nightingale would keep her under control. He just hoped Bea would find nursing as satisfying as she'd thought it would be.

At least he could return to Nettlecombe knowing two of his daughters were settled. Louisa kept busy with her charitable works as well as planning her wedding. Seeing her fretting about Henry was distressing and he wondered if she'd read about the Russian siege of Silistria in the newspaper. Once home, he would try and reassure her. As for Sarah and Maria, he'd missed the little minxes and couldn't wait to see them again. And, of course, Ellery would be there with his enthusiastic greeting. At least he'd get some welcome kisses even if they were of the warm and wet variety.

Reaching for his case, he extracted some papers then sat back to peruse them. There had been several applicants for the position of estate manager and his agent had furnished him with details of the two most suitable. One was older and experienced in traditional procedures of estate management, the other was younger and keen to adopt more modern methods. He would keep an open mind and see which impressed him the most.

Sitting back in his seat, he looked out at the rolling hills which, even in summer, were lush and green. Almost before he knew it, they were passing through the archway topped with the stone griffins that guarded Nettlecombe.

As soon as the carriage drew to a halt, Edwin climbed down and stretched. The Jacobean manor with its grey stones and mullioned windows bathed in the rosy glow of the early evening sun had never looked so welcoming.

'Good evening, my Lord,' the butler said, bowing as he opened the door. 'Welcome home.'

'Thank you, Ferris. I am ready for a good stiff drink after my long journey.'

'Puppy!'

'Papa.' Sarah and Maria came thundering down the stairs and threw themselves into his arms.

'My, you are pleased to see me,' Edwin said, grinning delightedly at their enthusiasm.

'We are, for being the kindest of Papas you will have brought us something nice,' Sarah told him, staring up at him assuredly.

'I missed you, Puppy,' Maria told him, nodding her head so enthusiastically, a lock of fair hair escaped its velvet ribbon. 'And I like presents.'

Edwin smiled. 'Well, we shall have to see if there is anything in my bag later.'

'Welcome home, Edwin, I hope you had a good trip,' Nanny greeted him. 'Now, girls, it is time to get ready for bed. Miss Birkett will expect you at your desks all ready to learn when she returns tomorrow.'

'But Puppy's only just come home,' Maria told her.

'If you're in bed when I come to kiss you goodnight, I might have a little surprise for you,' Edwin promised.

'You spoil them, Edwin,' Nanny told him as they ran off squealing with delight. 'Cook has prepared your favourite Sole Véronique.'

'Wonderful, I'll look forward to that.'

'No doubt you wish to check the letters that are waiting on your desk, so I'll have a drink sent in. Louisa has been visiting Captain Beauchamp's parents but promised to return in time for supper.'

Edwin nodded, then strode down the hallway, inhaling the familiar fragrance of beeswax and roses. He paused by the hideous clock. Why had he put up with it for so long?

'Please see this monstrosity is disposed of immediately,' he told Ferris. Nodding to his ancestors as he passed, he continued his way along the hallway. A quick flick through the post while he drank his aperitif then he'd take the girls their presents, he thought, grinning as he imagined their smiles of delight.

However, opening his study door, he was met with a heavy silence. Frowning, he stared at the rug before the grate. 'Well, you wouldn't lie there with no fire blazing, would you, old boy?' he said softly. 'Come on, Ellery, your master's home.' When there was still no response, he bent and peered under the desk. There lay his faithful friend, still as a stone. His companion through thick and thin had departed this life.

Hunkering down, he threw his arms around his faithful pet and sobbed.

Chapter 23

The following day, as the carriage rocked its way through the lanes of Combe, Louisa Farringdon stared out of the window. June's warm weather had encouraged the lace makers to work on their pillows in front of their cottages. Having stopped at the school house to collect the sprigs Lily had made for her veil, Louisa was now on her way to see Jane Haydon for a consultation about her wedding underpinnings. Whilst her interfering stepmother was out of the way, she was taking the opportunity to prepare her trousseau.

She'd offered to stay at home with Papa, for poor Ellery's death had hit him hard. The Labrador had been around for most of her life, and they were going to miss his devoted yet undemanding presence enormously. Edwin had insisted she keep her appointments, saying he too had things to attend to, and, sad though it was, there was no reason to let anyone down. However, she had promised to return home by noon when they would hold a service in the rose garden where they'd decided to lay their dear pet to rest. She would then spend the rest of the day with her Papa, perhaps take a walk around the estate and catch up on their news.

Louisa looked down at the sprigs in her lap. Such intricate work, each one with a motif of her favourite flowers. Now, whilst Lily made the others incorporating the two family's coats of arms, Louisa needed to decide in what order she wanted these sewn together for her veil. If only Victoria and Bea were here to advise. Still, the Beauchamps were to take afternoon tea at Nettlecombe next week and she knew her future mother-in-law would be delighted to help. It was strange how on hearing Charlotte was in London for the Season, they'd decided to pay a visit. Although she'd voiced her concerns that making plans for their wedding might be deemed frivolous when Henry was away fighting, they had disagreed, saying it would help them all to have something positive to think about.

Automatically her hand reached for his dress button that she kept in her pocket or beneath her pillow at night. She missed him more each day, she thought, stroking it lovingly. It was agonizing waiting to hear from him and the little information she'd gleaned about the war wasn't reassuring. Papa had told her not to believe everything she read for it wasn't good news that sold papers, therefore reports were often exaggerated or embellished. That didn't stop her from worrying though.

Driving past the Sam Gill Hall, she smiled as Quick urged the horses to go faster. Having set her bonnet at the foot-man, Ida Somers sought every opportunity to flatter and charm him, and the poor man was embarrassed beyond belief. However, he had no need to worry, for Louisa wasn't stopping today. Although she would have to visit the women soon, for worryingly orders had declined.

Louisa must have spent longer musing than she realized, for suddenly they were pulling to a halt outside the corsetiere shop with its sign in neat gilt script. To her delight, there were new accessories in the window, although her discerning eye noted they seemed somewhat spread out. Perhaps that was the latest way of displaying merchandise, she mused, pushing open the door and inhaling the delightful flower fragrance she loved so much.

As the bell ceased its jangling, she was greeted by Miss Haydon herself and Louisa was pleased to see that she was looking less strained than on her previous visit.

'Good afternoon, Lady Louisa,' Jane greeted her.

'Louisa please, Jane,' she admonished. 'I trust you are well?'

'Yes, thank you. Miss Brown is on her way from the workroom to attend the shop, so we won't be interrupted.'

'There is no hurry,' Louisa assured her. 'I see you have different accessories in your window display.'

'I have added a few new lines, for it is important to be up to the minute, isn't it?' she asked, looking to Louisa for confirmation.

'It certainly is. Perhaps you could show me once I have selected the silk and satin for my underpinnings,' she said, turning to the bolts of fabric on the shelf behind the counter.

'I have finished, Miss Haydon,' announced the young apprentice, appearing in the doorway. She was clutching a huge folder and Louisa noticed how she'd blossomed since her last visit.

'Thank you, Miss Brown, I will take that with me. If you would like to come into the Receiving Room, Louisa, you can select your fabric in comfort. May I offer you some refreshment?'

'A glass of lemonade would be most welcome,' she replied.

Jane nodded to the young girl and then showed Louisa through.

'It is lovely and cool in here after the heat of the sun,' she said, looking appreciatively around the room with its tasteful pink furnishings.

'Please make yourself comfortable and I'll show you our samples book. Every page holds a square of the fabric we have in stock.'

'What a splendid idea,' Louisa smiled, taking the book from her. 'I don't remember this from before, but then I suppose you used to visit us at Nettlecombe and could only carry a few samples of silk. Not that I would expect you to visit us now after . . . well, the accident,' she hastened to assure her. 'You know why I am here this morning; are you sure it won't be distressing for you?'

'No, of course not,' Jane reassured her. 'It must be exciting planning the outfits for your wedding.'

'It is and yet it isn't. This is the ideal opportunity as Step Mama is away and cannot interfere, yet I can't help feeling it's precipitous when Henry is away fighting in the Crimea. I mean, I have no way of knowing when he'll be back, or even if . . . ' her voice trailed away. 'Forgive me, I don't wish to be melancholic, especially when I know you are busy. Perhaps you could show me some of those new accessories you were telling me about.'

'Of course,' Jane replied, moving over to the table. 'This is a chemisette or modesty piece,' she said, holding up the cotton sample. 'It fits inside your day dress and is less bulky than a camisole. Of course, it can be made in whatever fabric and colour you choose. These dress preservers are, well, self-explanatory, and these are engageantes, or detachable sleeves. I have samples here in broderie anglaise, another in lace.'

'May I take a closer look?' Louisa asked, taking them from her. 'These are beautiful and a pair in lace would look superb with that beautiful gown you made for Victoria. Apparently, she made a great impression on the ton when she appeared in it. In fact, I shall commission a pair to be sent to her. How soon could they be ready?' To her surprise, Jane hesitated and seemed to be pondering.

'In about four or five days,' she said eventually.

'That would be too late, I'm afraid, for apparently Victoria is to attend an important society function and has a suitor she is particularly taken with.'

'I could run up a pair like those this evening,' Jane offered, gesturing to broderie anglaise, 'but I fear they wouldn't be right for the dress either.'

'Forgive my ignorance, but perhaps you could explain why?'

'The lace I have in stock, whilst good, is not fine enough to make sleeves that would complement the gossamer silk of Victoria's gown. The white would be too stark against the golden sheen the thread gives it. I could try steeping it in some diluted tea to dull it down, but that would take time.'

'I see. And the broderie anglaise is the same?'

'That isn't as bright, but it is the thickness of the material that's really the problem; it wouldn't lie flat enough. Of course, both would go well with a stronger colour fabric.'

'I understand Victoria has been specially asked to wear her presentation gown.'

'Well, here we is, freshly made with me own fair hands. We hadn't got all the right ingredients, so I says to meself, yous better concoct something similar quick,' Millie announced, glasses jingling as she pushed the door open with her bottom. 'Hello, Lady Louisa, how is yous?'

'I am well, thank you, Millie. And yourself?' Louisa asked, smiling at the maid who, although irrepressible, was always eager to please.

'I got a follower so am well happy. Have you heard from your fella yet?'

'That will be all, Millie,' Jane said sharply.

'Thank you for the cold drink, it is just what I need on a hot day like this,' Louisa said, taking a sip. 'Goodness, that certainly has a tang. It is delicious though.' As the girl beamed and left, Jane shook her head in frustration.

'I'm sorry.'

'Don't be. What Millie said has just given me the most marvellous idea. Although I would use the word improvise rather than concoct. I called to collect the sprigs for my bridal veil earlier.' She reached inside her bag and pulled out a parcel. 'This pillow lace is more of a creamy colour so I wonder if you could use some of these to create a pair of engageantes. You said you could make them right away if you had the right fabric, and Victoria would receive them in time for her special party. My underpinnings can wait and, I would, of course, pay you extra for the inconvenience.'

'Well,' Jane said, taking the sprigs and studying them carefully, 'this lacework is exquisite and would work. Would it matter which motifs I used?'

'No, whichever looks best. I'll leave it to your judgement.'

'Do you wish to see the engageantes before I dispatch them?'

'Goodness no, your samples are splendid, and you will know better than I the style to best complement her gown. If you could have them sent to this address as soon as they are finished, I'd be most obliged,' Louisa said, taking a card from her reticule and passing it over. 'Actually, I wouldn't mind some myself. Perhaps you could make a pair in broderie anglaise for my day dresses; I can collect them when I call in for my fitting.'

'I'll get the diary and we can make another appointment. Would you care for another glass of lemon before you leave?'

'No, thank you,' Louisa replied quickly. 'I really should be going. I'm afraid Ellery died yesterday, and Papa is naturally upset so I don't wish to leave him for too long.'

'Oh, that is a shame. He was a lovely dog,' Jane said, remembering the docile pet who'd followed them from room to room.

'He was also very old. Not that it's much consolation as we do miss him.'

'Please tell Lord Farringdon I am truly sorry for his loss.'

Having finally found free time in her diary for the following month, Louisa booked her consultation then made her way through to the shop.

'Please thank Millie for the most unusual drink. Now do invoice me for your time today as well as those engageantes for Victoria.'

'As you've provided the lace, I shall just charge a nominal sum for the sewing,' Jane told her.

'Thank you. I know Victoria will be thrilled. Apparently, she has acquired quite a reputation for being dressed à la mode. Well, until next month then . . . oh, I nearly forgot, Papa asked how you were finding the sewing machine?'

'It's made a huge difference,' Millie said, stopping on her way to collect the tray. 'Theys can make much more.'

'Yes, please, thank Lord Farringdon and tell him he can collect it at any time,' Jane replied stiffly.

'But surely if you're finding it useful, it would make sense to keep it? I know Papa is grateful that you helped Victoria with her beautiful debut dress.'

'I really appreciate his kindness but couldn't possibly keep it. Thank you anyway.'

'As you wish,' Louisa replied, trying not to smile as Millie stood behind Jane rolling her eyes. Obviously, the girl thought her employer was being foolish. Still, it wasn't her place to argue.

*

Jane waited until the little bell had finished tinkling before turning to face the maid.

'How many times must I warn you not to interfere, Millie?'

'Well, it makes no sense to say His Lordship can have the machine back when it's always whirring away all day like nobody's business.'

'I have my pride,' Jane replied.

'And as I've told yous before, pride don't pay the bills.

Anyhows, what will happen when yous gets lots more orders for them sleeves and modesty pieces?'

'I'll manage,' Jane replied. 'Now go and tidy the Receiving Room. I have a client this afternoon. By the way, what was in that lemon drink you made?'

'Well, of course we had no lemons as such, so I nipped and asked her next door if I could borrow some citric acid. She'd seen Lady Louisa getting out of her carriage and was only too happy to help. Then I had to get fresh water from the pump before I added—'

'That's all right, Millie,' Jane said, holding up her hand. 'I don't know how you manage to produce half the things you do but appreciate you trying to help.'

'Well, yous needs looking after. Yous didn't even charge Her Ladyship for the postage to send the parcel to Victoria. This is meant to be a business, you know.'

Jane groaned. As usual Millie was right, but she'd been working until the small hours cutting out squares of fabric and compiling her sample book. She'd been impressed with what Mr Fairfax had shown her and wanted to implement it straightaway. She'd even included examples of the ones delivered by Fairfax's driver. For, as promised, her order had been delivered on time. It had been heart-wrenching handing over Sam's precious bobbin, but instinct told her the man would keep his word and return it when she had paid what she owed. She just hoped she'd be able to meet the deadline, for the fabric she'd purchased had cost far more than anticipated. From now on, she would list every service provided, including postage and make sure she charged for them.

Sighing, she glanced around the shop, automatically

checking everything was tidy but, as ever, Hope had been diligent. The window display was looking sparse though and would need to be replenished with the accessories they were currently making.

'I have paperwork to do, so go up to the workroom and make another chemisette,' she told the girl who'd been nervously watching her exchange with Millie. 'We might as well utilize the machine whilst it's here.'

'What Millie says does make sense, doesn't it?' Hope ventured, before scuttling away.

Wondering if the girls were ganging up on her, Jane went through to the Receiving Room and picked up the lace sprigs. Not only were they beautifully made, but they were also exactly the right colour. If she ensured the motifs were artistically arranged, the engageantes would be eye-catching and suitable for society functions. Of course, she would have to work late into the night again to fulfil her promise to Louisa, for she was fitting a new client for her underpinnings this afternoon.

While these accessories were meant to be an extension to her product range, her bespoke corsets were still her primary source of income. But Louisa was a good client, and Jane prided herself on the service she provided. Stifling a yawn, she couldn't help wondering if she'd taken on too much.

Chapter 24

Victoria peeled back the soft pink paper and gasped as she took out the pair of lace sleeves, scattering a flurry of rose petals over the settee.

'Oh my; engageantes,' she exclaimed, pulling them on and staring at her reflection in the mirror over the fireplace. 'Aren't these simply gorgeous? The lacework is so intricate.'

'They'll go beautifully with your golden gown for Aunt Dorothea's house party next weekend. I'd love a pair like that,' Hester sighed. 'I suppose that's a gift from yet another admirer?'

'Don't be silly, Hester; suitors don't buy presents like this. It wouldn't be proper. Remember what we read in Step Mama's book?'

'Ah yes. Rule 5: A young lady must only accept suitable gifts such as books, confectionery, flowers, or sheet music,' she intoned, giving a fair imitation of Charlotte. 'So, who did send them then?'

'From the fragrant rose petals in the packaging, I should imagine Jane Haydon fashioned them. You know the lady who made my dress. Yet the lace looks similar in design to that Louisa is having made for her veil. She showed Bea and I some sample sprigs a few weeks ago.' Victoria scrutinized the gift card and nodded. 'Just as I thought. These are a gift from my sister, sewn by Jane with lace made by Lily from Combe. She is extremely talented and helped make the lace for Queen Victoria's wedding dress and train.'

'Ooh la, you do move in illustrious circles,' Hester laughed.

'Ha, ha, I must have been all of four years old when she married.'

'Even so, you are lucky to have sisters. I'm glad you are here for the Season, Victoria; it makes everything more fun.'

It was Saturday morning and, as usual, Charlotte had sent them to study the rules of etiquette in the book she had meticulously prepared. Although they knew it was an excuse to be rid of them so she could prepare for wherever she mysteriously disappeared to each weekend, they were only too happy to play along, for it gave them time to plan what they would wear for their carriage ride with Tristan and Roscoe. Since their alleged surprise meeting in Hyde Park, it had become customary for them all to spend the time together without Charlotte's constant harping.

Emmeline and Dorothea were happy to act as chaperones as it gave them the opportunity to exchange the latest gossip arising from social events they'd attended during the week. They would then return to Dorothea's house for afternoon tea, after which the four friends would take a stroll around the gardens, each couple walking a different gravelled path.

It was Victoria's favourite time of the week, for whilst they'd meet at balls and soirees, this afforded them precious time alone to talk or, on reaching the privacy of the pergola, receive his kisses. Victoria felt her body growing hot at the thought. She was startled out of her reverie by angry voices coming from the next room.

'This simply will not do, Charlotte.'

'But I'm not asking for much, Nicholas, and Edwin will understand that I need to look my best.' Recognizing her stepmother's wheedling tones, Victoria stared at Hester and raised her brows.

'The answer is no, Charlotte. You have more new outfits delivered each week than Emmeline has bought in all the years we've been married.'

'And it shows,' she sneered. 'Why, her dresses are so out-moded I'm surprised she's allowed into the homes of the ton. What kind of man are you, expecting her to—'

'That's enough,' he cut in. 'Emmeline is a well-respected member of the community who gives freely of her time to charitable works. Which is more than can be said for the way you are spending yours.' There was a loud crash as the door slammed, followed by the thundering of footsteps up the stairs.

'That's Step Mama's usual trick when she doesn't get her own way,' Victoria sighed. 'I am astonished she thinks she needs yet more ensembles.'

'Finance and frocks are very important to her, aren't they? It's true that Mother doesn't have many, but she always looks presentable. Father will never tolerate anyone bad-mouthing her. Still, it's not like him to blow his stack.'

'Perhaps we'd better look busy in case he comes in here,' Victoria said, repacking her present and picking up the dreaded book. 'Where did we get to? Ah, Rule 16: Give your suitor your undivided attention, listen avidly to his responses for it is your duty to make him feel he is the most important man in the room. A flutter of eyelashes will make him go weak at the knees.'

'Gracious, I just chatter away about anything and anyone. Besides, Roscoe would only think I'd got something in my eye if I fluttered my lashes at him,' Hester snorted then sat up quickly as the door opened and her father appeared.

'Everything all right in here?' Although he smiled, the set of his chin told a different story.

'We're fine, Father. Is everything all right with you? Can I call for a cup of tea or coffee?'

'Thank you my dear, but I'm just on my way out. Are you girls going for your Saturday afternoon ride in the park with Aunt Dorothea?'

'We are, Father. After we have learnt the Rules of Etiquette Aunt Charlotte has written out for us,' Hester replied, picking up the book and waving it at him. He opened his mouth to say something, thought better of it and shook his head.

'Well, enjoy yourselves. I'll see you at supper.'

'There Father goes, striding down the street as if the devil were after him. Oh, and look, here comes Aunt Charlotte. She's peering around like she doesn't wish to be seen, now she's hurrying towards the mews.'

'Must be going out in the carriage. And, despite all she said to Uncle, she's wearing another new outfit,' Victoria exclaimed, joining her cousin at the window. 'That's probably what made Uncle cross.'

'Well, at least we know the coast is clear. To make sure, we'll read one more wretched rule and then discuss what we are going to wear this afternoon. I can't wait to see Roscoe.' Victoria smiled at her cousin's animated expression, for she was impatient to be with Tristan again.

'Rule 17: One may accept a chaste kiss on the forehead or hand but never on the cheek,' she snorted, throwing it down in disgust. 'I wouldn't mind settling for any kiss, chaste or otherwise from Roscoe. I swear blind he still sees me as the young girl with grazed knees he used to play with. Why, Victoria, is it hot in here or is that a flush I see on those forbidden cheeks?'

Luckily, she was saved from replying for Hester was checking the little clock. 'Heavens, look at the time. We haven't decided what we're wearing, and Chambers will be all of a dither.'

'We'd better go upstairs, Vanny will be waiting too,' Victoria replied, snatching up her parcel and the book. 'I'm sure she knows where Step Mama goes, you know, for when I mention it, she always turns away and mutters something unintelligible.'

In her room, any feelings of disquiet about her stepmother's actions were soon replaced by the tingle of excitement at the thought of seeing Tristan again. She already knew she loved him and that he was the man she wanted to marry. And, to encourage him, she would wear her brightest, most eye-catching outfit.

'Don't you think it strange how Step Mama disappears every Saturday afternoon and on Wednesday too?' she asked, staring at Vanny in the mirror.

'I'm not really . . . ' the maid began, concentrating on the top of Victoria's head, then muttering as she dropped a hair pin on the floor.

Before she could question her further, Hester appeared in the doorway. Dressed in bronze, she looked as vibrant as her personality.

'I'll see you downstairs,' she cried, seeing her cousin wasn't ready.

Victoria fought down her impatience as Vanny placed the bonnet trimmed with amethyst ribbons on to her head and pinned it carefully in place, all the while avoiding looking in the mirror. Pulling on her buff kid gloves, she could tell the maid was clearly flustered. There was no time now, but she vowed to tackle her about Charlotte when she returned.

'My sister sent these to wear with my gown for Lady Dorothea's house party,' she said, indicating the parcel on her dressing table. 'Please see they are packed ready,' she said, before hurrying down the stairs.

However, to her surprise, only the barouche was waiting, and it had its top drawn up, which was unusual for their perambulation around the park on a sunny afternoon. To her consternation Lady Dorothea was alone.

'Good afternoon, Victoria. Please do not look so crest-fallen, the others have gone on ahead and Tristan will be joining us at the house for afternoon tea. I thought it would be a good opportunity for us to have a little chat,' the woman said. As she gestured for Victoria to take the seat opposite, the scent of lily of the valley wafted around the carriage.

'I see. How nice,' Victoria said, forcing a smile as she smoothed down her skirts.

'How are you, my dear?' Although the woman smiled cordially, Victoria couldn't help sensing something was wrong.

'I'm very well, thank you, Lady Dorothea, and I trust you are too.'

'The weather is so frightfully hot, the air fetid and as for the dust and flies . . . ' she threw her hands up in despair. 'Let us say that is one reason for having the canopy up today. I shall be relieved to be leaving for my country home next week.' She held her lace handkerchief to her nose and inhaled deeply.

'You won't be returning to London then?' Victoria asked.

'Good heavens, no. The Season might last into August but only fools stay in the city beyond the end of June. I cannot wait to return to the clean air and delights of my estates. One trembles to think what pleasures will be forthcoming from the hot houses and the blossoms in the gardens will be something to behold. There will be displays in every room. I can think of nothing more appealing than having time to assemble artistic arrangements, bands of blue flowers with swathes of silver foliage, veils of violets and lilac interspersed with layers of lemons and ribbons of reds.'

'Isn't it amazing how all nature's colours blend harmoniously together when the same ones from a paintbox can clash?' Victoria cried.

'Ah, so you have an appreciation of all things flora too?' Dorothea asked, her eyes gleaming with delight.

'I do indeed. When Mama was alive . . . ' she trailed off, remembering Charlotte and not wishing to sound insensitive.

'Your Mama loved flowers too,' Dorothea nodded, her voice softer.

'We had them in every room as well,' Victoria admitted.

'A home filled with the fragrance of flowers is a happy

one. And talking of homes brings me nicely onto to the other reason for having the top up.' She tapped it with her closed parasol then turned to Victoria, her expression serious. 'One can't be too careful; prying eyes and pricking ears are everywhere. Now, Emmeline has kindly given you her guest suite for the Season and, as her best friend and Hester's godmother, I need to ensure her kind hospitality is not being abused.'

'I'm not sure I understand.' Victoria frowned at the abrupt change in the woman's manner.

'I am sorry if I sound blunt, but society rules are clear. Now that you and Hester are launched, there cannot be any hint of any impropriety.'

Victoria's heart sank like a stone. Had she been spotted accepting Tristan's kisses in the gardens, or worse, returning them? Feeling her cheeks growing hot, she turned her head.

'It is imperative that nothing anyone is . . . may be doing, besmirches our good names. I feel it prudent to mention this in case I need to withdraw my invitation.'

'Withdraw your invitation?' Victoria gasped, staring at Dorothea in dismay. That would mean not seeing Tristan or spending time with him at his family home in Surrey. She'd been so looking forward to getting to know him better, furthering their relationship. Why, in her dreams she'd even gone as far as hoping . . .

'Indeed,' Dorothea's strident tones penetrated her musing. 'The ball I host at our country seat is the talk of the Season, even if I do say so myself. Anyone who is anyone is invited. Hester is my beloved godchild, and I simply will not have her associating with anyone who . . . well, let us say, is not upholding the rules. Do I make myself clear?' Dorothea turned the full force of her gaze upon her, then before Victoria could ask exactly what she meant, the woman sighed.

'And that's the third reason for having the top up – cats and dogs.'

Victoria frowned, then saw it had begun to rain. Before long it was thundering on the roof, huge drops bouncing off onto the street.

'Still, at least it will flush some of the muck away.' The woman smiled as though the previous conversation hadn't taken place, but Victoria could only nod for the change of weather meant her walk in the gardens with Tristan couldn't take place. Quite apart from wishing to be alone with him, she also needed to ask him what his mother had meant.

Chapter 25

The following week, Victoria gazed around the drawing room of Lady Dorothea's country home, taking in the fine furnishings that were elegant rather than extravagant, its French doors opening onto the sweeping lawns. It was decorated in the Style of the Adam Brothers with scalloped ceilings, elaborate plasterwork and sconces on the walls affixed with wax candles. The decor was painted soft green, the covers a dusky pink while the rich carpet in a buttery hue all complemented the sweet peas that were artistically arranged on the table.

'This is delightful, Lady Dorothea,' Charlotte enthused. 'Pray what do you call this room?'

'The Green Room, of course. I have no time for people who use grandiose names,' she replied, a little smile playing at the corners of her mouth. Victoria saw Emmeline and Hester exchange knowing looks. 'Do make yourselves comfortable, I am sure you must require sustenance after your journey.'

Once refreshments had been enjoyed, Dorothea excused herself to speak with the housekeeper, leaving Tristan to show them around the parterre garden. It was bordered by neatly clipped boxwood and, as the others stood admiring the colourful shrubs, he turned to Victoria and winked.

'Mother enjoyed discussing floral arrangements with you last week. It is a huge passion of hers and you clearly made a good impression, as you have with me,' he added, dropping his voice so the others didn't hear.

Victoria smiled, relief flooding through her. After her discussion with Lady Dorothea in the barouche, she'd spent all week worrying their invitation to Sunningdale would be withdrawn. There had been no opportunity to ask Tristan what his mother had meant, but, upon reflection, perhaps that was no bad thing. She might be naive in the ways of the ton, but she didn't need to make it apparent.

'What are you two whispering about?' Charlotte's imperious tones cut through the air, spoiling their private moment.

'I was just explaining to Victoria that the Celtic knot garden planted with heaths and lavenders around the floral sundial is a particular favourite of Mother's, Lady Farringdon. Still, as with most parterres, the overall view is best afforded from the upper terrace. Perhaps you would care to see it from there?'

'And leave you and Victoria by yourselves? I think not. I wasn't born yesterday, you know.' Feeling Tristan grin, Victoria didn't dare look at him. 'I am here to chaperone and, as you must surely be aware by now, I am not one to shirk my responsibilities,' Charlotte told them.

'Except on Saturdays and Wednesday afternoons,' he muttered. 'Of course not,' he replied politely. 'Perhaps you would care to stroll further down to the gardens and visit the maze?'

'That would be great fun,' Hester exclaimed. 'We can shake off the wardens,' she whispered to Roscoe.

'Don't you think we should stay near the house for when the other guests arrive?' Charlotte asked.

'That won't be necessary, Lady Farringdon. Nobody else is due until tomorrow.'

'Dorothea kindly invited us to arrive a day early so that Hester and Victoria can relax before the grand ball,' Emmeline explained.

'I should make the most of it, for the house will be awash with people from then until noon on Monday,' Tristan told them. 'Even Giles will be gracing us with his presence at some point,' he added.

'Oh, that will be nice,' Charlotte replied, her voice unnaturally high.

Victoria shot her a puzzled look, but the woman had already composed herself.

'I really should see if there is anything I can do to assist. Dorothea is well organized, of course, but there is always much to oversee.' Emmeline glanced uncertainly from the little group to the magnificent Georgian manor house, its honey-coloured stone turrets rising majestically into the glorious cobalt sky.

'As you wish, Emmeline. I shall continue my chaperoning duties. It wouldn't do to leave young ladies by themselves.'

Emmeline made her way back to the house and Charlotte purposefully placed herself between Tristan and Victoria as they continued their way through the manicured gardens. Trying not to feel resentful, Victoria peered around, inhaling the fragrant herbs pleasingly planted in symmetrical rows in the smaller kitchen knot garden. However, Charlotte's mind was on other things.

'How much land do you have here?' she asked, staring around.

'About eighty-five acres, give or take the odd one,' Tristan replied, giving a nonchalant shrug of his shoulders. 'Of course, we have others in Cornwall and the Highlands of Scotland, plus the houses in London.'

'All to be passed on to your brother Giles?'

'When he marries, yes.'

'And what about you, Tristan? Presumably, you have some provision, or do you have to make your own living?' she asked, scrutinizing him closely.

'Step Mama,' Victoria exclaimed.

'The latter, Lady Farringdon. Which is why you'll find me travelling to sunny climes and treading the grapes,' he replied, winking at Victoria. 'Behind those hedges are the hot houses with our own vines. Regrettably, our grapes are not yet ready to be picked so I am unable to give you a demonstration.'

'Really,' Charlotte retorted with a grimace.

'Beyond you'll see the walled kitchen garden,' Tristan continued, giving her no opportunity to question him further. 'And the singing you can hear is coming from the linnets in the aviary over there,' he told them, gesturing to a long, tall cage. But Charlotte, busy processing all he'd said, didn't respond. As they walked on in silence carefully avoiding the strutting peacocks, Hester and Victoria exchanged knowing glances.

'Here is our maze, roughly translated as a delirium or delusion for obvious reasons,' Tristan announced. 'I know you've both had the pleasure of exploring it before,' he added turning to Rosco and Hester.

'And we got utterly lost,' she giggled.

'Goodness, it looks vast,' Victoria exclaimed, staring at the sea of clipped hedging stretching out before them.

'Nine thousand yews, multiple paths, some with dead ends as you would expect, with bridges thrown in to confuse. But here is the point. In the centre is a Greek urn containing rare abalone shells. The first person to emerge from the maze with one is the winner. Lady Marchington holds the record at thirty-five minutes, and it hasn't been beaten in a decade. Still, I admit it is complicated; perhaps a bit much for a beginner. What do you think, Lady Farringdon?' He turned towards her, blue eyes sparkling with mischief.

'Good heavens, young man, I've been in more elaborate mazes than this,' Charlotte retorted.

'Indeed? Then you obviously know that the trick is to always turn right,' he told her.

'Elementary, young man,' Charlotte scoffed, waving her hand at him. 'Come along, Victoria, Hester, we'll show him,' she ordered, setting off briskly along the first path.

Trying not to laugh at her fierce expression, they duly followed. It was strangely still and cool inside and intrigued by the various twists and turns and crunch of needles beneath her feet, Victoria didn't notice the boys weren't following.

A tap on her arm made her jump and her eyes widened when she saw Tristan holding back a branch and beckoning. She glanced round but Charlotte had already disappeared and, heart beating faster she let him lead her further into the opening until they were completely hidden within the foliage.

'I've missed you so much,' he murmured, gazing at her longingly. 'It was agony making polite conversation in the drawing room last weekend when all I wanted was for us to be alone in the shade of the pergola. Tell me you missed me too.'

'I missed my rose,' she teased only to chuckle delightedly when he produced a perfect red bud from behind his back.

'Never let it be said Tristan Newton Berwick disappoints his lady,' he declared, bowing solemnly as he presented it to her. His lady? Her heart flipped yet she couldn't resist teasing him.

'Ah, but I was disappointed not to see you at Lady Darlington's soiree.'

'And risk being eaten alive?' He shuddered. 'It appears she has me lined up for her precious Primrose who, being prim by nature, is no fun at all. Her mother does not approve of dancing either, in case there should be a touching of flesh.' He raised his brows theatrically. 'At least tomorrow I will equitably be able to hold you close,' he smiled. 'In the meantime, am I to be rewarded for risking my life plucking one of Mother's finest blooms?' he asked, holding out his arms towards her.

'What about Step Mama?' Victoria murmured, torn between desire and duty. 'She'll be looking for us by now and—'

'Will get hopelessly lost,' he cut in. 'Turning right all the time is a red herring.' Gently he lifted her hand and placed a kiss in her palm before pulling her close. As the woody fragrance of yew mingled with the tang of his citrusy cologne, and the cool air was suffused by the heat of his body, she could resist no longer.

All thought of her stepmother and Dorothea's caution disappeared as she willingly gave herself up to his embrace. His lips moved to her cheek, and she raised her face to accept.

Blow the etiquette rules, she thought, trembling as he trailed featherlight kisses tantalizingly down her neck until he reached her throat.

It was only when they heard Charlotte calling that reason returned, and reluctantly they broke apart. Still their gazes locked, and unable to look away, she blushed, aware of a new intensity of feeling between them. His eyes were navy with emotion, the air around them charged with excitement, the future filled with promise.

'Victoria, I demand you come here at once.' Her stepmother's voice sounded again, this time higher pitched and more insistent.

'We'd better go before she works herself into a frenzy,' Victoria sighed.

'Never mind, we have the best part of tomorrow before the guests start arriving. I'm sure we can steal away, even if only for a short time.' He gave a wicked grin and Victoria's heart flipped. She couldn't think of anything she'd like better.

'Victoria!'

'Come on,' he said, lifting a branch behind them. 'This leads right to the centre so it will look as though we've been searching for the shell. Here, take this,' he said, delving into his pocket and drawing out an abalone shell.

'Where on earth have you been?' Charlotte asked as they appeared on the path beside her. Her eyes narrowed as she took in Victoria's flushed face.

'Victoria's found the shell,' Tristan declared jubilantly.

'Oh, well done,' Roscoe cried from behind them. He drew out his pocket watch and, with a wink at Tristan, cried, 'And, in only twenty minutes, which means she's broken

Lady Marchington's record.' As the others cheered, Charlotte stared sceptically from Tristan to Victoria.

'Don't think you've heard the last of this,' she hissed, taking Victoria's arm, and drawing her away. 'Clearly, we need to discuss your future before you end up making a complete fool of yourself. Tomorrow morning you will accompany me in my carriage.'

'But I have already made plans . . . ' Victoria began, staring at her stepmother in dismay.

'Then you can unmake them.'

Victoria's heart sank; how was it possible to go from elation to despair in such a short space of time?

*

To Victoria's astonishment, her stepmother greeted her warmly when she climbed into the coach the following morning. It really was difficult keeping up with the woman's changing moods.

'Ah, there you are my dear.' Charlotte smiled. She was wearing another outfit Victoria had never seen before and seemed impatient to get going.

'Is it really necessary to go out this morning? I really feel we should be helping Aunt Dorothea with the preparations,' Victoria ventured, in a last attempt to stay at the house.

'That is what servants are for, Victoria, and why you have taken to calling that pompous woman, Aunt, I do not know.'

'She invited me to, actually. Besides, I like her.'

'As you do that second son of hers. Honestly, Victoria,

there is little point in being launched into society with the opportunity of making a good marriage, if you squander it on someone who needs to earn a living. And by treading grapes.' She grimaced.

'He doesn't actually tread them, Step Mama.'

'But he said he did. I really don't know what your father would say.'

'Papa's first thought would be for my happiness. Then, like everyone at supper last night, he would compliment Tristan on his splendid choice of wines. He is obviously knowledgeable in his field.'

'And, left to your own devices, that is where you'll end up living: in a field. Talking of choices, the ones you make now will influence the rest of your life. Goodness, whatever is the coachman doing,' she grumbled as the carriage lurched to avoid an oncoming carriage. Then, in an instant, her stepmother's expression changed, her face flushing as she gave a secret little smile. Victoria peered out of the window to see what had caused the change in her demeanour, but the carriage was already disappearing into the distance. Before she had time to ponder further, they were drawing to a halt in front of a stone property. Curiously, it had an array of coloured bottles displayed in the bow windows.

'Come along, I have a surprise for you,' Charlotte said, allowing the coachman to help her down.

A chime signalled their arrival as they opened the door. Stepping into the dim interior where glass-fronted mahogany cabinets lined the walls, Victoria saw they displayed more of the fascinating little bottles.

'Good morning, may I be of assistance?' a dark-haired

young man asked, appearing from a back room. He was wearing a white coat and seemed flustered.

'Monsieur Florian Juan? Lady Farringdon. We have an appointment,' Charlotte said impatiently as the man stared blankly.

'Actually I—' he began but Charlotte held up her hand impatiently.

'My stepdaughter, Victoria, requires her own fragrance made for an important ball. A maid was dispatched to notify you yesterday. You come recommended by the Countess of Kilcoyle.'

'Lady Dorothea, a lovely lady and valued client of our house,' the man inclined his head graciously.

'Yes, yes, well, I'll leave you in Mr Juan's capable hands, Victoria. I shall return in, say, three hours' time. That should give you long enough to create something bespoke. Good day to you.'

Before either the man or Victoria could respond, Charlotte had swept from the establishment, the chime pealing again as the door closed behind her.

'I'm sorry, Lady Victoria, but there seems to be some mistake. It is Monsieur Florian who is the master perfumer and on Saturdays he attends his shop in London. I am his apprentice, Gabriel.'

'Oh, I see. Well, perhaps I could take one of these perfumes with me?' Victoria asked, staring at the bottles on display while thinking perhaps she would get to see Tristan after all.

'Impossible, everything is created for the individual client.' Gabriel shrugged. 'I am sorry, but I did not know you were coming here today.'

'If it's any consolation I didn't either,' Victoria told him, turning to go. Then she saw the carriage was no longer outside. 'Oh no, Step Mama has already left. I have no idea where I am or how to get back to Lady Dorothea's house.'

'I am here by myself and cannot leave the shop.' Gabriel shrugged again. You will have wait here until she returns.'

'But I . . .' Victoria began, then realized she had no choice. 'Thank you, that is most kind.' She tried not to sigh as the opportunity of seeing Tristan slipped away.

'I always take a hot drink into the garden at this time and inspect the flowers; you are welcome to join me,' offered Gabriel, who had been watching her anxiously.

'That would be lovely, thank you.'

'Please, you follow me.'

The room behind the shop was like nothing Victoria had ever seen before. There were two strange-looking copper vessels that steamed and hissed in one corner, whilst on the table pipettes and glass tubes were set out. Shelves containing phials of different-coloured liquids lined the walls, and the aroma wafting around was divine. As Victoria stared about her in fascination, Gabriel went over and lifted a blackened kettle from the fire.

'This is where you make perfume?' she asked.

'It is where I distil the essences to be blended, yes. Your coffee,' he said passing her an earthenware mug. 'We will see the flowers, now.'

She followed him outside, her eyes widening in delight at the profusion of colours.

'Goodness, what an amazing array,' she cried, taking in the roses, geraniums, lilies, lilac, lavender, and all manner of other plants. 'Do you use all these flowers and herbs?'

'If they attract the butterflies and bees then they are good enough for the perfume making,' he replied, delighted by her enthusiasm. 'However, it is in the blending that we create the different aromas. When is it, this ball of yours?'

'This evening,' Victoria told him and watched as his dark brows shot up to his hairline.

'Impossible,' he cried, throwing up his hands in horror. 'A woman needs to select the fragrances that suit her personality, so that wherever she goes, she is instantly recognizable. Is unforgettable.'

'How intriguing,' she cried. 'Tell me more.'

'The essences selected have to work in harmony with each other. It is like creating a symphony.'

By the time Charlotte returned, Victoria's head was buzzing like the bees in the flower heads. She didn't even notice the woman was later than promised. With Gabriel's help, she was not only going to be recognizable but unforgettable.

Chapter 26

Charlotte was preoccupied on the journey back, staring out of the window, and saying nothing. Resigned to her stepmother's unpredictable moods, Victoria thought back over her morning and everything she'd learned from Gabriel. What a nice man and how knowledgeable. She couldn't wait for her parcel to arrive. Or to share details of her visit with Aunt Dorothea. It was strange she hadn't mentioned the appointment and that the perfumier himself hadn't been there.

It was late afternoon by the time they arrived back at Sunningdale. As the butler solemnly admitted them, the fragrance of sweet peas and roses from the elaborate arrangement on the highly polished hall table wafted their way.

'We'll go straight to our rooms and prepare for this evening,' Charlotte told Victoria briskly.

'Shouldn't we tell Aunt Dorothea or Aunt Emmeline we have returned?' Victoria asked. 'There might still be something we can do to help.' Before her stepmother could reply, Hester came hurrying into the hallway. Her flame curls had already been dressed in preparation for the ball, although she had yet to change.

'Where have you been?' she cried. 'Aunt Dorothea's really worried.'

'But she knew where we were going, didn't she?' Victoria said, turning to her stepmother, only to find the woman was already disappearing up the stairs.

'Never mind,' Hester said, raising her eyes. 'Mother is waiting for you. Poor Tristan was quite put out when you didn't appear this morning,' she added, pushing open the door to the comfortable drawing room that was bathed in the rays of the afternoon sun.

'There you are, Victoria,' Emmeline said. 'Your Uncle thought you'd like to wear these tonight. I was going to give them to you earlier but . . . well, never mind.' She handed Victoria the box containing her pearls.

'Perhaps you'd explain where you and that stepmother of yours disappeared today? I should have thought it good manners to inform us you were going out,' Dorothea said, sweeping into the room and confronting Victoria with her candid stare. 'Emmeline has been out of her mind worrying something untoward happened.'

'But I thought you already knew, Aunt Dorothea,' she frowned.

'All I know is that Benson informed me Charlotte requested breakfast be brought up to your rooms, after which you went out in your carriage.'

'We went to see the perfumier, Monsieur Florian. Step Mama told me you'd recommended him, said a servant had been dispatched with a message yesterday.'

'Had I recommended the services of Monsieur Florian to Lady Farringdon, which I can assure you I did not, my servants have all been far too busy with preparations for the weekend to be running around the countryside on extraneous errands.'

There was no doubt she was telling the truth and Victoria thought back to Gabriel's shocked expression when they'd arrived.

'Why don't you girls sit down, and Victoria can tell us exactly where she's been?' Emmeline suggested. They did as she suggested, and Victoria proceeded to explain.

'Then Step Mama left saying she had an appointment and would return in three hours when I would have my own perfume for this evening.'

'A woman of Lady Farringdon's standing would have known it takes weeks if not months to produce a bespoke fragrance. Besides, Monsieur Florian is always to be found in his Jermyn Street premises on a Saturday.' Then she frowned. 'Did you say she left you alone with Gabriel for three hours?' Dorothea exclaimed, her eyes widening in horror.

'Well, it was nearer four hours by the time she returned,' Victoria admitted.

'And you say this Gabriel had no knowledge of this supposed appointment?'

'No. It could have been embarrassing but he was so kind, showing me his wonderful garden and explaining how perfume is made. It is so interesting,' Victoria enthused.

'It is, especially to one who appreciates flowers,' Dorothea agreed, smiling for the first time. 'Well, it is getting late, I suggest you girls go and make yourselves beautiful for tonight.'

'I really am sorry to have caused you to worry,' Victoria

said, rising to her feet. 'I did tell Step Mama we should stay and help you with the preparations but . . . '

'She needed to meet with her . . . appointment,' Dorothea finished, exchanging a look with Emmeline. 'Well, at least you have come to no harm and now I look forward to seeing you both dressed in all your finery. As Giles has yet to arrive, Tristan will receive our guests with me; you girls can go straight to the ballroom.'

As the door shut behind them, Victoria heard Dorothea's voice.

'This has gone too far. She must go. I will not have the family name besmirched.'

Go? But where? And what about Tristan? Victoria's heart plummeted. She had been so entranced with the flowers and hearing how perfume was made, she hadn't even thought about being left alone with a strange man. But surely that had been her stepmother's fault?

'Golly. I've never heard Aunt so cross,' Hester exclaimed. 'But how fascinating to find out how perfume is made. Ah, there's Tristan.'

'So, the wanderer returns,' he remarked coolly.

'Don't be like that, Tris,' Hester groaned. 'Victoria thought we knew Charlotte was taking her out. Anyway, I must go and change,' she added, tripping lightly up the stairs.

'You weren't trying to avoid me then?' he asked, his expression softening as he stared at Victoria.

'Of course not. I didn't want to go out, but Step Mama insisted.'

'I see. Well, there's no time to talk now; I must receive the guests with Mother. Let me mark your card; I won't get another opportunity until the festivities are under way and by then you won't have any dances left.'

'But it's upstairs in my room,' Victoria began then jumped as the card landed with a clatter on the floor beside her. They looked up to see Hester on the landing, grinning wickedly.

'Good old Hes.' He smiled as he retrieved the card and quickly marked it. Then, as he passed it back, his hand lingered on hers, sending a shiver of excitement shooting through her. 'I cannot wait for the first dance. Just ensure Charlotte doesn't whisk you away anywhere else.'

'I will,' she murmured, hoping her aunt wouldn't have her sent away immediately.

Glancing at the card, her heart skipped when she saw he had again defied protocol and marked it three times. Pulses racing and heart singing, she hurried up the wide staircase. She was dying to spend time with Tristan and, if she was already in the ballroom when Dorothea had received her guests, she couldn't throw her out, could she?

The room she been allocated for her stay was sumptuous, with pink peony drapes, four-poster bed and a moss-green carpet so soft her feet just sank into it. The heady fragrance of honeysuckle floating in through the open window made her think of home. However, her mind was on her gown rather than the surroundings. It was vital she look her best, for Dorothea's balls were renowned, and ladies far more beautiful than she would be attending.

Dressed in her golden gown complete with the engageantes, she sat at her dressing table, watching in the mirror as Vanny fastened the strand of pearls around her neck. Was it her imagination or did the maid seem nervous again this evening?

'Did you have a good day, Vanny?' she asked. The maid picked up the brush and began smoothing Victoria's hair before answering.

'Yes, thank you, m'lady.'

'And have you been out anywhere since we arrived?' The maid hesitated then, on the pretext of selecting more hair pins, turned away. 'Do you know anything about an appointment with Monsieur Florian?' The maid's hands stilled then she picked up a piece of lace that matched the engageantes.

'This was also in the parcel, m'lady, and I thought it would be perfect to weave through your hair.'

'Yes, it will, thank you. How long have you worked for my family, Vanny?'

'Since before the new mistress came.'

'Then surely you owe to it me to be truthful?'

'I have to do what I'm told or—'

'Aren't you ready yet? The guests are beginning to arrive,' Hester exclaimed as she burst into the room, clearly impatient to be downstairs. 'Oh my, you look absolutely gorgeous,' she exclaimed. 'Those lace sleeves make your gown look quite regal.'

'We will speak further tomorrow,' Victoria told the maid, who nodded and scuttled away. Sliding into her dancing slippers, she checked her appearance in the full-length gilt mirror on the wall, then turned to Hester. 'You look divine in that emerald green.'

'Thank you. I hope Ross agrees,' she sighed.

A procession of carriages had been arriving for the past hour and it was clear the guests waiting to be received were all well connected and dressed accordingly.

They made their way through the ballroom where Charlotte and Emmeline were waiting with the other chaperones. To Victoria's dismay, her stepmother was glaring at her sister, and, as they approached, she saw why. Her Aunt, wearing a deep-pink dress that lent colour to her cheeks, looked soft and feminine. Beside her, Charlotte, in the white dress she had worn the day of the presentation, looked harsh and drawn even in the candlelight.

'Father insisted Mother have a new dress for tonight and Aunt Dorothea got her own modiste to come here. It was only finished and fitted this afternoon,' Hester whispered.

'What beautiful young ladies,' Emmeline greeted them. 'Aren't they a credit to us?' she asked Charlotte.

'I see you are wearing the Farringdon pearls,' Charlotte snapped, ignoring the question, and transferring her glare to Victoria. 'You can give them to me for safe keeping after the ball tonight.'

'Nicholas was only too happy to retrieve them from the bank and will return them to the safety box on our return,' Emmeline said quickly, aware they were attracting attention. 'Now, I know I've said it before, Victoria, but that gown is magnificent and those lace sleeves simply exquisite. Wherever did you get them?'

'They were made by Jane Haydon, the lady who sewed my gown, but the lace was made by Lily from Combe,' Victoria replied.

'Lily only made the lace for Queen Victoria's wedding dress and veil,' Hester exclaimed, her excited voice causing more heads to turn as guests peered at Victoria's outfit, eagerly awaiting more information to be imparted.

'How interesting,' Dorothea remarked, catching the tail end of the conversation as she joined them. She was wearing a spectacular gown in claret trimmed with black lace, diamonds studded through her silver hair sparkling in the light as she moved. 'I'm surprised you haven't mentioned this, Lady Farringdon, but then you do rather have a habit of keeping things to yourself.'

'I do not see the need to discuss family affairs,' Charlotte replied, coolly.

'Normally I would agree. However, as circumstances dictate otherwise, I will speak with you in the drawing room after breakfast tomorrow morning.'

Looking indignant, Charlotte opened her mouth to respond but, at that moment, the orchestra struck up a grand march. Tristan, resplendent in his dark jacket and snowy white shirt, appeared at their side.

'Please excuse us, Lady Farringdon.' Bowing politely, he proffered his arm and led Victoria towards the couples already on the dance floor.

'Alone at last,' he quipped, gazing at her intently so that her heart skipped, and heedless of the press of couples around them, made her feel as if they were in their own world. 'May I tell you how especially gorgeous you are looking tonight?' he murmured as they glided in harmony across the floor.

'Indeed, you may,' she agreed, smiling up at him.

All too soon, the music tailed off and Tristan was leading her from the floor.

'It irks me to have to relinquish you into the arms of another,' he sighed. 'Still, I have claimed the dance before the interval so we can have supper together as well. Until then, as host, I must do my duty, for goodness knows where Giles has got to.' They walked back to where Charlotte was waiting with the other chaperones, and it was clear from her expression that her mood hadn't improved. 'Here she is, safe and sound, Lady Farringdon,' Tristan grinned, bowed then disappeared into the crowd to claim his next partner.

'Thank you,' she replied stiffly, peering anxiously around.

'Are you expecting someone, Step Mama?' Victoria asked.

'What? Er, no, of course not,' she replied quickly. 'Now where was I? Ah, yes, you should be concentrating on making a better match than one with a second son.'

'Lady Farringdon, Lord Chalfont at your service,' an older man said, bowing low. 'I believe I have the honour of the next dance,' he added, hazel eyes gleaming as he turned to Victoria. Forcing a smile, she allowed him to lead her back to the floor. She saw Tristan had been claimed by the woman they'd seen at Lady Alice's recital, and she was clearly intent on pressing him to dance with one of her daughters.

'Hortence, Phoebe and Ophelia are all such treasures.' The woman's high-pitched voice cut through the thrum of voices. 'Which one would you like to dance with first?' The fair-haired one displaying ample bosom, intent on increasing her chances, discreetly edged her bodice lower. However, it seemed Tristan was either immune to her charms or didn't notice.

'Forgive me but I have already claimed someone for this dance so regret I must decline your kind offer.'

Victoria stifled a giggle as the girls pouted and the woman looked affronted.

What was it with these domineering mothers? When I have

daughters of my own, I shall permit them to choose their own suitors, she decided. Goodness, where had that thought come from, she wondered, relieved to see the dance with the oily Lord Chalfont was a formal cotillion which required frequent changing of partners.

When she was returned to Charlotte, her stepmother again pointed out the importance of effecting a good marriage.

'There is more to life than making a match with someone undesirable,' Victoria sighed, sick of the subject.

'Listen to me,' Charlotte hissed. 'The most eligible bachelors in the land are here tonight. Your extravagant outfit has caught the attention of some of them, so you'd be well advised to capitalize on that.'

Knowing she'd already made her choice, Victoria let her stepmother drone on while she waited impatiently for Tristan to claim her again. The air, with its expensive perfume and pomade, cigar smoke wafting in from the terrace, felt cloying. She was just wondering if she had time to step outside for a breath of fresh air when a buzz of excitement rippled through the room and a tall figure appeared in front of them. He looked familiar and yet different somehow.

'Lady Farringdon, might I present myself, Lord Newton Berwick at your service.' The man bowed low then turned the full force of his smile upon Victoria.

'I believe this is our dance?'

'I think you must be mistaken for I am already claimed for this one,' she stuttered.

'And the name beside it is Newton Berwick.'

'Yes, but—' she began, glancing at the card on her wrist where Tristan had merely signed his surname.

'I am Giles Newton Berwick, so shall we?' he continued, proffering his arm. His eyes, although blue like his brother's, had a steely, determined look.

Victoria glanced around but could see no sign of Tristan. However, she did catch the self-satisfied grin on her step-mother's face and, if she hadn't known better, she'd have thought this had been planned.

'Come along, Victoria, it is rude to keep the gentleman waiting,' Charlotte prompted, giving her a push.

Everyone seemed to be looking at them and, knowing she couldn't risk making a fuss, Victoria allowed herself to be led onto the dance floor.

Chapter 27

Although Victoria looked for Tristan on the dance floor, the press of bodies in their finery was so dense she could see no sign of him. Dorothea's ball was certainly living up to its reputation of being the most popular of the Season.

'Might I compliment you on your elegance, Lady Victoria,' Giles said, causing her to focus her attention on him. She smiled enigmatically but didn't respond. 'In fact, you are easily the most beautiful lady in the room tonight,' he added, turning the full force of his charm upon her.

'Do you always scatter compliments like apple blossom on the breeze, my Lord?'

He stared at her for a moment then laughed out loud, causing people to stare.

'Elegant, beautiful and droll. What a delightful mix.' He smiled, showing even teeth that gleamed against his tanned skin. 'There is no need for formality on such an auspicious occasion; the name is Giles.'

Luckily, there was no further opportunity for talking, and she sighed with relief when the dance finished, and he led her from the floor. Ignoring the envious looks of the other women who were following their every move, Victoria began walking back towards Charlotte, only to find herself gently propelled towards the edge of the room.

'No point in queuing when one doesn't have to.' Before she could object, she found herself in an anteroom where the supper table was set with pristine white damask cloths. Gleaming silverware platters were laden with wafer-thin cold meats, breads, and pats of golden butter each topped with the family crest. Dainty fruit tartlets, cream and cheeses with glistening grapes graced the sideboards. More intent on scanning the people who were now lining up at the other entrance for sight of Tristan than worrying about the food, Victoria automatically allowed the waiter to serve her a selection.

'Let us find a quiet corner and you can tell me about yourself.'

'But Step Mama—' she began.

'—is craning her neck and watching our every move gleefully, so I hardly think you need worry,' he chuckled. 'Ah, I espy a table over there.' As he strode purposefully across the room, acknowledging the many guests who greeted him, Victoria followed, her glance darting left and right. Then she spotted Tristan and her heart leapt only to sink to her golden slippers when she saw him chatting to a beautiful young woman, her ebony hair swept up in jewelled combs. She was accompanied by a distinguished man with silver hair who she assumed must be her father. Tristan was looking so animated and entranced by what the woman was saying, he didn't even notice Victoria. So that was why he hadn't claimed their dance, she thought, sinking into the chair that was pulled out for her. Noticing her expression, Giles raised his brow and shrugged.

'A bit of a heartbreaker, our Tristan, I'm afraid,' he said, attacking his supper with enthusiasm.

'I see,' she murmured. How foolish she had been to believe what he'd said, she reflected morosely, looking down at her plate and feeling sick. She couldn't manage a morsel. Giles, busy regaling her with tales of his travels, didn't even notice. Unlike his brother who'd always sought her opinion, he obviously expected her to listen attentively. Just when she thought she would scream with frustration, the orchestra struck up, signalling that dancing was about to resume.

'Allow me to escort you back to Lady Farringdon. I shall, of course, claim you for the last dance.' He smiled magnanimously, clearly expecting her to be flattered. How conceited he was, she thought, hurrying across the room as quickly as she dared.

Charlotte was agog, but before she could ask any questions, Victoria was claimed by a lean young man in uniform. Almost involuntarily her gaze scanned the floor, but of Tristan there was no sign, and by the time Giles sought her for the last dance, her spirits were as low as the candles burning in the sconces.

'My dear Victoria,' he said, when the orchestra stopped playing, and he escorted her from the floor. 'Be assured, tonight is just the beginning. I know what I want, and that is you. Rest assured, I never let anything, or anyone, stand in my way.' He shot a triumphant grin across the room and Victoria looked up to see Tristan staring at them, his expression inscrutable. Instinctively, she wanted to go and challenge him about the dark-haired woman, but pride made her hesitate. Then, before she could change her mind, he'd disappeared into the crowd.

'I expect he was seeking you out to tell you he's been called away on business. That's his usual trick,' Giles murmured. 'Ah, Lady Farringdon, I beg permission to court your charming daughter.'

'Permission granted, Lord Newton Berwick,' she replied. They exchanged a knowing look that made Victoria think again that this had somehow been planned. 'We are guests here until Monday when we return to Chester Square. We look forward to welcoming you, Lord Newton Berwick.'

'Thank you, Lady Farringdon.' He bowed then turned to Victoria. 'It has been a delightful evening. I look forward to seeing you again very shortly.' His blue eyes so like Tristan's in colour, yet lacking the humour, gazed at her intently and she felt a shiver slide down her spine. Not if I see you first, she wanted to shout, but propriety came to the fore and she smiled demurely.

After a night punctuated by dreams of Tristan holding out his arms towards her, only for him to turn into Giles when she reached him, Victoria was late waking. She was staring up at the ceiling and wondering what could have gone wrong between her and Tristan when Charlotte burst into her room.

'For heaven's sake,' she remonstrated when she saw Victoria still in bed. 'Get up and dressed in your travelling outfit. We are leaving immediately.' Victoria was about to protest, but it was obvious from the tight set of her face that the woman was in a filthy temper. Frowning, she put all thoughts of Tristan aside, clambered out of bed and dressed.

'Shouldn't we say goodbye to Aunt Dorothea and thank her

for her hospitality before we leave?' she asked, as Charlotte ushered her outside where their coach was waiting.

'Come along,' her stepmother urged, all but pushing her inside.

'But I understood we were staying until tomorrow,' Victoria said, as soon as they were ensconced in their carriage.

'I refuse to stay where we are not welcome. That Dorothea is so high and mighty.'

'Whatever do you mean? What about Aunt Emmeline and Hester? And where is Vanny?' Victoria asked, staring in dismay at the beautiful house as they pulled away. Then a movement at the drawing room window caught her eye. Surely that was Tristan. Her heart flipped then she shook herself. If it was, then he was probably making sure she left before meeting his new paramour.

'Your aunt and cousin are staying on for a few days longer. Apparently, there are relatives they wish to visit. Or so they said.' Her stepmother sniffed.

'And Vanny?'

'Had to go home. Her father is ill,' her stepmother replied, waving her fan frantically. 'Goodness, it is so hot.'

'But . . . ' Victoria frowned, something stirring at the back of her mind.

'She caught a lift with the carter first thing,' Charlotte said, waving her hand as if that was the end of the matter. 'It's that goddammed righteous Dorothea.'

'Ah yes. You had a meeting with Aunt Dorothea this morning. Perhaps if you explained what she said, I might understand why we have to leave.'

'How many times must I tell you that woman is not your

aunt,' Charlotte snapped. 'As for the things she said, I've a good mind to sue her for slander.'

'What exactly did she say?' Victoria asked, her head beginning to spin.

'It's really of no consequence,' Charlotte sighed, closing her eyes.

How typical of her stepmother to start a conversation only to stop when it suited her, Victoria thought, staring out of the window. They were making their way through the Surrey countryside with its abundance of tall, leafy trees, and, reminded of the greenery of Devonshire, she had a sudden desire to be back there.

'I'd like to return to Nettlecombe rather than London,' Victoria announced.

'Don't be ridiculous,' Charlotte hissed, her eyes snapping open. 'There are at least six weeks of the Season left. And Giles has obviously taken a shine to you,' she added, a satisfied smile spreading across her face. 'Such a charming young man and to think he will become an earl when he marries, inherit the estates.' Her eyes gleamed at the prospect. 'Even you must see the advantage of marrying the brother with prospects rather than the one in trade. Treading grapes, I mean what kind of job is that?' she tutted.

'Tristan was only teasing you, Step Mama. He is a connoisseur and has his—'

'I consider his attitude juvenile,' Charlotte interjected, waving her hand dismissively. 'Giles is a man of the world.'

'And you know that from your brief meeting last night?' she asked, eyeing her stepmother shrewdly, but Charlotte turned to look out of the window.

Honestly, the woman was as arrogant as Giles. He might be blonde and blue-eyed like his brother, but, unlike Tristan, who was warm and funny, his cool air of superiority got under her skin. Besides, it wasn't Tristan's fault he'd been born the younger son. Except he now clearly preferred the company of a raven-haired beauty.

'Well, Giles won't be keen to call now we've had to leave Sunningdale a day early,' Victoria threw out, grateful for one small mercy at least.

'And why exactly do you think we've had to leave?' Charlotte asked, shooting her a penetrating stare.

'I can only think it is because Aunt Dorothea disapproved.'

'Of what exactly?'

'My behaviour. It was not dignified for me to spend all that time alone with Gabriel.'

'Ah,' Charlotte replied, visibly relaxing back in her seat, a little smile playing at her lips. 'She certainly mentioned Saturday in no uncertain terms.' Victoria was about to say that being left alone hadn't been her idea, but her stepmother hadn't finished. 'However, we will say no more about it. I won't even mention it to your father – as long as you agree to receive Giles as your suitor,' she added magnanimously.

Victoria stared at her in dismay. That was blackmail. Not only did she have to spend the rest of the Season in London, but she was expected to entertain Giles even though he made her skin crawl. Yet, what choice did she have? Her Papa was a good, kind man and she couldn't bear the thought of disappointing him.

'Very well,' she sighed, turning away so she didn't have to see the look of satisfaction spreading across her stepmother's face. She might have agreed to this unpalatable arrangement, but when they returned to Chester Square, she would ensure her diary was filled with appointments. Then she remembered Tristan and the raven-haired beauty. The endless round of parties and balls had already begun to pall and, without him, they would be unbearable. She needed to find a more satisfying way to spend the rest of her time in London. When Aunt Emmeline returned, she would ask to help at Haven House again. She wanted to help those poor women, who through no fault of their own, found themselves in the direst of situations.

As they continued their journey, an uncomfortable silence filled the carriage. Victoria thought back over the past weekend. She was sorry if she'd disappointed Aunt Dorothea and when she wrote thanking her for her hospitality, she would apologize and reiterate that it had been her stepmother who had arranged that morning and there was no way she could have changed the events.

She would also write to Louisa, thanking her for her engageantes, explain how well they'd had been received and that many ladies had asked where they could purchase similar. If her sister mentioned that to Jane, it would surely help her business. She would ask Louisa to check Vanny had arrived safely back in Combe for it worried her that she had caught a lift by carter. One heard such awful stories about women travelling alone and it was such a long way back to Devonshire.

Chapter 28

At Nettlecombe Manor, Louisa and her father had finished breakfast and adjourned to the bright airy sunroom, or Citrine Room as Charlotte insisted it be called. Now they were basking in the warmth of the early morning rays whilst they finished their coffee and perused the morning mail.

'Goodness, Victoria says Vanny's father has been taken ill and she has had to return home. I thought her mother was a widow and Vanny had to provide for her?'

'I'm sure that is the case,' Edwin agreed, peering over his own correspondence at her.

'I shall check when I visit Combe this morning. I'm surprised Step Mama hasn't sent for Shears to replace her.'

'True.'

'You seem preoccupied, Papa. Are you quite well?' Louisa asked, knowing how much he was missing his faithful friend.

'Sorry, my dear,' he replied. 'This is a reply from Blackmore accepting the job of estate manager. He is free to take up the position at Michaelmas which is a relief as poor Wilf and Edith are anxious to move on. Still, it's only a matter of weeks until then.'

'You elected for the younger man then?'

'Hmm. Gorwyn had a lot of experience, but times are changing and Nettlecombe needs to move with them. Talking of moving, have you heard anything from Henry?'

'A letter arrived from him yesterday. Do you remember reading about Silistria in the newspapers? Apparently, his regiment along with other British and French Allies gathered at a place near the coast, then set off to relieve the poor people in the town, but by the time they reached the outskirts, the Russians had all left. He said they were able to help feed some of the starving families though.'

'It must be a comfort to know he is safe and well.'

'Oh yes, and perhaps his regiment can come home now. Who knows, they might even be making their way back to the boat,' she cried excitedly, her fingers automatically reaching for the button in her pocket.

'Don't get your hopes up, Louisa,' Edwin cautioned. 'Things may well have changed since then. Doesn't mail from the Crimea take some weeks to arrive?' Frowning, Louisa reached into her pocket again. Checking the envelope, her spirits sank when she saw he was right.

'Well, it can't be much longer,' she told him determinedly. 'It is fortuitous I have a consultation with Jane Haydon this morning for I really must get my trousseau organized. After our enforced separation, I just know Henry will want us to marry as soon as he returns.' She frowned as a strange expression crossed her father's face.

'Don't you agree, Papa?'

'Sorry, my dear, of course I do. It was you mentioning Miss Haydon that put me in mind of that sewing machine.

I thought that by insisting she accept it as a gesture of good-will, I was helping, but, upon reflection, I fear I might have appeared somewhat pompous.'

'Oh goodness, Papa, I quite forgot,' Louisa cried, staring at him in dismay. 'On my last visit Jane mentioned you could collect it any time. Although Millie, her maid, seemed to have other ideas.'

'Well, Miss Haydon is in charge, so ask Quick to bring it back with you,' he said.

'Why, Papa, I do believe you have a soft spot for Miss Haydon,' Louisa teased.

'I admire her courage. Carrying on her business after Sam was killed can't have been easy. I was merely endeavouring to help, as I would you and your sisters.' Quickly finishing his coffee, he rose to his feet. 'I'm off to the quarry for my appointment with Wakeley. I presume you will be taking the cart as usual.'

'Yes, Papa. I have no wish to look as if I'm lording it over the workers. I'll leave that to you,' she quipped.

It was a relief to have her charitable works to concentrate her attentions on, Louisa mused, as they drew up outside the village hall. She was missing Henry more each day, although hopefully he would soon be on his way home. Nettlecombe seemed very quiet without her sisters. Still, Victoria and her stepmother would be returning around the middle of next month, so she intended making the most of the opportunity to choose her trousseau without Charlotte's interference.

As she entered the hall, the savoury smell of broth simmering greeted her, yet the mood of the women was despondent.

'Good morning, everyone,' she called cheerfully.

'Is it?' Rosa replied gloomily as she tried to soothe her fretful baby. The others muttered in agreement.

'Whatever is wrong?' Louisa asked, looking at the little group who unusually were huddled together rather than sewing.

'Leah's dead and the work's drying up,' Ida Somers told her bluntly.

'Oh, poor Leah,' Louisa murmured, her heart going out to the unfortunate woman who'd spent her last months in the local asylum after contracting syphilis.

''Tis kindest really. Had warts the size of winkles all over 'er tatie trap and even up her behind,' Flo grimaced. 'Made her chaynee-eyed an' all.'

'I heard it sent her gurt noodled,' Lizzie sighed. 'Made her act silly,' she added, seeing Louisa looking perplexed.

'If that don't make you all think on about going with strange men then I don't know what will,' Ida Somers snorted.

'Perhaps we should say a prayer for her,' Louisa suggested.

'Fat lot of good that'll do 'er now,' Ida snorted. 'Better you pray for some more orders.'

'We ain't stupid and knows if we don't get more work in, we'll have to close,' Rosa said, cuddling her baby tighter.

'Goodness, it's not that bad, surely? What about that order from the fishermen?' Louisa asked.

'Nearly finished it, ain't we? Let's face it, there's only so many shirts and vests a man can wear,' Ida sighed.

'Or afford,' Jeannie ventured.

'If there ain't nothing for us to do, there'll be no money for rent or food,' Flo muttered.

'We'll all be out on our ears like 'er up back along.'

'Pardon, Jeannie?' Louisa asked the woman, wishing they wouldn't lapse into their dialect when they got agitated.

'Old Mrs Vanstone. Her daughter's been given the boot. Well, yer should know,' Ida sniffed, staring at Louisa reproachfully.

'As I understand it, Vanny, er, Miss Vanstone told my stepmother she had to return home as her father's ill.'

'What father? He's bin stiff in the ground this ten year or more.'

'Clearly there has been some mistake,' Louisa replied. 'Have you enough work to be getting on with today?'

'Just about,' Ida replied.

'Well, you can carry on with that whilst I go and see Mrs Vanstone. After that, I have an appointment in Salthaven so will put my thinking cap on during the journey. The broth smells as delicious as always, Lizzie,' Louisa smiled.

'Thank yer,' she mumbled. 'At least we knows the kids won't go hungry this day.'

'Don't worry, I promise they will continue to be fed, whatever happens,' she assured them. 'And I will endeavour to obtain more orders,' she added, as she took her leave. Though where they would come from, she had no idea.

'Mrs Vanstone's home please?' she called to Quick. He nodded then looked nervously over her shoulder, obviously expecting Ida Somers to appear. The woman must be feeling despondent for she clearly hadn't given the man a thought.

The cart rocked its way over the rutted narrow lane that led to the beach side of the hamlet, and, moments later, they were pulling up outside a thatched one-up, one-down cottage.

'Lady Louisa,' Vanny gasped, the colour draining from her face when she saw her visitor.

'Hello, Vanny, may I come in, please?'

The girl nodded and opened the door wider.

Louisa stepped straight into the tiny, dark living room which, as in so many cottages, served as the kitchen as well. Then she noticed an older woman on a day bed by the window, pillow and bobbins on her lap.

'Excuse me for not getting up on account of I can't,' she muttered, dark eyes hostile. ''Tis shameful the way yer treated my girl. Left alone in the middle of nowhere like that, having to make hers way home without no money.'

Louisa turned to Vanny. 'Surely not?' She frowned. 'Until I received a letter from Victoria this morning, I thought you were still in London. Tell me exactly what happened.'

'Yes, m'lady,' Vanny replied nervously, gesturing for Louisa to take a seat on the old rush stool beside the empty grate. She began speaking, hesitant at first, then, like a dam being breached, the story came tumbling out. Louisa listened carefully, her eyes growing ever wider.

'Let me get this straight. When you first arrived in London, you saw my stepmother riding with another man in her carriage and she forbade you to mention it?'

'Yes, m'lady, said I'd be sent packing if I said anything, which was a joke as that is exactly what happened anyway. And then she took up with a young man, titled as well. Met at his house in London many times, then there was that day in Surrey. The Countess of Kilcoyle found out she was seeing someone, but Lady Farringdon refused to tell her whom, so was sent packing.'

'And does Victoria know about all this?'

'I think she suspects something, but I've tried to avoid her questions. It's not seemly, is it? And goodness knows what His Lordship will say when he finds out.'

'We must try and make sure he doesn't,' Louisa told her.

''Tis a disgrace. When yer thinks how quick Her Ladyship were to judge them quarry workers' widows too,' Mrs Vanstone tutted. 'And them poor as church mice. Mind, we all be poverty stricken round these parts. Lived in this cot since me and my Alf was wed and always managed to pay our rent on time even though the roof lets rain in. Suppose it's the workhouse for us now,' she muttered, letting out a long sigh.

'Certainly not, Mrs Vanstone,' Louisa assured her, opening her reticule, and counting out several coins. 'Please take this to tide you over. And no, Mrs Vanstone, it is not charity, merely wages owed with a little extra for inconvenience,' she added as the older woman opened her mouth to protest. 'Spend the day with your mother, Vanny, and then report back to work tomorrow.' She turned to go and then stopped. 'I trust that I can rely on your discretion. Perhaps you could say you were needed back at the manor? Heaven knows I have certainly missed you.'

'Of course, and thank you, m'lady.'

'That's beautiful lace you make, Mrs Vanstone,' she said, admiring the work on the woman's pillow.

'Idden much call for it since them machines was installed up Tivvy way. Journeyman acts like he's doin' us a favour taking it off our hands, and for such a pittance he might as well not bother.'

'Well, I'll wish you good day and can only apologize again for the trouble you've both been put to.'

Really, she could kill that stepmother of hers, Louisa fumed, as the cart wended its way towards Salthaven. What an example to set Victoria when she was meant to be acting as chaperone for the Season. She would go to London and confront Charlotte, for dear Papa must never find out how she'd deceived him.

*

As the new client dithered over her choice of fabric, Jane forced herself to remain calm. Mrs Smythe's considerable bulk, which had taken time and effort to size for her new corset, was now spread over most of the chaise, her cloying cologne overpowering the delicate fragrance of rose. The Receiving Room, usually an oasis of calm, felt congested as one grumble followed another.

'I feel somewhat dismayed at the lack of choice,' the woman sighed, turning the pages of the folder containing samples of those Jane had left in stock.

'More fabric is being delivered next month, Mrs Smythe,' Jane told her, crossing her fingers, and hoping that would be true. 'What about this lovely apricot? The colour would sit well against your skin giving it a nice glow.'

'A glow?' she cried, staring at Jane in horror. 'I'll have you know I have the porcelain skin of my youth and require something that highlights the fact.'

Jane wanted to protest, as the woman had obviously left her youth behind many years ago, but assumed a professional smile. 'Of course, Madam. Have you considered this ivory?' she suggested, mentally working out just how much she had left in the workroom. Not only would the corset require extra fabric, but the seams would also need double stitching to ensure the garment didn't burst when the woman bent over. Not for the first time lately, she blessed having the machine.

'It's hardly inspiring, is it?'

'But the delicate sheen would enhance your porcelain skin, which is the look you are hoping to achieve.' Jane smiled, her lips feeling as if they'd been pinned into place. 'And of course, you will need boning, I would suggest baleen as—'

'Good heavens, girl, are you mad? A figure like mine doesn't require boning.' The woman's eyes bulged indignantly.

And no professional corsetiere who valued her reputation would dream of letting a woman of such size wear one of her creations without it, Jane thought.

'Begging your pardon, madam, the greatest ladies of society insist on having better quality than steel in their underpinnings and naturally, I assumed, that being one yourself, you would wish for baleen.'

'Well, naturally. Now, I have a luncheon engagement so must take my leave.' The woman struggled from the chaise and Jane tried not to wince as the springs protested.

'Miss Brown, please make an appointment for Mrs Smythe to be fitted next week,' Jane said, leading the way back to the shop. 'I shall be in the Receiving Room when Lady Louisa arrives,' she added, satisfied when her client looked suitably impressed.

As the stress of the past weeks caught up with her, Jane sank onto the chaise and put her head in her hands. The last client might have been trying but she had a valid point. Business had been brisk and, with the extra accessories they'd been making, fabric was dwindling.

Hope had been working flat out on the machine to keep up with orders for these extra lines, which meant her training for making corsets had fallen behind. Whilst the girl never complained, it was what she'd primarily been apprenticed to learn, and it was only a matter of time before Lady Connaught found out.

Although she'd been trying to put money aside, with clients still too slow in settling their invoices, she had been unable to meet the deadline for paying Mr Fairfax's bill in full. Not only had she forfeited Sam's precious bobbin, but she'd also incurred interest on her outstanding debt, for the merchant's driver had been adamant they were the terms she had agreed to. He'd warned that if she didn't make up the payment next time, the interest would be compounded. With the threat of her debts spiralling out of control, she wondered again what had possessed her to go direct to the warehouse. Despite her best intentions, instead of expanding her emporium, it seemed she might be about to lose it.

Chapter 29

The jangling of the shop bell brought Jane back to the present and she jumped to her feet just as Hope showed Louisa Farringdon into the Receiving Room.

'Good morning, Lady, I mean Louisa,' Jane greeted her. 'Please make yourself comfortable,' she added, gesturing to the chaise.

'Good morning, Jane, I trust you are well,' she replied, taking a seat, and smoothing down the skirts of her blue moire silk day dress. The ribbons of her deep bonnet matched perfectly, and Jane could only marvel at how elegantly turned out she was. 'Oh, I do love the fragrance in here, it reminds me of the garden at Nettlecombe.' Jane smiled politely, thankful for the sea breeze that had freshened the room after her last client.

'I see some items in your window have a reserved notice on them. How wonderful that your business is thriving,' Louisa enthused.

Jane smiled. If she did but know it, those tickets were pinned to garments that she'd made for display purposes only. Not having enough stocks to ensure replacement when a client made a purchase, she'd devised the idea of enticing clients to try before they buy. The small deposit she asked to secure the order went some way towards payment to the merchant Mr Fairfax. It was working well but she still had a huge amount to find before his driver called again.

'I had a letter from Victoria this morning extolling the beauty of those engageantes you made,' Louisa told her. 'Apparently, they were much admired at the Countess of Kilcoyle's ball.'

'I'm pleased she liked them. In fact, I have received orders for similar ones.'

'Really? That's marvellous,' Louisa enthused.

'It would appear Victoria felt able to recommend my services to the ladies of London which is an honour, especially as there are so many modistes and corsetieres in the city,' Jane told her, realizing more appreciation was expected.

'Ah, but not as skilled, nor having your vision. You really do have a talent for being forward-thinking; those chemisettes on your mannequins are quite inspired. Who would have thought trimming the neckline like that would make them look so desirable, and of course, they are much less cumbersome than camisoles. But I digress, today I must concentrate on my trousseau, for Henry could be coming home soon.'

'You have heard from him?' Jane asked, noticing her animated look.

'I received a letter only yesterday. Apparently by the time his regiment reached the Russian positions, they had already deserted, so, with no one to fight, it seems logical they will return, don't you think?'

Knowing it wasn't her place to say that things might have

moved on since then, Jane smiled and answered diplomatically.

'I hope you soon receive the news you are waiting for. In the meantime, having forfeited your last consultation for Victoria's engageantes, shall we focus on your underpinnings? Are you having your wedding gown made in the style you showed me, or have you changed your mind?'

'Oh no, I knew as soon as I saw the illustration that it was the one,' she said, opening her reticule and passing the drawing to Jane.

'It is beautiful and will be perfect for your delicate frame,' Jane replied, studying the elegant silhouette of the white fitted lace bodice with a band of embroidered flowers at the waist, from which silk skirts gently flowed. 'And you still intend wearing the long veil with it?'

'Yes, Lily said she could make more lace in time. I think she was secretly delighted to think her work was going to be seen by the ton. Goodness, if we are hoping to bring the date forward, I shall have to encourage her to get on with it. As the ceremony will be in the chapel at Nettlecombe the date won't prove a problem.'

'That's good,' Jane said, opening her book and jotting down some notes. 'I already have your personal details, but we did not finalize your actual requirements last time, did we?'

'No, I'm afraid I got distracted by those beautiful new accessories of yours.'

'I have your broderie anglaise engageantes ready, but perhaps we should continue with our review first. If you were to select underpinnings in pearlescent fabric rather than stark white, there would be no danger of anything showing through the delicate silk. I know the skirts will be flowing but, on your special day, all you want to be concentrating on is Henry, not the people peering at you from behind as you make your vows.'

'Goodness, you really do think of everything, don't you?' Louisa said, clearly impressed.

'I try,' she said, picking up her pattern book. 'Now, to give you a streamlined and sleek appearance, the design of your corset will need to be smooth and with as little embellishment as possible. Although you will need something less . . . functional, shall we say, for when you change out of your wedding gown.'

'Goodness, I hadn't even thought of that,' Louisa giggled, a rosy flush creeping across her cheeks. 'This sounds more fun. Shall we concentrate on that one first? In fact, I shall choose fabric for them both whilst I'm here. Let me see your folder,' she added, flicking through the samples.

'I can always order more if you have anything particular in mind,' she ventured, crossing her fingers under her notebook.

There was a sudden clash of crockery as Millie, despite Jane's request not to, pushed open the door with her bottom.

'Hello, Lady Louisa, I saved yous the last piece of me sponge cake, but I'm afraid there's no lemon drink so it's tea today.'

'Hello, Millie. It is lovely to see you again and tea would be most acceptable. How is that young man of yours?'

'Ooh, he's wonderful. I was invited to meet his ma, and she made me very welcome. I never knew me own mother, so it'll be lovely to have one when we wed.'

'You're to be married? Congratulations,' Louisa said, clapping her hands delightedly.

'You never said anything before,' Jane reproached.

'Well, yous been so busy,' she chirped.

'We'll have a good chat later then. That will be all for now,' Jane told her.

'Goodness, I nearly forgot,' Louisa cried. 'Papa said you must have thought him pompous insisting you keep that sewing machine, although, to be fair, he did think he was helping. Anyway, you will be pleased to hear we can relieve you of it today. Can you ask Quick to load it onto the cart, Millie?'

'Oh,' Jane murmured, trying to hide her dismay. She had come to rely on that machine, but having protested to Lord Farringdon, she could hardly object.

'Pride,' Millie muttered, pausing in the doorway.

'Did you say something, Millie?' Louisa asked.

'I said yous will make a beautiful bride, my lady,' the maid replied, pointing to the illustration on the table. 'I'll go and tell Quick then, shall I?' she asked Jane who could only nod in agreement.

'Doesn't she look happy?' Louisa smiled as the maid left. 'It will pose a problem for you though, won't it?'

'Oh?'

'Well, it is customary for a bride to move in with her new husband after the ceremony.'

'Yes, of course,' Jane replied. She really would have to have that discussion with Millie. Fancy her not saying anything. They'd always been like sisters, hadn't they?

'Now, we were looking at fabrics for your corsets.' She smiled, resuming her professional manner.

Conscious of the thumps and bumps as the machine was manoeuvred down the stairs, Jane tried to focus on Louisa's requirements. Having decided on the design and materials for the underpinnings, they moved on to accoutrements, and it seemed Louisa wanted at least two of everything. Meticulously listing the items and prices in her notebook, Jane tried not to shudder at the amount of fabric it was all going to take. Who would have thought a sizeable commission would cause such anxiety?

'Thank you, Jane, you have been a great help and I know I can leave everything in your capable hands,' Louisa said eventually. 'Would it be too much to ask that you prioritize my commission?'

'I can assure you everything will be ready in good time, Lady Louisa. Although we are currently snowed under with new orders. Even with Hope working late into the evenings, there aren't enough hours in the day.'

'That's a good problem to have, isn't it? Not like my poor ladies in Combe who are completing their last contract as we speak. Still, that is my predicament, and one I need to address,' she said, rising to her feet.

'Seems to me yous could help each other,' Millie said, making her usual timely entrance. 'I mean, thinks about it,' she added as they both looked askance. 'Yous got too many orders,' she told Jane. 'And Lady Louisa's lot ain't got enough.'

'Goodness, Millie, you never cease to amaze me,' Louisa cried before Jane could reply. 'That could just solve both our problem, at least for the immediate future.'

'But it takes years to learn how to make corsets,' Jane protested, finally finding her voice.

'Of course it does,' Millie agreed. 'But Hope could show them how to make basic modesty pieces, chemisettes and gown preservers, leaving yous free to make and fit the corsets.'

'And if Hope could also demonstrate how the sewing machine works, that would be really helpful,' Louisa said, clearly thrilled at the solution that had been suggested.

'Oh, I nearly forgot your engageantes,' Jane murmured, hurrying over to the cupboard in the corner. Things were moving so quickly she needed time to process her thoughts. However, oblivious to Jane's quandary, Louisa followed her, exclaiming with delight when she saw the sleeves.

'Exquisite,' she exclaimed, holding them up to the window. 'No wonder Victoria was thrilled.'

'These are the broderie anglaise version. I don't have any of that beautiful lace you provided for those.'

'Nevertheless, they are simply gorgeous and will lend a different look to my gowns.'

'Them nobs want her lace sleeves an' all. You should see all the letters with their fancy seals she's received,' Millie told her.

'That's because they know Lily made the lace for the Queen's wedding dress,' Jane interjected.

'Indeed? Then I will speak to Lily about obtaining more.'

'That would be most helpful,' Jane replied, her spirits lifting. Society ladies liked being seen wearing celebrated items and were prepared to pay well.

'Now, could you spare Hope tomorrow afternoon? I will, of course, send Quick to collect her and ensure she is returned safely at the end of the day.'

'Well, I, er . . .'

'Yous don't have any appointments tomorrow 'cos yous

needs to work on them corsets,' Millie offered, oblivious to Jane's quandary.

'But clients may call into the shop . . . ' she began.

'Then have no fear 'cos Millie's here,' the maid chirped, making Louisa smile.

'That's settled then. The women will be relieved to hear they have enough work to keep them employed for the foreseeable future. It's a matter of pride that they can pay their bills,' she told Jane, unaware she was touching on a sore point. 'Send the fabric along with Hope and include a list of what each item sells for then we can work out a fair price for everyone. Isn't this a truly marvellous idea?'

'I'm glad you think so,' Jane murmured.

'I apologize for staying longer than planned, but I'm sure you agree this will be to our mutual benefit. Now, how soon can I return to try on my bridal underpinnings? I really would like it to be soon, for once the women have started their new venture, I need to depart for London.'

'Ooh, is yous goin' to some of them balls with all the toffs?' Millie asked.

'Something like that, Millie,' Louisa said, smiling. 'Good day to you, Jane; you can add the engageantes to my invoice which I know will come to a healthy sum. How astonishing to think my Quarry Crafters will be in business with your emporium.'

'Indeed,' Jane replied. 'If you could let me know about the lace, I'd be grateful, and, of course, should your workers encounter any problems, then you know where I am.'

By the time Louisa had left, it was obvious from Hope's excitement that Millie had already said something.

'Do you really think I'm skilled enough to teach other people how to sew accessories and use the machine?' she gasped.

'Yes, Hope, I do. You are a very capable seamstress. And, when you return, I will have more time to teach you more about corset making.'

'I'd love a chemisette like this,' Millie murmured, running her fingers longingly over the fabric on the mannequin. 'My Bert would think me a real lady,' she giggled.

'Well, take it. We can deduct a little each week from your wages,' Jane offered, still feeling guilty that she'd been too busy to hear her maid's news.

'What wages?' the girl snorted. 'Yous hasn't paid me for three weeks.'

Jane stared at her in dismay. Had she really been so bound up in business she'd forgotten to pay her staff?

'We will have a discussion over supper, and then I shall pay you everything I owe you,' Jane promised, taking herself back to the Receiving Room.

For the second time that day, she sank onto the chaise, her head spinning. No sooner did she make progress than something else came along. It wasn't fair on Millie or Hope to let her worries overshadow everything else. But what had she got herself into now? While Jane appreciated Louisa's sense of responsibility towards the widows, she felt as if she'd been swept along without time to consider. Sending sufficient fabric to Combe would leave her barely enough for the commissions she'd already received. Or a machine to reinforce the seams on Mrs Smythe's corset. With even more people relying on her, she sincerely hoped Louisa would be able to source that lace. She could then charge premium prices for her engageantes.

It was good having a healthy order book and women assisting to make the simpler garments, which would at least be under Ida Somers' critical eye. However the fact remained that she was still short of silk for the corsets which made up the bulk of her business. Although she hated the idea, there was only one thing she could do. Going over to her dresser, she took out the little tin box where she'd squirrelled away every spare coin she could towards the sum she owed Mr Fairfax.

Chapter 30

Jane glowered at the locked gates of the warehouse. She'd been waiting since daybreak and now the ships moored alongside the wharf had all been unloaded. Surely Mr Fairfax should have been here by now? Having worked all night on the corset for his lady friend, using up precious silk into the bargain, she'd then made the long journey here. She hadn't even dared snatch a couple of hours' rest in case she overslept. Now she was bone-weary, her stomach gnawed with hunger and the constant shouting and clattering of heavy crates being transported was making her head throb. It had taken every ounce of courage she possessed to come here, and her spirits plummeted at what had obviously been a waste of time and effort.

'No good standing there, my lovely,' a voice called. Looking up she saw a young man in mismatched jacket and trousers leaning against a barrow. 'Fairfax won't be coming today. Got word his ship sunk in the Irish Sea. Big gale blew up and it keeled over, taking the crew and all his cloth with it.'

'Oh no,' Jane gasped, her hand going to her mouth in horror.

'Friend of his, are you?' he asked, eyeing her up and down knowingly.

'No, I came here on business, to obtain fabric.'

The man grinned. 'Well, now, this could just be your lucky day, 'cos Joey here has some of the finest,' he told her, pulling back the ragged cover with a flourish. Jane stared at the bales of cloth in an assortment of garish colours. Even from where she was standing, Jane could see they were shoddy.

'Thank you, but I will wait until Mr Fairfax returns,' she said, walking quickly away.

'Joey's willing to do a special deal for such a lovely lady,' he called after her, but she ignored him. A group of sailors embarking from a nearby ship jeered and whistled, but she tightened her shawl around her shoulders and lengthened her stride. Come hell or high water, she would never subject herself to this again, she vowed.

The walk back to Salthaven was gruelling. Vehicles clattered by yet no sympathetic carter stopped to offer her a lift. Her thoughts raced in time to the pounding of her steps. Why had she rashly made up that corset when her stocks of silk were dwindling alarmingly? Why had she wasted time on this ill-conceived quest? She didn't have enough money to pay Mr Fairfax in full, and with hindsight, it was obvious he was not the sort of man to be persuaded by a corset that had been part of the bargain for her earlier order. As if to add insult to injury, fat drops of rain began to fall, quickly turning the road to mud.

Putting the parcel inside her shawl, she pressed on knowing she needed to get back in time in time to select the fabric for Hope to take to Combe. With corsets and engageantes to complete herself, she didn't dare risk the girl taking too much. However well-intentioned Millie's suggestion the Quarry Crafters help with the orders had been, Jane wished she'd put her foot down. She might be snowed under but at least she had been in control of her own business. Or thought she had. It was unforgivable she should have forgotten to pay Millie, even if the maid had been delighted to be given the chemisette as an early wedding gift. She would make time to have a good chat with her whilst Hope was in Combe.

By the time she reached the road that led to Salthaven, the rain was coming down in sheets, turning the ruts in the road to fetid pools. Lost in thought, it was some moments before she realized a carriage had drawn up alongside.

'Miss Haydon?' She looked up from under her bedraggled bonnet to see a figure peering through the window of the liveried carriage.

'Good morning, Lord Farringdon,' she replied, conscious she must look a sight.

'May I offer you a lift?' he said, proffering his gloved hand. 'Driver, divert to Miss Haydon's Emporium in Salthaven. Goodness, you are drenched.' She stared at the water dripping from her shawl, the clumps of mud clinging to her skirts and quickly made to withdraw. 'Not that it matters one jot,' he said, gallantly.

'But it will dirty your seat,' she murmured.

'It's survived worse,' he assured her. 'Whatever are you doing walking in weather like this?'

'I needed to see about some fabric,' she replied, hearing the concern in his voice but not wishing him to know her problems.

As she carefully placed the wrapped corset on the seat beside her, he smiled.

'Well, at least your mission was successful. I hear from Louisa that your work has become popular with the ladies of London.' Hearing the admiration in his voice, Jane smiled. 'She came home last evening positively brimming with excitement about the wedding. Although personally I feel she is being somewhat presumptuous thinking Henry will return any time soon. The reports coming out of Crimea would suggest the contrary.'

'I feared as much,' Jane sighed.

'However, there is no need for us to disillusion her, is there?' As his hazel eyes stared beseechingly, she shook her head.

'Of course not, Lord Farringdon.' Satisfied, he sat back in his seat. 'I was sorry to hear about Ellery,' Jane ventured.

'Thank you. I must confess to missing him more than . . . well, more with each passing day,' he amended quickly. 'It is silly to be upset really. The poor fellow reached a good old age but, well, you get so fond of your pets, don't you?'

'I can only imagine, for I have never had any myself.'

'Really?' he asked, staring at her in surprise.

'Madame Pittier always said fur and fabric didn't mix,' she explained.

'I suppose that makes sense, especially as I understand she had a penchant for French silk of quality. Ah, nearly there,' he said before Jane could reply. 'Louisa tells me she has commissioned you to make the garments for her trousseau,' he said.

'Yes, and I am most grateful. However, I remember Lady

Farringdon mentioning an apricot rose and quite forgot to ask if that colour needed to be incorporated in any of the trimmings. I know how important it is to some people that things co-ordinate.'

'Ah yes, the rose,' Edwin sighed. 'It was actually grown with Louisa's betrothal celebrations in mind. Charlotte, well . . . let us just say she assumed it was for her. I asked for a new one to be cultivated, but regrettably, the gardener informs me it will be next year before it is sufficiently established.' He looked so despondent Jane hastened to assure him.

'Perhaps it could be a present for their first anniversary? She would have her own gardens by then.'

'That is a marvellous idea, Miss Haydon,' he replied, brightening. 'I do apologize for burdening you with my concerns, but you are extremely easy to talk to.' Jane smiled for the truth was she found him easy to talk to as well.

'No wonder you are such a successful business-woman.' His look of respect made her feel a fraud and she was about to tell him she was anything but, yet common sense prevailed. You didn't share financial concerns with someone you invoiced, no matter how tempting it was.

'Louisa tells me she got carried away with all the things she commissioned so . . . ' His hand went to his inside pocket and Jane's heart leapt. Then, he hesitated and shook his head. 'Forgive me, I was going to offer to pay you something in advance but having already offended you by insisting you keep the sewing machine, I now know better and will wait until you send me the invoice.'

'Thank you,' she managed to stammer.

'At least the machine is now out of your way. It is encouraging to know it will be put to good use by Louisa's ladies, as I think of them,' he said, oblivious to her thoughts. 'Well, here we are,' he added, as they pulled up outside her establishment.

'Thank you for the lift, Lord Farringdon,' she murmured, climbing quickly out of the coach. Millie was right, her stupid pride would be her downfall. Yet, pride didn't pay the bills and a contribution to funds would have helped her predicament enormously. Still, she only had herself to blame, didn't she?

*

As the cart rattled its way to Combe, Louisa was processing everything Vanny had told her. Luckily, her Papa had left for a meeting, and she'd been able to question the maid without fear of him overhearing. Having extracted further details of her stepmother's behaviour, it appeared she had been acting without propriety ever since Victoria had arrived in London, if not before. Her mouth tightened in rage. How could she treat her Papa so despicably? And to put Vanny in such an insidious position was unforgivable.

Although the maid thought Victoria suspected something was amiss, she was sure she wasn't aware of the facts. Knowing a mere whisper would ruin her sister's reputation with the ton made it imperative she confront her stepmother at the earliest opportunity. Papa would think it perfectly normal for Louisa to visit her sister, for they'd always been close.

Before she could leave, though, she needed to ensure the women knew what they had to do and that they produced work of the high standard Miss Haydon expected.

Her first stop was at Lily's cottage to make some enquiries.

She felt bad about the way Vanny had been treated and hoped she might be able to help her mother by way of recompense, which in turn would help Jane Haydon. She could only imagine the envious looks Victoria's engageantes had attracted at the Countess of Kilcoyle's ball.

Luckily, it had stopped raining and, mindful of the puddles, she stepped carefully from the cart, instructing Quick to continue to Salthaven to collect Hope. The church clock began striking the noon hour and the school door burst open, discharging exuberant children eager for their luncheon. She watched them swarm towards the hall, knowing the women would also have stopped working, for village life was regulated by that clock.

'Do you have a moment?' she asked, walking over to Lily, and, thinking of her husband, added, 'I won't keep you long as I know Tom will be eager for his meal.'

'Lady Louisa, how lovely to see you. I hope the lace proved satisfactory?'

'More than satisfactory, it has been very well received in London and that is what I wish to speak with you about, as well as my veil, of course.'

Briefly, Louisa explained about engageantes, and how the orders from the society ladies were for lace rather than broderie anglaise. Lily listened carefully then smiled.

'I think half the lace makers round here were involved in the commission for Queen Victoria's wedding, although, of course, some of the older ones have passed on now and many are in their dotage.'

'I understand Mrs Vanstone still works her pillow, as you call it, although she said she doesn't get paid much.'

'No,' Lily sighed. 'The faster output of machine-made lace makes it more profitable, although the quality is not as fine,' she declared. 'I presume you wish to assist after what happened to Vanny?'

'You mean, you know?'

'Not the detail, and I wouldn't pry. Tom saw her walking along the Sidmouth Road in a terribly distressed state and offered her a lift.'

'Well, your presumption is right,' Louisa sighed. 'And I am sure you will hear if my plan works out. In the meantime, I know you are busy with the school, but would you be able to replenish those sprigs for my veil soon? I'll obviously recompense you for the short notice. It would appear Henry could be on his way home soon and there will no need to delay our wedding.'

'Really?' Lily replied, looking surprised. 'Well, that would be good news. I will make a start this very evening.'

'Thank you. Good day to you, Tom,' she called, seeing the blacksmith crossing the lane from the forge opposite.

Walking towards the hall, she thought how wonderful it would be for both Mrs Vanstone and Jane Haydon if her plan worked out. Suddenly she felt she was being watched and spinning round saw Wise Woman Winnie, black cat perched on her shoulder, standing at her garden gate.

'Hello, Winnie,' she called.

'Lady Louisa, I fear you are not heeding my words, making plans for your betrothal after I had that seeing. I told you everything has its season. There will be no wedding 'til the mist lifts.' The cat leaned closer to Louisa, its luminous amber eyes peering into hers. Shivers prickled her spine but whether it was from the cat or its owner's prophecy, Louisa couldn't tell.

'Thank you for your wise words, Winnie. If you'll excuse me, the Quarry Crafters are waiting.' Knowing Winnie meant well, Louisa turned her attention to what she was going to tell the women.

Needless to say, Ida Somers had already imparted the news, and the women were agog to hear more. As the children headed back to school, Louisa suggested they all sit down while she outlined the details.

'Cors we've never used one of those before,' Rosa said, pointing to the sewing machine that had been placed by the row of tables.

'Hope, Miss Haydon's apprentice, will show us all when she arrives,' Louisa told them.

'I'da hopes it don't take as long to learn as when yer first started,' Ida Somers groaned. 'I'da took ages to get yer all sewing with a needle, let alone that fearsome beast.'

'Well, everyone has more experience now,' Louisa said diplomatically. 'Hope is bringing fabric with her so, while we wait for her to arrive, I'll show you the patterns for the accessories you will be making.'

'Yer having a laugh, ain't yer?' Flo cried, picking up the sample modesty piece. 'This ain't got no back.'

'Cos it goes in the front of yer day gown,' Ida Somers told her.

'But I wears this one all the time,' Lizzie replied, staring down at her homespun.

'And this is a chemisette, which is worn as an ornamental under-bodice. That is why it is unconnected at the sides,' Louisa explained, holding up the garment.

'I presume they'll be for the society ladies 'cos they's the only ones who can afford to have so many clothes?' Rosa asked Louisa.

'Indeed, and I understand they have already placed orders,' she confirmed.

'Probably best if we start with the gown preservers,' Ida said, picking up one of the shaped pads. 'Sort of work up our own sweat,' she chortled.

Hearing the cart clatter to a halt outside, Louisa sighed with relief. Fond of the widows she might be, but there was no denying their lives were very different.

'I'da goin' to help Hope with her stuff – and see me handsome driver,' the woman announced, jumping up from her chair and hurrying outside. But it seemed the girl didn't need any assistance for she was merely clutching a single carpet bag.

'Is Quick bringing in the rest of the fabric?' Louisa asked.

'It's all here, m'lady. Miss Haydon said it would be better to practise on calico first.'

Louisa frowned. How long would it be before they progressed to the using the finer fabric and she could leave for London?

Chapter 31

'Lord Giles Newton Berwick,' Jarvis solemnly announced, standing aside as the tall, fair-haired man strutted into the drawing room. His haughty demeanour along with the dark blue of his jacket reminded Victoria of the peacocks on the lawn at Sunningdale, and she had to bite her lip to prevent herself from laughing out loud.

'My Lord, welcome to our humble abode,' Charlotte said, treating him to her most gracious smile, 'or temporary abode, I should say, for, as you know, we reside in our manor house in Devonshire and are merely here for the Season.'

Goodness, even for her stepmother, she was overdoing the lady of the manor bit, surely, Victoria thought.

'Lady Farringdon, how wonderful to see you again,' Giles said, hiding his smile behind a low bow and almost crushing the enormous bouquet he was clutching. 'And temporary, or not, the vista is quite charming,' he added, staring meaningfully at Victoria as he proffered the beribboned flowers with a flourish.

'Thank you,' she said, taking the ostentatious arrangement and passing it to the butler who discreetly bore it away.

She sighed inwardly. It had obviously cost a small fortune, but blowsy blooms were not to her taste. She couldn't help comparing them to the simple but perfect red rosebud imbued with sweet fragrance that his brother had presented to her. 'I hope the countess and your, er, family are well,' she asked Giles, seeing her stepmother signalling for her to make conversation.

'Mother still has a houseful so is in her element,' he laughed. 'And Tristan has returned to his work.'

'Treading grapes, isn't it?' Charlotte asked, giving a disparaging laugh.

'Oh, he's always trampling on something: grapes . . . hearts. It's the thrill of the chase with our Tristan, with never a thought for those he might hurt.' Giles shook his head and stared at Victoria. Seeing the triumphant gleam in his eyes, she forced her lips into a smile, determined not to let him see his words had wounded.

'Do be seated,' Charlotte invited, gesturing to the row of velvet-covered upright chairs set out for visitors. Ignoring them, he settled himself on the sofa opposite the chaise they were occupying.

'I will get straight to the point, Lady Farringdon,' he began. 'Although you have graciously given your blessing for me to court Victoria, when I want something, I move at speed, and noblesse oblige dictates I seek the permission of Lord Farringdon.'

'Papa is in Devonshire,' Victoria replied quickly, her spirits rising at the thought that this would discourage or at least delay further development of their courtship. However, she'd reckoned without her stepmother's dogged determination.

'That is most considerate, not to say honourable, Giles. I may call you Giles?'

'Indeed, you may, Lady Farringdon.'

'Edwin – Lord Farringdon, that is – and I both desire the best for our dear Victoria's future, and I can assure you he has utmost faith in my judgement.'

Dear Victoria? Since when had her stepmother referred to her as that, she wondered, staring at the woman in astonishment.

Ignoring her look, Charlotte continued. 'You may therefore proceed with this courtship forthwith. The Season has passed its peak, after all; in fact, many couples have already announced their betrothal.'

'Step Mama,' Victoria exclaimed, mortified by the woman's cogency, 'there is no hurry . . . '

'On the contrary, Victoria,' Giles said, leaning forward and giving her the benefit of his most charming smile. 'As I have already said, when I decide I want something, nothing will stand in my way.' He turned to Charlotte. 'Until I have had the chance to meet Lord Farringdon, perhaps I might speak with Nicholas; he is Victoria's uncle, after all.'

In the ensuing silence, Victoria watched the conflicting expressions flitting across her stepmother's face. She could hardly tell him that on their return from Surrey they'd had a blazing row resulting in him storming out of the house.

'Nicholas is staying at his club until Emmeline and Hester return. He shares the same moral code as yourself, Giles, and says it would be improper for him to be here alone with two attractive young ladies.'

Victoria shook her head, as the glib lie slipped from her stepmother's lips.

'Admirable of the chap. Anyway, the point of my visit, apart from taking the opportunity of seeing you both again, is to invite you to join me for a celebratory tea at Gunter's in Berkeley Square tomorrow afternoon.'

'Celebratory?' Victoria frowned.

'Indeed. We must celebrate the beginning of our courtship in style, must we not?'

'But there is no hurry. I mean I am not ready—' Victoria began.

'Oh, but you are. You are out in society, after all?' Giles told her. He turned the full force of his gaze upon her, and Victoria was struck again by the cool and calculating look in his eyes. He was clearly a man used to getting his own way. And her stepmother was actively encouraging him.

*

As the maître d' fawned and showed them to the best table in the elegant tea rooms, a delicious array of delectable sandwiches, fancies and cream cakes on tiered silver stands were set out before them. Giles was at his most charming, ensuring the waiter kept their cups and plates replenished whilst regaling them with anecdotes.

'Pineapples, or pines as they used to be known, were an exotic luxury, so prohibitively expensive, people would hire them to use as the centrepiece for their dinner parties. They would then return them uneaten the next day to claim a refund, would you believe.'

'That sounds to me like people living beyond their means,' Charlotte said piously. 'When I entertain, I encourage my guests to consume anything on offer. I mean, it is my duty as hostess. The pineapples grown in the hot houses at Nettlecombe are to be enjoyed.'

'Quite right too,' Giles agreed. 'Don't you agree, Victoria?'

'Actually, I feel more than a little sympathy for those people who felt they needed to go to such lengths to impress their guests.'

'Ah, but you must agree, it is about the appearance, or at least the perception,' Giles replied, his smile so condescending, Victoria shuddered.

'How I agree. I have always taught Victoria and her sisters that appearance and perception are paramount,' Charlotte enthused and, as she turned the full force of her gaze on Giles, Victoria thought how alike they were. And how at ease they seemed in each other's company. Like old friends. 'Isn't that right, Victoria?' The woman's voice penetrated her thoughts.

'Oh, er, yes, Step Mama,' she replied.

'Don't worry, I will see she is schooled in the ways of a good wife and hostess before . . . well, you know.' She gave him a beguiling smile. 'That reminds me, have you seen the announcement of Lady Arabella's engagement in *The Times*?'

'Indeed, I have, Lady Farringdon,' he replied, dabbing a crumb from his lip with his snowy linen napkin.

'Seemingly, not a day goes by without someone becoming betrothed,' Charlotte sighed.

'Step Mama, really,' Victoria exclaimed, mortified by her insistence on pursuing the subject of matrimony.

'I was merely saying,' she said, holding up her hands in surrender.

'I believe in doing things in style. Making a statement.

Saving the best until last. In fact, from now on, I want you to wear your golden gown everywhere we go,' Giles replied, leaning closer to Victoria so that she caught the full impact of his musky cologne. It was heavy and cloying and she couldn't help comparing it to the fresh, citrusy tang of Tristan's.

'Really? How intriguing,' Charlotte exclaimed, her eyes agog. 'Do enlighten us.'

'I believe we should make our announcement at the end of the Season. A grand finale, as it were. Future Earl gains Golden Girl of the Season,' he announced grandly so that the people at the nearby tables turned to look. As Victoria, who had been nibbling at a pastry, stared at him in horror, a crumb caught in her throat causing her to cough.

'My word, Giles, I do believe Victoria is quite overcome by your splendid suggestion,' Charlotte gushed, kicking her under the table whilst shooting her a warning look.

'I think I need some fresh air,' Victoria gasped, rising quickly to her feet.

'Dear girl, she is completely overcome with delight,' she heard Charlotte explain as she hurried outside. There it was again, that use of the word dear, implying they had a close relationship. Victoria could only wonder at the woman's hypocrisy.

Breathing in the fresh air, she sought the shelter of the plane trees that graced the square. Several carriages were drawn up, their occupants enjoying ice creams in the welcome shade whilst waiters scurried about, attending their every need. But Victoria hardly noticed; she felt as if a stone had settled in her stomach. Like a fly caught in a spider's web, she could feel the silk thread slowly being wrapped around her, helplessly waiting until it came in for the kill. Unable to stand it a moment longer, she jumped into the Farringdon carriage and ordered the coachman to take her back to Chester Square immediately. If Charlotte liked Giles so much, she could go home with him.

Hoping for some peace and quiet in which to gather her thoughts, she snatched her post and calling cards from the silver salver in the hallway and ran upstairs. Flicking through the envelopes, her heart flopped when she saw there was nothing from Tristan. Heedless of her smart afternoon attire, she threw herself onto the bed and, cuddling her beloved Miss Darcey, closed her eyes.

It was less than an hour later when her bedroom door burst open and an enraged Charlotte stormed in.

'How dare you abandon His Lordship like that,' she screamed. With her eyes blazing and hands on hips she looked like Boudica advancing into battle. 'Not only did he treat us to afternoon refreshments in arguably the most prestigious tea house in London, but he made his intentions of proposing to you abundantly clear.'

'I have been thinking things over and do not have any intention of marrying him, Step Mama,' Victoria said, propping herself up on her pillow.

'Now, you listen to me, young lady, we have an agreement; unless you want your Papa to find out about your impropriety in Surrey that so appalled the Countess of Kilcoyle, you will go out with Giles every time he invites you, otherwise . . . ' She left the sentence hanging in the air.

'Quite apart from the fact we hardly know each other,

I don't love him. Could never love him. Surely as a woman you must understand that; after all, you and Papa love each other,' she appealed.

'Love?' Charlotte spat. 'It is about duty. Besides, your father has never really loved me.'

'That's rubbish, he gives you everything you want,' Victoria cried. 'He panders to your every whim.'

Charlotte shook her head, a look of bleakness shadowing her eyes, but it was gone so quickly, Victoria thought she must have imagined it. 'That is hardly the same thing. Living with him is like walking in the shadow of a ghost. Your dear papa loved Beatrice, still loves her. I never stood a chance.'

Victoria stared at her stepmother in disbelief.

'Your Papa already feels let down not having an heir for his beloved Nettlecombe Manor. Don't you let him down too; it might be more than he could bear. He has high hopes of you marrying well. And an earl would make him exceedingly proud.' She shot Victoria a candid look then walked towards the door. 'But you are a sensible girl, aware of your duty. I know you will do the right thing, for him at least. Oh, by the way, as Nicholas is not here, you'd better give me the Farringdon pearls for safe keeping.'

In the space of a minute, Victoria had gone from anger to guilt and back to anger again. How could the woman be so calculating?

'I appear to have left them at Aunt Dorothea's,' she murmured, staring down at her lap.

'Surely not? How could you be so careless?' Charlotte snapped, peering around the room as if they might materialize in front of her.

'It wasn't my fault I had to pack so quickly,' Victoria retorted.

'For goodness' sake, Victoria, it is time you stopped cuddling dolls and concentrated on the things that matter in life. Like Giles. Write to Emmeline straight away and ask her to bring them when she returns,' Charlotte snapped. 'They are mine, after all.'

'Not if I have anything to do with it,' Victoria murmured, cuddling her doll tighter.

'You can also write to Giles, thanking him for his hospitality this afternoon. Tell him you will be delighted to accompany him to the opera house on Saturday evening.'

'What? But I have no int—'

'Do it, Victoria, or I shall be forced to write a letter myself, to your Papa,' she warned. 'Besides, I have already accepted the invitation, so it is only good manners for you to say how much you are looking forward to seeing him again.' With a satisfied smile, she sailed from the room.

No sooner had the door closed behind her than Victoria lifted the feathered hat from her doll's head and retrieved the string of South Sea pearls. 'You'll keep them safe for me, won't you, Miss Darcey,' she whispered, running her fingers lovingly over the lustrous gems. The doll stared back at her, rosebud mouth smiling and blue eyes twinkling as if to reassure her. But the twinkling eyes only served to remind her of Tristan, and she threw herself back on the bed, cuddling both the pearls and her doll tightly to her chest. What had the ebony-haired woman got that she hadn't? Or was he, like Giles suggested, a womanizer who delighted in the thrill of the chase?

Unable to bear her thoughts any longer, she wound the pearls back under the hat, readjusted the feathers and placed Miss Darcey on her bed again. Thinking she might as well attend to her mail, she picked up a thick envelope addressed in a female hand and quickly slit it open.

Dear Lady Farringdon,

I have a rather important and somewhat urgent matter I need to discuss with you. With that in mind I wish to call to see you on Thursday afternoon at two o'clock. I do hope you will forgive my impetuosity, but this really cannot wait.

Yours faithfully,
Eleanor Barrington

How intriguing, Victoria thought. She didn't recognize the name and wondered what the woman could possibly want. Well, it was Thursday tomorrow, which seemed a little presumptuous of this Eleanor Barrington, but at least it would give her the excuse of not having to receive any suitors.

Chapter 32

At breakfast the next morning, Victoria's stepmother wasted no time in reminding her of the wonderful opportunity she was being presented with.

'It is your duty to accept Giles' proposal the moment it is offered.'

'But it is all so sudden. I hardly know the man. I am not ready,' Victoria protested, feeling the room closing in on her.

'And that is just the way he wants you. Malleable, ready to be moulded to his requirements.'

'What, like some pet dog, you mean,' Victoria muttered. 'Surely, I have some say in all this?'

'Indeed, you do not. Need I remind you that the whole point of your coming out is for men to bid for you? You will never get a better offer than this. Women who do not secure a husband in their first Season can face a lifetime of spinster-hood,' Charlotte warned, fixing her with a glacial stare. 'You would be ostracized by polite society, never willingly invited to gatherings. In short, you would become a lonely old woman.'

Victoria laughed. 'Really, Step Mama, I am only eighteen.'

'And will attain your nineteenth birthday in two months' time. Clearly you do not understand the minds and workings of men. They like young flesh and next year there will be a new delivery of debutantes ripe for the taking. You are a virgin, I take it?'

Victoria shook her head at the woman's audacity.

'You are not?' the woman screeched, misunderstanding the gesture. 'I knew letting you roam the garden with that good-for-nothing grape picker was a mistake.' Her hand went to her throat, her eyelids fluttering closed. A moment later they snapped open again. 'Keep quiet and nobody need ever know any different. You will act the innocent, do you understand?'

'I have no need to act the innocent, Step Mama, because I am. However, I have heard more than enough, and this subject is at an end,' she declared.

'Very well, as long as you remember our pact. It is your choice, Victoria: you can either bring honour or disgrace on the Farringdon family.'

'All right, Step Mama, I hear you.' Victoria sighed, knowing when she was beaten. Poor Papa had enough on his plate without having to worry about her.

'Good, that is settled. One day, when you are happily ensconced in your castle entertaining and being entertained by the crème de la crème, you will thank me for this advice. Now, did you send a letter to Giles apologizing for your hasty departure yesterday, telling him how much you are looking forward to seeing him again on Saturday?'

'Yes, Step Mama.'

'Well, see that you tell the new maid that you intend wearing your gold gown so that she has it looking pristine.'

'I cannot wear that to the opera,' Victoria exclaimed, looking aghast. 'It is not appropriate.'

'Fiddlesticks. Giles has decreed you wear it at each event you attend in order that the announcement of your betrothal has maximum impact.'

'But—'

'There are no buts. You will wear it and that's the end of the matter. Whatever will he think if you can't obey the first simple request he makes of his future wife,' she said, dabbing her mouth delicately with her napkin and rising to her feet. 'Now, I am off to see Madame Helene about my outfit for your betrothal celebrations. Being the finest modiste in London, her engagement diary was fully booked but luckily when I explained the importance of the occasion, an appointment was found for me.'

'But how could you have possibly known? Giles hasn't even proposed yet . . . ' Victoria began, staring at her in surprise.

Charlotte gave a secret little smile. 'Preparation, Victoria. Think ahead, be prepared and you will sail efficiently and effortlessly through life. Now, whilst I am gone, I suggest you read this book I have prepared for you.' Looking as if she was passing over the crown jewels themselves, she presented Victoria with a burgundy leather-bound volume and swept from the room.

As the door closed behind her, Victoria looked down at the title penned in her elaborate script: *Acceptable Behaviour for a Society Wife*. Sighing, she turned to the first page.

*Remember you now belong to your husband. It is your
duty to do as he decrees, dress the way he requests, be
an entertaining and competent hostess.
Remember the rubrics . . .*

She sighed again, then quickly flicked through the pages that
listed rule after rule on how to conduct herself as a society
wife. She already knew she was expected to obey her husband
and that, on marriage, her assets would become his, but it
seemed she was expected to give him her soul as well. How
she wished Hester was here. What a scream they'd have
reading through these ridiculous rules together. She missed
her cousin and hoped it wouldn't be long before she returned
from Surrey. Thinking of Sunningdale immediately brought
an image of Tristan to mind, the happy afternoon they'd
spent exploring the garden, their embrace in the maze. She
sighed and shook her head. It was no good going down that
path when he'd obviously gone down another. Smiling wryly,
she jumped as a knock on the door startled her back to the
present.

'This has just arrived for you, Lady Victoria,' Jarvis
announced, placing a small package on the table before her.

'Thank you,' she said, reaching for the card that was
affixed. It was from Gabriel saying that, having listened to her
likes and wishes, he had created the perfume just for her. He
sincerely hoped she would like it and it would work its magic.

Blushing, as she remembered just how much she had
revealed in his workshop that Saturday morning, she was
thankful her stepmother hadn't been there. But then it was
because of the woman's behaviour she'd been forced into this

pact. Pushing those thoughts aside, she opened the box and gasped at the beautiful glass bottle etched with a delicate flower. Carefully lifting the crystal stopper, she inhaled. Immediately, the delightful fragrance of a summer garden in bloom filled her senses, reminding her again of that afternoon at Sunningdale with Tristan.

Gabriel had completely captured the essence of what she wanted, and she was thrilled. He'd even named it *Inoublie*, the French for 'unforgettable', as that was what she'd told him she wanted to be. She let out a bitter laugh. How ironic when Tristan obviously thought her the exact opposite. Blinking away the tears, she replaced the bottle in its box and took it upstairs to her room.

Hiding it at the back of her dressing table drawer, she rang for the new maid. Whilst the girl was eager to please, she had yet to anticipate Victoria's needs as Vanny had. How happy she had been to hear from Louisa that their lady's maid had been reinstated at Nettlecombe. She couldn't wait for her sister to arrive and tell her exactly what had transpired.

'Yes, m'lady?' the young girl asked.

'I need to make myself presentable for my visitor, Jones. As I don't know what she wishes to see me about, I shall play safe and wear my amethyst silk.'

*

'Miss Eleanor Barrington.' Jarvis announced.

Victoria looked up as the woman was shown into the drawing room, her eyes widening in astonishment, the smile of welcome freezing on her lips. It was the ebony-haired beauty from the ball at Sunningdale. Stylishly dressed in a deep-blue skirt with matching jacket and a crisp white blouse pinned at the neck with a sapphire brooch, she was even more stunning close up. No wonder Tristan had been enchanted by her. Good manners prevailing, she forced a smile.

'Good afternoon, Miss Barrington. Please do take a seat.' She gestured to the chaise opposite.

'Lady Farringdon, it is good of you to see me. You won't remember me, but I was a guest at the ball at Sunningdale. The countess kindly invited me. She knew of my interest, you see.'

In her son, of course, Victoria thought, trying to push away the image of them sitting close together.

'It was a delightful evening. Now, you said in your letter, you had something urgent you wished to discuss with me.'

'Yes, forgive me. It is about your beautiful gown. The fabric caught my eye when you were dancing in the candlelight, and I begged Tristan mercilessly to introduce me to you. Being the darling he is, he agreed, but when he went to find you, you were on the dance floor with his brother. Obviously, he couldn't interrupt although it was obvious Tristan wasn't happy. Anyway, we returned to Sunningdale the next day in the hope of seeing you but were told you had already left. I was so disappointed, my husband all but begged Tristan for your address. You see, I am an historian, specializing in material woven by the Huguenots. I have quite a collection of their various patterns,' she finished by way of explanation. But Victoria's mind was reeling.

'Your husband?'

'Yes, Maurice likes nothing better than the whisper of

a mystery. Well, he does own a newspaper. Ah, you are puzzling over my name. Here are my details,' she said, opening her reticule and extracting a card. 'I set up my little business before we married and, as I was gaining a reputation for my work, I continued using my maiden name. My married name is Wolverstone. Maurice is always joking that when I become rich, he will retire.'

For the first time that afternoon, Victoria's smile was genuine. Suddenly, the day seemed brighter, her heart began to sing. So, she wasn't with Tristan, after all.

'May I ask where you purchased the gown? It is quite exquisite and has obviously been sewn by a very talented dressmaker.'

'It was made by a seamstress in Devonshire, and she had the fabric in her storeroom,' Victoria said carefully, not wishing to give out Jane Haydon's name until she knew more about this woman. 'It was all very last minute and needed to be white silk for my presentation. I must admit she did a superb job.'

'She did indeed, especially as I believe the fabric to be pail red, which is notorious to work.'

'That is a funny name,' Victoria responded, recalling the letter she had translated for Jane.

'Distinctive, which is why I think the silk might have been woven by someone of Huguenot descent. This technique uses metallic threads that come alive by candlelight.'

'Well, that is certainly true of my golden gown,' Victoria agreed.

'I am already in possession of two gowns from that period, one made with orange thread, known as frost gold, the other blue, which is known as frost silver and shines like rime by the light of a candle. Lady Farringdon, would it be possible for me to see your gown?'

'Victoria, please, and I see no reason why you shouldn't,' she replied, pulling the bell for her maid. She would have let her see anything now she knew Tristan wasn't interested in her. Yet, if he wasn't, why hadn't he been in touch? There was no time to dwell on the subject for Jones appeared in the doorway.

'Please set out my golden gown in the drawing room next door,' she said. 'Then ask for refreshments to be ready for when we return.'

'This is extremely kind of you,' her visitor said. 'To be honest, I wasn't sure you would see me. That is, I thought your stepmother might object.'

'Luckily she is visiting her modiste,' Victoria grinned conspiratorially. 'Although I do have some say in what happens around here,' she added for good measure, if only to reassure herself. 'Come on, let us go through.' Victoria smiled, leading the way.

Jones was just finishing smoothing out the dress on the large walnut table, and the dark wood enhanced the fabric making it gleam.

'Oh my,' Eleanor exclaimed, excited and reverential at the same time. 'May I touch? I have worn white gloves especially, just in case.'

'Of course,' Victoria agreed, both amused and heartened by the woman's enthusiasm. It was some moments later when her visitor stepped back and nodded.

'I'm pretty sure this is a fine example of the pail red. It has the distinctive weave of the other metallic threaded fabrics I mentioned earlier.'

'You seem somewhat animated if you don't mind my mentioning it,' Victoria said. 'Perhaps some tea might be beneficial?'

'Yes, thank you,' the woman replied, yet she seemed reluctant to leave the gown, turning back to gaze at it from the doorway.

'Well, I am ready for refreshment,' Victoria prompted, leading the way back to the drawing room. 'Then you can tell me more.'

Whilst they had been gone, the tea things had been set out and Jarvis stood waiting. Although Victoria could see her visitor was bursting to ask questions, she refrained until their drink had been poured.

'Do at least have a scone; Cook has a very light touch,' Victoria urged, as the cake stand was proffered.

'Thank you but I am far too excited to eat anything,' Eleanor Barrington replied. She took a quick sip of tea then replaced her cup and saucer back on the table. 'This pattern was first designed by James Leman who become a master weaver. If this is the genuine example of his work that I believe it to be, it would complete my collection of his three metallic threaded designs. So, Lady Farringdon . . . Victoria, would you be prepared to sell it? I would pay a fair price.'

'Goodness, I would have to think about that. I mean the Season doesn't finish until the middle of next month.'

'When all the men return to their estates for the glorious twelfth and the grouse shooting.'

'Quite so. Between you and me, I find London is growing

ever hotter and malodourous, and cannot wait to return to the fresher air of Devonshire. It might rain more there, but I truly never want to live anywhere else.'

'What, even when you marry?' Eleanor asked. Then seeing Victoria's shocked expression, she promptly apologized.

'Sorry, me and my big mouth. Maurice always says I'm far too nosy, but I dare say it's to do with the nature of my work. Asking questions comes naturally.' She smiled ruefully.

'I can see that,' Victoria replied and, although she smiled, her visitor's words had got her thinking. Where was she going to live when she married?

'I know what I have said has come as a shock and you need time to think about selling your gown. Even if you were to agree, it couldn't be until the Season ends, but I wonder . . .' her voice trailed off and she fidgeted awkwardly in her seat.

'What do you wonder, Eleanor?' Victoria frowned.

'It is a terrible cheek, but could I perhaps borrow it, just for a couple of days or so? It would give me the opportunity to verify the threads and weave.'

Victoria opened her mouth to refuse, then reconsidered. She'd had more than enough of being dictated to, and if the gown wasn't here, she couldn't wear it to the opera, could she?

'Why not. I'll get Jones to pack it up. Is your carriage waiting outside?'

'I came by hansom cab and asked for it to return in . . .' she looked at the clock on the mantel and let out a squeal. 'About ten minutes.'

Once again Victoria tugged on the bell pull and instructed Jones to place the dress, carefully but speedily, into the box that was in her dressing room.

'That is so kind,' Eleanor gushed. 'And once I have completed my investigations, I will personally return it. I just wish I could find out how the fabric came to be in Devonshire.'

'Here is the card for Jane Haydon. She is the lady who supplied the silk and made my gown. If anyone can assist, it will be she. I will pen a note telling her she can expect to hear from you.'

Chapter 33

Although she had been here for over two months now and had adjusted to the regime of life at the Hospital for Gentlewomen During Illness and went about her work diligently, Bea was becoming increasingly dissatisfied. Most of the patients were friendly and appreciated the comfort she provided, but surely there was more to nursing than changing beds, washing, feeding, and pandering to their ill humours and megrims? Helping Ruby's Nan prepare and distil her remedies and seeing the benefits derived from them had made her eager to learn more about diagnosing and treating illness.

Inside the hospital the air was hot and humid, making the smell of chloride of lime that pervaded the building even stronger. The herbal aroma from Nan's balm that protected her hands from the worst of all the washing and scrubbing was infinitely preferable. Placing the last of the breakfast things on the hatch ready for them to be winched back down to the kitchen, she wiped her brow.

'Blimey, it's stickier than the porridge on them poor patients' plates. Me dress is sticking to me body and it's only nine o'clock,' Ruby moaned, hastily depositing her crockery then flapping her apron in front of her face to create a breeze. 'And it's old Lennox's day for doing his rounds so we'll have to rush around like blue ars—'

'Nurse Farringdon, report to ward three straight away.' Miss Ratcliffe's strident tones boomed down the corridor, interrupting their conversation. 'And kindly refrain from asking any more questions. You know how it annoys the doctor.'

'Yes, Matron,' Bea replied. How was she expected to learn if she couldn't enquire what was being diagnosed and prescribed?

'See yer later,' Ruby muttered, quickly disappearing in the other direction.

Walking briskly towards the ward, Bea saw that the early morning mist had given way to low cloud trapping what little air there was, while the open windows only served to let in buzzing bluebottles and other winged insects that feasted on the rubbish outside. There had been another outbreak of cholera on the outskirts of the city, and she recalled her discussion with Ruby's Nan about miasmata, particles in the air from decomposing matter, that travelled through the air causing illness. The woman had dismissed the theory, saying if that were the case everyone who breathed would be infected. Bea had to admit she had a point and hoped to ask the superintendent for her thoughts on the matter. However, Miss Nightingale was incredibly busy, and she had only caught fleeting glances of her hurrying about her business.

'At last, Nurse,' Dr Lennox snapped when she walked into the room. 'I have been waiting to examine Miss Pavey's knee.'

He looked pointedly at the clock then gestured impatiently to the bed.

'Yes, Doctor,' Bea replied, stifling a sigh as she pulled back the covers and carefully removed the dressing. If the man was in that much of a hurry, then surely he could have done it himself, she thought, eyeing the angry-looking sore with dismay.

'I think—' she began, only to be cut off as the physician held up his hand.

'You are not paid to think,' he replied, his voice so patronizing she had to control the childish impulse to put out her tongue. 'Ah. Hmm,' he murmured, then pressed the woman's skin causing her to cry out in pain and reach for Bea's hand.

'Surely if you . . . ' she ventured, unable to bear seeing unnecessary suffering. The doctor straightened, and despite his diminutive stature, managed to tower over her.

'So, Nurse Farringdon, not content with considering yourself an authority on nutrition, you now presume to have a superior knowledge of leg ulcers than I, the physician.' His bulging eyes glistened with contempt.

'Not at all, Doctor. However, when Firecracker, my horse, had—' she began.

'You dare to compare my patient with a horse?' he bellowed, his stethoscope bouncing wildly as he threw up his hands in disbelief.

'I only meant the pustule on the leg was—'

'Stand aside until I have finished my ministrations then you can make the bed, which is what you are employed to do,' he ordered.

'But I like Nurse holding my hand. It helps,' Miss Pavey ventured, sitting up straighter and glowering at the man.

'Oh, very well,' he sighed. 'But let us be clear who is trained to treat disease and disorder, and who is merely here to assist with the housekeeping.' As he bent again to study the festering sore, the woman shot Bea a sympathetic look. Then her grip tightened, and she squealed as her leg was twisted this way and that. 'Hmm, nothing one of my powders won't cure,' the man finally pronounced. 'Put the dressing back in place, Nurse, whilst I write a prescription for the apothecary.'

'But surely it needs a clean—' Bea began, remembering what she'd been taught. He leaned closer, his face red as the blood that was dripping onto the sheet.

'Go and report to Matron,' he snapped, flapping his hand as if she was a bothersome fly. 'Tell her to send me a nurse who knows her place and doesn't pester with inane questions.'

Fighting down her anger, Bea exited the room with as much dignity as she could muster. Physician or not, he had no right to speak to her like that. Remembering Firecracker had given her a sudden longing for home. How she missed him and wished she was back in the lush green of Devonshire, the wind in her hair as she put him through his paces.

'Don't let him get to you,' Salena murmured as Bea strode down the corridor, her face like thunder.

'But he treats me like a servant,' she protested.

'That's what we are to him. The secret is to smile and nod, then when he's gone carry on as you would normally. It's the only way with the likes of him, and I should know,' she grinned ruefully, her teeth gleaming ivory against her chocolate skin.

'But that sore is infected. It needs a poultice to draw out the poison, yet the doctor has written a prescription for one of his powders and I can't see how that will help.' She shrugged helplessly.

'Look, Bea, just agree with what he says, administer his powders as and when the apothecary dispenses them. If, in the meantime, something needs immediate attention, well, you know what to do . . . ' she gave a wink. 'Anyway, good news, Dr Lennox is moving on. My, you should see his replacement.' Salena grinned and rolled her eyes. 'Dark, broodingly handsome. I tell you, if I wasn't a happily married woman . . . ' she chuckled, then sobered as they heard footsteps approaching.

'If you nurses don't have any work to do, I can soon find you some.' They jumped as the figure of Matron materialized beside them. 'I thought I told you to assist Dr Lennox,' she added, fixing her penetrating stare on Bea.

'I did, Matron, but he's sent me to see you.'

'Which means that, despite my warning, you gave him the benefit of your wonderful wisdom,' she tutted and pursed her lips.

'All I said was— Bea began.

'Nurse Farringdon has explained what is required so I shall go and assist the doctor straight away,' Salena murmured, quickly disappearing in the direction Bea had just come from.

'I don't know what I'm going to do with you, Nurse, I really don't,' Matron sighed, holding up her hand as Bea opened her mouth to reply. 'I know you are well intentioned and wish to learn, but the first tenet of becoming a good nurse is discipline. Until you can do as you are told immediately and without question, you will not progress. Do I make myself clear?'

'Yes, Matron,' Bea replied, knowing it was no use arguing.

'There are pots waiting to be emptied and cleaned in the sluice. As they are inanimate objects and can't be questioned, you can make yourself useful in there. By the time you have done that, Dr Lennox will have finished his rounds and you can take the luncheon trays around.'

Bea's spirits sank. Was she never going to be anything better than a glorified skivvy?

Whether it was the heat getting to her, or the superior, high-handed attitude of Dr Lennox, by the time Bea pushed open the heavy door, her mood was as foul as the piles of pots that awaited her. Surely it wasn't asking too much to expect some sort of nursing training, she fumed, emptying the patients' morning detritus with more force than necessary. If she'd wanted to spend her time as a cleaner, she would have applied to become one. Although that seemed even more of a thankless task, she thought, remembering the women on their hands and knees, scrubbing the floors in the entrance hall, whilst people trampled mud all over them. When one had dared complain, an officious-looking man had pointed to the door saying if she wasn't happy, she could leave as others would be only too glad of her job.

Raging at the unfairness shown to women, she banged the pots in the sink with unnecessary force.

'Is everything all right in here?' an anxious voice asked. Whirling round, her elbow knocked a pot that was still waiting to be emptied. It hit the floor and she could only watch helplessly as the disgusting contents spread over the red quarry tiling.

'You made me jump,' Bea cried, as she found herself staring straight into the dark eyes of a good-looking young man.

'Oops,' he chuckled.

'It's not funny, especially in this weather,' she retorted, mortified at her carelessness.

'No, of course not. Sorry for startling you, but the door was open, and I was going to ask for directions to ward seven.'

Bea looked down, ashamed. Not only had she let her bad mood show, but she'd left the door open which was completely against hospital hygiene rules. She was about to apologize but he'd already picked up a cloth and was clearing up the mess. Quickly she bent to help but he shook his head.

'All done,' he announced, throwing the filthy cloth into the empty pot, and returning it to the side. As he carefully washed his hands, Bea couldn't help noticing how long his fingers were, how manicured his nails. Sensing her watching, he turned and smiled. 'I'd better be going if you can show me the way.'

Bea pointed him in the right direction but, before she could thank him, he disappeared through the door, carefully closing it behind him. What a nice man. He must have come to see one of the patients, she thought, wondering which of the governesses in ward seven would be the lucky recipient. Determined to make up for her petulance, she set about cleaning the pots until they shone.

An influx of patients over the next few days meant Bea was too busy changing bed linen, ferrying food and making sure they were comfortable to worry about Dr Lennox and his condescending attitude. She was surprised, therefore, when having been summoned to take a pot to ward three, she saw Dr Lennox attending to Miss Pavey, another man by his side.

'As you can see, the ulcer, which was badly infected, is now healing nicely. All down to my powders, of course,' he crowed.

'Well,' Bea exclaimed, knowing full well it had been the poultice Salena had applied that had drawn out the pus.

'Did you say something, Nurse?' Dr Lennox demanded, a scowl on his face as he turned to face her. Then the other man straightened, his dark eyes twinkling with amusement as he gazed at Bea.

'Hello again,' he murmured. Bea's stomach flipped as she recognized the handsome man she'd encountered in the sluice. 'Dr Gascoine, newly appointed,' he elaborated. Her heart flopped. Supposing he told Dr Lennox she'd left the door open?

'Can we concentrate on the job in hand? Time is money,' Dr Lennox growled.

'Of course, sir,' he replied gravely, darting a wink at Bea before turning back to Miss Pavey's knee. 'You say it was the powder that caused this miraculous healing?'

'Indeed. Now, my boy, you have the benefit of my wisdom for the rest of the day, so observe closely and learn.'

'Are you going to be much longer, Doctor, only my bladder's bursting,' Miss Pavey cried.

'Nurse, attend to, er, that . . . ' Dr Lennox grimaced, waving his hand at the pot in Bea's hand. 'Then see the dressing is replaced and the bed made properly. Your hospital corners were all askew last time.'

'But—' Bea began, about to remind him that he'd dismissed her before she'd finished last week, but he had already turned to leave.

'Make sure you keep these nurses in their place, Dr Gascoine. Especially that one. She's a troublemaker. Does nothing but ask questions. Fancies herself a doctor, if you ask me. As if a mere female would be intelligent enough to . . . '

The rest of his sentence was lost as he headed towards the door. Incensed, Bea raised the pot and was just taking aim when the young man turned round. He held his hands up in mock surrender and, ashamed to be caught out once again, she lowered her arm.

'I was just going to say that I think a woman doctor would be of great benefit to medicine,' he murmured. 'And as long as you refrain from throwing those pots, I'm sure we are going to get along just fine.'

Bea smiled, her spirits rising. She thought they would get along just fine too.

'I think you've made a conquest there, Nurse,' Miss Pavey said, sitting up straighter in the bed and grinning broadly. 'But please could I have that pot now?'

Chapter 34

'Nurse Farringdon, Dr Gascoine informs me he is having difficulty orientating himself to the layout of the wards so you will accompany him on his rounds this morning,' Miss Ratcliffe said. 'Although I'd appreciate you not bombarding him with too many questions on his first day of duty.' Whilst her expression was serious, Bea detected a slight twinkle in her eye.

'Yes, Matron,' she replied, spirits soaring. Making her way from the room, she ignored the envious looks of the other nurses. She wanted to learn and was going to make the most of this opportunity.

'Right, lead on, Nurse,' Dr Gascoine said, looking up from the notes he was studying and smiling. 'I believe I am to see Miss Carter who is suffering from headaches and an irritating cough first.' He tucked the file under his arm and began striding down the corridor.

'I thought you didn't know where the wards were,' Bea cried.

'Ah, you've caught me out,' he admitted. 'Frankly, I find your enthusiasm heartening and feedback from patients informs me you are one of the most popular nurses here, so who better to accompany me on my first day solo, as it were. Although, I had the benefit of Dr Lennox's wisdom, of course.' He shot her a rueful look, and she couldn't help but grin. 'How are you finding nursing here?'

'Honestly? I'm finding it all a little tame and not what I'd envisaged. Whilst most of the patients are pleasant and grateful for all we do, none of them are really that ill, are they?'

'Well, as they have to produce a certificate from their physician confirming they have no infectious disease or mental illness before they can be admitted, I suppose they can't be. However, we must remember that their ailments seem serious to them. We must respect that and do everything we can to make them feel better. Now, I believe our first patient is in here,' he added, knocking and pushing open the door.

'Good morning, Miss Carter, and how are you feeling today?' he asked cheerily. A pretty woman in her mid-twenties, she stared at him dolefully.

'Those megrims are plaguing me, Doctor, and I've been coughing so much it's made my, er, front hurt,' she replied, staring quickly at Bea.

'Don't worry, Miss Carter, Doctor here will make you better,' she replied.

'He isn't going to touch my, well, you know,' the woman cried, panic flaring in her eyes as she covered her chest with her hands.

'Of course not, Miss Carter,' Dr Gascoine reassured her. 'I'm just going to have a little listen through this,' he told her, holding up his stethoscope. 'Now, hold Nurse Farringdon's hand and no talking or it will look as though I'm listening in to a private conversation,' he joked. Reassured, the woman lay back against her pillow. 'There, that didn't hurt, did it?'

'No,' she admitted. 'But I don't want one of them leather plaster things with opium on my chest. My grandmother died because of that. She was still coughing up phlegm too.'

'Indeed? Do coughs run in your family then?'

'Yes, we've all got weak chests and this cough is racking,' she admitted.

'I see. Well, Miss Carter, your cough is not racking, as you put it, and you certainly do not require a plaster of that nature. As for your megrims, all our inner workings are connected so I'm sure one is exacerbating the other.'

'Really? My, I had never thought of that,' the woman exclaimed. 'You are clever, Doctor.'

'It is what I am trained for. I will get something made up to treat both your ailments and will call in and see you again soon to make sure it is working.'

'Thank you, Doctor.' She smiled, relief evident in her voice. 'How long do you think I will be in here?'

'A week, maybe two. We must ensure you are on the mend before you are discharged.'

'Oh,' she sighed.

'I expect being a governess you are missing your charge,' Bea said, patting her hand reassuringly. 'Don't worry, you will soon be back home and part of the family again.'

'I am missing Master William, although he runs me a merry dance,' she said, shaking her head. 'The strange thing about being a governess is that you are by yourself really, above the servants yet not part of the family. It can be quite lonely in the evenings.'

'Goodness, I've never thought of it like that before,' Bea told her, thinking of Nanny, who'd always seemed like one of the family to her. 'Now lie back and relax. I'll bring your medicine to you as soon as it has been dispensed.'

In the corridor, Dr Gascoine turned to Bea.

'Well, Nurse, what is your diagnosis and recommended treatment for Miss Carter?'

'You are asking for my opinion?' she cried, staring at him in surprise.

'I am. Did you not want to learn more?'

'Goodness, yes,' she answered, grinning. 'Nanny gave us honey for a tickly cough or there's always sticklewort. As for the megrims, lavender would relieve anxiety and help her relax,' she told him. Then, remembering what Ruby's Nan had said, she added, 'Although of course you might not believe in the old remedies.'

'Whilst medicine has made enormous advances, I still see value in the natural ways and don't see why they cannot be used together. You are certainly on the right track. Oh, and by the way, Dr Lennox was wrong about women in medicine for in 1849 Elizabeth Blackwell gained her medical degree in America.'

'Really? So there is hope after all?'

He laughed. 'Indeed. Hope, study and a lot of hard work. Now, on to the next patient.'

*

'I'm looking forward to meeting your family,' Ruby said, as they made their way through the busy streets. 'I hopes I don't let you down though.'

'Whyever would you?' Bea asked, staring at her friend in

surprise. 'Your Nan always makes me welcome, so now it's my turn to reciprocate. You'll love Victoria, and my cousin Hester's a hoot.'

'And you're pretty chirpy yourself since Dr Gascoine started,' Ruby said, grinning. 'Don't think we haven't all noticed how he seeks you out.'

'I've learned so much from him. His approach to dealing with patients is completely different.'

'And your interest has nothing to do with his handsome looks, I suppose?' she teased, darting Bea a knowing look.

It was another sweltering July day and they hurried along the busy streets, each holding one of Nan's perfumed pouches to their noses to ward off the noxious odours that seemed stronger every time they ventured out of the hospital. Soot from the countless chimneys cast a pall over everything and, before long, Bea felt as if she was covered in smuts. She would have hailed a hansom but was conscious that Ruby would insist on paying her share, even though she could ill afford it. She was coming to realize how important pride was to the people she worked with.

'I'm surprised your family hasn't returned to their country house to escape all this,' Ruby said, gesturing to the piles of horse dung and garbage that littered the roads and walkways.

'Papa and Louisa are in Devonshire, but Step Mama insists Victoria remains in London until the Season ends.'

Thankfully, the closer they got to Chester Square, the better the streets became, no doubt because of the street cleaners that worked tirelessly to clear the detritus. It was funny how she was now aware of things she'd never even considered before.

It had been an age since she'd last seen her sister and Bea

couldn't wait to hear all the details about the high life of society.

'Here we are,' she said, indicating a town house with its arched windows and black railings.

'Coo, it's a tall one, isn't it?' Ruby gasped, staring up at the five storeys. 'And it's got a basement,' she added, peering through the palings. Which floor's your family got?'

'Aunt and Uncle occupy them all although Step Mama and Victoria are staying for the Season,' Bea told her, tripping up the steps and ringing the bell.

They were admitted by the footman and Bea smiled at Ruby's wide-eyed gaze as he took their cloaks.

'Blimey, you can see your face in them floor tiles,' she murmured, staring around the spacious hallway. 'This hall's bigger than Nan's whole home. And she'd love these,' she added, pointing to the bright blooms in the large vase on the mahogany table.

'Bea, come on up,' Victoria called from the top of the stairs. 'Oh, it is lovely to see you again,' she greeted her sister.

'It seems like for ever,' Bea cried, returning her embrace. 'And this is my friend Ruby Grey. Ruby, meet my sister Victoria.'

'Charmed, I'm sure,' Ruby murmured, dipping a bob.

'We don't go in for all that,' Bea chuckled. 'Well, Step Mama might. Where is the old . . . I mean is she waiting in the drawing room?'

'Step Mama always goes out on Saturday, which means we can chat in peace. Aunt Emmeline and Hester are still in Surrey and Uncle is staying at his club until they return. Now take a seat while I ring for some refreshments and then you must tell me all about life as a nurse.'

'I'd rather hear about your beaus and balls,' Bea told her.

'And I'd love to see the golden dress that was in the illustrated paper,' Ruby cried, sinking into the chaise with a sigh.

'Ah well, there is a story to that,' Victoria admitted, nodding as the footman and a maid appeared bearing silver salvers.

'Well, come on then. Tell all,' Bea urged as soon as they were settled with their drinks. 'How many handsome suitors have come calling and have any made a bid for you?'

'Ugh, that sounds like you're being bought,' Ruby said, grimacing. 'I thought it was all romance and dancing in the moonlight with you nobs. Begging your pardon, your ladyship.'

'That's all right, Ruby. And please call me Victoria. I've had many suitors but only one, called Tristan, whom I really liked, but that didn't work out. However, his older brother Giles has declared his interest and Step Mama insists I must accept the moment he proposes. His mother is a countess, and he will become an earl so . . . ' She shrugged.

'Enough said,' Bea sympathized. 'What is he like? I mean you do like him enough to marry?'

'Like? You like a cat or a dog. Surely you're meant to love the man you marry?' Ruby cried. 'I mean you have to . . . well, you know,' she stuttered, her cheeks flushing.

'Step Mama has other ideas,' Victoria sighed. 'It is all about duty and family honour.'

'Everything is about appearance with Charlotte. You'll understand better when you meet her,' Bea told Ruby. 'Although Papa won't want you to wed someone you're not happy with, Victoria. Tell us about the dress,' she urged, hating to see her sister looking uncomfortable. 'It is the one Jane Haydon made, I take it?'

'Yes, it is,' Victoria nodded, brightening. 'And it has been well received in society, which is why Giles insists I wear it every time I'm seen out with him.'

'Blimey, he sounds arrogant,' Ruby muttered. 'Not sure I'd want to marry someone who tells me what to wear. In fact, I couldn't. You should stand up for yourself, girl.'

'Well, it is funny you should say that.' Victoria smiled and proceeded to tell them about her visit from Miss Barrington. 'Step Mama was apoplectic when I admitted I'd let her take the gown away so that she could check the fabric was the pail-red thread. And Giles was livid when I appeared in emerald-green velvet, saying I had completely ruined the image he was creating.'

'But you're pretty as a picture. He should be proud to be seen with you, whatever you choose to wear,' Ruby declared hotly. 'I've heard me lather talk about them threads that shine in the candlelight. He has a stall on Spitalfields Market and I'm sure he said it was something to do with them Huguenots. They were wonderful weavers apparently, worked out of the market and, although it was all a long time ago, they are still well regarded. I could ask him if you like?'

'I told Miss Barrington I would pass on any information so that would be very helpful, Ruby. Thank you. Hm, who is your lather?' Victoria frowned.

'Me father,' Ruby laughed, shaking her head. 'It's the way we speak in our part of London.'

'I see. Well, I have also written to Jane Haydon saying

Miss Barrington will be in touch with her; perhaps I should let Louisa know as well.'

'Good idea. I've heard from Louisa myself, and she is hoping to visit soon. Wouldn't it be lovely if we could all get together? There is so much to tell you, however, that's enough about me. Tell me about life at the hospital. Are you enjoying nursing?'

'Oh yes, especially now Dr Gascoine has joined us.'

'He's really handsome and has taken a shine to Bea,' Ruby chuckled.

'Do tell me more,' Victoria urged, sitting forward in her seat.

Bea explained how the doctor encouraged her nursing, then went on to tell her about helping Ruby's Nan make her herbal remedies.

'That sounds fascinating. When we visited Surrey, I had the pleasure of watching a perfumer making fragrances from flowers. In fact—' She was interrupted mid-sentence as Charlotte burst into the room, wrinkling her nose in distaste.

'What on earth is that dreadful smell? Oh, Beatrice, it is you.'

'Thank you, Step Mama, and good afternoon to you too,' Bea responded. 'This is my friend and fellow nurse Ruby Grey. Ruby, meet my stepmother, Charlotte Farringdon.'

'Lady Farringdon please,' Charlotte retorted.

'Pleased to meet you, Lady Farringdon,' Ruby greeted her.

'Goodness, your voice does jar on one's nerves. Surely someone has suggested you modulate it. Now, will someone please tell me what that obnoxious odour is?'

'Didn't notice it until a couple of minutes ago,' Ruby muttered, looking pointedly at Charlotte.

'It's probably the chloride of lime they use to keep the hospital clean. It clings to our clothes and hair somewhat,' Bea said quickly.

'Hospital? Keep it clean? Dear heavens, I hope you haven't brought some deadly disease into the house.'

'We cure our patients, not kill them,' Ruby retorted.

'Well, you'd better go back to them then,' Charlotte snapped. 'Victoria, it is time you began making yourself beautiful for Giles. He is going to be an earl, you know,' she added, turning to Beatrice.

'Yes, we heard,' she replied. 'The question is, will he make Victoria happy?'

'It is Victoria's duty to make a good marriage. And it should be yours too, Beatrice,' she sniffed.

'Papa gave his consent for me to become a nurse,' Bea told her. 'The question is, does he know about this Giles?'

'Do not concern yourself, Beatrice, I am taking care of everything,' Charlotte told her.

'That's what worries me,' Bea replied. 'Are you sure this is what you want?' she asked Victoria.

'If it isn't, you should say so now. Have the courage to marry who you really want; you'll never be happy else,' Ruby insisted.

'Fiddlesticks, girl. It is patently clear you do not have the first idea of what constitutes a decent marriage. Now it is time you left so that Victoria can prepare for her evening engagement with Giles,' Charlotte said, flapping her hands at them.

'I will show you out,' Victoria said, jumping to her feet and leading the way out. 'There's still so much to discuss, Bea; can we meet for afternoon tea when Louisa arrives?'

'Of course. I was expecting to find you happy as a lark, yet you look as if you have the weight of the world on your shoulders. Don't let Step Mama bully you, Victoria. This Giles cannot make a formal proposal until he has spoken to Papa,' Bea whispered, throwing her arms around her sister's shoulders.

If only life were that easy, Victoria thought.

Chapter 35

Jane's mind was whirling as she checked the Receiving Room was tidy for Lady Connaught's visit. Word of her lace engageantes was still spreading amongst the society ladies of London and commissions arrived seemingly with every post. Meanwhile, her reputation for making quality corsets that fitted well ensured her appointment book was full for the foreseeable future. With so much to do, she regretted the impetuous stand she'd made about not keeping the sewing machine.

With more orders than fabric to fulfil them, and a visit from the merchant's agent imminent, she was racking her brains as to how to persuade him to let her have more. Yet, deep down, she knew it was futile, for whilst she still owed money, there was no hope of placing any more orders or getting back her beloved bobbin. Mr Fairfax might still be away, but his men ensured business kept running in his absence and they were not known for having sympathetic natures. With a sigh, she returned her thoughts to the present.

If Lady Connaught decided to place a commission, she was going to be in a terrible predicament. As her patron, she quite rightly expected priority treatment, but Jane couldn't magic fabric out of thin air, especially that of the quality the woman was used to.

'Lady Connaught, Miss Haydon,' Hope announced. Elegant in her favourite pastel pink dress, the lady glided into the room.

'Lady Connaught, how lovely to see you. Ask Millie to bring in refreshments, please, Miss Brown.'

'I can't tell you how much it pleases me to see your business flourishing, my dear,' she said, taking the seat Jane proffered. 'Your window display is positively tantalizing and those delightful engageantes make me wish I were a young debutante again. Such an ingenious idea to incorporate our local pillow lace. It is far superior to that made by machinery and wonderful to think our lovely ladies are gainfully employed once again. Obviously, my fears that you weren't coping were groundless.'

'I appreciate your concern, Lady Connaught, and, actually, you—'

'No, you have my admiration, and I am the first to admit when I have been wrong,' Lady Connaught said, holding up her hand to prevent Jane saying any more. 'I understand from Lady Louisa that you are also keeping her Quarry Crafters at Combe busy. It is so important that those women can earn a wage and feed their children.'

'Actually, it was Lady Louisa's idea to use the pillow lace,' Jane told her, thinking it wrong to accept the credit herself.

'Well, you obviously work well together, and I am pleased she has something useful to occupy her mind. I gather she is anticipating the early return of Captain Beauchamp but reports on the Crimean War would suggest otherwise. We shall just have to pray for his safe homecoming. Now, I notice young Hope is blossoming, which leads me to—'

'Here we is, Lady C, yous favourite sponge cake,' Millie chirped, entering the room backwards as was her way, no matter how many times Jane asked her not to.

'Good morning, Millicent. How lovely to see you again, and cake in the morning, what a delightful and sinful treat.'

'A bit of what yous fancy and all that. My Bert says when we's wed he's going to be the best fed man in Salthaven, although I'm not to tell his ma that, of course,' she giggled.

'You mean you are betrothed, Millie? My sincere congratulations.'

'Ta, Lady C. Cors, I don't want to leave Jane here in the lurch, so I told Bert, he'll have to bide his time but yous know what men's like, they want their—'

'Thank you, Millie, I will pour,' Jane said quickly.

'Yous always says that, even when yous eyelids is dropping of a night.'

'Goodness, what wonderful news. Millie is so good-hearted she'll make a wonderful wife and mother. However, I do hope you are not overdoing things,' Lady Connaught said, studying Jane closely after the maid had left.

'Not at all, Millie is prone to exaggeration,' Jane replied, not for the first time wishing the girl would hold her counsel.

'Hmm,' Lady Connaught murmured. 'Having expanded business so successfully, you must be really busy. As I was saying earlier, Hope is doing so well under your tutelage, and I remember what you said about opening a sewing school. Oh, not yet,' she said quickly, as Jane looked alarmed. 'However, I was hoping you might consider taking on another girl from the orphanage. Sunny, so named because she is always smiling, was another unfortunate abandoned baby. She is twelve years old, bright, with neat stitching. However, she is also suffering the same unwanted attention of the housemaster. Really that man needs stringing up, but of course, he denies any wrongdoing, and these things can never be proven.'

'I feel sorry for this Sunny, of course, but—' Jane began, wondering if she dare broach the delicate subject of money. Extra sponsorship could be the answer to her problem.

'Good, that's settled then,' Lady Connaught said, finishing her cake and sighing contentedly. 'That Millie does have a light hand. Now don't you worry about funding. Hope tells me she is earning her keep now, so I will transfer my sponsorship to Sunny. I will send her along to see you tomorrow.'

'Thank you,' Jane replied faintly, wondering why she was surprised at the speed with which Lady Connaught accomplished her missions. 'I'll show you out,' she added as the woman rose to her feet.

'I can save you the bother of finding a replacement for Millie too. There are any number of bright girls at the home who would jump at the opportunity. Despite the training they receive, some still end up in the workhouse and I always feel a sense of achievement when I can prevent that from happening. In fact, when you are ready to open your sewing school, we could work in partnership to that end. Now, I really must go. I will make an appointment with Hope for a consultation in the autumn. My, the seasons change so quickly, do they not?'

Yes, they did, Jane thought, as Lady Connaught made her elegant exit. Although it was only July, the reminder that autumn wasn't far away was another concern, for Michaelmas was when the next quarter's rent was due. It was also the end of her first six months of trading when she was expected to show a profit. And now she had to fund Hope's wages as well. Although it was true the girl was beginning to earn her keep, she still needed training and overseeing, as would this new girl Sunny. She felt like a swan, serene on the surface yet frantically paddling under the water to keep afloat.

'Oh, Madame Pittier, how did you manage?' she cried, picking up the glass bowl of petals and inhaling the reviving fragrance of eau de rose.

'*By careful management and not running before I could walk. Keep going, keep sewing, you will win through.*'

'How I wish I could believe you,' she sighed.

'*Help others and others will help you.*' As if she was standing beside her, Jane heard her gentle words of encouragement.

'Thank you, Madame, but despite having kept on going and sewing, the only way I seem to be going is backwards.' But the room was heavy with silence.

Jane sighed. The last thing she wanted was Madame to be disappointed in her, but what more could she do? While she wanted to help the poor girls from the orphanage, and had derived enormous satisfaction from training Hope, she still had her business to run and corsets to sew. Nevertheless, she stared around, visualizing the room full of young apprentices eager to learn. As she wouldn't be marrying and having children of her own, they could become her family. A tingle of excitement ran up her spine.

Then she caught sight of the card on the mantel and reality returned. Lady Victoria had written introducing a Miss

Barrington, who apparently studied the origins of historical gowns and fabrics. The woman wished to call on her to discuss Victoria's debut gown and had made an appointment to visit this afternoon. She could barely spare the time to entertain someone who was unlikely to become a client, and yet she could hardly refuse a request from Victoria. Jane glanced at the clock; there was just time to finish sewing the corset for tomorrow's client. She would do as Madame advised: keep on going and keep on sewing, and see where it got her.

*

'Miss Barrington,' Hope announced, stepping back as the dark-haired woman dressed in dark-blue afternoon attire stepped into the room. 'Will you be wanting refreshments, only it is Millie's afternoon off?'

'Please do not worry on my account,' the woman said quickly. 'Thank you so much for seeing me, Miss Haydon.' Her smile was warm, and Jane took to her immediately.

'It is my pleasure, Miss Barrington. Won't you take a seat,' she replied, gesturing to the chaise.

'Please call me Eleanor. What a beautiful room, and so fragrant, just like your lovely shop.'

'Thank you, Eleanor. And you must call me Jane. Lady Victoria wrote telling me you are interested in her debut gown.'

'Oh, indeed I am. It is beautiful, exquisitely stitched and, believe you me, I have seen many gorgeous gowns. I am a collector, you see, interested in the history of fabric and it has now been confirmed that the thread running through

334

the silk is pail red,' Miss Barrington told her excitedly. 'This particular pattern was first designed by a Huguenot weaver, James Leman.'

Jane frowned. 'I'm afraid the name means nothing to me.'

'It wouldn't to most people. I've become known for seeking out the origins of unusual weaves and have been fortunate to be shown old patterns by someone who currently has a stall in Spitalfields. They are very proud of their history there, you see. Could you possibly tell me how this particular fabric came to be in your possession?'

'It belonged to my old employer who sadly died and left me her business. I was going to use it for my own wedding gown, but my betrothed was killed earlier this year.'

'I am so sorry,' the woman murmured. 'That must have been terrible for you. And yet you used it to make Lady Victoria's debut gown?'

'She needed one made urgently and it was the only suitable silk in my workroom . . . ' Jane shrugged. 'I couldn't disappoint her.'

'If you don't mind me saying, that was incredibly generous of you.'

'She paid me for making it, so . . . ' Jane continued, blinking back the tears the mention of Sam still invoked.

'Lady Victoria did mention that. Also, that you found a letter with the fabric?'

'Goodness, I'd forgotten about that,' Jane exclaimed.

'Would it be possible for me to see it? For authenticity, or provenance, as we call it in the business.'

'You can, although it is written in French,' Jane said, going over to the desk and taking out the yellowing sheet of paper she'd placed inside a book for safe keeping. 'Madame was named Rosetta,' she added, handing it over. There was silence as Eleanor read then reread the letter.

'You'll know that this is a love letter, of course,' she cried, her eyes glittering with excitement. 'And it certainly confirms the origin of the fabric. Was this hidden inside?'

'Actually, it was in a parcel containing mother of pearl buttons.'

'The ones on the dress?'

Jane nodded. 'They were a perfect match.'

'Oh, this just gets better and better,' Eleanor cried. 'I've been puzzling how this particular fabric could have been woven so long after Leman's demise. Being a master weaver, he obviously passed the pattern on to another. And Jean Pittier says here he was trained by a master. I cannot tell you how thrilling this is.'

'Would Jean Pittier have been of Huguenot descent?'

'His name would suggest it likely. Why do you ask?'

'Because when I first unwrapped the fabric, I heard the clattering of looms and men's voices singing in a foreign tongue. The same thing happened when I found the package under the table, then again when I was sewing the gown. Yet as soon as it was finished, they just disappeared. I thought perhaps I was going mad.'

'I am sure that was not the case. Do you think it was a portent?'

'Well, Madame Pittier was prone to believe in things like that. In fact, I am sure I have heard her voice too, at times. Do you think me fanciful?'

'Indeed, I do not. You would be surprised at the strange

336

things that have occurred when spirits from the past have a message or wish to make their feelings known. You say Madame Pittier, so if she got to marry this, Jean . . . sorry, I am now being too inquisitive.'

'Not at all. Madame told me her beloved had died before they could wed. Madame is a name used as a mark of respect for women in business, and I always assumed her own surname was Pittier. However, it would appear she assumed his name.'

'How tragic and yet it is such a romantic story, is it not?' Eleanor leaned forward in her chair. 'It would be an honour to display the gown with the pail-red thread along with its history. I've already been fortunate enough to acquire the other two in this collection, one in the orange indicating frost gold, the other in blue, frost silver. This gown would go on public display, and you would, of course, be invited to the opening night. So, what do you say, Jane? Would you be willing to sell it to me? I will pay you a fair price.'

'You would have to discuss that with Lady Victoria. It is her gown, after all, and she paid me a fair price for the silk and making it.'

'But that was before she knew its true value. You see, it is worth twenty times that amount.'

'Gracious me,' Jane murmured, her hand flying to her mouth. She'd thought Victoria had been more than generous and had been happy with the sum pressed upon her.

'Lady Victoria is happy for me to have it for my collection but insists it only right the money be paid to you.' She picked up her reticule and drew out an envelope. 'Please take it. You will be making so many people happy if you agree.'

Jane stared at the package and could tell by the thickness

it contained a large sum. Enough to pay her bills, buy more fabric, pay Hope's wages. She reached out her hand then snatched it back.

'It doesn't seem right,' she whispered.

'But it is. That fabric was yours and it is only because you so generously allowed Lady Victoria to have it that the truth of it became known. If you could agree to let me keep the letter to show alongside the gown . . . oh, my goodness, in all the excitement, I quite forgot, I have a letter she's penned to you, to that effect.'

As Jane read the heartfelt message from Victoria telling her how badly she felt for paying her so little for the fabric and begging her to accept its true worth so that her conscience would be clear, she felt her resistance fading.

'Just think what this would do for your business,' Eleanor murmured, watching Jane carefully as dangled the envelope before her.

'Thank you, I shall accept and will write to Lady Victoria telling her that I intend using the money to set up an apprentice sewing school for girls from local orphanages. Hopefully she will see that it will give them a good start in life and keep them from the workhouse.'

'Well done, Jane. Didn't I always say, do good to others and good will come to you.'

Jane Haydon, Proprietor and Patron, had a certain ring to it. Jane smiled, happy to give real purpose to her life and happy to be able to retrieve her beloved bobbin.

Chapter 36

'Oh, Louisa, am I pleased to see you,' Victoria told her sister as they settled on the chairs in the upstairs sitting room, a tray of tea and biscuits before them. 'It has been so lonely with only the servants in the house. And that monstrosity is driving me mad,' she added, gesturing to the gold and pink porcelain timepiece with its scroll and floral decoration on the mantel.

'It is somewhat loud, isn't it?' Louisa said, shaking her head at the cherub trumpeting the hour. Then she frowned and turned to her sister. 'Wait a minute, did you say you've been by yourself? I thought Step Mama was meant to be your chaperone.'

'That's the strange thing. She was positively relishing that duty, hobnobbing with the ton, encouraging – no, insisting – I accept the suit of a future earl. Then she went out in the carriage yesterday and never returned.'

'You mean she simply abandoned you?' Louisa frowned. 'Where is Aunt Emmeline?'

'She and Hester are due to return from Surrey later today.'

'What about Uncle Nicholas?'

'He and Step Mama had a terrible row when we arrived back from Sunningdale. I was sent up here and couldn't hear the exact words, but the gist was he wasn't prepared to be part of any impropriety. He stormed out, saying he would be staying at his club until Aunt Emmeline returned.' She was too embarrassed to admit she was afraid he'd been referring to her own behaviour.

'You mean he knows what Step Mama's been up to?' Louisa asked. 'Vanny's told me about her outings with this Alexander Clarke and—'

'I must confess I had my suspicions,' Victoria cut in. 'He worked with Uncle Nicholas, but I understand he was sent packing weeks ago. Although, that hasn't stopped Step Mama going out by herself.'

'Really?' Louisa asked, a frown puckering her brow.

'Yes, but tell me how Vanny is? Step Mama said she had to go home as her father was ill, yet I'm sure she told us he died years ago.'

'And that is true. However, it seems someone saw Step Mama out with another man in Surrey. Fearing it was Vanny she sent her packing. Thankfully, no harm came to her, but I was outraged when I heard how dreadfully she'd been treated.'

'I knew Vanny was keeping something from me and tried to speak to her about it on a couple of occasions, but with so much happening . . . ' Victoria shrugged. 'Wait a minute, did you say Step Mama was seen with another man in Surrey?' she asked, frowning as she thought back to that weekend at Dorothea's. They had only been at Sunningdale for a couple of days and having spent Friday all together, Charlotte could only have met him on the Saturday. Had taking her to the perfumery been her stepmother's alibi?

'I did, and if word gets back to Papa, the tittle-tattle and shame would destroy him. That is why I have come here to have it out with her, and I intend waiting until she returns.'

'Goodness, Louisa, you are brave. I wonder who this other man is?'

'Some dastardly low life with no morals, I should think, although Vanny did mention she thought him titled,' Louisa replied. 'Anyway, she is safely back at Nettlecombe Manor and now her mother is gainfully employed making the lace for Jane Haydon's engageantes. At least something good has come out of the situation. I really thought I had a reasonable understanding of the families of Combe, but this has made me realize how little I really know about how they have to live.'

'I know what you mean; I helped Aunt Emmeline at Haven House, the refuge she set up, and the state of the poor women there beggars belief.'

'Anyway, to happier things, how has the Season been?'

'I don't think I'm cut out for society life with its endless balls, boring soirees, and excruciating recitals.' She grimaced. 'It's all so calculated. You can think yourself lucky to have missed the marriage mart. Have you heard from Henry?'

'Not for a while.' Louisa sighed. 'To be honest, I've been deluding myself he will be returning soon, when the reality is the war is escalating.' She shrugged. 'Anyhow, what about you, sister dear? Vanny told me about Lord Newton Berwick.'

'Which one?' Victoria said bitterly. She leaned forward in her seat, and, like a dam bursting, the events of the past

341

weeks came pouring out, although she still couldn't bring herself to mention the pact she'd been coerced into agreeing to.

'Let me get this right, Tristan Newton Berwick, the man you thought was as smitten as you, and whom Vanny told me about, has been usurped by his elder brother, Giles. He has made a bid for you which Step Mama is actively encouraging because he will inherit a title?'

'Along with vast estates all over the country,' Victoria added.

'Clearly you are not enamoured with the idea which leads me to believe you are still yearning for Tristan.'

'I can't help it,' Victoria admitted. 'He was full of fun and good humour. I could have sworn he felt the same as I did. Obviously, I was mistaken. By comparison, Giles is cold and arrogant. Frankly, he is beginning to force his wishes, ably assisted by Step Mama, of course.'

'I see. Giles cannot make his suit until he has spoken to Papa, who hopes you will make a favourable marriage, but would never want you to be unhappy.'

'That is what Bea said when she visited. By the way, she suggested we all meet for tea one afternoon.'

'I'd like that,' Louisa said. 'We have never been apart for this long before, have we? Don't worry, things have a habit of working out.'

'I can't see how. Tristan has made it plain I am forgettable when I so wanted to be the opposite.' Her eyes narrowed as she thought of the bespoke fragrance and how those hours spent with the perfumer were now being used against her. She'd never kept anything from her sister before yet her look of disgust and disappointment was more than she could bear.

It would make no difference that she'd had no choice in the matter, etiquette decreed nice young ladies never spent time alone with a male. Reputations had been ruined for less.

'There really is no escaping the woman, is there?' Louisa murmured, grimacing at the portrait over the fireplace. Before she could answer, there was a knock, and the door was thrown open.

'Victoria, you'll never guess . . . ' her cousin cried. 'Oh, hello Louisa, how lovely to see you.'

'Hester, you've obviously had a lovely time; you're positively glowing,' Victoria cried.

'I have and I am,' she cried, her eyes shining. 'Ross has been so attentive, and you'll never guess what? He is coming to see Father this weekend.'

'That is wonderful news. I am delighted for you. Roscoe is Giles and Tristan's cousin,' Victoria told her sister.

'Talking of Tristan, he was bereft when he discovered you'd left the house without saying goodbye. He . . . oh heavens, I almost forgot, Mother wishes to speak with you straightaway. I'll keep Louisa company and we'll have a good catch-up when you return. How is Captain Beauchamp?' she asked, turning her attention to Louisa.

As she made her way downstairs, Victoria felt sick as she recalled that last conversation with Lady Dorothea in the drawing room at Sunningdale. Was she to be sent home in disgrace after all? She could hardly admit her stepmother had agreed to keep quiet about her behaviour on the understanding she agreed to marry Giles.

'Ah, come in, Victoria,' Emmeline said, looking up as Victoria nervously entered the room. It didn't help that her aunt was looking serious. 'Sit down,' she instructed, indicating the chair opposite. 'I am sorry it has come to this, but you must understand I cannot condone impropriety. With Roscoe about to ask for Hester's hand in marriage, her father and I cannot risk any untoward scandalmongering and—'

'I can only apologize once again for my behaviour, Aunt Emmeline,' Victoria said, rising to her feet.

'Your behaviour, Victoria?' The woman frowned and gestured for her to sit down again.

'I honestly didn't know Step Mama was going to leave me at the perfumiers by myself. If it hadn't been a strange town, I would have returned to Sunningdale immediately and—'

'That was unfortunate,' Emmeline interjected, 'but Dorothea and I realize the situation was not of your making. My dear, it is not your behaviour we are questioning, but that of Charlotte. The morning after the ball, Dorothea expressly warned her to desist, or she would have to leave Sunningdale forthwith. As no assurance was given, she was summarily dismissed.'

'You mean, we didn't have to leave early because of me?'

'No, of course not.' Emmeline's frown deepened. 'Though what Charlotte was thinking of leaving you alone with Monsieur Florian's apprentice like that . . . ' she shook her head. 'My dear, I need to ask if your stepmother has been out by herself since you returned?'

Victoria hesitated. What should she say?

'It is important that you answer truthfully,' her aunt urged.

'Very well. Yes, she has. In fact, she went out again yesterday and has yet to return.'

'You mean Charlotte left you alone in the house overnight?'

Emmeline exclaimed. 'This really is too much. Although Nicholas insisted she was up to no good. Have you attended any functions recently?'

'We've been to Gunter's and attended the opera with Giles Newton Berwick.'

'I have to say, I'm surprised at you switching allegiance from one brother to the other. But that is your prerogative, of course.'

If Victoria didn't know better, she would have thought her aunt was disappointed. She was dying to ask about Tristan, but her aunt's look of disapproval kept her quiet. Besides, had he wanted to see her, he knew where she was staying, didn't he? Now she knew it was her stepmother and not herself who was in disgrace, she didn't wish to say anything that would further upset her aunt.

'Victoria, I need to ask you something of a somewhat, er, delicate nature. Do you know who your stepmother has been meeting on these excursions?'

Victoria swallowed but knew she owed it to her aunt to be truthful. 'I believe she was seeing Mr Clarke,' she ventured.

'Yes, my dear, but that was some time ago and Mr Clarke has returned to Sussex. No, I am referring to more recent outings. You see, there has been suggestion . . . well, never mind.' Emmeline leaned forward in her seat and, lowering her voice, asked, 'Do you know if she has been seeing someone else? Oh, this is embarrassing but I wouldn't ask if it wasn't so important.'

Seeing the anguish in her eyes, Victoria realized she owed it to her aunt to tell her the little she knew.

'Step Mama has been getting dressed up and acting very

secretively. My maid told Louisa she'd been seen with someone in Surrey but didn't know the details. Although, apparently, that was why Vanny was sent packing.'

'I see.' Emmeline let out a long sigh. 'And you have no idea where Charlotte was going yesterday?'

'No, she just said she would see me later, except of course, she didn't.'

'Thank you for your honesty. I know this hasn't been easy for you. I think it would be a good idea for you to go back upstairs whilst I speak with Nicholas. This situation must be sorted before word gets out. The servants are sworn to secrecy about Her Ladyship's movements, but even so . . . ' She shrugged. 'Anyway, my dear, I hear your sister has arrived; please convey my apologies for not being here to welcome her and do tell her I look forward to seeing her later. It will give you girls a chance to catch up and Hester is bursting to tell you her exciting news. I will send for you all later when we've decided what is to be done.'

'Yes, Aunt,' she murmured. Her head spinning, and needing some time to think, she took herself up to her room. Although her aunt hadn't been specific, she had inferred her stepmother had a lover. Someone she'd met with in Surrey, too. And that was why Dorothea had sent her home.

She sank onto her bed, trying to remember Charlotte's exact words on that journey. With hindsight, she realized the woman hadn't actually said anything, letting Victoria assume the blame for their early departure. Clearly, she'd twisted Dorothea's words to suit her own needs and consequently she was now practically betrothed to the ghastly Giles Newton Berwick.

'I thought I heard you come back upstairs.' Looking up, she saw Hester hovering in the doorway. 'I hope your chat with Mother cleared the air. She really is fond of you and was upset you'd left Sunningdale so hastily. As was Tristan.'

'Well, I'm sure it didn't take him long to find someone else to pay court to. According to Giles, it is the thrill of the chase he enjoys,' she retorted.

Hester frowned. 'I rather think you are doing Tristan an injustice. I've told you before, Giles has always wanted everything Tristan has.'

'So, Tristan hasn't returned to his work then?'

'Well, yes, he has, because there was a—'

'Look, Hester, I know you mean well but I really don't want to talk about it, all right?'

'Well, it is your business.' She shrugged. 'I just thought . . . well, anyway, Louisa and I have been chatting all things marriage and it's made us hungry. Do come and join us for cake and lemonade.' Looking at her cousin's eager expression, Victoria felt a stab of remorse. It wasn't Hester's fault she'd been inveigled into her stepmother's web of deceit.

'I'm dying to hear all about Roscoe,' Victoria said, forcing a smile as she followed her cousin from the room. 'Is that why you stayed away so long?'

Although she had little appetite, she took her place at the table alongside Louisa and duly listened as Hester happily recounted how Roscoe had taken her for rides in the Surrey countryside and plied her with gifts.

'Why, he even paid Mother and I compliments, sometimes without even making his customary jokes,' she exclaimed. As the subject moved on to wedding arrangements, Victoria marvelled at how much Louisa and Hester had in common. Perhaps that was what love did for you, she thought, feeling a pang. But as talk turned to dress designs, Victoria, having had enough, turned the subject away from matrimony.

'I must tell you about my debut gown,' she said, then proceeded to relate details of her visit from Eleanor Barrington.

'Tristan mentioned she was a collector who thought the fabric had significant meaning. They were both disappointed when they heard you'd left Sunningdale,' Hester said, giving Victoria a pointed look.

'Well, I'm glad for Jane Haydon,' Louisa said. 'Giving up the fabric she'd intended for her own wedding gown was a truly altruistic thing to do. She works hard and, having recently expanded her business, I'm sure the money will come in useful.'

'But how could you bear to give up the beautiful dress that made you debutante of this Season?' Hester exclaimed in disbelief.

'Giles insisted I wear it every time we go out together and, frankly, I am pleased to see the back of it.'

'Gracious, he does sound domineering,' Louisa murmured. Before any more could be said, they were interrupted by a knock on the door.

'Your father and mother request your presence in the drawing room, Miss Hester, and would be obliged if your guests would also attend,' Jarvis solemnly announced.

'That sounds ominous,' Hester murmured, leading the way.

To their surprise, Nicholas and Emmeline were not alone. Edwin Farringdon was pacing the room, pale-faced and solemn. Something was obviously wrong.

'Papa,' Victoria cried, hurrying over and taking his arm, 'are you all right?'

'I thought you were at home,' Louisa murmured.

'Sit down, girls, I'm afraid something dreadful has happened.' Glancing at each other uneasily, they settled quickly on the chaise. 'The coach your stepmother was travelling in was involved in an accident yesterday. She was trapped in the wreckage, and I'm afraid she perished.'

Chapter 37

'Where is Papa?' Victoria asked, as, still reeling from shock, they sat toying with their breakfast.

'He has gone with your uncle to speak to the authorities. As you can imagine, there are details to establish, formalities to go through. Now, if you have all finished eating, I suggest we go through to the drawing room. I need to write a letter to Dorothea informing her of the accident, and an hour's reflection will be good for the soul,' Emmeline told them.

'But Mother, Charlotte was not a nice—' Hester began.

'That is no way to speak of your aunt. Whatever her faults, one must never speak ill of the dead. You will sit and reflect on her good points,' Emmeline chided, seating herself at the escritoire in the corner of the room.

'Did she have any?' Hester muttered, sinking into one of the armchairs.

'I'm trying hard to think of one,' Victoria whispered only for Louisa to shake her head.

She closed her eyes but all she could see was the triumphant gleam in her stepmother's eyes as she discussed their pact. Yet only she knew of it, and she was no longer here to tell Papa.

To her shame, all she could feel was a sense of relief. Whilst she hoped the woman hadn't suffered, it would be hypocritical of her to think she had any fond memories. She wondered how her father was faring. How awful it must be for him.

Finally, after what seemed an inordinately long time, the scratching of nib on paper ceased and, clutching her letter, Emmeline rose from her seat.

'As it would be inappropriate for me to go to Haven House this afternoon, I must arrange for someone else to cover my shift. I will return shortly.'

As soon as the door had closed, Louisa spoke, her expression serious.

'I have said a prayer for Step Mama but confess my thoughts have been about poor Papa. If word gets out about these, er, illicit relationships, he will be humiliated beyond belief. Why, he could even be shunned by society. He is a good man and doesn't deserve that, so I propose we keep this to ourselves.'

'I agree,' Victoria said, relieved that she wasn't the only one whose thoughts hadn't been focused on their stepmother. 'Aunt Emmeline told me the servants have already been sworn to secrecy about her covert movements. Always supposing we can trust them to be discreet.'

'None of them would defy Mother,' Hester declared hotly. 'Apart from the fact they admire her and receive a fair wage, Mother places great value upon integrity and they know they would be instantly dismissed if they talked. I'll be sure to tell her what we've agreed when—' The insistent ringing of the front doorbell stopped her mid-sentence. 'Heavens, who could be calling today?'

There was the sound of muffled voices then Aunt Emmeline appeared, Giles following in her wake.

'You have a visitor, Lady Victoria,' she announced formally. 'Lord Newton Berwick, may I present Lady Louisa, her sister, and Hester, of course, you know.'

'It is a pleasure to meet you, Lady Louisa, and good to see you again, Hester,' he said, perfecting a small bow. 'Please accept my condolences for your sad loss.'

'Goodness, you've heard already?' Victoria exclaimed. 'I dare say you can tell by our attire we are not receiving visitors.'

'Other than your betrothed,' Giles beamed. 'Although I have to say, Victoria, that black dress does you no favours at all.'

'I suggest you sit at the table in the window; we will remain at this end of the room,' Emmeline suggested quickly, as Louisa shot him a disapproving look.

'Having heard your father had arrived, I thought it prudent to call and see him, although I understand he is presently not at home.'

'He is speaking with the authorities about the accident,' Victoria told him.

'Then I shall wait,' he replied. As he placed his top hat on the chair next to him, Victoria noticed the graze on his forehead.

'You have hurt yourself?' Victoria asked, her good manners coming to the fore.

'It is nothing,' he said, looking uncomfortable. Almost immediately he resumed his dictatorial manner. 'The sooner your father gives permission for our betrothal the sooner we can make arrangements.'

'You seem to overlook the fact that I am in mourning for Step Mama.'

'But it is what she wanted, what we planned, she promised—' As if he was suddenly aware he was being watched, he ground to a halt.

'There can be no thought of betrothal for at least a year,' Victoria told him, ignoring his outburst.

'That is preposterous. Your birthday is in November and you agreed we would marry then,' he blustered.

'I have never agreed to anything. It was you and Step Mama who decided we would become betrothed, and, of course, that is always provided Papa gives his permission.'

'Of course he will, you silly girl,' he snapped. 'You'll never get a better offer.'

'Please do not speak to my sister like that,' Louisa cried, rising to her feet.

'Yes, Giles, remember your manners,' Emmeline scolded. 'Victoria is correct. There can be no thought of betrothal until she has observed the correct period of mourning, which will last for at least a year. Still, I'm sure you will agree Victoria is well worth waiting for.'

'Wait for a year? But that's impossible,' he shouted, colour infusing his face.

'Of course it isn't. Or has it something to do with the fact that your inheritance requires that status before you attain your twenty-fifth birthday on the first of December?' she asked, staring meaningfully at him.

'As I say, it is impossible for me to wait that long,' he said, ignoring Emmeline and turning to face Victoria. 'It is crucial we marry this year. I'm sure, under the circumstances, your father will agree to waive this period of mourning. It is somewhat archaic anyway, is it not?'

Victoria stared at him, noting the anger sparking in his eyes, lips set in a tight line.

'Even if what Aunt Emmeline says is true, which you have chosen to ignore, I could never consider the suit of any man so disrespectful of my grieving. Please ask Jarvis to show Lord Newton Berwick out, Aunt Emmeline.'

'Now, look here, there's no need to be hasty. You will become one of the richest ladies in the land and—'

'One of the unhappiest,' Victoria replied. 'Ah, Jarvis, Lord Newton Berwick is leaving.'

'But I . . . ' Giles began, then seeing she meant it, his eyes narrowed. 'You'll regret this,' he roared, snatching up his hat.

'I doubt that very much,' Victoria said, turning her back on him as he stormed from the room.

'Well, I never,' Aunt Emmeline exclaimed, and no one knew if she was commenting on the man's audacity or Victoria's spirited rebuttal.

*

'Please accept our condolences,' the chief inspector murmured as Edwin and Nicholas were shown from his office. 'As I've already said, we shall be continuing our inquiries and will keep you informed of any developments.'

'Thank you,' Edwin replied, his mind still processing all he'd been told.

'Come on, old chap, you need a stiff drink. My club's just around the corner.'

Once seated at a table set discreetly at the back of the room with its plush leather furnishings, Edwin swirled the amber liquid in his glass before taking a swig.

'Nasty business,' Nicholas muttered. 'I wonder what spooked the horses,' he added, his analytical mind going over what they'd been told.

'A dog, wild animal? With the unfortunate coachman copping it too, I doubt we'll ever know,' Edwin sighed. 'Not a very nice way to end your life though, upside down in a ditch with a broken neck. I would never have wished that upon her.'

Nicholas signalled for more drinks, and they lapsed into silence, neither wishing to voice their feelings. Like an elephant in the room, the reason why Charlotte should have been riding alone in a carriage with another man hung between them.

'I wonder if they'll find out who it was,' Edwin finally burst out.

'Whoever he was, fleeing like that was a cowardly thing to do. The inspector said he likely sustained some sort of injury but . . . ' Nicholas shrugged.

'But if he could run away, it couldn't have been anything serious. Look, Nicholas, my prime concern at the moment is the girls, and I really don't think there is any need for them to know to know their stepmother was killed on an outing with her lover.'

'Steady on, old chap, we don't know that for sure,' Nicholas blustered.

Edwin stared candidly at his brother-in-law then shook his head.

'I appreciate you trying to spare my feelings but having already heard that Charlotte frequently went out by herself,

I . . . well, I'm not a fool. Or maybe I am.' He took another gulp of his drink to steady himself. 'When formalities have been completed and Charlotte's body is released, I will see she is given a decent burial, but it will not be in the grounds of the family chapel at Nettlecombe.'

Chapter 38

Even for August, the weather was hot with brilliant sun shining from a cloudless sky as the Farringdon family and their staff assembled in the graveyard beside the chapel at Nettlecombe Manor.

Edwin watched dry-eyed as the coffin was lowered into the freshly dug hole. If asked, he could say in all truthfulness that Charlotte was in there, albeit in her painted glory. Only he and Nicholas knew they were burying her picture and not a body. Unable to bear the thought of her being near his beloved Beatrice and venerable ancestors, he'd arranged for her to be buried in a churchyard in London. Still, as Charlotte herself had been fond of saying, it was all about appearances and perception.

Looking at his daughters standing with their heads respectfully bowed, he doubted they had shed a single tear over her demise. He couldn't blame them. Whilst he was sad, it was because of the bad choice he'd made rather than for any loss. If he were truthful, he'd felt more grief when Ellery had died. At least his beloved pet had been loyal and given his love freely.

At a signal from the vicar, he stepped forward and tossed

a yellow Charlotte rose onto the coffin, bowed his head then stepped back again. A token tribute, he thought.

'*Ashes to ashes.*' As the vicar intoned the time-honoured words, Edwin's glance returned to his family. Although nobody had been able to identify the man seen running away from the accident, the police were still making inquiries. Sarah and Maria were standing beside their governess, Miss Birkett, looking bemused. Charlotte had never paid them much attention and they hadn't missed her when she was in London, so, for them, life would continue as normal.

'*Dust to dust.*' Edwin clenched his hands. How he wished this farce was over. Deception didn't come easy to him, yet it would look strange if Charlotte wasn't seen to be laid to rest on family ground.

'Stay strong, Edwin, you are doing the right thing,' Nicholas whispered in his ear.

'*Grant that our sister may sleep here in peace until you waken her, for you are the resurrection and the life.*'

Then it was over and as the gravediggers stepped forward to complete their job, his younger daughters broke away from their governess and came hurtling towards him.

'Puppy, Mama's gone to live in heaven now. Is that far away?' Maria asked.

'A fair way, yes,' Edwin replied. 'We'll look for her amongst the stars tonight.'

'Oh, goody, we'll have to stay up late then. Are we having cake for tea?' Sarah asked.

'Don't worry, Edwin, the young are resilient,' Nanny said, catching hold of their hands and shooing them back to the long-suffering Miss Birkett. 'And so are you. One should never speak ill of the departed, but you are now free to continue your life as you wish.' She lowered her voice. 'And young enough to meet a decent young lady.'

'Nanny, please,' Edwin spluttered. 'I'm far too old.'

'Fiddlesticks. There's many a fine tune left, young Edwin, and Nettlecombe needs a son and heir.'

'Are you all right, Papa?' He turned to see his three elder daughters watching him anxiously.

'Yes, I am. Although it is a sad day of course,' he added quickly.

'Perhaps Step Mama will be happy now,' Louisa sighed, patting his arm.

'Well, if she isn't happy in heaven, I don't know where she will be,' Victoria murmured. 'Always supposing that is where she's gone.' Having escaped justice on earth, she hoped the woman had gone to the dark and miserable place she deserved and would be held accountable for her dreadful actions in the afterlife.

'At the hospital we are taught not to judge or dispense morals but to offer help and sympathy,' Bea said. 'However, I'm finding it difficult to think that way today.'

'Well, wherever she is, we must hope she's at peace,' Edwin told them. 'Now, I understand you have invited the staff to join us in the great hall for the wake.'

'Mama always included the staff on these occasions, and we thought it time they were involved in family gatherings again,' Louisa told him, looking and sounding so like her mother, Edwin couldn't help smiling.

'I'm afraid I must return to London immediately, Papa. There has been an outbreak of cholera in Westminster and

Miss Nightingale has been called upon to help. She requires my assistance, which means that at last she must see that I have the qualities to become a proper nurse,' Beatrice replied.

'Cholera?' Victoria cried. 'But that is deadly, surely?'

'It can be, but it is my job to help. I was only granted leave of absence because it was a family funeral and the superintendent agreed I should be here to support Papa.'

'Which is greatly appreciated. Go and do your duty knowing I am proud of you, my daughter,' Edwin told her, pulling her close for a moment.

'Thank you, Papa. That means a lot to me.'

'Quick will drive you to the railway station at Exeter. Travelling by train will be far quicker than going by road.'

'That will be a great help, Papa. Oh, and before I go, there's one more thing . . . did you know that gypsy curses can be lifted?'

'No, I didn't,' Edwin replied, surprised at the change of subject.

'Apparently, it's all to do with kindness. Ruby's Nan said if you grant them your blessing to camp on Nettlecombe land, the curse will be revoked.'

'You really think it is that simple?' he chuckled, then seeing her hurt expression, he nodded. 'Well, it would be worth trying, I suppose.'

He smiled fondly at his daughters. What fine young ladies they were, each one eager to help and support him. And he would do anything for them too. They were young with their lives before them. Why burden them with his secret? Skeletons were meant to be kept hidden and keeping details of their stepmother's paramour from them had been the right thing to do.

Chapter 39

Dressed in her black gown, Victoria breathed in the sweet smell of fresh grass that still glistened like jewels after last night's rain. She ran her fingers along the string of pearls at her collar, the only brightness to relieve both her sombre mood and attire. Although they were dutifully marking the mourning period, it was difficult to feel much sorrow for a woman who'd been cold and controlling. However, Papa would have questioned any break with tradition, and, determined to keep any whisper of their stepmother's disgraceful behaviour from him, it was necessary to appear respectful. The fact that it had been Charlotte herself who had said it was all about appearance and perception brought a wry smile to her lips. Despite her resolve not to think about him, it was missing Tristan that was the cause of her low mood.

Whilst it was lovely to be back home and free from the clutches of the arrogant Giles Newton Berwick, she couldn't contain the feelings of restlessness that had stolen over these past weeks. Idly, she plucked a late-blooming rose only for the red velvet petals to bring back memories of Tristan. With a pang, she tossed the flower into her trug. Why couldn't her treacherous heart accept he had moved on to pastures new and that was what she needed to do too?

Louisa was admirably giving of her time to the Quarry Crafters until Henry came home and Beatrice was following her vocation to nurse the sick. But what could she do? What interested her, excited her even? Although she had volunteered her services at the alms houses in the next village, that still didn't fill her waking hours.

She stared around the flower beds, deciding which autumn blooms to collect for the manor. Now she no longer had to pander to Charlotte's vagaries, she enjoyed placing flower arrangements in every room. How Gabriel would love all the different varieties head gardener Reed and his team proudly cultivated. That was it! She would learn how to distil and blend them into perfume. It might take time, but it would be fun and satisfying. Once she had perfected the art, she would fill beautiful little bottles to give to friends and family. And she would give her fragrances flower names rather than stupid ones like *Unforgettable* or *Inoublie*.

As her heart gave another pang, she forced her thoughts back to the present. There were botanical books in their library, and, as soon as she had collected enough flowers for the house, she would go and look through them. She would also write to Gabriel, requesting advice on how to get started. Buoyed by her thoughts, she took up her secateurs and snipped another bloom.

'A rose by any other name would smell as sweet.'

Victoria froze. Surely her ears had deceived her. Heart pounding, she spun round to see Tristan standing on the lawn behind her. There was no mistaking the look of love burning from his bright-blue eyes.

'What are you doing here?' she asked, nerves making her voice sound harsh as she smoothed down her skirts. Instantly, his expression turned wary.

'I know you are in mourning, but I wanted to come and offer my condolences. Whilst it is some weeks since the accident, I have been away and only heard about it upon my return.'

'Ah yes, I remember now, you left during Aunt Dorothea's ball.'

'It was actually the day after, and I left after being told you and your stepmother had returned to London. Without saying goodbye, which was incredibly rude for such a well-brought-up young lady.'

'Me rude?' she cried. 'What about you? Marking my card then not appearing to claim your dance, leaving me in the embarrassing situation of having to accept your brother's offer.' Pent-up anger of the past weeks came rushing out in a torrent and she took a steadying breath.

'Ah yes,' he replied, mimicking her earlier remark. 'My dear brother who made it clear that, being eldest and technically the host of Mother's ball, had prior claim on any lady he desired. Which naturally, being Giles, was the very one I did.'

She stared at him, looking for signs he might be lying, but he looked so earnest, so sincere, and far too serious for the man she remembered.

'Well, what about Ele—' she was about to say Eleanor Barrington then remembered her visit and the reason for it. Frustrated, she moved towards a row of brightly coloured dahlias.

'Eleanor Barrington was enquiring about your golden

gown,' he said, guessing what she'd been about to say. 'And, being the polite host, I was assisting. But then you already know that.'

'Well, yes, but your brother said you move from one woman to another. Apparently, it's the thrill of the chase you enjoy.'

'My brother has a lot to answer for,' he replied curtly. 'If you must know, we had an almighty row after he claimed that last dance. It is no secret he always wants what I have. Not that I am implying I had you, of course,' he added quickly.

'I should hope not,' she retorted. She turned away, blindly plucking at a flower so that he couldn't see her flushing cheeks.

'A perfect pink bloom,' he murmured. Too late she realized she'd picked another rose and, despite her resolve, was transported back to that first time he had called upon her. But that was months ago, and, since the ball, he had been very conspicuous by his absence. As she thought of the hours she'd spent thinking of him, dreaming about him, her anger returned.

'Thank you for your condolences but I think you have forgotten we are alone out here,' she reminded him.

'Oh, didn't I say? That sweet lady you call Nanny received me. I was given the once-over then told she would be watching my every move.' He gestured towards the manor and, sure enough, Nanny waved back. 'So, you can be assured your reputation is safe, Lady Victoria. And, being the perfect gentleman, I shall, of course, act with propriety.' Noting the twinkle in his eye, she felt her lips twitch, then remembering she was cross with him, endeavoured to look impassive.

'Trust you to run away, you mean. Where did you go anyway?' she asked, curiosity getting the better of her.

'You mean the wonderful Giles didn't tell you? The warehouse holding my stocks caught fire and the whole lot went up with such a bang it put Guy Fawkes to shame. I've had to work round the clock sourcing replacement wine supplies for my patrons before they made alternative arrangements. Competition is fierce and once you lose your client base it is very difficult to get back.'

'Heavens,' she murmured. 'I had no idea.'

'But I wrote explaining, saying I might be away for some time but would call upon you the moment I returned.'

'But I never received anything. Which is strange as Aunt Emmeline was meticulous about checking and distributing the mail.' She frowned. 'But then she did stay on in Surrey, and, in her absence, Jarvis gave the correspondence to Step Mama. Oh, you don't think . . . ?' Surely not even Charlotte would have kept a letter from her? But the truth was glaringly obvious for, by then, arrangements were being made for her betrothal to Giles.

'I can see that, despite your protestation, you do believe me. Whatever her reasons, and I see now what they were, it will serve no purpose for us to think ill of the dead, nor to dwell on the past. As I no longer need worry about your scorning my outpourings of the heart, for that is what I wrote in an attempt to explain my feelings towards you, would it be too much to ask, dearest Victoria, whether you would consider accepting my suit? After your period of mourning, of course.'

'Oh,' she cried, her pulses racing, heart singing. However, she didn't intend making it easy for him and kept her expression deadpan.

'I realize you need time to consider and will give you all of five . . . seconds,' he finished, lips twitching.

'Tristan Newton Berwick, you are . . . you are . . . an idiot,' she exclaimed, laughing despite herself.

'Dare I take that to mean you accept?' he asked.

'You may escort me around the grounds whilst I consider,' she told him, handing him her trug.

'My lady doth drive a hard bargain,' he told a statue as they passed.

'But is worth pursuing,' a voice murmured. Startled, he looked over his shoulder to see Nanny standing beside the hot house. The woman really did mean what she said about watching his every move, he thought. Knowing they were being trailed, he turned the conversation to their surroundings.

'Aunt Dorothea would love these gardens, you know,' he said, as they headed to the grounds beyond.

'We don't have a maze though,' she said, smiling coyly up at him.

'I'm sure we could make use of that shrubbery,' he said, pointing ahead. Then he stopped dead. 'Goodness, are those grapevines by any chance?' he asked, squinting into the distance.

'Apparently the Romans brought them and established vineyards here. Obviously, it was some considerable time ago and, as you can see, they have been sadly neglected. As have I,' she sighed.

'If the lady would but give me her answer, I might be able to rectify that last matter at least,' he replied, turning to face her.

Seeing the love blazing from his eyes, she could resist no longer.

'Yes, Tristan, you have permission to speak with Papa,' she told him, delighted by his beaming smile yet bemused by his restraint. 'Aren't you going to . . . well, you know, shouldn't we seal our agreement as it were?' she ventured.

'Not whilst we are being watched. My goodness, how long has it been since I've been worried about incurring the wrath of a nanny?' he muttered as the woman walked towards them.

'I thought you should know that your father has returned, Lady Victoria. Oh, and that Cookson has prepared something special for luncheon,' she added, her eyes twinkling knowingly. They watched as she made her way back to the house, leaving them to follow.

Which they did, but only after detouring to the privacy of the rose arbour where they sealed their agreement in a most satisfactory and unforgettable way.

Chapter 40

With new puppy Jasper pulling eagerly at his lead, Edwin strode down the wide driveway, where the leaves on the lime trees were gleaming yellow in the early autumn sunshine. How he loved this mellow time of year, when the hedges were laden with nature's bounty and the harvest safely gathered in. Blackmore, the new estate manager, had taken up his position that morning. Young, full of enthusiasm and eager to implement his plans, Edwin had high expectations for the future of Nettlecombe. He was also happy knowing Wilfred and Edith were safely installed in their cottage in Combe.

What a turbulent summer it had been, yet, for the first time in ages, he felt a sense of hope rising inside him.

Having come to terms with Charlotte's activities, he was thankful details had not been made public. Of course, a generous donation to the newspaper magnate, Maurice Wolverstone, for his benevolent fund, had helped, but it was worth it to ensure his daughters never discovered their step-mother had betrayed him with another man. A scandal like that would be sure to ruin their reputations. Whilst Edwin had been hurt by Charlotte's behaviour, time and reflection made him realize she would never have been satisfied with the attention of just one man. Neither had she been a natural mother, seeing the children as competition for his attention. Unlike the seagulls circling above that mate for life and are fiercely protective of their young, Charlotte had been more of a hummingbird, brightly flitting from one person to another in her quest for admiration, whilst woefully neglecting her family.

Which made Emmeline's revelation after the service in the chapel – that Charlotte had confided she felt bad for not giving him an heir for Nettlecombe – poignant. Had Charlotte voiced her disappointment to him, would it have made a difference? He would never know.

Still, that was in the past and the future spread out before him. With five lovely daughters and two future weddings to concentrate on, he had much to be thankful for.

Louisa was still working with the Quarry Crafters, ensuring the women were gainfully employed and their children fed, whilst she waited for her beloved Captain Henry Beauchamp to return from the Crimea. News had just been received that the British had inflicted a heavy defeat on the Russians at Alma, although there had been allied casualties. He was awaiting further news, praying that Henry had escaped unscathed, before telling Louisa anything. In the meantime, he was encouraging her to proceed with the plans she was making for their wedding, hoping they would be fulfilled in the not-too-distant future.

Victoria and Tristan Newton Berwick had an agreement, and he'd given his permission for them to become betrothed when the period of mourning came to an end. Of course, the mourning was a farce, but necessary to maintain social convention and if his secret were to be kept, appearances needed to be upheld. Still, they were young and hadn't known each other long so it would give them time to ensure their feelings were strong enough to endure.

In the meantime, under Louisa's auspices, Victoria was learning the intricacies of running a household. She was also highly regarded at the alms houses where her cheerful nature and floral posies were gratefully received by the older folk. Although some of the aromas emanating from the still room these days were questionable, to say the least.

Bea, meanwhile, was helping Miss Nightingale nurse those unfortunate victims succumbing to cholera in the city. The outbreak had predominantly affected the poorest areas and those women working the streets. Whilst Edwin was fearful for her safety, he was immensely proud of the selfless contribution she was making and prayed for her safe return to Nettlecombe when the outbreak had been contained.

Walking on, he passed the lane leading down to the quarry. Jasper eagerly sniffed the sea air, tugging on his lead to head in that direction.

'Another day, boy. You need to be trained before I can take you to the works or you'll be off down one of the caves after a rabbit,' Edwin told him. 'Besides, the men are enjoying time off to attend the Michaelmas Day fair today.' Production had been healthy and, with the order book filling, he could afford to be generous. Jasper whined then barked as a low-flying pheasant crossed their path. 'I can see I am going to have my work cut out with you.'

Although he tried to sound firm and authoritative, he was happy to have a companion by his side once more.

In the lower field, brightly painted wagons and stalls adorned with fluttering flags spread its length. The fair was already underway, the music of the fiddler playing lifted his spirits and he smiled at the sound of children laughing at the tricks of the jester. The aroma of frying onions and sausages tempted him to join in the celebrations. He would bring Maria and Sarah here later, let them have fun, enjoy the festivities, and mingle with the villagers. They might be little monkeys, but they were growing up fast and needed to find out what life was like outside the classroom.

The sight of bright cornflowers, or bachelor's buttons as they were known round these parts, put him in mind of Jane Haydon and how indebted he was for her help in preparing Victoria's debut gown. Remembering her indignation when he'd dared to suggest she keep the sewing machine still made him smile. Thankfully, it was now being put to good use by the Quarry Crafters. What a good idea it had been them joining forces with the young corsetiere, for both businesses were now thriving.

On hearing Jane Haydon was to use the money she'd received for the pail-red fabric to open a school for apprentices, he'd offered his services as a patron. It was time he involved himself in another charitable cause and they didn't come any worthier than ensuring young girls were given the opportunity to earn a living, enabling them to make their own way in the world.

A group of women sitting on the steps of their vardos waved to him as he passed. He'd been sceptical when Bea had told him that curses could be lifted by kindness. Only time would tell if it had worked, but it was worth a try. Anyway, he'd missed the travelling folk with their stories of far-flung places, and it was good to have them back on Nettlecombe land again. Charlotte would have had a fit, of course, but she was no longer here, and it was yet another indication that life had moved on.

Nanny assured Edwin that he was still young enough to make another marriage, even sire more children. Although he had thought the idea preposterous, suddenly he wasn't so sure. A tingle of excitement ran up his spine. Who knew what the future held?

In the meantime, seeing the grounds of Nettlecombe thronging with family and staff, and the villagers of Combe mixing with the itinerant folk made him happy, very happy indeed. Like the changing seasons that moved life ever onwards, he would make it his mission to ensure the Farringdon family were happy, and their fortune assured.

Acknowledgements

Pern: Your meticulous research and many reviving cups of tea are much appreciated.

Teresa Chris: Your continued support and nuggets about the upper classes were invaluable.

Kate Mills and her wonderful team at HQ: You are all a joy to work with and I thank you from the bottom of my heart for making my stories the best they can be.

BWC: How lovely it has been to resume our meetings in person. Your input, as ever, has been invaluable.

ONE PLACE. MANY STORIES

Bold, innovative and
empowering publishing.

FOLLOW US ON:

@HQStories